## "DAMN YOU, COUGAR," ROZ RASPED SHAKILY.

"I was thinking the same thing myself," he muttered in self-contempt. He wanted to devour the taste of her, commit each curve and swell to tormenting memory, but that was sure to only make matters worse. Damn, she was so tantalizingly close and yet so intolerably far away that he was shaking with the need of her. Him! The man whom legend claimed was carved from rock.

"I hate what you do to me, Yank," Cougar growled, staring down at her dewy mouth, starving for a taste of her. "This was the last thing I wanted."

"Good. That makes us even. Now turn me loose," Roz demanded.

If only he could turn her loose, Cougar mused. Every time he came near this woman he discarded all the good sense he had spent thirty years cultivating. And because he couldn't restrain himself when he was with this intriguing female, he was going to spend another hellish day, craving a taste of her, inhaling her alluring scent that cl̲i̲n̲g̲ ̲t̲o̲ ̲h̲i̲s̲ ̲s̲k̲i̲n. Then he would lecture himself for refusi̲ ̲ ̲ ̲ ̲ ̲ ̲ ̲ ̲ ̲h̲a̲n̲d̲s̲ ̲o̲f̲f̲ ̲ ̲ ̲ ̲len temptation. Yes, he wa̲ ̲ ̲ ̲ ̲ ̲ ̲ ̲ ̲ ̲ ̲ ̲ ̲mself later . . .

Bu

Pinna̲ ̲ ̲ ̲ ̲ ̲ ̲ ̲ ̲ ̲ ̲ ̲ ̲ ̲ ̲ this first book in a series of exciting romances w̲i̲t̲h̲ the hero takes center stage. Experience love through *his* eyes and rapture in *his* arms. Discover romance as you never have before . . . with the hero of your dreams. Let Cougar sweep you away on an adventure of the heart and soul and let yourself revel in the sensual feel of . . .

### A MAN'S TOUCH

# A MAN'S TOUCH
## Debra Falcon

**PINNACLE BOOKS**
**WINDSOR PUBLISHING CORP.**

PINNACLE BOOKS are published by

Windsor Publishing Corp.
850 Third Avenue
New York, NY 10022

First Printing: August, 1994

Printed in the United States of America

*This book is dedicated to my husband Ed and our children, Christie, Jill and Kurt with much love.*

*A very special thanks to my editor, Jennifer Sawyer. Your time, effort and assistance are greatly appreciated.*

# *One*

The sound of picks, axes and shovels clanked against granite rock and echoed around the tree-lined canyon. Cougar halted his steed and scowled at the newly established mining camp that spoiled what had once been a peaceful section of the mountain range near his ranch.

"White men," he muttered sourly.

The three mountain lions that were his constant traveling companions growled in agreement.

Cougar did not appreciate civilization crowding in on him. Never had, never would. Since the days when he was growing up in Cheyenne camps, whites were always breathing down his neck, pushing him, taking over what wasn't theirs.

And Cougar was half white. He hated that most of all. It was the curse of his life, knowing the white side of his heritage was responsible for the slaughter and confinement of his proud Cheyenne clansmen.

Cougar glanced at the small herd of cattle that had paused to graze on the summer grasses of the valley— recently become a prospector's haven. The cattle had drawn the attention of the sweaty argonauts who had

come West to dig for silver and gold. They would find
no riches here in this obscure canyon, but Cougar
wouldn't bother telling the fools so. It was none of his
business what these white men did, as long as they gave
him a wide berth. If they didn't, then Cougar—like the
butchering army that massacred all those he called family—gave no quarter.

"Beef!" one of the prospectors yelled, tossing his
shovel aside to come running.

The man had only taken ten steps before Cougar and
his snarling companions moved alongside the grazing
herd to block his approach.

A hush descended over the crowd of miners as Cougar and his trio of black mountain lions stood like sentinels over the cattle and the string of horses that trailed
behind.

The prospector who had rashly dashed forward took
several retreating steps when the cats stalked him.

"Jeb, you better back off," an old argonaut advised.
"I don't reckon you know who you're about to tangle
with. Better to be hungry than dead."

Cougar cast a cool glance toward the gray-haired argonaut who had practically tiptoed forward to clutch his
young partner's arm. Cougar could see the apprehensive
lines bracketing the old man's mouth when he tried to
manufacture a smile. Cougar, however, didn't make
things any easier on his new acquaintances. He simply
sat on his mount, staring at the two men who came
closer to him than most men dared to come.

"Jeb didn't mean no harm," the old codger declared
with a smile that displayed the lack of two front teeth.
"He's new in these hills, don't ya know. Came all the

way from Illinois, ya see. Reckon he don't know who you be."

*Cougar* didn't reckon *he* knew who he be, either. A misfit? Most certainly. A man whose reputation had a remarkable knack for preceding him wherever he went? Obviously. But whoever Cougar was, he had no place in white man's society. The past eight years had taught him that, taught him more than he wanted to know about the customs and characteristics of white men and their double standards.

"Would you sell us one of your calves—?" Jeb grunted uncomfortably when his partner gouged him in the ribs for voicing the bold request. "We haven't had beef for weeks."

Cougar didn't bother to reply. He didn't have to. The gray-haired prospector answered for him.

"Cougar don't sell nothin' to nobody, Jeb," Elijah Quinn told his young partner. " 'Cept to those nice folk down the mountain at Howard Station. If you want a plate of beef, then you can buy it from them . . . if we ever find a trace of gold up here to pay for it."

While Elijah Quinn was explaining the way things were, Cougar's gaze swung around the camp of tents. He could see the other miners whispering to each other, carrying tales of Cougar's past feats, making him bigger than life with their exaggerated gossip. Of course, he didn't give a damn which stories about his past were circulating through camp, so long as he was allowed plenty of breathing space. Those legends of the Colorado Cat Man had proved to be a shield that kept unwanted companions at bay. And that's the way Cougar preferred to live his life—

alone. He had learned the hard way, to depend on no one but himself, to expect nothing.

Following that philosophy, Cougar was never disappointed. A man lived the way he knew how and then he departed to the Great Spirit's Hanging Road in the Sky, or to the white man's heaven or hell. Cougar was still trying to figure out where he would spend his afterlife, since he had one foot planted in Indian culture and one foot reluctantly stuck in white civilization. To Cougar's way of thinking, this was the hell he had been condemned to by the criminals he had tracked during his years of bounty hunting.

*And for all these years of hell and damnation he had the white men to thank.*

"You just go on your way, Mr. Cougar," Elijah generously offered. "You won't find no trouble here. We're peace-lovin' men, just out to seek our fortunes."

After Elijah tipped his hat in a courteous gesture—a gesture which Cougar never had understood—Cougar gave the command to the cats poised beside his horse. The cats gave a soft, whistling call that put the grazing cattle in motion. The herd moseyed down the dirt path that led up to the summit east of the plunging canyon.

The cluster of men who congregated to spin tales of the legendary Cat Man parted to let the cattle herd and string of horses pass. Cougar spoke not one word while he was being appraised. He purposely kept his distance, letting the miners believe what they wanted about him. It made no difference to him; nothing did these days. Harsh experience had left such thick calluses on Cougar's heart and soul that he wasn't sure he remembered how to *feel,* only to react and exist. Those he knew as family and friends were long gone and he had tried to bury their memories with them.


Cougar herded his cattle and horses up the steep incline that overlooked the new mining camp. When he heard the scrabble of footsteps on the outcropping of rock above him, he automatically grabbed for his pistol. An excited voice called his name, and what little emotion he still felt stirred when the dark-eyed, tousle-haired boy appeared on the ledge.

"Cougar!" Caleb Howard waved his spindly arms in expansive gestures to gain the half-breed's attention. "Ma said you'd be coming when the moon was full again. Sure enough, you're back!"

Caleb wandered too near the edge of the bluff in his eagerness to greet the legendary gunslinger who came and went through the mountains like a skipping wind. Pebbles dribbled over the cliff, pelting the cattle. The startled herd tossed up their heads and stampeded up the slope to avoid the shower of rocks.

Before Cougar could bring the alarmed herd under control, he heard a feminine shriek down the trail. The black cats responded with their customary wail that was reminiscent of a woman screaming in terror. Cougar scowled when the string of horses behind him balked, very nearly jerking him off his mount and dislodging his arm from its socket.

"Miss Gaylord!" Caleb yelped in dismay and disappeared from the overhanging cliff.

Cougar didn't know who Miss Gaylord was and he didn't much care. What annoyed him was the fact that his well-behaved herd of cattle were scattering around the meadow like a flock of ducks and his well-trained horses were whinnying in alarm as they collided and scrabbled to prevent themselves from toppling over the bluff and plunging into the Ponderosa pines below.

By the time Cougar brought the horses under control and led them up to level ground, cattle were strung hither and yon. Young Caleb Howard was crouched beside a bundle of cotton skirts and shapely legs. A broken easel lay in the grass and paper cartwheeled across the meadow, propelled by the wind. Bottles of paint were strewn beside a discarded pallet smeared with paint.

Cougar frowned, bemused by the peculiar scene. But when Caleb propped the upended female into a sitting position, Cougar could guess what had happened when his startled cattle thundered up the path.

His squinting gaze dropped to the gaily adorned woman who was arranging her plumed hat on a pile of disheveled silver-blond hair. The scooped neck of the pink muslin gown drooped low on the woman's generous bosom. Petticoats flapped in the wind, displaying her well-proportioned legs. Eyes as clear and blue as a mountain stream blinked up at the young lad who was fussing over her.

A jolt of immediate awareness struck Cougar like a lightning bolt when he stared down at such bewitching beauty. For several seconds Cougar permitted himself to admire the tantalizing scenery before stark reality descended on him.

*Contrast.* That was the first word that popped to mind when he peered at this curvaceous female with startling blue eyes and hair like a river of sparkling moonbeams.

In an instant Cougar realized that Miss Gaylord was everything he was not—refinement, elegance, delicacy. She reminded Cougar of a misplaced lily in a prickly cactus patch—totally and completely out of her element in these unforgiving mountains. She was, he thought, an absurdity.

"Are you all right, Miss Gaylord?" Caleb questioned as he tried to hoist Rozalie to her feet.

Rozalie Gaylord swayed dizzily as Caleb yanked on her arm. She had hit her head on a rock when she stumbled away from the cattle that thundered toward her from out of nowhere.

A gasp gurgled in Roz's throat and clung to her lips when her blurred gaze landed on the dark figure that rose up from the boulders. Jet black hair, held in place by a leather headband, gleamed in the afternoon light. Roz noticed a broad muscular chest, crisscrossed by two bandoleers that contained enough ammunition to blow up the federal mint in Denver. The scars from three bullets marred what was otherwise utter masculine perfection.

Fringed buckskin breeches and knee-high moccasins completed an ensemble that was unlike any Roz had ever seen. A shield, sporting a cougar's paw print and decorated with eagle feathers, hung beside the colorful saddle blanket that was strapped to the coal black steed.

The man's ominous profile, outlined by the blaring sun, caused Roz to teeter on wobbly legs. But for Caleb's supporting arm, Roz would have landed on her backside after she stumbled on the trailing hem of her dress.

"Dear God!" Roz wheezed as her vision cleared, re-

vealing even more of the foreboding image that reminded her of the devil himself.

Roz blinked once and then twice to ensure that her
faulty vision hadn't deceived her. What she had assumed
to be swaying shadows among the jagged rocks were
three solid black mountain lions that lunged off the
ledge to circle the horse's legs. Her gaze elevated, magnetically drawn to this . . . this creature who looked to
be half man and half . . . Roz didn't know what!

For a half minute Roz merely stood there gazing into
the bright sunlight, memorizing the hard, angular features of the half-dressed man who had paused ten feet
away from her. The pumas continued to circle like restless shadows, prompting Roz to skittishly move away.

When the nearest cat hunkered down in front of the
steed and its master, and let loose with an unearthly
scream that sent chills ricocheting down Roz's backbone,
she wobbled backward. The eerie sound echoed around
the canyon, halting the racket of picks and shovels.

The brisk wind that swept across the summit died
abruptly. The second two-hundred-pound cat sank down
beside the first and lifted its broad head. And suddenly
all three cougars were caterwauling loud enough to raise
the dead and startle the last breath out of the dying.
The wild sound rose higher and higher, racing around
the canyon rim, hanging in the air until it evaporated
into deathly silence.

Roz stood there, clinging to Caleb, who didn't seem
the least bit intimidated by the man and his squalling
cats. Roz, however, was having difficulty adjusting to
the sight of the wild animals and the foreboding image
of the man who sat there glaring at her with eyes that

perfectly matched the golden gleam of the panthers' eyes.

In all her twenty-one years, Roz could honestly say that she had never been so spellbound by a vision that, as far as she knew, had risen right up from the rock walls that surrounded her. There was something about him that inspired mystical thoughts—some phenomenal, dominating force emanating from him that formed a fascinating aura . . .

When those piercing amber eyes burned over her, Roz swore he had sucked the breath right out of her. The look on the man's chiseled face was so hard, so utterly devoid of emotion that she felt she was indeed staring at a bronze statue perched above the plunging chasm. Till the day she died, she would not forget that first, devastating impression, that stony vision poised before a backdrop of craggy boulders, Ponderosa pines and jagged mountain crests.

Without a word of greeting or even the semblance of a smile, the rider reined his black steed sideways. A quiet summons in a foreign tongue brought the powerful black cats obediently behind him.

Roz watched the half-naked rider assemble the cattle herd as if they were regimented troops. The cats prowled the perimeters like posted guards, ever conscious of what transpired around them—just like their formidable master . . .

"Who the blazes is that man?" Roz asked the world at large.

"Cougar," Cal answered.

"Not the cats, Cal," Roz patiently corrected her young companion. "The *man*."

Cal tilted his suntanned face upward and smiled a smile that affected every miniature feature on his face. *"He* is *Cougar.* Ma says some folks call him the Colorado Cat Man." Cal leaned close to convey a confidential comment. "I've heard some of the passengers at the stage station say he's the devil himself, traveling with his ghost cats, but that ain't true."

Roz glanced across the high mountain meadow at the brawny giant. She vaguely recalled the tales she had heard from the travelers who passed through Howard Station. She had shrugged them off as local folklore and hadn't given the stories another thought. Now she realized that the tales carried a great deal of truth.

*"Isn't* true," Roz said belatedly.

"You don't think so, either?"

"No, I mean that you should use *isn't* rather than *ain't."*

Cal wrinkled his pug nose. "I know Ma asked you to straighten out my English while you was—"

*"Were—"*

"—here," Cal continued. "But Cougar says it don't— doesn't matter what a man says or how he says it. It's what he *does* that counts."

"You are well acquainted with Cougar, are you?" Roz inquired as she knelt to gather the bottles of paint and canvas that were strewn around her like casualties of a stampede.

"Me and him are—"

"He and I, Cal," she patiently amended.

Cal inhaled a deep breath and began again. "He and I are good friends, even if Cougar don't—doesn't claim to have many of them. He likes me."

One certainly could not have determined *that* by the look on Cougar's rugged face, Roz mused. The Stone Man had offered Cal no more than a cool glance before riding off to gather his cattle. And furthermore, the inconsiderate lout hadn't even bothered to apologize for demolishing Roz's easel and ruining her painting of the mining camp that was tucked in the spectacular valley below. There was a hoofprint in the canvas where a carefully sketched tent should have been!

While Roz was walking around, collecting her art supplies, a sharp whistle sent Cal bounding across the meadow. Roz muttered under her breath. If that heathen ever tried to call *her* with a whistle she would certainly have something to say about that!

A mischievous thought caused Roz to smile as she plucked up the red paint and returned it to its proper place. On a dare, she would paint a smile on Cougar's full mouth. She would also paint a shirt on that incredibly masculine chest. It was too distracting by half.

When Roz glanced over her shoulder to monitor Cougar's activities, she was shocked to see him riding off with Cal perched behind him. The rude heathen hadn't offered to help her gather her supplies after they had been sent flying and she had been mowed down by his herd. Nor had he bothered to inform her that he was taking Cal only God knew where!

Roz bolted to her feet, hiked up her hindering skirts and dashed off. "Come back here this instant!" she shouted, one arm flapping like laundry on a clothesline. "What do you think you're doing with that boy!"

Cougar halted his steed, watching the bundle of pink fluff scurry toward him. From his bird's-eye view he was granted an unhindered display of cleavage. The tantalizing sight reminded him that he may have only been half white but he was *all* man. Cougar didn't appreciate the scintillating sensations this delicate vision of femininity stirred in him. He didn't enjoy admiring and craving something that was so far off limits to him that it couldn't even qualify as temptation. *Forbidden* was nearer the mark.

*Temptation,* in Cougar's estimation, was that which teased a man into taking what he knew he should leave alone. *Forbidden* was that which, if taken, could become a torment that would haunt a man's days and nights. Miss Gaylord was definitely forbidden fruit. She could be looked upon but never touched. Her cultured accent and refined beauty indicated generations of blue-blooded breeding. She was out of his reach, and Cougar shouldn't even be thinking what he was thinking or craving what he was wanting. It was completely out of the question.

Panting for breath, Roz stumbled to a halt when the three snarling cats bade her to stop where she was—or else. Breasts heaving, Roz peered into those cold golden eyes and struggled for composure. "Excuse me, but just where do you think you're taking Cal? His mother entrusted him into my care and I promised to keep an eye on him."

Cougar looked down his nose and snorted derisively. "Lady, you can't even defend yourself against a herd of cattle. The boy is better off with me, even on one of my bad days."

"You have good ones?" Roz smarted off.

Cougar cocked a dark brow in response to the snippy retort. He wasn't accustomed to having anyone sass him.

The fact that this mere slip of a woman dared to cross him caught him off guard.

Cal tapped Cougar on the shoulder. "She don't—doesn't know you like I do," he explained. "I didn't have time to tell her everything before you whistled at me."

"And that's another thing, sir," Roz piped up. "You don't call a twelve-year-old boy with a whistle. It's degrading. Cal is not one of your pet panthers that comes to heel at your command!"

Cougar's brows jackknifed. Not only did decent, respectable women from civilization *not* speak to him, they *never* lectured him. In fact, his usual contact with females was the kind made in a prone position on the beds in bordellos. Those encounters had been few and far between, and usually with paramours who had imbibed so much whiskey they didn't know or care who he was.

"It's okay, Miss Gaylord," Cal spoke up good-naturedly. "Me and Cougar are friends."

"Cougar and *I* are friends,"

*"We* are *not* friends, paleface," Cougar grunted disrespectfully.

Roz threw up her hands in exasperation. "Fine, we are not friends. Just give me the boy and you can go on your way."

"No."

Roz blinked at the stern baritone voice. "Cal happens to be my responsibility."

"Not anymore," Cougar assured her as he nudged the black gelding eastward. "You look to be the kind who has her hands full taking care of herself."

On that parting shot, Cougar trotted off with Cal happily clinging to him.

Cal glanced over his shoulder and sighed. "Ain't Miss Gaylord the prettiest thing you ever saw, Cougar? Ma says she never met a real live lady before Roz came along. She's from New York, you know."

"No, I didn't know." Cougar replied in a voice of disinterest which didn't discourage the gregarious youngster who was known to talk a man's leg off and drill a barrage of questions when he was in one of his frequent inquisitive moods.

"She's a painter," Caleb continued as he settled himself comfortably behind the brawny half-breed.

"So I gathered."

"A good one, too. The painting she was doing of the mining camp looked wonderful until your calf stepped in the middle of it—"

"Which would not have happened if you hadn't been flapping your arms like a goose," Cougar cut in gruffly. "An Indian knows never to startle animals."

"I'm not an Indian," Cal reminded him.

Cougar glanced over his shoulder at the shaggy-haired boy who had eyes like a doe. "Someday, knowing what an Indian knows might save your life."

"You mean like the time you sensed trouble ahead and sent your horse and the cougars down the trail while you sneaked up on that outlaw from behind to gun him down?"

Cougar frowned darkly. "Where did you hear that?"

"From some of the men who were taking their meal at the station. I've heard lots of stories about the days when you were a gunslinger tracking criminals." Cal wrapped his arms tightly around Cougar's lean waist when the trail descended at a steep grade. "Pa says you was—were the best there ever was, bar none."

"Your pa talks too much," Cougar muttered.

"He's not really my pa, you know."

"I know."

"Don't know who my kin is," Cal added quietly.

"Neither do I."

Caleb stared at Cougar's broad back. "You're a bastard, too?"

Cougar jerked his head around and glowered at the chattering lad. "You shouldn't be talking like that, kid. Your ma will have you chewing on soap for supper."

"Well, *are* you?" Cal persisted.

"Don't you ever get tired of yammering?"

"Nope," Cal answered proudly. "I can talk day and night. Want to hear me?"

"No, I'll take your word for it."

"Are you going to take me fishing, like you promised last time you was—were here?"

The boy, Cougar decided, had the memory of an elephant. Cal never forgot a promise. Too bad he would grow up to be a white man—and they never kept a promise. But Cal wasn't going to be like that if Cougar had anything to do with it.

Cougar well remembered when the Indian agent at the reservation decided to make a white man out of him. And in turn, Black Kettle, peace chief of the Cheyenne, promised to make an Indian out of the agent. The novel experiment had worked well for the agent. Benjamin Hunter learned to think and reason like a Cheyenne, learned the rituals and customs that motivated the tribe. Benjamin had come to understand Indians better than most white men and he had been the one who taught Cougar how to behave like the whites when it was to his advantage to do so.

And then the soldiers came to the peaceful camp on the Washita River, invading like menacing hordes, murdering women and children who'd never raised a hand against Custer and his cavalry.

To this day Cougar could still smell the coppery scent of blood flowing like a river, hear the bark of rifles and the haunting screams of the dying . . .

And that was the day everything inside Cougar died . . .

"Cougar? Are you okay?" Caleb questioned after the long silence. "Are we going fishing?"

Cougar made a pact with himself, there and then. This talkative orphan who had been taken in by the Howards was *not* going to grow up to be like most white men. Caleb would know and understand the ways of the Indian. He would view the world through two sets of eyes, just as Cougar did. Cougar would teach this lad what Cal's adopted father couldn't teach him. And for all the worthless souls Cougar had sent to the white man's hell with his pistol, rifle and knife, there would be one young man in the next generation who wouldn't spit his last words in an Indian's face, or sneer with contempt. The prejudices that separated Indian from white would dissolve only when there were enough Caleb Howards in the world to judge a man by his worth, not by the color of his skin.

"We'll go fishing and hunting, Cal," Cougar said finally. "Indian style."

"What does that mean?"

"You'll find out after your pa and I cut out the calves he wants and he takes his pick of this string of horses."

Cal's tanned face brightened with anticipation. "Did you bring me the pony you promised last time you were here?"

"Don't Indians always keep their word?"

"Of course they do. Indians never lie."

Cougar nodded somberly, assured that his subtle attempts to alter Caleb's attitudes had been successful. This impressionable lad and his parents were Cougar's only tie to civilization, his one attempt to keep in touch with his white heritage. It was all Cougar could manage after the vicious bloodletting on the Washita.

For each worthless outlaw Cougar had struck down in the name of white man's justice, he counted the lives of the Cheyenne who fell beneath the Army's rifles and bayonets. Cougar had never quite evened the score, but he had reached the point where killing no longer affected what was left of his conscience. He could launch murderers and thieves into hell without batting an eyelash. He could watch a man breathe his last breath while cursing Cougar's name, and feel absolutely nothing at all, not even vengeful satisfaction.

And when Cougar had used up all that was left of his very soul, he had walked away from his dangerous profession of manhunting. He was still looking for a purpose in his isolated life, a purpose he had yet to find. The mountain cabin on his ranch that he shared with Gray Eagle, a fugitive from the massacre on the Washita, brought a certain sense of belonging and inner peace. Cougar's contact with Caleb and his family granted him limited pleasure. And in between were the bitter memories, the blood-stained visions that haunted his sleep.

Some memories never died, Cougar reminded himself grimly, only the massacred Cheyenne clan who made them did . . .

# Two

Cougar stared pensively at the bowl-shaped valley while he trailed the cattle down the narrow path. Howard Stage Station and Trading Post were always a hubbub of activity. Gideon Howard had situated his ranch against the towering peaks to ward off the chill of icy winter winds, and Francene's famous homecooked meals lured travelers, miners and news reporters to this majestic meadow that set against a backdrop of rocky peaks. This was the stage lines' central location in the foothills of the Rockies, the site where paths diverged in all directions.

Francene's and Gideon's industriousness had paid off financially. They provided the essentials of food, lodging and travel connections. The only thing Howard's home station lacked that Finnegan's Station—located fifteen miles to the south—provided was a bordello.

The Howards were as close to being family as anyone in Cougar's life. Cougar had once broken up a fight between drunken prospectors who had tried to wreck the trading post. The Howards had insisted on paying Cougar for his trouble, but all he had asked in return was one of Francene's famous meals. Four years past, when Cougar had been seriously wounded during an ambush, Francene and Gideon had taken him in and nursed him back to health.

The friendship had strengthened while Cougar recovered from the three bullet wounds. After he'd healed, he went after the outlaw gang that had bushwhacked him. The outlaws' trail of death and destruction had come to a quick end, and Cougar had collected a staggering amount of bounty money for his trouble.

Cougar never forgot the kindness the Howards had bestowed on him or the lively young boy they had taken into their fold when Cal's unwed mother abandoned him in the Denver streets. Since those days, Cougar came to Howard Station to sell beef and well-trained horses for the stages.

Even though the visitors at the inn and trading post took a wide berth around Cougar, the Howards always welcomed him. He had grown to respect the fifty-year-old Gideon who had been injured during his stint in the Civil War. Although Gideon walked with a stiff left leg and leaned heavily on a cane, he was still an ambitious businessman who labored long and hard to provide for his family. Gideon had suffered a kind of torment similar to what Cougar had experienced. Though they rarely spoke of past horrors, there was a bond of mutual respect and understanding.

As for the forty-four-year-old Francene Howard, Cougar had nothing but polite respect. While most white women looked down their noses at Cougar, as if he were a freak from a traveling circus, Francene treated him like a younger brother. Cougar had come to expect a welcoming smile from Francene each time he showed up.

Yes, Cougar mused, feeling Caleb's arms anchor

around his waist as they made their final descent into the valley. This was Cougar's adopted family, his link with white civilization, the one place he could come and feel accepted.

"Cougar! It's about time you showed up!"

As anticipated, Francene Howard waved in enthusiastic greeting when she spied the herd of cattle and the approaching rider. Cougar raised an arm in response before glancing toward the barn to see Gideon limp outside.

"I've been expecting you for at least a week," Francene said as she strode off the porch, pausing the customary distance from the black cats that milled around Cougar. "Cal has been asking about you for a full month."

Cougar reached around behind him to lift the youngster from his horse and set him to the ground.

Francene blinked in surprise. "Cal? Did something happen? Where's Roz?"

The mention of the alluring woman Cougar had encountered the previous hour spoiled his disposition. Rozalie Gaylord had come to mind once or twice during the ride, even while Cal was rattling nonstop, leaping from one subject to another like a mountain goat. Cougar didn't enjoy being preoccupied with that curvaceous blonde. He had written Rozalie off the moment he met her, even if his male body had paid no attention to the good advice sent down by his brain.

"Cougar didn't bring Miss Gaylord, just me," Caleb contributed as he nonchalantly strolled past the black pumas. When he paused to pat the nearest cat on the head, Cougar's sharp command left Caleb's hand dangling in midair. "Sorry, Cougar, I forgot. Don't touch the cats, right?"

"Right," Cougar confirmed.

Francene cupped her hand over her eyes and squinted into the sunlight. "What did you think of our Miss Gaylord, Cougar?"

"I didn't think of her at all," Cougar said with a gruff snort, aware that he was lying through his teeth. And here he had told Cal that Indians never lied. Well, Cougar was half white, after all. Didn't that entitle him to a few *white* lies? Fact was, he had thought about Rozalie aplenty . . . and resented every moment of it.

"Cougar looked at Miss Gaylord a lot, though," Caleb said, adding his unwanted two cents' worth.

Cougar glared the loose-lipped lad into silence. There were times—like now—when Cougar wished Cal wasn't compelled to share his every thought with the world. Cougar was going to have to break the kid of that bad habit. They would discuss the importance of silence while he was teaching Cal to hunt and fish.

Francene smiled knowingly. "Roz is a very attractive and sophisticated young lady. It would be difficult not to notice her. And she has an exceptional talent as an artist and illustrator. *Harper's Weekly* and *Scribner's Monthly* have paid her handsomely to do articles and illustrations on Western life."

Cougar stared somberly at Francene. "Why?"

"Why?" Francene smiled at the rough-edged half-breed whom she had come to call a friend. "Well, because folks in the East are curious about our way of life and the activities of mining camps. Ours is almost another civilization in itself, after all."

"And what does a New Yorker know about our way of life?" Cougar snorted sardonically. "She might *see* what we are, but she can never understand what makes us what we are. Only a Westerner can describe Western life."

Francene frowned curiously at Cougar's clipped tone. "Did you have a disagreement with Roz?"

"She's here; that's all." Cougar signaled to the cats to drive the cattle toward the corral bringing an end to the subject of Roz Gaylord.

While Gideon and Cougar separated the cattle, Francene pivoted around and strode inside to tend the meal she had placed on the stove. The evening stage was due to arrive in an hour. Several of the patrons at the inn were waiting to catch the stage bound for Colorado Springs.

"Mama, how come Cougar don't—doesn't like Miss Gaylord when everybody else does?" Cal questioned as he followed in Francene's wake.

"Cougar likes Roz just fine."

"But he said he didn't."

Francene wrapped her arm affectionately around her adopted son and herded him into the trading post. "It's often hard to tell what Cougar likes and doesn't like."

"But he likes me. I know he does," Cal said proudly. "And he likes you and Pa."

"But that's a different kind of *like*," Francene clarified.

"How is it different?"

Francene heaved an exasperated sigh. "Just set the plates on the table for me. Like your friend Cougar says—you ask too many questions."

* * *

Gideon Howard limped around the corral, assessing the dozen head of fattened steers Cougar had brought for sale. "I'll take six of them," he decided. "The summer months are always our busiest season at the station. We can barely keep enough food in stock to feed the flocks of travelers who pass through here. I'm going to have to butcher a calf tomorrow. It's a good thing you showed up when you did."

"What about the horses?" Cougar questioned, indicating the string of mustangs that were tethered beside the gate.

"I can use a half dozen of them, too. These rugged roads through the mountain passes are hard on livestock," Gideon said as he absently rubbed his stiff left leg. "Two of our best teams came up lame after being pushed too hard. The drivers have been trying to outrun those renegades who are preying on the coaches. I heard a gang of thieves attacked a stage near Denver last week and made off with a strongbox containing one thousand dollars in gold dust."

Gideon propped himself against the corral and swiped a beefy hand through his crop of silver-brown hair. "According to reports, the stage line is hauling a gold consignment to the Denver mint next week. We'll need all the fresh, sturdy horses we can get, if those thieves get wind of that information."

"I suppose General Cook and his Rocky Mountain Detectives have been tracking the thieves," Cougar grumbled before he ambled over to separate half the cattle into the adjoining pen.

Gideon nodded affirmatively. "I've heard that the posse has been on the gang's trail for three weeks without much luck." He eyed Cougar's powerful physique and the bandoleers that crisscrossed his muscled back. "But since they don't have your tracking ability, the posse always seems to arrive in time to console the survivors of holdups and bury the latest victims."

Cougar fastened the gate behind the cattle and pivoted to face Gideon. "I retired from that line of work."

"And there hasn't been anybody of your caliber to take your place," Gideon declared. "Folks still tell stories about your phenomenal feats. You and your cats have become a living legend in these parts."

Cougar's reply was a cynical snort. He would just as soon not have his name bandied about.

"Well, all the same, there's a hefty bounty on this gang of outlaws. The posse would gladly split the reward with you if you and your cats would track the desperados down."

"I—" Cougar's voice trailed off when something—or someone—caught the corner of his eye just below the crest of rocks where the road circled the jutting mountain. Cougar intended to look the other way, he really did. But there was something instinctively intriguing about the delicate blonde who was certainly a feast for the eyes. She drew Cougar's eyes and thoughts and held them fast, much to his dismay.

It must have been because Roz Gaylord was the first full-fledged lady Cougar had ever met. Her regal bearing and eloquent manner of speech indicated intelligence nurtured and groomed with years of formal education. Pedigree was stamped all over her—from her fair complexion to the expensive lace petticoats that peeked from beneath the hem of her gown.

Attractive though Francene Howard was, she was a dim glow in comparison to the lovely Rozalie Gaylord. It annoyed Cougar to no end that this woman's appearance had such a potent effect on him.

*Forbidden,* Cougar reminded himself, even as his gaze flooded over her shapely figure, missing not even the smallest detail.

Gideon chuckled when he noticed where Cougar's eyes had strayed. "Now there's the touchstone," he said, replacing his Stetson on his head. "If Roz attracts *your* attention, then her effect on every male traveler who passes through here is no fluke."

Willfully, Cougar dragged his gaze back to Gideon and frowned, puzzled.

Gideon hobbled toward the corral gate, still grinning in amusement. "Men have been falling all over themselves to sit by Roz at the dining table. They follow her around like panting puppies, always eager to assist her, no matter what she happens to be doing. I figured most of these poor prospectors were starved for affection. But if Roz distracts even *you,* then there's not a damned thing wrong with all the rest of us who can't help but admire her stunning beauty."

"You're married," Cougar pointed out gruffly.

Gideon nodded positively. "I'm *very* married. I love my wife the way I've never loved another living soul. Don't ever doubt that. But . . ." Gideon glanced in Roz's direction and grinned. "Even the good book doesn't say there's anything wrong with paying visual respect to a beautiful woman. It's like enjoying a breathtaking view of magnificent scenery. *Not* to look would be like ignoring one of the seven wonders of the world."

Cougar strode over to untie his horse and lead it into the barn. "That particular white woman doesn't fit in here," he muttered. "The Yankee would be better off if she packed up and went back East."

Gideon snickered at Cougar's scowling tone. "As I recall, you once said you didn't fit in here, either. But you keep coming back for our hospitality and we keep looking forward to having you here."

Cougar flung Gideon a hard glare. "I may not be back again if you open your home to bits of fluff like this one. Thinking of opening a bordello here, just like Finnegan's Station?"

Gideon jerked upright, his smile vanishing in two shakes. "Now hold on there, Cougar. You know I call you my friend and that you are always welcome in my home anytime you please. But don't even think that Roz is *that* kind of woman! She attended one of the finest schools in the East and graduated with honors. She was recognized for her artistic and literary abilities, too. After her pa died she came West because she has no family left. Roz inherited a fortune that had those Eastern dandies stampeding all over each other to offer marriage proposals. She came here to paint and to mourn in peace. She's a true lady and don't you ever try to convince yourself otherwise."

Cougar's thick brow elevated at Gideon's explosive tone. Hell's jangling bells, if one didn't know better, one would have thought this ex-Confederate soldier had adopted Roz as his daughter. That really shouldn't surprise Cougar, now that he thought about it. Gideon had taken in the young orphan and made friends with a halfbreed whom no one ever wanted around unless he was ridding towns and mining camps of riffraff. Folks tolerated Cougar when he could resolve their problems. And afterwards, the townsfolk couldn't wait to shovel him out of their way.

When Gideon limped off to assist Roz from her horse, Cougar propelled himself toward the barn. Maybe everything in breeches clamored to Rozalie Gaylord, but Cougar sure as hell wasn't about to. Roz was a prissy Easterner who was obviously accustomed to preferential treatment from men. She wouldn't get it from Cougar. The less association with Roz the better Cougar liked it.

The Howards could take in all the strays they wanted, but that didn't mean Cougar had to bend over backward to be nice. Besides, most folks expected him to be mean and nasty, living up to his ominous reputation as the stalking Cat Man.

And furthermore, Cougar was *not* going to sniff around those fluffy, pastel pink skirts like every other man within a hundred miles. Roz didn't need another male companion and he didn't need her.

Cougar needed no one . . .

The warning growl of the ever-present cats caused the other horses in the stables to dance uneasily in their stalls. Out of reflexive habit, Cougar wheeled around, his pistol leaping from holster to hand in less than a heartbeat.

A shocked gasp flew off Roz's lips when she found herself staring at the silver barrel of a pistol and saw the three black shadows swirling around Cougar's buckskin-clad legs. Cougar had a most appalling way of alienating people, she decided. He was as wary of mankind as his unusual pets, and probably just as deadly, if the stories she had heard were true. More and more, Roz was beginning to think they were.

Cougar shoved his pistol into his holster and strode forward. "I'll take care of the horse, Yank. You better prance back to the trading post before you get dirt on those fancy shoes of yours."

Before Cougar could snatch the gray mare's reins from Roz's hands, she tucked them behind her back and lifted a defiant chin. "I have learned to care for horses myself, thank you very much."

Cougar wheeled around, refusing to endure the visual torment of a woman so far off limits to him that it was ridiculous to entertain the erotic thoughts that kept dancing in his head.

"All I want from you is an apology for being unnecessarily rude and inconsiderate," Roz declared, surveying the sleek lines of Cougar's back and the powerful columns of his legs that were emphasized by the close-fitting buckskin. "You ruined my painting and I'm sure you would like to apologize for it."

"You thought wrong, paleface," Cougar scowled as he reached beneath his horse to unfasten the cinch. "You were practically camped out in the middle of the damned road. What the hell did you expect? For me and anyone else who came along to climb up the side of the mountain to bypass you?"

Roz clenched her teeth. She was not going to be intimidated by this cantankerous rapscallion, even if he had guard lions waiting to pounce at his command. "Now see here, Cougar. You act as if you think you

own this whole blessed territory. I have just as much
right to set up my easel and sketch as you have to—"

Roz's words evaporated on her lips when Cougar
rounded on her, wearing a snarl to match his accompanying cats. *"My* people laid claim to this entire territory,
as well as that of Wyoming, Nebraska and Kansas," he
growled into her peaked face. "That was before *your*
people decided they liked the looks of the place and
took it over, any way they could. They came with rifles,
poison and disease. Now, the only land *my* people are
allowed to have are the regions *your* people haven't figured out what to do with yet. And mark my words, *Miss
Gaylord,* when the whites decide Indian Territory appeals to them, they'll take that, too!"

Roz found herself staring up at six-foot-two inches
and two hundred pounds of virility. She tried to ignore
him. "And that is all my fault?" Roz asked, bracing
herself against his stormy glare and thundering voice.
"Just because you carry a grudge then *I* am supposed
to be your scapegoat, is that it?"

Cougar stepped back apace when he realized Roz was
right. He had become accustomed to blaming all whites
for the despicable actions of their government and society. Maybe it wasn't this woman's fault that his people
had been mistreated and confined to those loathsome
prisons called reservations, but damn it, there was something about this fetching blue-eyed blonde that infuriated
him.

The fact that Cougar had backed off enough to give
her breathing space prompted Roz to take *her* frustra-
tions out on him, just as he had aired his griefs on her.
Turn about was fair play.

"And by the same token, I suppose I should resent *you* personally since I have recently found myself overrun with marriage proposals, simply because I had the misfortune of inheriting scads of money. Since most men are eager to separate me from my fortune, it surely must follow that *you,* like *them,* are a shallow mercenary, motivated only by greed, who cares nothing for my feelings or my wishes."

Cougar blinked, fascinated by the woman's impressive command of the English language and her crisp Eastern accent. Her intelligence and culture were as obvious as a wart on the end of one's nose. Physically, Roz was no match for Cougar, but intellectually? He began to wonder.

"And now, Mr. Cougar—"

"Just Cougar," he amended gruffly.

"And now *Just Cougar,* if you will excuse me, I will stable the mare before going inside to help Francene put the finishing touches on supper." Roz lifted a delicate chin and her blue eyes sparked with undeniable spirit. "And after the dishes are washed, and you have undoubtedly had the chance to bite the head off of everyone within snapping distance, because we have committed the ultimate sin of being born white, I would like to sketch you and your cats for my journals. I want the world to see what a madman looks like."

When Roz tried to brush past him, Cougar's steely hand clamped around her elbow, jerking her back to his side. Roz found herself peering into a sneer that had the black cats cowering in the corner. It had the same effect on Roz, but she was angry enough to defy him on general principle alone.

"I won't *sit* for you, Yank, and I sure as hell won't come to heel." There, that should get her goat, thought Cougar.

Roz marshalled her courage and held up her free hand, bound and determined to draw the battle lines—here and now. "Would you like to take a bite out of my finger to prove to me that you are as uncivilized as you want me to believe? Go ahead, if it makes you feel better. By all means, add another frightening tale to the legends circulating about you. I've already heard it said that you once fed the outlaw you tracked to your man-eating lions. And of course, let's not forget that tall tale of how Dead Man's Mountain came to have its name, and how you strung up three murderers, Indian style, and left them for the buzzards on some lonely stretch of road. And I would be remiss if I failed to mention how the legendary Cat Man cut the heart out of—"

It was increasingly apparent that Roz didn't own a goat that could be gotten. Of course, coming from New York, Cougar should have realized that. She, however, was getting *his* goat! "That's enough!" Cougar growled, baring his teeth.

"Ouch!" Roz wailed in pain when his viselike grip very nearly crushed the bone in her arm.

"For your information, I don't track outlaws anymore," he muttered at her.

"No?" Roz said through a grimace. "But aren't you still crucifying the rest of us for sins we haven't committed—?"

Cougar told himself the ultimate reason he snaked an arm around Roz's waist and hauled her against him was to intimidate her into silence and frighten her into keeping her distance from him in the future.

Damn, now he was also lying to *himself.* His white heritage was really corrupting him!

Despite the mental tug of war raging inside him, Cougar felt his body clench with need as he stared at her petal-soft mouth, craving a taste of her. The feel of her creamy breasts mashing against his bare chest caused a jolt of awareness to sizzle through him. Cougar hated his impulsive attraction and yet was unable to control the rousing needs that pulsated through him, as Roz writhed against his suddenly sensitive body in her attempt to escape his imprisoning embrace.

It was a long moment before Cougar summoned the willpower to set the forbidden beauty away from him, though he was compelled to keep his fingers clasped around her wrist, granting himself the simplest of touches.

Now he'd really done it, damn it. The feel of her soft feminine body pressed familiarly to his burned on his flesh. Cougar struck out against the bittersweet pleasure that was already beginning to torment him, struck out at the frustration of knowing this woman had the power to shatter his self-restraint as if it never existed.

"Lady, unless you want to find yourself flat on your back in the straw, I suggest you leave me the hell alone from here on out," Cougar muttered into her stunned expression. "And you are not going to immortalize me on canvas so your Eastern cronies will have one more excuse to restrict my kind until we have to ask permission from whites to even breathe! The less we see of each other the better, and I better not see myself on canvas!"

"And I refuse to be bullied about by a man, any man—especially the likes of you!" Roz spluttered. "Just because I'm a woman is no excuse for you or any other man to think you can talk down to me and treat me like a second-class citizen! I want only one thing from you and one thing only—an apology for damaging my art equipment and my painting. That is common courtesy, *Just Cougar.* I demand no less from you and I expect nothing more. For sure and certain, I wish none of your attention, because it appears to be as shallow as that of every other man who wants only one thing from a woman, no matter what civilization he hails from!"

Her blue eyes glittered with frustration. Roz tried to jerk her arm from Cougar's grasp, but it was a waste of energy. "Let me go!"

Cougar was annoyed. He didn't like this sassy female, but the man in him hungered for a taste of her. It had been a long time since he'd had a woman. That, Cougar assured himself, was the *only* reason Rozalie Gaylord so easily aroused him. The minute he touched her, his masculine body had reacted primitively. When he stared into those luminous blue eyes and got lost in their glittering depths, he forgot she was off limits. When he ventured too close, the scent of jasmine clogged his senses. He had reacted to pure male instinct. Hell and damnation. For a man who prided himself on his unflappable self-control, he'd certainly lost it with this feisty female.

Truth be told, Cougar didn't know why he felt the need to vent all his frustration on her. Maybe she was right, though he was loath to admit it. Maybe he *was* making her a scapegoat for his smoldering resentment. And maybe he had used his anger as a shield against this fierce physical attraction. Not that it had worked worth a damn, he reminded himself disgustedly. It galled Cougar to admit that he wasn't really fighting Roz. The greatest enemy he faced, he realized with a start, was *himself* . . .

Roz's thick-lashed gaze swept up when she felt the stranglehold on her arm relax. She met those glistening amber eyes and watched a muscle leap in his clenched jaw. She inclined her head to survey him from a different angle, studying his profile in the slanting light that filtered into the shadowed stables. Although Cougar still reminded her of a sculpture carved in stone, she sensed a subtle and intriguing change in him. She wondered, if—beneath that burning hatred for a world that had not been shaped to his specifications—Cougar actually harbored other emotions. When he hauled her up against him, she thought she had felt something other than his frustration.

But it was very difficult to tell, Roz thought. Cougar had such a hard, callous shell that it wouldn't be easy to penetrate his protective shield. And yet, there was something disturbingly appealing about him, even if Roz would have preferred to shoot herself in the hand rather than admit it to him.

Roz was reminded of the English fairy tale about a kiss that had transformed a monster into a prince. If she tested the whimsical theory on Cougar he would probably still scowl at her like a fire-breathing dragon.

The thought put a trace of a smile on her lips. Why, Roz wondered, did a *woman*'s basic nature compel her to change a *man*'s basic nature? Why was she suddenly determined to offer Cougar tenderness when he seemed perfectly content to remain locked in his stony shell?

Impulsively, Roz reached up to limn his high cheekbones, the stern lines that bracketed his sensuous mouth. He jerked away from her as if her touch had branded him with fire. Fascinated, Roz touched him again, noting that this time he didn't retreat, that he was appraising her with an unfathomable expression. The untouchable Cougar had yielded, if only slightly, to gentleness. But to Roz, it was as if she had accomplished a remarkable feat. She had touched this half-wild creature who understood hatred far better than he understood tender affection.

Spellbound, she traced the curve of his mouth with her forefinger before her hand glided down the column of his neck to span the breadth of his muscular chest.

Cougar was right, Roz decided. To sketch this impressive mass of living strength on canvas might immortalize him, but it would be impossible to capture his raw power and dominating force. Perhaps Cougar scoffed at the legends that circulated about him, but she could sense a uniqueness about him. And if she were to be honest with herself, she would admit that she resented her inability to match him. He would always be his own man in a world that granted very little space to women. She envied him that.

A sigh escaped Roz's lips as she dropped the gray mare's reins in his hand and stepped away. As intriguing

as she found this man, for reasons she couldn't satisfactorily explain, she recognized the futility of trying to
befriend him. She was as alone in this world as he was,
but Cougar didn't want or need her underfoot. She
would make no further attempt at a truce. They would
grant each other their own space, nothing more.

"Although we seem to have nothing in common, I
have the feeling you and I are more alike than you want
to admit, *Just Cougar.*"

"Doubt it, Yankee," he grunted.

When Roz turned and walked away, Cougar stood
there for the longest time, lost to the lingering sensations provoked by her gentle touch. Everything in him
rebelled against letting her walk out when he ached to
know the pleasure a woman like Roz could provide. But
that, Cougar quickly reminded himself, would breed disaster of the worst sort. He and Rozalie Gaylord were
galaxies apart. If he dared to step over the line again
and follow the call of his rioting male body, he expected
to encounter another of the disappointments that life
seemed so determined to deal him. The pleasure he
might discover would become a torment. One thing he
knew for certain was that he and this enchanting bluestocking had no future together.

Besides, he told himself fiercely, he could appease
his lusts with any woman. It need not be this delicate
nymph. As Gideon had emphatically pointed out, Roz
was not the kind of woman whom a man took to his
bed and then walked away without looking back. But
still . . .

"Cougar, when are we going fishing? And which one
of those ponies is mine?"

Cougar glanced over his shoulder to see Caleb poised in the entryway. He was almost relieved to be sharing the chattering youngster's companionship. Caleb and his incessant questions were the distraction Cougar desperately needed right now. His body was throbbing in places he would like to forget he had.

Introducing Cal to his new pony would keep Cougar plenty busy. Too bad the piebald colt couldn't talk. Sure as hell, Cougar was going to get stuck answering a thousand and one questions.

# Three

"Thanks for taking Cal hunting and fishing yesterday," Gideon said as he and Cougar tossed hay into the mangers in the barn. He paused to lean against the nearest stall, absently massaging his stiff leg. "Francene and I find ourselves doing such a thriving business that we don't have as much time to spend with Cal as we would like."

Cougar continued to fill the mangers with straw. "I'm trying to teach Cal not to talk so much. He still frightens the game away during a hunt."

Gideon chuckled as he picked up his pitchfork. "He is full of questions, isn't he?"

Yes, thought Cougar. The boy had posed several disturbing questions that Cougar preferred not to answer— all of them pertained to Rozalie Gaylord.

The previous evening, while Cougar was ensconced at the far end of the table—Cal being the only diner who dared to come near him—the other travelers had flocked around Roz's end of the table. When she stood up to leave, men scrambled to their feet, bowing and scraping over her as if she were visiting royalty. For the most part, Cougar had stared at his plate and tried to keep his eyes to himself. He was the *only* man who had made the effort.

Later that evening, when Cougar returned from taking the cats to feed, he had seen Roz poised on a wooden crate. She had been sketching three men lounging on the porch, taking their evening smoke. Cougar had tried to go about his own business, but he found his eyes straying to the silhouette beside the gleaming lantern. All in all, Cougar had worn himself out trying not to notice everything that shapely female said and did. It greatly disturbed him that *ignoring* her demanded such conscious effort . . .

The sound of a distant bugle put the sprawling cats on their feet and sent a chill down Cougar's spine. He wondered if the day would ever come when a bugle call wouldn't incite nightmares of the morning charge that left the Cheyenne camp on the Washita River running with blood.

Gideon set his pitchfork aside when he heard the signal of the approaching stage. "The coach is late. I hope they didn't have trouble along the route—"

Before Gideon could collect the fresh horses, Cougar surged in front of him to tend the task. As always, the cats followed obediently behind him. Gideon backed up apace to let the formidable foursome pass.

"You don't have to do that, Cougar."

Cougar's only reply was a shrug.

Gideon noted the impressive speed with which Cougar hitched the harnesses in place and sent the horses down the aisle. The cats had been trained to work with livestock, and were as efficient as dogs, moving the steeds toward the barn exit. To say that Gideon was impressed was an understatement. It never ceased to amaze him that those black cats responded dutifully to Cougar's clipped commands.

As vicious as mountain lions could be in their own domain, Cougar had domesticated the orphaned cubs at such an early age that they thought *he* was their mother. Although Mexican tigers—as cougars were often called—were independent loners in their native habitat, these coal black cats had formed a clan and never strayed far from Cougar.

"Just how the hell do you do that?" Gideon questioned after Cougar gave a command in the Cheyenne tongue and the cats herded the horses outside.

Cougar turned questioning amber eyes to Gideon. "Do what?"

"How did you train those cats to be so well behaved . . . ?" His voice trailed off when he saw Cougar's attention drift toward the trading post where Roz stood watching the cats hold the horses in position. A wry smile pursed Gideon's lips. Despite Cougar's attempt to ignore the Howards' guest, the half-breed's unwilling interest showed. Loath though Cougar would be to admit it, he was definitely distracted by the stunning blue-eyed blonde.

Cougar scowled when he realized where his gaze had strayed. With a muttered oath, he tethered the horses by the corral. When he pivoted around, Roz was bent over her sketch pad, working fastidiously while a group of travelers hovered over her like flies buzzing around honey.

By the time the coach arrived Roz had completed whatever she had been sketching. The waiting passengers were praising her exceptional talent and voicing their forlorn farewells to her. Cougar grumbled sourly. He had never seen grown men drool over a woman to such disgusting extremes. It was nauseating.

When the stage rolled to a halt and another group of men stepped down, the spellbinding process began again, much to Cougar's annoyance. He and his oversize cats were usually the first thing strangers noticed. Suddenly Cougar had been upstaged by the curvaceous blonde in azure blue satin. Not that Cougar wanted the wary attention he usually received, but it only served to prove what fools white men were. Lust, it seemed, was a stronger instinct than danger.

It was several minutes before the three dusty passengers noticed Cougar and his cats standing at a distance. Cougar knew the instant one of the new arrivals recognized him—by reputation at least. The older man hastily passed Cougar's name to his companion who made a sweeping circle to reach the trading post.

While Cougar was given his customary wide berth, Rozalie Gaylord was surrounded like a queen in her court. Although the congregation of men cast apprehensive glances at Cougar at regular intervals, they were "oohing" and "ahing" over whatever sketch Roz had made.

Cougar wheeled away to hitch the fresh team to the whiffletree of the coach. His gaze landed on the two riders who had followed the stage along its northern route. A niggling sense of uneasiness rippled through Cougar as he readied the team of horses. Instinct warned him to keep a watchful eye on the strangers. Cougar had dealt with enough trouble over the years to smell it when it approached. The scraggly-haired riders looked like trouble waiting to happen. Their well-worn holsters were indication enough that these two men lived by their gunhands.

It wouldn't have surprised Cougar to learn that both of these hombres' faces had been sketched on wanted posters. But these days, that wasn't Cougar's concern. He had retired from the business of reducing the population of criminals in white man's society. Now, he didn't go looking for trouble, even for the money he could acquire . . . But then again, he wasn't about to back away from a problem, either . . .

The riders' gazes swung to Cougar, widening in obvious recognition when they spotted the prowling cats beside the corral. The men muttered something to each other as they swung from their saddles. Cougar surveyed the pot-bellied Mexican and his wiry comrade whose cheek was bulging with such a large wad of tobacco that he resembled a squirrel. If those two new arrivals were honest, hard-working prospectors then Cougar was a fairy-tale prince!

Cougar went about the business of leading the laboring team of horses to water, but he monitored the long riders' activities continuously. The two men kept to themselves while they appraised the trading post, barn and wayside inn.

Pretty damned curious, weren't they? thought Cougar. If he didn't know better he would have sworn the vaquero and his tobacco-chewing sidekick were considering buying the damned place.

The strangers lost interest in Cougar when Roz emerged from the flock of men who congregated around her. The rotund Mexican and his skinny friend followed her with their eyes until she disappeared into the shadows within the barn.

For the life of him, Cougar didn't know why his footsteps took him into the barn after he had fiercely vowed to avoid Roz like the plague. But suddenly there he was, five steps behind her. Before she could set her sketch pad aside to saddle the mare, Cougar opened the stall gate.

Roz wheeled around when she heard the creaking door. She hadn't realized Cougar and his cats had followed her until she found the foursome standing as close as her own shadow.

"Why do you do that?" Roz squeaked, staring up at the tower of living strength who could loom with the same intimidation as a mountain.

Cougar glanced in her general direction. "Why do I do what, Yank?"

Roz gnashed her teeth at the nickname he had given her. "Why do you sneak up without the slightest warning? Do you enjoy scaring people half to death?"

Cougar shrugged a bare shoulder before sliding the bit into the gray mare's mouth. While the horse crunched and rolled the bit, Cougar slung the saddle blanket in place. "Keep your distance from the two long riders," he ordered her.

Roz blinked at the abrupt change in topics. "Why?"

"Because I don't trust them."

"You don't trust anyone, *Just Cougar*," she flung back at him. "Why should the Mexican and his friend be any different?"

"I have a bad feeling about them," was all Cougar said as he eased the saddle onto the mare.

"The same bad feeling you have about me?"

Cougar paused from his task and glanced down at the prim beauty who had the infuriating knack of putting his male body on alert in nothing flat. He knew exactly how every other man felt when he ventured close to this beguiling female.

"Well?" Roz prompted when he tarried so long in thought.

"Yes," Cougar grumbled. "The same bad feeling."

When he spied the sketch Roz had made of him with his cats, he stalked over to snatch it away. The scowl he was presently wearing was identical to the one in the sketch. The portrait made him look as though he were carved from stone. And maybe he was, but he didn't appreciate seeing the hard expression staring back at him. And oddly enough, it bothered him to know this sketch was Roz's perception of him.

"I told you not to draw me," Cougar snapped abrasively.

"Why? Because you don't like what you see?" When Cougar muttered and tried to rip the paper from the pad, Roz jerked it from his hand and held it behind her back. Her chin tilted to a belligerent angle. "You ruined my painting of the mining camp, but you are *not* going to destroy my work today," she told him in no uncertain terms.

Cougar took one ominous step forward. "Give me the sketch, Yank," he ground out menacingly.

Roz tore the drawing from the pad, as if she meant to obey the growling giant. And then, with a look of supreme defiance, she rolled it up and stuffed it down the front of her gown. "No."

Cougar bared his teeth and the cats loomed closer, sensing his rising anger. "Give . . . me . . . the sketch, Yank," he demanded slowly and succinctly.

Roz's delicate chin went airborne. "I said . . . *no.*"

"Don't make me fetch it myself," he hissed in threat.

"Try it and I'll scream the barn down, *Just Cougar.*"

"It won't do you a damned bit of good."

"There are seven men outside, not counting Gideon, who would come running to my rescue."

"And they wouldn't make it through the door before my cats slashed them to ribbons," Cougar guaranteed.

Blue eyes clashed with glittering gold. "You wouldn't dare."

"Don't ever challenge me, Yank. The last four men who did that are buried beneath the bluff called Devil's Mountain with an X marking their eternal resting places. I don't make idle threats. I make deadly promises."

"I see. So I am going to be drawn and quartered, just because I dared to sketch your likeness? Dear God, it must be true that Westerners *do* gun each other down for simply looking at each other the wrong way!" she said in mock horror.

"Lady, you are getting on my bad side," Cougar gritted out. "Don't push it."

Roz peered up into those icy amber eyes. Common sense urged her to submit. Feminine pride refused to let her back down. She was *not* going to be browbeaten by this formidable rascal, even if every man at the stage station tucked his tail between his legs and slinked away from Cougar. The way Roz had it figured, Cougar would already have crammed his hand down the front of her gown to retrieve the sketch if he were as ruthless toward women as he was rumored to be toward men.

And besides, it was the principle of the thing, Roz reminded herself. It was *her* sketch, after all. She had every right to draw whatever she pleased without Cougar's snarling censorship.

"Give me the drawing . . . *now,*" Cougar repeated gruffly. "Don't make me hurt you, Yank."

Roz pivoted toward the mare, only to be whirled around to face Cougar's unpleasant snarl. She realized she had underestimated him. When he dared to reach for the rolled sketch, Roz reflexively clamped her hand over his, unintentionally mashing his hand against her breast. Her quick intake of breath only made matters worse.

Cougar meant to move his hand immediately, really he did. But his fingertips had obviously developed minds of their own. For what seemed an eternity, Cougar found himself staring down into wide sapphire eyes, feeling Roz's accelerated heartbeat pounding against his palm.

Cougar tried to draw a breath, but he was overwhelmed by the alluring scent of expensive perfume. His gaze dropped to the creamy swells displayed to their best advantage by the scoop-necked gown. His thumb grazed the fabric of her gown and chemise that concealed the beaded peak beneath and his fingers gently contracted around her soft flesh. He heard Roz's breath catch and he felt riveting arousal pulsate through his body.

Before Cougar realized what he was doing, his free hand had curled around her hip, guiding her against his hardened flesh. His attention focused on those heart-shaped lips that he had desperately wanted to taste the previous day—and hadn't. When her mouth parted on a shocked gasp, his dark head moved toward hers, lingering only a hairbreadth away. Cougar was lost to the forbidden fantasy that had been hounding him, fighting compelling temptation.

The appetizing feel of her lush body molded to his, sent burgeoning need exploding through him. Cougar's mouth hovered above hers while self-restraint warred with hungry desire. He wanted to crush this fragile female in his arms; he wanted to push her away. Torment . . .

"Damn you, Cougar," Roz rasped shakily.

"I was thinking the same thing myself," he muttered in self-contempt. He wanted to devour the taste of her, commit each curve and swell to tormenting memory, but that was sure to only make matters worse. Damn, she was so tantalizingly close and yet so intolerably far away that he was shaking with the need of her. Him—the man whom legend claimed was carved from rock.

Cougar's knees threatened to buckle beneath him. Not that he would have minded. Sprawling in the straw with this impossible temptress in his arms had tremendous appeal at the moment. And this was not, Cougar realized, one of his saner moments.

"I hate what you do to me, Yank," Cougar growled, staring down at her dewy mouth, starving for a taste of her. "This was the last thing I wanted."

"Good. That makes us even. Now turn me loose," Roz demanded.

If only he *could* turn her loose, Cougar mused. Every time he came near this woman he discarded all the good sense he had spent thirty years cultivating. And because he couldn't restrain himself when he was with this intriguing female, he was going to spend another hellish day, craving a taste of her, inhaling her alluring scent that clung to his skin. Then he would lecture himself for refusing to keep his hands off forbidden temptation. Yes, he was definitely going to despise himself later . . .

But not now . . .

Cougar felt his body quiver with unfulfilled passion, wished for intimacies that would satisfy the raging fire in his blood. *Just one taste of her luscious lips, one more touch of fragrant skin,* Cougar told himself. Then he would retreat to his own space and convince himself that he'd had more than enough. And never again would he let forbidden desire get the best of him.

At least not twice in the same day . . .

Damn! Now even his better judgment was making concessions! Cougar was shocked by his own betraying thoughts, craving a kiss that would probably become a worse addiction than white man's whiskey . . .

"Cougar? Are we going hunting again this morning?"

Cougar unhanded Roz so quickly that she had to grope for the top rail of the stall to support her legs. While Roz struggled to regain her composure, Cougar battled to get himself in hand. He was not about to wheel around to confront Caleb while the bulge in his buckskin breeches was so glaringly apparent. Caleb would demand to know what Cougar had stashed in his breeches. The kid had a million questions.

"I'll be outside in a minute," Cougar replied without glancing at the youngster. "Go help Gideon load the passengers' luggage on the coach."

Cal surveyed Cougar's rigid backbone and frowned curiously. "Is something wrong? Your voice sounds funny."

Cougar gritted his teeth, his gaze transfixed on Roz's heaving breasts that he had measured with his hand, until her imprint had burned into his skin. "Nothing is wrong, Cal. Do as you're told."

When Cal trooped off, Cougar outstretched the very hand that had been molded to Roz's breast. "The picture, Yank."

"Go to hell, Cougar," Roz snapped as she surged past him to mount the mare.

"The saddle isn't—"

Before Cougar could voice his warning, Roz stuffed a foot in the stirrup and tried to pull herself onto the mare. What was to have been a hasty departure evolved into a startled shriek that reverberated off the rafters. Roz—and the saddle—slid sideways. The cats squalled in unison, the unholy sound exploding in the barn. When Roz tried to twist around to anchor herself to the sidestepping steed she found herself clutching air. Before she nosedived to the ground, brawny arms fastened around her. Roz clamped onto the bandoleer that curled over Cougar's shoulder and raked her hair from her eyes to determine which way was up.

A passel of men gathered at the barn door before Cougar could set Roz to her feet. Gideon's gray brows elevated in amusement when he saw Cougar cradling Roz in his arms while the black cats milled around his legs.

"Is everything all right in here?" Gideon questioned, hazel eyes twinkling.

"The Yank forgot to fasten the girth before she mounted the mare," Cougar explained awkwardly, setting Roz upright.

"You okay, Roz?" Gideon inquired.

Roz rearranged her twisted gown and gathered her dignity. "I'm fine, thank you, Gideon. A careless oversight on my part, is all."

"Pa? How come Cougar was hugging Miss Gaylord?" Cal asked.

Inwardly Cougar groaned. He was going to stitch that kid's mouth shut, first chance he got.

"That wasn't a hug," Roz explained, her voice one octave higher than normal. "I fell and Cougar caught me. End of story."

When the men drifted away, Roz reached for the saddle, only to have it scooped out of her arms. In stilted silence, Cougar fastened it in place.

"I want that sketch, Yank," Cougar demanded.

"Over my dead body."

"Don't tempt me, woman," he snarled at her—and at himself for yielding to overwhelming temptation.

Roz climbed into the saddle and practically ran Cougar down in her haste to escape him. He had the good sense to step out of the way when she spurred the gray mare and took off like a speeding bullet.

A puckered scowl gathered on Cougar's bronzed features as he watched Roz trot off. When he noticed the discarded sketch pad, he scooped it up and waved it overhead. "You forgot something, Yank!" he hollered at her.

Back stiff as a flag pole, Roz pulled the mare to a halt and twisted to see the looming giant emerge from the shadows of the barn. When Cougar strode forward, Roz plucked up the sketch pad, taking great care not to touch the hands that had glided over her flesh in disturbingly provocative caresses.

"Thank you," she said, staring at the cats, not at him.

"You're welcome. Now give me the sketch."

"I'll only make another one."

"And I'll take it away, too."

"You haven't retrieved the first one yet."

Tawny eyes purposely fastened on her bosom. "The day isn't over, Yank."

Roz peered at the sinewy hulk of man who had introduced her to sensations she never knew existed—and wished she still didn't! She should have been offended and outraged by what had transpired between them. Instead, she was *outraged* that she *hadn't* been offended and repulsed. Roz could almost feel his bold caresses flooding over her and she was unbridled by the recurring sensations the memory provoked. Although she resented the fact that this uncivilized heathen stirred her physically, she could not deny her vivid responses to him.

Why him? she wondered incredulously. Although Roz had never been impressed or flattered when other men doted over her, she certainly did not appreciate being treated so disrespectfully. Cougar ridiculed her, tormented her . . . and drew her against her will.

A pity that, Roz mused as she reined the mare down the path. Cougar was all wrong for her. She wasn't woman enough to stir a self-reliant, hard-bitten man like him, and she was every kind of fool if she allowed this ill-fated fascination to take root and grow. Cougar had made it clear that he had no use for a tenderfoot who was out of her element in the rough-and-tumble West.

When Roz disappeared from sight, Cougar resumed the task of tossing hay into the stalls. What was there about that prissy female that disturbed him so much? Every encounter incited his begrudging awareness. He was miffed that Roz didn't shrink away from him the way most folks did.

Cougar preferred to maintain a cautious distance between himself and members of white society. It was safe; it felt natural. Unfortunately, that sophisticated blonde refused to behave like her male counterparts. She defied him, challenged him . . . and aroused him to the extreme. To see her was to want her in the worst way and Cougar resented every sensation that throbbed through his male body, even *now,* for crying out loud!

Why hadn't he reached down her bodice to retrieve that sketch, as he had intended to do? It wasn't as if he couldn't have overpowered her any time he pleased. He really should have pressed the advantage of his size and strength. Maybe Roz would have realized that her stubborn feminine pride and contrariness were no match for him. Maybe she would have taken the customary wide berth around him like everybody else.

Cougar had gone too easy on that woman. His mistake. He wouldn't let it happen again. He was not going to take her femininity into consideration from here on out, he promised himself. He knew better than to let anyone gain an advantage over him. He had permitted that mere slip of a woman to get to him. It was downright infuriating to realize that he had allowed her—*allowed her,* mind you—to win this skirmish. The woman was going to ruin his bad reputation if he didn't watch out.

No one, he mused with an irritated scowl, was ever going to call Cougar a *pussycat* who could be tamed by a woman. And that was exactly what was going to happen if he didn't get control of that sassy female . . . and himself.

# Four

"Brace yourself," Cougar instructed Cal, who was staring down the sight of the rifle he cradled in his spindly arms.

"This thing sure is heavy," Cal said as he scooted his feet farther apart to steady himself.

"And it kicks like a mule," Cougar warned. "Have you sighted your target?"

"Yes, sir."

"Then squeeze the trigger."

The rifle exploded. Cal slammed back against Cougar who was positioned behind him. The barrel dropped toward the ground when Cal reached up to massage his aching shoulder.

"Damn, I missed."

"Don't cuss," Cougar ordered sternly.

"Why not? All the men around the trading post do."

"You're not a man yet. It isn't allowed."

"When am I going to be a man?"

"When you stop asking so many questions. Now, pay attention to the business at hand."

Cal dragged the repeating rifle back to position, as Cougar had taught him to do, and stared at the paper target nailed to the tree. "You like Miss Gaylord, don't you?" he asked out of the blue.

"No."

"Then how come you were hugging her in the barn?"

"That wasn't a hug," Cougar said through gritted teeth. "We already explained about that. What I wanted to do was strangle her for being so careless."

"How come?"

"Aim the damned rifle and clam up," Cougar growled in exasperation.

"Yes, sir."

"What's with this *sir* business?"

"Miss Gaylord says that's the polite way to address a man," Cal said before he squeezed the trigger, missing the tree by a mile.

Cougar detected a presence behind him, even before the cats issued their characteristic warning. He pivoted to see Roz perched on a boulder, making another hurried sketch. He could guess who was the subject of her latest illustration. Damn her, she was purposely trying to annoy him . . . and it was working . . .

The rifle cracked in the silence and Cougar grunted uncomfortably when Cal's bony elbow caught him in the groin. Curse that woman, she was nothing but an unwelcome distraction, sneaking up and sketching him when she didn't think he was looking!

Before Cougar could stalk over to shoo Roz on her way, she gathered her feet beneath her and scooped up her art supplies. With her glorious blond head tilted to a self-satisfied angle, she hiked up the hill toward the trading post.

That female was all but daring him to voice another

objection to being sketched for her stupid journal on Western life. Cougar was already a legendary tale on wagging tongues. He had no desire to have his scowling face plastered on the pages of some damned Eastern magazine.

"That's enough practice for today, Cal." Cougar snatched the rifle from the boy's hands. "Go help your pa with the chores."

Cal's face fell in disappointment. "What are you going to do?"

"I'm going to feed the cats."

"Can I come with you?"

"No."

"I won't get in your way if you let me come. I won't even ask any questions," Cal promised faithfully.

"It's almost dark. You hightail it back home," Cougar commanded in a tone that invited no argument.

With his lower lip sagging, Cal gathered the string of fish he and Cougar had caught in the stream below the trading post. Reluctantly, he trudged off.

As night gathered around him, Cougar sent a soft command to the cats. He preferred to stalk the darkness with the panthers rather than hover around the trading post where the other men congregated to fawn over Rozalie Gaylord. The previous night had presented yet another spectacle of a fairy princess surrounded by her admiring suitors. It still amazed Cougar that white men made such a big to-do over Roz. Well, she wasn't going to find Cougar trailing behind her. He had better things to do.

Cougar had kept a watchful eye on the two strangers who went by the name of Vito Guerero and Skeet

Thomas. True, the men had made no trouble while they gathered trail supplies and loitered around the home station. But in Cougar's estimation, the men's nonchalant behavior was cause for suspicion. Vito and Skeet didn't appear to be in a great hurry to leave, even after purchasing enough staples and supplies to sustain them in the wilderness for a week.

The men were just *around*. That made Cougar leery of them. The instinct that had kept Cougar alive while he was stalking dangerous criminals kept hounding him. Something wasn't right. Too bad he was so damned distracted by that curvaceous blonde not to spend more time speculating about what Vito and Skeet were up to.

Cougar discarded his suspicions when he heard the piercing cry of wounded rabbits and the pumas' ferocious snarls. The haunting sounds assured Cougar that the cats had found their evening meal.

Cougar wished the hell he could satisfy his . . .

Another scream sliced the silence. At first, Cougar thought it was the cry of one of his cats. But *this* particular sound went through Cougar like a cold chill, putting his keen senses on full alert. The call of the panther had often been likened to a woman's terrified scream, but Cougar was reasonably certain this sound *was* a woman's terrified scream. The second shriek put Cougar in motion. He charged toward the frightening sound that came in the opposite direction of the feeding pumas.

Cougar slid his dagger from its sheath and darted between the clumps of trees. His astute gaze swept his surroundings, searching for the source of the alarming sounds. He had lived with the cats so long that he had learned to think and react like them each time he sensed lurking danger. Cougar was accustomed to handling trouble, and he had learned to find it before it found him. Tonight, he had the inescapable feeling that trouble had struck that misplaced Yankee who didn't have the good sense to pack up and go home where she belonged.

Roz's arms flailed wildly, battling her assailants. She had thought Cougar had sneaked up on her while she was bent over a sketch in profound concentration. But she should have known better. Cougar moved with phenomenal silence—like his soundless, prowling cats.

The man who latched onto her and tried to clamp his grimy hand over her mouth was *not* after the sketches she had drawn. He and his foul-smelling companion wanted something else.

In desperation, Roz bit savagely at the fingers that covered the lower portion of her face. When Vito Guerero retracted his hand, she screamed bloody murder— for all the good it did her. Before she could scrabble up the hill to safety, Skeet Thomas grabbed her by the hair of her head and yanked her backward, sending her tumbling in a tangle of hampering skirts and petticoats. Roz found herself flat on her back, staring up at the bulky Mexican who grinned devilishly at her.

"I'll hold her down," Skeet insisted as his hand clamped bruisingly on her breast. "Just be quick about taking her. I want my turn."

Roz managed a half scream before Skeet crushed his free hand over her mouth, mashing her lips against her teeth, preventing her from taking a chunk out of his fingers. Revulsion flooded through Roz when Skeet groped beneath the bodice of her gown, while Vito dropped to his knees to lift her skirt. The sound of rending cloth had Roz writhing frantically for freedom. She could smell whiskey on Vito's and Skeet's breath, smell the pungent odor of dirt and sweat that clung to them.

Her terrified gasp died in her throat when Skeet shoved her head sideways, wrenching her neck to discourage her from struggling against the inevitable.

"Hold still, unless you want your head twisted off your shoulders," Skeet sneered down at her. "You're wasting your energy fighting us."

Cool air flooded over Roz when Vito tugged at her undergarments and jabbed her legs farther apart with his knees. She tried to scream again, but the only sound to reach her ears was the drumming of her own pulse and the sinister laughter of her assailants.

All Roz had wanted when she wandered down from the trading post was the privacy to sketch by the light of the lantern she had brought with her. She had needed to be alone with her thoughts and now her privacy had been invaded. And worse, she was about to be molested by these drunken ruffians who had been lurking around her for two days . . .

Nausea nearly gagged Roz when Vito's fingers pinched into the tender flesh of her thigh. His left hand clamped over her breast, bruising tender skin. Skeet continued his degrading gropes and muttered impatiently for Vito to finish his turn. When Vito's mouth replaced Skeet's hand on her lips, Roz felt revulsion crest over her like a tidal wave. Wildly, she kicked and twisted, lashing out with every ounce of strength she possessed.

"Bastards!" she railed when Vito came up for breath.

"Stop fighting," Vito demanded brusquely. "You're going to like it as much as we do. You've been flaunting that gorgeous body of yours for two days and we intend to give you what you've been wanting."

Roz's furious screech was stifled when Vito sprawled on her, knocking out her breath. He cursed the confining layers of clothes he had to fight his way through to take what he wanted. Roz arched her back and braced her feet, bucking in attempt to hurl him aside, but Skeet held her down while Vito pinned her beneath his bulky weight.

The awful realization that she could not prevent what was about to happen poured over Roz. She could feel the vile monster surging toward her with disgusting intent while his lusty companion pawed at her for his own fiendish enjoyment. Roz squeezed back the tears that pooled in her eyes and struggled against impossible odds. If she were to be sexually abused, by damn, she was going to battle to the bitter end.

Just when Roz feared she had met with humiliating defeat the heavy weight of Vito's body rose like an apparition and cartwheeled sideways. A muffled grunt erupted from Skeet's lips when flesh connected with flesh, sending him somersaulting backward.

Cursing foully, Vito Guerero rolled to his feet, snatching his dagger from its sheath. He scurried toward Skeet Thomas who had retrieved his knife from his boot. Both men stood poised for an oncoming attack, cursing the interruption that deprived them of their demonic amusement.

A growl that sounded inhuman caught Roz's attention. Her goggle-eyed gaze swung to the imposing figure of the man who had appeared from out of nowhere. For a second Roz didn't recognize the incongruous form that moved like a disembodied spirit. There was something strange about this creature, something so wild and vicious in the stealthy movements that Roz was prepared to swear her rescuer *was* a panther.

An eerie shiver skittered through her soul as she watched the lithe predator coil into a crouch. Another guttural growl erupted from the foreboding shadow as it inched closer to the two men who stood shoulder to shoulder, waiting attack.

"Back off," Vito hissed as he and Skeet held their daggers in front of them like shields.

Vito was not about to draw his pistol. He had heard Cougar was lightning-quick with either hand. Vito didn't want to discover—first-hand—if this gunfighter could drop two men before they could breathe their last breath.

"We've got no fight with you. We just wanted our turns with the woman," Skeet insisted.

The only response was another passionless, unnerving snarl.

Roz sat up shakily, dragging her torn clothes modestly around her, hugging her knees to her chest. She watched the crouched figure shift position. It was as if Cougar had changed forms before Roz's very eyes! He had become so much like the black mountain lions that were his constant companions that they could have been born from the same litter! Dear God, she was beginning to believe every incredible legend about this mystical creature!

It was obvious that Vito and Skeet were asking themselves the same thing and wondering *who* or *what* they were dealing with. They were having no more luck reasoning with Cougar in his present state than they could have communicated with a wild animal.

Out of desperation, Vito lunged forward to distract his opponent while Skeet darted sideways to attack from the flank. The theory that the best defense was an aggressive offense proved to be a miscalculation. A swipe of Cougar's dagger had Vito howling in pain. With unerring efficiency, Cougar had slashed Vito's trigger finger, slicing the tendons around his knuckles. The dagger dropped with a thud and he recoiled against the nearest tree, cradling his wounded hand against his paunchy belly.

"Christ!" Skeet gasped, unable to believe the swiftness with which Cougar had struck. He muttered an obscenity when the stealthy half-breed wheeled on him. "Come on, friend. We were just having our fun with the woman. If you want a turn with her, we'll help you hold her down. She's a feisty little thing, but she won't be a match for the three of us—"

Skeet yelped in agony when the shadowy figure leaped forward, cutting a slice across Skeet's thigh before he had time to react. Swearing bitterly, Skeet grabbed his bloody leg and tried to parry with his own knife. The blade struck only air as the dark creature flitted away like a breath of wind.

When Vito tried to reverse direction to make his escape, Cougar blocked his path. Hissing in pain, Skeet dragged himself up against a tree for support, unable to come to his companion's aid.

Roz winced when Vito's bulky body was slammed onto the ground and his breath gushed out in a *whoosh*. Cougar's dagger gleamed in the faint light as the blade came to rest against Vito's throat. Vito's curse transformed into a wail when the sharp blade cut a swath from his left ear to the point just a hairbreadth from his jugular.

Watching Vito fall beneath Cougar's deadly attack put Skeet to flight. He dragged his injured leg in his haste to reach the horses that were tethered in the trees.

The guttural sounds that gurgled in Vito's throat brought Roz to her feet. "No!"

"Yes, Yank," came the cold, hollow voice. "The only rehabilitation for murderers and rapists is death."

Despite the chilling effect of Cougar's snarl, Roz dashed forward to clutch at his arm. But the instant she touched Cougar, she instinctively snatched her hand away. It was as if she had touched stone!

The smell of Vito's blood was in the air, a coppery scent that caused Roz's stomach to lurch in revulsion. As much as she despised what Vito and Skeet tried to do to her, she couldn't tolerate watching Vito's throat being slit from ear to ear.

"Let him go," she whispered brokenly.

"Go back to the trading post if you don't want to watch," came the emotionless voice.

"We'll leave right now, I swear it," Vito frantically pleaded. "We won't touch her again!"

Despite the terrifying sensations of touching Cougar

when he was in his deadliest form, Roz grabbed at his arm, pulling the dagger away from Vito's bleeding throat. The dam of carefully held emotion broke and Roz wilted to her knees, choking on sobs. She felt as if she were trapped in a nightmare, suffering a chill that went deeper than bone. The anguishing memory of groping hands crawling over her left her shuddering. Another sob escaped her lips and tears clouded her vision, blocking out both victim and avenger.

"Just get him away from me," Roz whimpered, clutching self-consciously at her gaping gown. "Both of you . . . get away from me."

Her voice evaporated when the sound of thundering hooves indicated that Skeet had made his mad dash to safety, leaving Vito to fend for himself as best he could.

A strange whistle call filled the silence that followed the retreating hoofbeats. Muffled sounds pounded the ground, catching Roz's attention. She cringed at the unsettling screeches that were reminiscent of her own desperate call for help. And then came the low, threatening growls that heralded the panthers' arrival.

Roz heard Vito thrashing his way to his feet to avoid another attack. The thud of his footsteps echoed in the stillness of the night as he scampered toward his horse. His steed whinnied when it caught the scent of the cats that Cougar had sent bounding after him.

"Call them back, Cougar," Roz implored between shuddering breaths.

"Why? So he can live to molest again? Let him die as he prefers to live—in violence and lust. Skeet already made his escape. Do you want both of them to go free after what they tried to do to you?"

"No, let them learn their lesson and live to remember the painful consequences," Roz murmured shakily.

With a harsh oath, Cougar let loose with another unnerving scream and the cats responded in kind. In the distance, Cougar heard the rapid pelting of hooves carrying Vito into the night to join his comrade. Cougar knew he shouldn't have been influenced by Roz's sobbing request. He had dealt with enough desperadoes in his time to know that mercy was a weakness in the world where demons resided. Cougar, like the panthers, knew instinctively that there was no turning back after he moved in for the kill. Not to finish what he began was to invite a worse kind of trouble—the kind that seethed with revenge.

Roz may have convinced herself that it was noble to spare men like Vito Guerero and Skeet Thomas, but Cougar knew better. The Skeet Thomases and Vito Guereros of the world only learned to be more cautious the next time they pounced on their victim. It was like teaching the devil new ways to torment mortal souls . . .

The sound of Roz's muffled sobs went through Cougar like a flaming arrow. He cursed the fact that this woman had the power to affect him in so many different ways. He had yielded to forbidden temptation *with* her and ignored his killer instincts *because* of her. What was even more baffling was that Cougar swore he could almost *feel* her horror when he rushed toward the terrified sound of her voice.

Odd, Cougar had almost forgotten what fear felt like. Even when he launched his attack against the two scruffy men, he had been mindful of Roz's revulsion, of what had happened to her. Such things had never bothered him before. Cougar had learned to ignore everything except instinct and cold logic, to strike without distraction. But he had been fully aware of Roz, affected by her touch, even when he sank into the dark depths of rigid mind and body control, just as the Cheyenne oracle had taught him to do before engaging in battle.

The teachings that prepared Cheyenne dog soldiers for war had been deeply ingrained in Cougar. Tracking down ruthless criminals reinforced the belief that he needed to be singly focused on his deadly tasks. But he had allowed the feelings of this hapless female to deter him, to dissuade him from doing what should have been done.

That wasn't good, not good a-tall, Cougar thought with a scowl.

"I'll take you back to the post," Cougar offered, reaching down to hoist Roz to her feet.

She shrank away from him as if his touch was fire. "No, I don't want anyone to see me like this," she choked out, swiping at the stream of tears that scalded her cheeks. "I don't want to face the curious glances and humiliating questions. Cal will have his share of them, too."

No greater truth had ever been spoken, Cougar mused. Cougar couldn't say that he blamed Roz for not wanting to confront the men at the inn or Cal's inevitable questions. She would be more self-conscious than she was now.

Despite Roz's whimpered objections, Cougar scooped her into his arms. "Stop struggling, Yank. I'm only taking you down to the stream so you can freshen up."

"Just put me down," she demanded between shuddering breaths. "I can walk."

Cougar frowned at the near-hysterical tone of her voice. She shrank away from him as if his touch was as offensive as Vito's and Skeet's. After the traumatic experience she had endured, Cougar predicted she probably wouldn't want a man close to her.

Roz had been badly frightened when Cougar had taken his fury out on Vito and Skeet. Cougar well remembered how she had jerked away from him while he loomed over Vito, intent on meting out deadly punishment. When the killer instinct coursed through Cougar it changed him. He knew that all too well. Many times in the past he had seen the fear in his victims' eyes while he loomed over them, emulating the effective skills of the mountain lion. He knew he could be terrifying when he reached so deep inside himself to control the spiritual and mental forces that the Cheyenne relied heavily upon during battle. And Roz hadn't even seen Cougar at his *worst,* and *still* it unnerved her.

Slashing the ligaments around Skeet's knee cap to slow him down and forcing Vito to submit was mere child's play compared to the depths Cougar had gone when clashing with deadly cutthroats. Cougar hadn't even called in his cats for the kill this time. If Roz thought he was terrifying when he became more of a cougar than a man, she would be horrified of him during extremely difficult situations.

"Put me down. Now!" Roz demanded between sobs.

Cougar set her to her feet, but her knees folded like an accordion. He latched onto her before she plunked into an unceremonious heap. Hooking an arm beneath her knees, he strode quickly toward the creek, despite her objections—and she still had plenty of them.

"Men are bastards," Roz spluttered when Cougar braced her up beside him. "All I ever wanted was to be left alone. You men seem to think that woman was placed on the planet to satisfy your urges or provide you with the money you believe you can swindle from us. I wish I were a man. I would give anything to have the size and strength to fight back. Then I would have all the freedom I want!"

Cougar eased Roz onto the grassy stream bank and tore off the trailing hem of her petticoat to use as a wet compress on her bruises and scrapes. Roz recoiled as if he meant to strike her as her attackers had done.

"Calm down, Yank," Cougar muttered, at a loss as how to handle this haunted female. Gentleness and kindness weren't exactly his forte and he felt ill-equipped to deal with Roz. Cougar had adjusted to the harsh cruelties of life, but Roz wasn't as experienced at coping with difficulty. Dealing with Roz in her state required patience and understanding, but Cougar didn't believe he had enough of either.

Roz sobbed quietly, clutching the tattered bodice against her breasts while she huddled beside the stream. She kept herself knotted in a tight ball while Cougar sank down to saturate the improvised cloth.

A soft whistle call brought the black cats to heel. While the catamounts drank from the creek, Cougar pivoted toward Roz. He froze in his tracks when he noticed the tears glistening in her luminous eyes, saw the wild tangle of silver blond hair that streamed over her bare shoulders like a waterfall of light and moonbeams.

Damn, even when she looked her worst, this nymph was utterly breathtaking. Was it little wonder that men from all walks of life had difficulty keeping their hands off her?

Despite the fact that Cougar had nothing whatsoever in common with this delicate sophisticate, he couldn't help but be intrigued by her. She was the loveliest creature he had ever seen. And when she was hurting, he could almost feel her pain and frustration.

*Almost.* Cougar had made a pact with himself eight years earlier never to *feel* anything again. Grief, fury and burning hatred had stolen his very soul and turned his aching heart to ice while he watched the Cheyenne slaughtered like a herd of buffalo.

The faint stirring of compassion deep inside Cougar was unfamiliar. He peered down at Roz, feeling helplessly inadequate. As much as he wanted to ease her suffering, he didn't know how to start, what to say. She was learning that life had a way of peeling off layers of the soul until there was nothing left. Despair was like a poison that stole the beat right out of the heart. Now *how,* Cougar asked himself, was he going to be the cheerful, encouraging companion Roz needed when he was the world's worst cynic?

Cougar squatted down on his haunches and gently pressed the compress against Roz's cheek. She reflexively pulled away from him and inhaled a shaky breath. The second time he tried to tend her wounds she was more receptive to the feel of the cool cloth on her scratched flesh. She reminded Cougar of the wild mustangs he and Gray Eagle had driven into the box canyon near the mountain cabin and patiently tamed to accept human touch. Any sudden movement alarmed the mustangs, as it alarmed Roz.

Cougar told himself to proceed slowly and deliberately until Roz accepted his ministrations without expecting him to pounce on her. He asked himself if he was going to regret giving so much of himself to ease her suffering. Probably. But teaching himself to be gentle was the sacrifice he had to make for this beguiling creature. Cougar definitely wasn't known for his abundance of engaging charm, but he was going to have to manufacture some real quick!

# *Five*

"Why are you still here when I've made it clear that I want to be alone?" Roz asked as Cougar glided the damp cloth down her arm to clean the scrape on her elbow. "Besides, I know perfectly well that you have no use whatsoever for me."

"Maybe I enjoy seeing you miserable, Yank," he said, trying out the sense of humor that had dried up a decade ago.

Roz muffled a sniff and nodded glumly. *"That* I can believe."

"I thought you would." When he slid the cloth across the scratch on her shoulder and breasts, Roz flinched and drew away. "Relax, I'm not going to do what they did."

The reminder caused Roz to shiver with uncontrollable revulsion. Cougar cursed his carelessness. He couldn't seem to find the right words when it came to Roz. But then, Cougar reminded himself, he was a man of action, not words. He was doing the best he could.

"If you're feeling better, I'll walk you back to the inn," he offered quietly.

Roz gave her head a fierce shake, sending the cascade

of silver-blond tangles rippling around her shoulders. "No, I would rather stay here."

"You plan to camp out on the ground for the night, do you?"

Roz glanced around, as if she had just realized where she was. "No, I suppose not."

"Do you feel like standing up now?"

"Do I have to?"

"No, I can carry you."

"I don't think that's a good idea."

"Why not?"

"Because—" Roz stared at some distant point. "Because . . ." She let out her breath in a rush, refusing to reply.

"Because I'm a man and all men are bastards?" he supplied.

"Something like that. And besides, I'm not even sure you're human, not after—"

Cougar pressed his forefinger to her trembling lips to shush her. His hand cupped her chin, forcing her to meet his level gaze. "If I intended to hurt you, doesn't it stand to reason that I would have done that already?"

"Not if you're waiting for me to let my guard down."

Cougar felt the hint of a smile tugging at his lips. Or at least he thought it might have been a smile. He wasn't sure, since he was out of practice. Impulsively, he reached out to trace her heart-shaped mouth, just as she had traced his that first day in the barn.

"Think about it, Yank. After what you saw me do to Vito Guerero and Skeet Thomas, do you really think I need to bother waiting for you to let your guard down?" he asked reasonably.

The tension that pulsed through Roz dissipated. Cougar could sense the difference immediately. To his surprise, Roz abruptly flung her arms around his neck and let out a wail that had the cats screaming in reply. Cougar felt Roz's tears burning against his bare shoulder, felt her ragged breath sawing in and out against the column of his throat. He cuddled her protectively in his arms while she cried her eyes out, expending every last ounce of her frustration.

This was an unprecedented experience for Cougar and he felt terribly awkward. Women *never* leaned on him for compassion. Nobody did. He was not a man who was considered to have a sympathetic bone in his body. More often than not, he had been labeled as a ruthless demon who had no conscience, no heart, no soul—at least none that anybody but the devil himself dared to claim. But when Roz clung to him as if he were her only salvation, Cougar could *feel* his pulse beating, assuring him that he still had a heart.

"I-I'm s-sorry," Roz whimpered, sniffed and then hiccupped against his neck. "You don't even l-like me"—hiccup—"and here I am b-blubbering all over you."

Cougar was positively certain now that it *was* a smile that quirked his lips. "It's all right, Yank. I was planning to bathe tonight anyway. I just hadn't planned to do it in your tears. But they are definitely warmer than the water in the creek."

Roz lifted her head from his shoulder. Though she couldn't recall seeing Cougar smile—ever—and wasn't sure he even knew how, the expression altered her perception of him. This man of stone looked more human than usual, definitely more human than he had when he launched his attack on Vito and Skeet.

It felt good to have his sinewy arms encircling her. Cougar didn't seem anywhere near as cold and hard as he had been when she touched him earlier. There was something phenomenal about the transformation he underwent—mentally and physically—when he was dealing with danger. As ruthless as he had been *then,* he was all gentle patience *now.*

Cougar inwardly flinched when he met those glistening blue eyes. "Don't look at me like that," Cougar scowled.

"Like what?"

"Like you want my mouth on yours," he said curtly.

Roz blinked those long-lashed blue eyes and Cougar inwardly groaned.

"Is that how I look?" she asked.

"That's the impression I'm getting, yes."

"And you find that as distasteful as I found Vito's slobbery kisses?"

"I didn't say that, Yank."

"Can I ask you something, Cougar?"

Cougar cursed himself when his index finger involuntarily lifted to trace her sensuous lips. He was getting in over his head here, even when he was smart enough to see the futility of becoming involved with this dainty bluestocking who wasn't a part of his world.

"Cougar?" she prompted, reaching up to limn the angular line of his jaw.

"Watch it, Yank," Cougar warned. "You might find yourself flat on your back again."

She gave her head a shake. "I don't think so."

"Why the hell not?"

"Because you aren't anything like those two men."

"You thought I was, five minutes ago," he reminded her.

"I've changed my mind."

Cougar swore his heart had slammed into his ribs and stuck there when those hypnotic eyes focused on him, glistening with the residue of tears. He was certain the willpower he had taken for granted for a decade wasn't as indestructible as he'd thought. But he was *not*—repeat with great emphasis—*not* going to kiss Roz and discover what he knew he was missing. If he did, he wasn't sure he could stop himself this time, even if Roz was confident that he could. He was sorry to report that he was not as invincible as legend hailed him to be—at least not when it came to Rozalie Gaylord. She was proving to be the one battle Cougar wasn't sure he could win.

"Wash their taste and touch away," Roz whispered, tilting her face to his. "I'd rather go to sleep thinking of *you* than awake to nightmares of *them* . . ."

Cougar could no more deny her hushed request than he could dig a hole to Hong Kong. He felt himself melting like hot candle wax. This was another mistake . . .

And he couldn't stop himself from making it . . .

The instant his lips slanted over hers, Cougar felt Roz's body relax against his. He wanted to crush her to him, to absorb her, but he was afraid she would be reminded of Vito's and Skeet's bruising touch. Cougar had never been more aware of the woman in his arms, so intently attuned to her wants, needs and desires. And when he felt Roz's dewy-soft lips part under his tender coaxing and heard her breath tear out on a ragged sigh, he knew he was losing the battle of mind over body.

Cougar cursed his instantaneous reaction, even as he fed on the taste and feel of her. She was all wrong for him, but she felt exactly right. Her pliant body felt like the other half of his—a custom fit of perfect contrasts.

Her satiny flesh blended into his hard contours—strength tempered with soft femininity. Her heartbeat became his own thundering pulse as his tongue penetrated her lips to drink his fill. She emulated each erotic gesture he made, offering back the pleasure he gave until Cougar's head was swimming with sensations he had never considered offering or expected to receive in return.

Damn, she was burning him up inside, changing him, making him long for more than simple fulfillment of physical need. She was thawing out the glacier that had been his heart, threatening to storm the barricade that surrounded his emotions.

Even though Cougar was aware of the danger of allowing himself to care about anyone again, he couldn't resist this bewitching female, couldn't resist trying to replace Vito's and Skeet's disrespectful gropes with gentle caresses that soothed and satisfied.

Suddenly he wanted Roz to go to bed with the remembered feel of his hands gliding over her, the taste of his kisses on her lips. He felt the overpowering desire to drive the frightening ordeal out of her mind and body, to prove to her that tender passion was nothing remotely close to mindless lust.

Roz felt Cougar's hand scale her ribs and swirl over the exposed peak of her breasts. She should have retreated, she knew. She shouldn't be granting him more privileges than she already had. She should resist, as she had resisted her assailants. But Cougar's caresses were nothing like Vito's and Skeet's. Cougar gave her immeasurable pleasure, and he touched her so tenderly that her body arched eagerly toward his cupping hand, craving more.

A fireburst of sensations blazed through Roz as his kisses trailed across her cheek and whispered over the swell of her breasts. Roz caught her breath when his tongue flicked at her beaded nipple. When he took it into his mouth and gently suckled, she felt herself unraveling. When his hand tunneled beneath the ragged hem of her skirt to trace her inner thigh, she melted instinctively beneath his languid touch.

"Tell me to stop, Roz," Cougar groaned as his fingertips drifted up the generous slope of her hip.

"I—" When his lips brushed the taut peaks of her breasts, Roz lost all power of speech. Sensations tumbled over her like the surf rushing to shore, erasing all except the pleasure that channeled through her untried body.

Cougar was discovering a rare kind of satisfaction with each kiss and caress he bestowed on Roz. In the past, sex had been a swift completion of basic urges in the arms of women who made their living catering to men. But this lovely maiden was like a delicious treat to his senses, a discovery of a new dimension. Roz's quivering reactions fascinated Cougar, gave him a sense of power he had never experienced. He suddenly became obsessed with pleasuring her until her every response echoed through him as if it were his own.

The honeyed taste of her lips was a craving he couldn't ignore. Her scent went to his head like strong wine. Each time his hand swirled over the flesh of her thigh he could feel the feminine heat of her body calling to him. He wanted to touch the secret fire that was burning for him—to reassure her and himself—that there could be more between a man and woman than the mere meeting of bodies to ease basic need.

Cougar vowed to touch her with the greatest of care, with the tenderness a refined beauty like Roz deserved. And when she trustingly relaxed beneath his feathery caresses, Cougar couldn't conceal the smile that parted his lips. Roz couldn't possibly know what a devastating effect that trusting response had on him. Cougar had difficulty believing it himself. It was as if she had placed her faith in him, certain he wouldn't hurt her.

And with that silent gift of trust came a responsibility Cougar had never accepted . . .

Heaven and hell, Cougar thought as his lips drifted from the dusky peaks to her petal-soft mouth. Knowing he could find heaven in this angel's arms when he knew he should keep his distance was nine kinds of hell. He wanted Roz so badly that he was shaking with need. He had dared too much already, and yet it wasn't enough to satisfy his monstrous needs.

He and Roz were both demanding so much from each other that Cougar feared he didn't have enough self-restraint to stop what had already gone too far. Now, he had made her want him; later they would both regret forging past the point of no return . . .

*Impossible contrasts. Forbidden . . .*

Damn, thought Cougar. Was that the sound of his

conscience? He wasn't sure he even had one these days. His male body was roiling with unappeased need and his dormant conscience had suddenly sprung to life to remind him that he didn't dare take possession of this tempting female, no matter how great the temptation, especially since Gideon looked upon her as if she were the daughter he never had.

Cougar squeezed his eyes shut and valiantly battled for control. He couldn't take her to bed and then send her back to her own world, as if she were no more than a challenge conquered. She would come to hate him for taking advantage of her vulnerability. She was only reaching out to him for compassion and he craved more than Roz knew how to give.

Cougar mightily cursed his unruly body and clung desperately to self-control. He was not looking forward to the cold bath he was going to have to take in the mountain stream. His male body was going to sizzle like a hot branding iron plunged into water.

When Roz tipped her head back to stare up at him in astounded disbelief, Cougar saw the livid passion in her wide eyes, a passion he had aroused without satisfying. The ache that throbbed through Cougar was almost enough to bring him back to his knees after he had gained his feet. Roz wobbled unsteadily beside him as he propelled her up the creek bank. Cougar was frustrated with himself for letting things go so far . . . And not far enough to satisfy his hungry yearnings.

"Cougar?" Roz whispered, befuddled by the abrupt change in his attitude toward her. "Why—?"

"There is nowhere for you and me to go from here,

Yank," Cougar cut in gruffly. "You're back on your feet. That's all that matters. Leave it at that."

Roz pulled up short and planted feet when he tried to uproot her from the spot. She studied the shadowed features that had turned back to stone, marveling at his ability to switch his emotions off and on whenever he pleased. Minutes ago he had been playfully tender and incredibly passionate. Now he resembled the craggy peaks of granite mountains silhouetted in moonlight— hard, distant, impenetrable.

Roz was stung by the humiliating thought that Cougar had touched her out of pity. He hadn't really wanted her at all—not the way he had made her want him. And truth be known, she wasn't sure she would have wanted to stop him from introducing her to the dimensions of delirious passion. She had been too vulnerable to think straight, and his mind-boggling caresses had scattered all logical thought. And yet, while she was oblivious to all except the indescribable pleasure he had given her, *he* was in perfect control. He had simply accommodated her because she had practically asked for it.

Roz was mortified beyond words and she was thankful the darkness hid the hot blush of embarrassment that flamed in her cheeks.

"And I presume you think I should thank you kindly for feeling sorry enough to distract me the way you did," she muttered, highly offended.

"Yank, I didn't say that—"

"You may as well have, damn it!" Roz blustered in interruption and she shook loose from his supporting arm. "And now I expect you're hoping I'll offer you part of my inheritance in payment for the lesson learned and services rendered, is that right?"

Cougar did a double take. Who said anything about money changing hands? Sure as hell not him! Roz was obviously getting hysterical, and in a most amusing sort of way. "You think I want to be paid for pleasuring you? It wasn't that big a deal, Yank."

Roz reared back an arm, obviously determined to leave her handprint on his face. Before she could make stinging contact, Cougar caught her wrist and brought it down to her side. That outraged her all the more.

"Damn your hard hide, Cougar!"

*Hard* hide was right, he thought as another smile—ones that were all too easy and naturally when he was with this temperamental imp—grazed his lips. *Cougar* was about to explode with the hungry need he had nobly refrained from fulfilling, and *she* was railing at him. It made no sense whatever. What the hell did she want from him anyway? Damned if he knew. Cougar never claimed to be an authority on women.

"Look, Yank, you've had a bad night—"

"A bad night?" Roz howled, near hysterics again. "I've had a bad life, thank you very much. Not that you care!"

His expression turned to stone as he grabbed her arm and propelled her forward. "Lady, you don't know what bad is. And I hope you never find out, because I'm not sure you're tough enough to survive when *bad* turns to the *very worst.*"

"I've had the misfortune of getting mixed up with you," she shot back. "That's bad enough—"

Cougar clamped his hand over her mouth when he

heard voices in the distance . . . "Ouch! Damn it," he hissed when she took a bite out of his finger. "Calm down before you alert the men who are out on the porch enjoying their evening smoke."

Roz went very still. The last thing she wanted was to encounter curious eyes right now. When she launched herself out of Cougar's arms and headed toward the back of the inn, Cougar stared incredulously after her.

"Where the hell are you going?"

"To my room."

Cougar sighed heavily and followed in her wake. He stopped short when he saw Roz clutch the back hem of her soiled dress and tuck it between her legs, drawing up the full skirt and securing it to the sash at her waist. Wearing makeshift breeches, she latched onto the rough-hewed beam, intent on shinnying up to the terrace.

"Here, Yank, let me help," Cougar insisted.

"I don't want your help," she flung at him as she inched up the beam. "And furthermore, I don't want you anywhere near me again—ever. In fact, I'm swearing off all men altogether after tonight!"

"That's not what that luscious body of yours was telling me awhile ago," he unmercifully riposted.

Roz clamped herself around the supporting column like a limpet to a rock. The murderous glare she leveled on him would have leveled a normal man. But then, Roz reminded herself, Cougar was anything but normal.

Cougar had accomplished his purpose well enough. He had driven a wedge between him and this woman who was far too great a temptation. He was going to have to cut his visit to Howard Station short, that was more than obvious. He couldn't trust himself with that blond-haired nymph. Now that he had touched her, he wouldn't be able to control the need to finish what they had begun in a moment of madness.

When Roz tossed her bare leg over the terrace rail and wheeled to glower down at him, like a fairy princess poised high atop her castle tower, Cougar felt another grin purse his lips. Roz was in a fit of temper. She had a lot of spunk when she was riled, probably because she was horribly spoiled and accustomed to having her own way.

"I hope you roast in hell, Cougar," she hurled at him.

"It was a pleasure meeting you, too, Yank. Give my warm regards to the other blue bloods when you get home."

With that, Cougar pivoted around and walked off to fetch his cats, still certain he was better off with his own kind. Rozalie Gaylord would *never* be *his* kind, nor he hers.

# Six

The thunder of approaching hooves put Jake Roche on immediate alert. He snapped his rifle into position, while standing guard outside the shack that he and his men had confiscated from the elderly prospector who had once inhabited it. The previous owner had no need of it now that he was resting six feet deep—compliments of Roche's raiders.

When Jake recognized Vito and Skeet, he set his rifle aside and strode off the stoop. "I thought you were staying until tomorrow to scout out the stage station," Jake snapped, watching his men swing from their winded mounts.

"We had an unexpected change of plans," Skeet grumbled before spitting an arc of tobacco.

"What went wrong?"

"Nothing except one mean son of a bitch who prowls with three black Mexican tigers," Vito scowled as he rubbed his injured hand.

When Vito stepped onto the porch, the side of his neck was illuminated by lantern light. Jake swallowed his breath. The grisly wound loomed so close to the jugular vein that it was a wonder Vito was still alive. As it was, Vito would bear a nasty scar that even a kerchief couldn't conceal. Dried blood was caked on the half-moon wound on the left side of his neck. An oblong bruise discolored his cheek. Vito did indeed look as if he had tangled with a bloodthirsty panther.

Jake turned his attention to Skeet Thomas who limped toward the cabin. Skeet's jaw also sported a bruise and his lips were swollen from the blow that had very nearly knocked his teeth down his throat. Ripped pants exposed a bloody slash which cut diagonally across his right thigh and dug deeply into his knee cap, making it impossible for him to walk without dragging his injured leg.

"I tell ya for sure, Jake, that half-breed bastard is damned scary when he's riled." Skeet hobbled into the cabin and dropped into the nearest chair. "There's no way we can take the incoming gold shipment from that station without losing several men. If Cougar doesn't ride out before the Wells Fargo consignment is due, we would be better off trying to hit the stage somewhere down the line. That hombre turned deadly real quick."

"Cougar?" Colby Jordan glanced up from the deck of cards he was dealing to the other confederates.

"You've heard of him?" Jake Roche questioned.

"Most folks in these parts have heard the legend, at the very least," Hudson Caine assured the leader of the band. "The man's reported to be half savage and half wildcat."

Jake's gray eyes narrowed. "What do you mean savage?"

"Injun," Colby Jordan clarified as he glanced at his poker hand. "And the part of him that ain't Cheyenne is said to be wildcat mean. Cougar took after the gang I once rode with a few years back and sent them all to hell. Some folks say he's the devil himself, gathering a few black souls to compensate for the one he ain't got. That manhunter never brought an outlaw back alive—" Colby glanced at Vito and Skeet. "How'd you two get out with your hides intact?"

Vito touched his sliced finger to the throbbing wound on his neck. "The lady we were trying to crawl on top of stopped Cougar from doing his worst."

Jake's thick brows flattened in a confused frown. "The bitch was sweet on you?"

Skeet snorted before snatching up a bottle and guzzling a drink of whiskey. "Nope. She was putting up one helluva fight."

"Then why'd she let you off the hook?" Hudson Caine wanted to know.

Vito shrugged a thick-bladed shoulder. "Too kind-hearted was my guess. An Easterner, she was. Too civilized to watch a man's throat slit wide open or see a man's leg amputated without anesthetic."

Jake paced the floor while the rest of the men mulled over their hands of cards. "Howard Station is ripe for the picking, especially with that gold shipment due to arrive in two days. How long is this Cougar character planning on staying, Skeet?"

"Dunno, Jake. The station owner said Cougar was going to herd the rest of his cattle and horses to Finnegan's station. Wherever Cougar goes, I don't wanna be there, I can tell ya for sure."

"Me neither," Vito grumbled. "When you get within five feet of that wild man, you're close enough to smell your own death. Next time he won't let me off the blade of his knife. He was all set to finish the job tonight.

I've got the uneasy feeling he won't be so generous next time me and Skeet meet up with him."

Jake turned to the taciturn man who sat in the corner, hurling his pearl-handled dagger at the wall. Burney Adair never had much to say. He was a quiet scout, one with whom Jake had served while he was riding with General Custer. They had both been court-martialed for mutilating those stinking savages during the Battle of the Washita. But then, Custer had gotten what he deserved for letting Roche and Adair shoulder the blame for the incident. Roche and Adair were still alive; Custer and the Seventh Cavalry had been slaughtered on the Little Bighorn.

"Burney, I want you to keep watch on Howard Station from a safe distance," Jake ordered. "If Cougar makes himself scarce before the gold arrives, we'll stick with our original plan."

"And if Cougar don't ride out?" Skeet Thomas wanted to know.

"Then we'll hit the next station on the line," Jake decided. "But Howard's is a home station. There are enough supplies in the trading post to keep us stocked for months. With that posse combing the countryside to find us, we might need to hole up in the mountains after this strike."

After Burney Adair had gathered his gear, Jake followed him outside. "Stay clear of the station," Jake instructed. "And don't carve up any dead bodies that might be linked to us."

"You think I have a fetish about my knife?" Burney snorted.

"I know damned well you do. Now is not the time to practice your carving."

"No," Burney agreed. "But maybe I'll have a chance to cut the Injun out of this Cougar fellow that's got Vito and Skeet running scared. I always did like to see an Injun sliced up for buzzard bait."

Jake shared Burney's obsessive hatred for Indians. They had both lost part of their kinfolk in raids, and they both shared the opinion that annihilation was the only way to deal with the Indian problem. But if that half-breed Vito and Skeet encountered was as deadly as rumor had it, Jake preferred to avoid the man if at all possible.

According to Vito and Skeet, the travelers at Howard Station wouldn't pose much of a threat during the holdup. There wasn't a good rifleman or pistolero among them. The proprietor, Vito reported, walked with a limp he had acquired during the Civil War. He was the only man at the station who might be competent with weapons.

If the Roche gang relied on the element of surprise to swoop down on the station, they would only have to cut down the stagecoach guards, driver and station owner. None of the men would be a match for Jake's confederates. All of them were proficient with rifles, pistols and whips. And of course, there was Burney Adair who derived wicked pleasure from taking a few slices out of his victims with his dagger.

"I'll send Hudson Caine out to relay your report," Jake said as Burney strode into the darkness.

Burney's reply was an inarticulate grunt. He was a man who let his dagger do his talking for him when he thought there was something that needed to be said.

\* \* \*

"How come you have to leave so soon?" Cal questioned Cougar. Disappointment was clearly evident on his face. "I thought you was—were going to teach me to ride my new pony and take me hunting."

"Next time, Cal," Cougar assured the crestfallen lad. "I have to sell the rest of the cattle and horses at Finnegan's Station . . ."

Cougar's voice trailed off when Roz emerged from the inn. Her appearance triggered bittersweet memories. Cougar had the impulsive urge to say his last good-bye, to part on a friendlier note than he had the previous evening. But that would serve no useful purpose for either of them. The only way for Cougar to keep his distance was to leave. He knew that, where that blue-eyed imp was concerned, he had no willpower.

"Miss Gaylord, Cougar is leaving!" Cal called out when he noticed where his idol's eyes had strayed.

Roz kept her gaze trained on a distant point beyond Cougar's bare shoulder. "So I see. Good-bye, *Just Cougar,*" she said in a tone that wavered with emotion.

After a short pause Roz reached inside her leather pouch and walked over to where Cougar sat upon his sturdy mountain pony, surrounded by the ever-present cats.

She extended the drawing she had made of him, staring no higher than his buckskin-clad knee. "Since you were so determined to have this, you can take it with my blessing."

The horse shifted beneath Cougar as he leaned out to accept the drawing. He grimaced at the hard, chiseled face that glared back at him from the sketch. He knew perfectly well that the illustration expressed Roz's perception of him, especially after last night. She had come to regret the intimacies they had shared, just as he'd foreseen.

It was better this way, Cougar told himself sensibly. He had nothing to offer a woman like Rozalie Gaylord, absolutely nothing at all. And she could never be anything to him except the place he came for physical satisfaction—which he certainly hadn't gotten because he had turned out to be more of a gentleman than he ever wanted to be.

This attraction would never last, Cougar assured himself. When Roz had finally coped with the loss of her father and completed her journals on the West, she would return to New York where she belonged. Cougar could give her no reason to stay, because there was nothing left in him to give anyone.

Life's bitter trials had drained the very heart and soul out of him. The tenderness Roz needed and deserved was not within him to give. Cougar had exhausted his small supply of it the previous evening and it still hadn't been enough.

Cougar didn't bother with a good-bye before he nudged his steed toward the corral to gather the calves and horses. He had said and done too much already.

"When are you coming back, Cougar?" Cal demanded to know.

"Before the first snow," Cougar promised.

"But this is just summer!" Cal bemoaned.

"I have things to do, Caleb."

"If your papa doesn't have chores for you to tend,

you can come to the meadow while I paint," Roz offered, refusing to glance in Cougar's direction.

The boy's gaze bounced back and forth between Cougar and Roz. "How come neither of you will look at each other?"

Roz muttered at the boy's keen powers of observation and tossed a manufactured smile in Cougar's general direction. "We're not ignoring each other at all, are we, Cougar?"

"Of course not, Yank. It was a pleasure to meet you."

"Same here," Roz said unenthusiastically.

With a nod to Cal, Cougar sent a quiet command to the pumas and then followed the small herd of livestock down the road. He hadn't meant to glance back, but Francene called and waved to him. Before Cougar could stop himself, his gaze strayed one last time to the alluring vision in mint green ruffles and lace.

Heaving a sigh, Cougar settled himself more comfortably on his steed and headed down the mountain. If nothing else, Cougar would think back on this trip to Howard Station as a time when he almost became human—for a few hours one night in a forbidden fantasy. He rather expected that Roz would refer to that particular memory as part of her nightmare.

It was for the best, Cougar convinced himself. By the time he returned to Howard Station Roz would be long gone.


Francene Howard stared after the lone rider until he disappeared from sight. "I thought Cougar was planning to stay a few more days," she said to her husband.

Gideon closed the corral gate and limped over to his wife, sliding his arm affectionately around her waist. "You know how Cougar is. When he gets the urge to go, he's gone."

"Well, he wouldn't be so restless if folks would treat him with a little more courtesy and less fear," Fran muttered. "They avoid him as if he were a leper, for heaven's sake! And I was so in hopes that Cougar and Roz—"

Gideon chuckled and gave his wife of twenty-five years a kiss to silence her. "You better keep your matchmaking tendencies to yourself, honey," he advised.

"I think Cougar deserves more than the lone-wolf life he leads," Francene grumbled. "Somebody needs to teach him how to smile again. I think Roz could be that someone. I've noticed the way she stares at him when she thinks no one is around."

Gideon sighed heavily. "Don't get your hopes up, hon. Some folks never learn to live with anything but loneliness. War can sometimes do that to a man. It took two years for me to get my life back into perspective, and I didn't live through anything near what Cougar has been through with the Indian massacres and his forays against the worst offenders of justice that this territory has seen. The man has had his soul damned near torn out of him, Fran. All he knows is how to survive."

"I still contend that a good woman would do wonders for him," Fran said with great conviction.

Gideon threw back his silver-brown head and laughed aloud. "There isn't a woman alive who can handle a man like Cougar. He's a living legend. What woman would want to compete with that?"

"All he needs is to learn how to love and care again," Francene contended.

"That is one tall order to fill. It's hard for love to grow from a seed that has never been planted. Cougar expects nothing from no one and he won't let anyone close enough to care."

"Maybe so, but still——"

"Pa?" Cal interrupted. "Miss Gaylord asked me if I could go with her while she paints. Can I?"

"Did you feed the hogs?" Gideon questioned.

"Yes, sir."

"Is the horse trough full to the brim?"

"Yes, sir."

Gideon nodded agreeably. "Just don't pester Roz while she's working."

"I won't," Cal assured his father. "She says I can paint today, right alongside her."

When Cal bounded toward Roz, who was leading the gray mare from the barn, Francene frowned pensively. She had noticed the change Roz had recently undergone. Roz was quieter than usual, paler, too. When Francene had asked if Roz knew what had become of Vito and Skeet at breakfast that morning, she had frozen up like a block of ice.

Dear Lord, Francene hoped those scraggly strangers hadn't tried to force their attention on Roz before they disappeared without a word. That's all that poor girl needed while she was recovering from the loss of her father.

Despite Francene's flaming curiosity, she turned back toward the inn to change the sheets and clean the rooms. She was going to have to fret over Roz's odd behavior while she worked, because there was a mountain of chores awaiting her.


Mimicking Roz's procedures, Cal stepped back from the canvas to survey his artistic creation. His pine tree was crooked and no amount of adjustment could correct the error.

"Perhaps you should thicken the base of your tree," Roz suggested, biting back an amused smile while her protégé fussed over his painting. Poor Caleb had no artistic talent whatsoever. His depth perception was sorely lacking, not to mention his inability to blend colors and deal with slanting shadows.

Cal strode forward to swipe a few bold strokes down the right side of his tree. His attempt to prop the pine tree upright offered little improvement. After comparing his painting to Roz's he set his brush aside and sighed in frustration.

"I'm never going to be a Rembrandt, or whoever that painter was you mentioned."

"Learning to paint takes time," Roz told him gently. "You have to develop a sense of depths, shapes and color."

"Well, I don't paint any better than I fire a rifle. Cougar says I've got the eyesight of a bat."

"That's wasn't a very nice thing for him to say," Roz sniffed.

"Cougar talks truth. He says I'm a better fisherman than hunter, and that I'm adequate with a lasso."

Roz went back to her landscape of thick pines and fir trees that reached into a vault of blue sky dotted with whispy clouds. "If it's all the same to you, I'd rather not hear anymore about what the great and wonderful Cougar has to say."

Caleb frowned, bemused. "How come you don't like Cougar? There's no other man like him in the whole territory."

"I do thank God for that. One Cougar around here is more than plenty."

"I'm going to grow up to be exactly like him—"

Roz wheeled around to brandish her paintbrush in Cal's startled face. "If you know what's good for you, young man, you will pattern yourself after your father."

"He ain't really my papa."

*"Isn't,"* she corrected before plowing on. "And Gideon is near enough to being your father to deserve your respect and your gratitude. He is generous and kind and he loves you just as much as if you were his own flesh-and-blood. The greater crime is having a father who cares more about himself and his own aspirations for you, one who ignores what *you* feel and what *you* need. And after he is gone forever, leaving only a last command as to how to handle the fortune he acquired—"

Roz snapped her mouth shut and pivoted toward her painting. She inhaled a cleansing breath and battled her churning emotions. "I'm sorry, Caleb. I didn't mean to preach at you. My point is that Gideon is a wonderful father and I wish mine had been more like him."

Cal studied the fetching young woman for a long moment. "Didn't your pa love you, Miss Gaylord?"

"No," she murmured ruefully. "He loved his money and prestige more. He became extremely upset with me when I refused to marry the man he selected for me, one whose wealth equally matched ours. It was Edward Gaylord's outraged anger with me that caused his heart to give out on him. That and his driving obsession to make money at every turn."

And there it was at last, Roz realized as she stared across the yawning canyon. There was the truth of her torment. She should not have unloaded it on a young boy. But after the incident the previous night, Roz had felt a stockpile of frustration bubbling inside her—old torments piling atop the new.

Roz had deeply resented her father's lack of attention, the absence of his love. Edward Gaylord had never had time for his daughter, only for his obsession. Since Roz's mother had died shortly after childbirth, Roz had turned to her father for affection. But no matter how much Roz tried to please him, to gain his attention, nothing worked—short of tantrums which he abhorred. Even as a child Roz had not been allowed to behave like a child. And when she had balked at the shallow aristocrat who bore Edward's stamp of approval as a son-in-law, her father had become furious with her.

The dreadful truth was that it was her fault that her father had collapsed, never to rise again. To this day, Roz could still hear him screeching at her, his face purple with rage. And when he wilted on the floor of his study, clutching his palpitating chest and snarling at her for openly defying him, Roz had been forced to accept her responsibility for the fatal attack.

When Edward realized he had made his last dollar, he had grabbed Roz by the sleeve and dragged her close, ordering her to ensure that his self-made fortune was secure, that no one other than a Gaylord would lay title to it. Roz had no idea what that remark implied and she'd had no time to question Edward. He had passed away, offering no last words of love, only another set of commands. And worse, Roz hadn't told Edward that all she had ever wanted was for him to love her.

Obviously love wasn't something most men understood. Edward Gaylord was a private and paranoid kind of man who had no room for love in his life. And neither did that stone-hearted Cougar who had torn Roz's emotions to shreds before he rode away, as if the tender moments they had shared meant absolutely nothing to him.

That was the very last time Rozalie Gaylord intended to reach out to *any* man for *any* reason. Men simply weren't worth a woman's effort. Now that Roz was financially independent she didn't have to answer to anyone and she was never going to again . . .

"Miss Gaylord!" Cal yelped, jostling her from her bitter reflections. "Your fir tree is beginning to look like mine."

Roz gaped at her painting in dismay. Sure enough, Cal was right. She had been so distracted by tormenting thoughts that she had failed to concentrate on her work.

"I think we should call it a day," Roz decided. "Neither of us is having much luck. I'm sure your mother could use extra help with her chores this afternoon. She said she was expecting extra guards and passengers with the gold shipment, as well as the supervisor who is inspecting stage stations."

Cal gathered his supplies and packed them in the leather pouch. When he spied the sketch Roz had done of him and Cougar at target practice, his face beamed with delight.

"Can I have this one, Miss Gaylord?"

Roz handed the drawing over to Cal. She had done too many sketches of that virile half-breed who had so little affection and concern for her that he hadn't even intended to tell her good-bye before he rode off. It was painfully clear that Cougar had simply toyed with her.

Roz was surprised Cougar hadn't taken everything she had to give when the situation presented itself. But then, knowing she didn't really appeal to him was explanation enough. Cougar appeared to be a man of particular tastes, and all he had felt for her—if he felt anything at all—was a smidgen of pity. That, Roz would have preferred to do without.

God, to think she had actually desired that heartless man! She must have been out of her mind last night. After what had happened, Roz didn't care if she ever saw Cougar again and she wasn't wasting another thought on him, either. His memory was ruining her artistic creativity. As far as she was concerned, those three black mountain lions were welcome to Cougar. They had more use for him than she did.


Burney Adair returned to the secluded shack in the mountains before Hudson Caine had time to ride out and check on him. Jake Roche met his right-hand man at the door with an expectant frown.

"Well, what did you find out?"

"The half-breed and his cats rode out this morning," Burney reported as he stepped from the stirrup.

"Good. We'll carry out our original plan. We'll position

ourselves in the hills around the station and strike as soon as the stage guards climb down from their perch."

"Are you sure that half-breed rode out and isn't coming back?" Vito demanded to know.

"He took off with a string of cattle and horses, heading south," Burney assured him.

Vito and Skeet breathed audible sighs of relief and absently massaged their mending wounds.

"If I never see that son of a bitch again that will be too soon for me," Skeet grumbled.

"You boys are getting soft," Jake taunted his confederates.

Vito snorted indignantly. "I'm *telling* you there is something downright scary about that half-breed when he is on the attack."

"Scary?" Colby Jordan snickered as he practiced snapping the whip he constantly carried with him. "Scarier than Roche's raiders?"

Vito nodded grimly. "I've heard the man called *El Gato Diablo*—the devil cat—and I've seen the look in those golden eyes at close range. It was like staring death in the face."

"Well, there's no need for you and Skeet to worry your pretty little heads over your cat man," Hudson mocked. "Burney said he was long gone."

No other news could have made Vito and Skeet happier than that, not even the anticipation of their share of the gold shipment. Till the day they died, they swore they wouldn't forget the unnerving sound of Cougar's voice—like an echo in stone. Neither would they forget the feel of Cougar's dagger slicing like sharp cat claws.

# Seven

The instant Cougar had transacted his business with the stage manager at Finnegan's Station, he made a bee-line toward the shanty that sat directly behind the rectangular stone building. Finnegan, a man of lusty appetite, had provided himself and travelers with a bordello to ease masculine needs. Cougar had frequented the combination saloon and bordello on occasion. He could not, however, remember a time when he was so determined to seek physical release. He had whetted his craving with a blue-eyed sophisticate and had found himself nobly backing away—at tremendous cost to his male body. Now he wished he had finished what he had started with Roz. She couldn't have hated him more one way or the other, he imagined.

Leaving the cats to feed near the creek that was located one mile north of Finnegan's Station, Cougar donned white man's clothes, following the advice of the Indian agent who had once told him to become white when it was to his best advantage. Cougar could act civilized when he felt like it. Or at least he had learned to look the part when he needed to.

The Hurdy Gurdy girls at Finnegan's Station voiced no objection when Cougar strolled into their cramped

parlor. Cougar drew several interested stares, but he settled on the buxom inamorata with dyed-blond hair who
hadn't been there the last time he passed through.

The way Cougar had it figured, the woman reminded
him enough of Roz Gaylord to satisfy the gnawing craving she had aroused in him. The only difference was
that the painted harlot wanted no more than his money
for the use of her body. Roz, on the other hand, was a
little too hard on emotions Cougar preferred to keep
dead and buried. He wasn't looking for lasting ties; he
was looking for temporary satisfaction.

The minute Cougar kicked the bedroom door shut and
peeled off his shirt, his female companion's dark eyes
widened. "Lord, mister, somebody put enough bullet
holes in you to stop a normal man dead in his tracks!"

"Some folks say I have the nine lives of a cat," Cougar murmured enigmatically.

"Yeah, well, honey, you look like you used up three
of those lives already," Dori Creighton insisted.

"I didn't come here to chitchat," Cougar muttered.

Dori shrugged a partially bare shoulder and flounced
on the bed. "Suit yourself. You're paying for whatever
you want." She held out her hand for the gold coin
Cougar dug from his pocket. "Just remember, no rough
stuff. Finnegan filled the last surly client's hide with
buckshot and told him not to come sniffing around his
girls again."

When Dori had tucked the coin in the jewelry box
beside the bed, she struck a provocative pose.

Cougar stared at the crimson red robe that boasted
feathers. The doxy reminded him of a plump hen. The
poor girl even had a cackle in the giggle that erupted

from her lips when Cougar eased down beside her. When she clutched his hand and clamped it against her ample bosom, Cougar cursed colorfully.

"What's your problem, sugar?" Dori questioned. "Did you want fast and furious?"

Nothing felt right about this impersonal encounter. That had never bothered Cougar until the previous night. He had always preferred complete emotional detachment when he eased his male needs. But he kept remembering how Roz had reacted to each exploring caress, how wildly exciting it had been to share each new experience with her.

Damnation, since when had he given a fig about gentle passion? And why should he care that the touch of this blond harlot didn't affect him the way Roz's did. It was over, damn it, and all that was important was easing his physical urges. This wasn't about *feeling;* it was about *doing.* All he wanted was pure and simple release . . .

Dori's cackling giggle jolted Cougar from his exasperating thoughts, and he jerked up his head to glare at her.

"Don't tell me you're married and are suddenly having misgivings about betraying your wife." Dori cast him another amused glance when he scowled at her. "She must be something special if you would turn down a quick tumble. I'm sure as the devil not going to tell her you strayed," she added with a conspiratory wink.

When Dori reached for him again, Cougar bounded to his feet, backing away from the bed. He had never been so frustrated in all his thirty years! And damn if he didn't feel as if he were betraying a precious memory. He hadn't even taken possession of Roz and he had no intention of it—ever. But Roz had been everything pure and sweet and innocent that life had to offer, and Cougar had never been remotely close to that kind of pleasure before . . . and he never would be again, most likely.

"You're leaving?" Dori chirped in disbelief when Cougar hurriedly shrugged on his shirt and grabbed his gunbelts.

"I'm leaving," Cougar gruffly confirmed.

Dori propped herself up on the bed and grinned mischievously. "Give my regards to the missus, sugar."

Cougar muttered something unintelligible and stamped out of the room. He couldn't believe he had turned her down. Why? Because of a half-formed memory, damn it! He must be out of his mind.

Still scowling at the curse Roz Gaylord had placed on him, Cougar stalked back to the parlor to buy himself a bottle of white man's fire water and two thick Mexican cigars. He was going to drink that woman's memory off his mind and burn the taste of her kisses away with tobacco. And when he was just one shot-glass away from oblivion, he would look Dori up. By then, his vision would be too blurred to remember those crystal clear blue eyes, and his body would be too numb to remember the forbidden dream that hadn't come true.

Intent on his purpose, Cougar rode back to the camp beside the trickling stream. He was still cursing the sound of Roz's sultry voice and the image that swam before his eyes when he passed out. The only affection he received was the lick of the pumas' sandpaper tongues before they bedded down on the left side of him, just as they always did.

* * *

Cougar didn't wake up; he came to, just as the sun climbed over the craggy summits of the Rockies. His frustrated growl set the cats to squalling in chorus. Cougar swore as the sound split his skull like an invisible hatchet.

Rolling onto his back, Cougar squinted at the dome of blue sky. Soon as he was able, he was going to march back to Finnegan's Station and finish what he had started—this time, at least. He was not a man who made a habit of leaving deeds half done and he sure as hell wasn't going to start a new policy, just because he had gotten hung up with that lovely Yankee who had taught him the difference between hurried lust and tender passion. He was going to forget Rozalie Gaylord by losing himself in another woman's arms.

The redhead this time, Cougar decided as he levered his sluggish body up on an elbow. He had sampled that one's charms the last time he came down from the mountains. He shouldn't have gone for the blonde. That had been his mistake.

That was the last thought to float across Cougar's pickled brain before he closed his eyes to give his hellish hangover the sleep it demanded . . .

The distant bugle call signaled the approach of the noon stage. Francene Howard scurried around the trading post in a flurry of last-minute activity. News had come down the line that a visiting dignitary was riding with the gold shipment. One of the Overland Express

supervisors—following the orders of the new superintendent—was inspecting the stage stations along the
route. Francene had been notified of the inspection the
previous evening and she vowed to make a good impression.

The home station had received high recommendations
the past six months and she intended to reclaim the title
of the best wayside inn and restaurant between Denver
and Colorado Springs. The new superintendent of the
Colorado division of Overland Express was said to be
a stickler for providing the best possible travel accom-
modations for passengers. According to the information
passed from station to station, the new superintendent
intended to upgrade meals, schedules and lodging. Although Francene had yet to meet the new superintendent
in person, she had heard he was a young, industrious
man who believed in working as hard as his attendants.

Francene intended to have a spotless report delivered
to the superintendent's desk. And when he came in person, as he planned to do within the next few months,
Francene vowed to roll out the red carpet. Any supervisor who was willing to make the rounds to personally
meet the employees and inspect the stations had
Francene's vote of approval. She would ensure he was
comfortable, well fed and made welcome.

By the time the pounding of hooves and jingle of
harnesses heralded the coach's arrival, Francene had her
best china sitting on the fresh linen tablecloth. The
chicken she had plucked and dressed at the crack of
dawn was frying in the skillets.

Francene had sent Roz off with a picnic basket and
a request to keep Caleb occupied until after the stage

had come and gone. Caleb had a habit of grilling travelers with questions while they dined. Francene decided to spare the stage supervisor from being placed on the firing line.

Francene had just stepped onto the porch when the guards climbed down from atop the coach. And then all hell broke loose. Gunfire came from all directions at once, ricocheting off the stone walls of the trading post and dancing in the dirt beside the coach. Passengers cursed when they were pinned down inside the coach, unable to reach the protective cover provided by the station. The guards tried to climb up to retrieve their rifles, but both men caught bullets before they could fire a single shot at the six masked men who thundered down from the hills with their pistols blazing.

"Gideon, no!" Francene screamed when she saw her husband reach for the pistol he carried on his hip.

Like a shot, Francene dashed toward the barn.

"Damn it, Fran, take cover," Gideon growled, shoving her inside the barn. But Francene wheeled to fling her arms around him, begging him not to invite gunplay.

Before the dust cleared the masked bandits had formed a circle around the area. The three men inside the coach were ordered out with hands held high. They were immediately relieved of their hardware. Two of the raiders bounded from their horses to check the inn and trading post, ensuring no one was lying in wait with weapons. The passengers were frisked for valuables before the leader turned his full attention on Gideon and Francene.

"You there, by the barn," Jake Roche snapped. "Come join your friends."

Cursing, Gideon limped forward on his cane, his wife cuddled protectively beside him. He was reminded of the day his infantry had been marched onto the battlefield, forced to surrender to the jeering Union Army that had outnumbered them three to one. The way Roche barked orders reminded Gideon of the arrogant Union soldiers who had lorded over their Confederate prisoners.

Gideon swore under his breath. He despised haughty airs, especially from a no-account desperado. But then, as now, Gideon was in no position to object, not when his beloved wife might be gunned down because of his belligerence.

"Where's the other woman and the kid?" Vito demanded to know.

Francene lifted her hostile gaze when she recognized the Mexican's accented voice and stocky build. Her gaze darted to the other familiar form that was perched beside Vito Guerero. "They aren't here," she said stiffly.

"I'll make sure," Vito volunteered as he swung to the ground.

While the desperadoes kept their weapons trained on their captives, Vito made a second search of the inn and post. When he came up empty-handed, Jake Roche issued the order for the stage supervisor to drag the strongbox down to the ground. The desperadoes opened fire on the lock and hurriedly loaded the pouches of gold in their saddlebags while their prisoners watched helplessly.

And then the celebrative looting began. Colby Jordan rode his horse into the trading post, lashing out with his whip to shatter the heirloom China, upending the carefully set table. While two of the thieves tied up the prisoners like a string of horses, the other desperadoes grabbed everything from the post they could carry. Whiskey, ammunition, blankets, hard tack and canned fruit were loaded on the horses Gideon had bought from Cougar.

Colby Jordan reined in his horse beside Gideon and guzzled another gulp of whiskey. He smirked at Gideon, whose face was clouded with frustrated fury. "What's a-matter old man? Afraid we're gonna spread your wife's legs and rut on her while you watch?"

Gideon took a menacing step forward, only to have Francene latch onto him and hold him at bay.

"Don't let him antagonize you," she insisted. "He's spoiling for a fight. Don't give it to him, Gideon."

Colby downed another drink, letting the whiskey dribble into his stubbled whiskers. "That's right, *Gideon,* don't give it to me. Let your wife do it for you."

Francene smothered a curse when Colby nudged his horse up beside her. With a flick of his wrist, he coiled the whip around Francene's waist and yanked her off the ground. What little restraint Gideon had mustered abandoned him when his wife was handled so roughly. Gideon felt the maddening urge to strike back for all the times he had been unable to fight while he was rotting away in that hellhole of a Union prison camp, suffering the ridicule of cruel guards. Gideon's wife was his greatest treasure and he refused to let her suffer as he had during that bloody damned war.

Howling with laughter, Colby jerked Francene up in front of him on his horse. "Come on, old man. You've already got one gimpy leg," he taunted. "Would you like the other leg to match?"

Gideon's hazel eyes burned with a fury that defied fear. When Colby clamped a hand over Francene's breast, rage boiled through him. The only weapon at his disposal was the cane in his fist. He swung it with all his might, catching Colby on the side of the head.

Colby let out a roar and a curse and pulled his pistol to fire at Gideon's thigh. When Gideon crumbled to the ground, Francene clawed at her captor, fighting her way free from the coiled whip. Then she launched herself off the horse to sprawl protectively on her downed husband.

"Leave him be!" she screeched wildly. "Just take what you want and go."

Her tear-misted gaze swung to the clump of men who had been tied behind the back of the coach like spare horses. Frustration ate away at Francene as she battled to protect Gideon, who was trying to push her away to attack his tormenting captor.

"Mount up," Jake Roche ordered his men.

"I think we should take the woman with us," Colby insisted.

Jake wouldn't have minded a little female companionship himself, and a hostage would go a long way in discouraging the posse of Rocky Mountain Detectives who had been scouting the area to locate them . . .

The sound of hoofbeats echoed through the canyon, causing Jake to swivel in his saddle, automatically grabbing for his pistols. "Who the devil is that?"

Gideon swore foully when he saw his adopted son and Roz Gaylord racing toward the station on the gray mare. It was obvious that they had heard the shots and had hightailed it back to the station. Their timing was terrible!

"We'll take that one with us." Skeet gestured toward Roz. "She owes me a turn with her."

While the men rode off to apprehend the twosome on the gray mare, Jake leaned out to slap the team of horses attached to the coach. The horses trotted off, forcing the string of men to jog behind to prevent being dragged through the dirt.

Francene didn't dare roll away from Gideon until the raiders had clattered off, for fear her husband would invite another bullet. In helpless fury Francene watched the pistoleros swarm around Roz and Caleb. Francene heard Roz's outraged screech and Caleb's terrified wail mingling with the curses of the captive men who had become entangled in their ropes and were being dragged by the runaway stagecoach.

It was as if the world had been thrust into the darkest regions of hell. Francene was just beginning to understand why Gideon had awakened to nightmares for two years after serving in the war. She knew she was doomed to suffer her own bad dreams, wondering if her son and Roz would return from their stint in hell.

Sobbing hysterically, Francene eased down to find Gideon's blood staining her gown. He shoved her hands away when she tried to inspect his wound.

"Get one of the horses out of the barn and stop that stage," Gideon told his sobbing wife. "Those men will be bloody pulps before too much longer. Now move!"

Blindly, Francene struggled to her feet, hesitant to leave her husband when his leg was covered with blood.

"I'll be fine," Gideon gritted out. "But those men don't have a prayer without you."

Biting back the tears, Francene dashed off to do as she had been told. The sight awaiting her, when she finally halted the stage, caused nauseated knots to coil in the pit of her stomach. All five men were scraped and bleeding after being dragged across the rocky road. Two men were unconscious and those who were still alert were spewing oaths and curses that consigned the Roche gang to eternal hell.

By the time Francene assisted the men into the coach and led the team back to the station, Gideon had crawled into the trading post to pull the burned chicken off the stove. A fog of smoke clouded the room that was strewn with fallen shelves, ransacked supplies and broken dishes.

Francene forced herself to think only of providing medical attention for her wounded husband and the injured travelers. Each time she dared to speculate on how Caleb and Roz were faring in the hands of those ruthless criminals, her skin crawled with revulsion. She was still fumbling around in a daze when the posse of ten men, lead by General Cook of the Rocky Mountain Detective Agency arrived at the station three hours later.

General Cook tried to interrogate Gideon while he was propped up in bed, but Gideon spouted his own commands. It was Gideon's intention to have one of the detectives fetch Cougar from the stage station located fifteen miles south.

When David Cook objected to the delay, Gideon all but shouted in his face. "By damn, you get Cougar up here now! Your whole damned posse isn't as good at tracking as Cougar is. A helluva lot of good your men did wandering around the countryside like Moses looking for the promised land!"

"Gideon, calm down," Francene beseeched as she sank down beside her raging husband. "The gang General Cook has been following has been evading posses for over six months."

"I don't give a damn about excuses," Gideon blustered in pain and frustration. "I want Cougar to track my son."

"As I heard it, the manhunter retired and refuses to take any more assignments, no matter how high the bounty," General Cook replied. "I offered him three assignments myself last winter and he flatly refused."

"Well, Cougar won't refuse me," Gideon guaranteed. "He owes me. You put a man on your fastest horse and skedaddle down to Finnegan's Station. You tell Cougar that Caleb and Roz have been taken hostage and he'll be here by dark!"

General Cook nodded to John Swenson who strode off to do as Gideon requested. Then and only then did Gideon settle back against the headboard to relate the incident in graphic detail. And while he did, Francene made her way to one of the vacant rooms in the inn to vent the tears she had held in check. She cried for her terrified son and the young woman whose life had surely become a living hell. She wept for the pain her husband was suffering and her lack of skill in removing the bullet that was deeply imbedded in his leg.

And finally, when there were no more tears left, Francene pulled herself together, washed her face and marched off to tend the chores that awaited her, praying that Cougar hadn't already left Finnegan's Station to disappear into the mountains he now called home.


Roz found herself strapped to the gray mare with Caleb secured behind her. Her hands had been anchored to the saddle horn and her feet to the stirrups. Cal's arms were wrapped around her waist and his body was meshed so tightly against her that she could feel every shuddering breath he had inhaled before he had cried himself to sleep a few minutes earlier. His head was resting against her shoulder as if it were his pillow.

By now, the fear Roz had experienced when she found herself surrounded by desperadoes had evaporated into emotional numbness. Hope had turned to futility. Lately, it seemed one torment was following closely on the heels of another . . . and another. Roz had yet to recover from the loss of her father and then the near rape. She hadn't learned to cope with her bittersweet encounter with Cougar. And now this! Roz would have asked herself what else could possibly go wrong, but she was afraid to find out.

Of course, the instant Vito and Skeet had yanked off their masks and smiled wolfishly at her, Roz knew what her fate was going to be. Having experienced Cougar's tenderness, even if it had been motivated by pity, would make the upcoming ordeals all the worse.

Cougar had taught her the difference between passion and abusive lust. Not that it mattered, Roz reminded herself dispiritedly. She would probably be just as dead when all was said and done. And not that Cougar would care when he came down from the mountains before the first winter snowflakes flew. By then, he probably wouldn't even remember her name or bother to lament her tragic death.

Roz dreaded enduring her fate, but her greatest fear was for Caleb. She felt personally responsible for him and she had blundered headfirst into trouble. Francene had entrusted her son to Roz's care while Francene readied the trading post for the stage line's dignitary. Instead of heading for cover when she heard the echoing shots, Roz had done the very last thing she should have done.

Dear God, Cougar was right. Roz didn't belong in the West. She didn't possess the necessary instincts or skills to rescue herself from the trouble she had gotten herself and Cal into. Gideon and Francene would be worried sick . . .

Roz winced when another tormenting thought stabbed through her aching heart like a knife. What if the Howards had been struck down by assassins' bullets? Roz hadn't been able to ascertain who had survived before the thundering brigade swooped down on her. There was no telling how much death and destruction the outlaws had wrought before they whisked their hostages up the winding trail into the mountains.

It was going to be difficult to keep her spirits from scraping rock bottom when the world had turned black. Hope seemed a fool's dream when Roz glanced at the six men who were armed to the teeth, toting enough supplies to feed an army for several months. And it was obvious that Vito Guerero and Skeet Thomas were planning to have their spiteful revenge on her. Their anticipatory grins said as much.

Roz wondered how her father would feel if he knew

that his only daughter had perished without heirs to pass down the fortune her father had made in shipping, land speculation and transportation. No doubt, that would be another disappointment Edward Gaylord would bring to Roz's attention when they met in the hereafter.

Roz had always believed money was no substitute for the true affection withheld by her strict, taciturn father. All she had ever wanted was to be loved for herself. She hadn't received her father's love, or had she received honest affection from the dozens of money-hungry suitors who offered marriage. And she hadn't even won the slightest bit of respect from the one man who had awakened her feminine desires, either. When Roz tried to count the blessings in her life to lift her spirits she came up empty-handed. She sincerely hoped her next life would turn out better than this one.

It was a shame she hadn't taken Cougar's cynical approach, instead of living on false hopes of a rosy future. If Cougar had been here, she imagined he would have told her to stop whining because life got no better.

Nothing affected the man of granite. He existed on a plane that heartache and suffering couldn't touch. The only pain Cougar ever experienced was physical, certainly not emotional. Cougar was like a cavern, filled with hollow tunnels that were lined with rock. He certainly wouldn't have been sitting here feeling sorry for himself. Of course, he would never have gotten himself into this perilous situation because of his phenomenal skills of self-defense.

*And to save yourself and Cal, you are going to have to become just like him,* Roz thought as the procession of riders trudged up the steep embankment.

Survival had to become Roz's sole purpose. This was what living hell was like, Roz decided. And if perchance she did survive this ordeal, she was taking the first train back to New York, just as Cougar suggested she do.

Cougar was absolutely right, this was no place for incompetent fools like her. And as Cal had reminded Roz, Cougar spoke the truth, even if you didn't enjoy hearing it. The bitter truth was that Roz was no more adept at protecting herself than Cal was at hitting targets with Cougar's oversized rifle.

Roz blinked back the mist of tears that clouded her eyes when she felt Cal stir behind her. She was going to have to make the supreme sacrifice to ensure Cal got out of this ordeal alive. He was young and he deserved the chance to grow into a man. She was going to have to convince these desperadoes to let him go, no matter what the cost to herself.

On that determined thought, Roz murmured comfortingly to Cal when she felt him sobbing quietly against her back. She was going to have to lie and tell him there was hope when she knew there was nothing ahead except inevitable calamity.

# Eight

Cougar descended from his camp in the foothills near Finnegan's Station. His head was still pounding like a tom-tom and his stomach pitched and rolled like a storm-tossed ship. It had taken the entire morning and half the afternoon to recover from his self-imposed torture. He was in the foulest of moods.

The piercing sunlight put a squint in his eyes and a snarl on his lips, but he was fiercely determined to get Roz Gaylord out of his system once and for all. He had already poisoned her memory by ingesting enough whiskey to kill a horse, and smoked enough tobacco to fog her taste and scent. Now he was going to burn away his hunger for her in the arms of the redhead.

Before Cougar reached the small settlement—consisting of a blacksmith's shop, stage station and bawdy house—a galloping rider appeared behind him, waving his arm in expansive gestures and shouting Cougar's name as if they were long lost friends. Cougar reined around to watch the bearded rider race toward him. The man skidded to a halt a safe distance away from the snarling black cats that had come bounding down the hill to investigate the yelps and shouts. Cougar frowned at the faintly familiar face beneath the gray Stetson.

"Cougar, you probably don't remember me, but we met in Denver a couple of years ago."

Cougar watched the rider pull off his hat and address him with a tentative smile. The man was ever mindful of the cats that had his mount dancing skittishly beneath him.

"Deputy John Swenson? Remember?" John prompted the formidable giant who looked as hostile as an entire Indian war party.

"I retired from manhunting a year ago," Cougar said without preamble. "You'll have to do your own dirty work, Swenson."

When those cold amber eyes bore down on him, John shifted uneasily in the saddle. "I realize that, Cougar, but I'm not a deputy these days. I'm riding with General David Cook of the Rocky Mountain Detective Agency."

Cougar let loose with a disrespectful snort. Cook and his detectives were none of his concern. And considering the black mood Cougar was in, John Swenson was damned fortunate Cougar hadn't bit his head off for bothering him with insignificant details. As far as Cougar was concerned, he could take care of himself, and if white folks couldn't do the same, that was their tough luck. Cougar had dealt with his share of criminals and dangerous crises. Let John Swenson and his sidekicks take their hitch at it.

"I take it there is some point to this lengthy reintroduction," Cougar grumbled unsociably.

John plunked his hat back on his sandy-blond head and nodded grimly. "I know you retired from bounty hunting—"

"You got that right," Cougar cut in.

"But Gideon Howard asked me to track you down."

Cougar went as still as stone. A deep sense of foreboding riveted him.

"Gideon says you owe him a favor."

"I do," Cougar confirmed. He owed Gideon his life after he dug out three bullets and patched him up.

"Well, Gideon said to tell you he was calling in the debt."

Cougar's mouth thinned in a fierce line. He knew Gideon well enough to know that whatever had happened was deadly serious. Gideon never asked for help if there was any conceivable way for him to manage on his own—stiff leg or no.

"Spit it out, Swenson," Cougar demanded bluntly. "What's the problem?"

John inhaled a deep breath to rattle off the sketchy details of the incident at Howard Station. "The Roche gang struck again—"

"Roche?" Cougar interrupted, his tawny eyes narrowing in a lethal stare.

John gulped at the glare that was directed at him and nodded affirmatively. "Jake Roche. Have you heard of him?"

The name went through Cougar like a penetrating dagger thrust into what had once been his heart. Vivid memories sprang to mind, visions of a bloody massacre that had taken the lives of women, children and weary old men who had grown tired of fighting the invading white menace.

Cougar could almost see that cocky bastard in his army uniform, charging toward the Cheyenne lodges, butchering everyone within his path. Hatred spurted through Cougar's veins—the same now as then.

"Roche and his raiders attacked Howard Station at noon," John hurriedly continued. "I don't have all the facts because I was ordered to leave in a flaming rush. But I do know Gideon took a bullet in his good leg while trying to protect his wife from molestation."

Cougar's fist curled into a knot on the reins and the muscles of his jaw clenched as he gritted a murderous curse to Jake Roche's name. "Go on, Swenson," he demanded.

"All the men traveling on the coach were tied up behind the stage and dragged halfway down the mountain. They were damned near skinned alive before Francene could rescue them."

Cougar's mood turned blacker than pitch while he waited to hear the rest of the gruesome tale.

"According to the passengers, Roche had decided to take Francene hostage since he knew our posse was closing in on him. But when the little boy and young woman returned to the station to determine what happened—"

"Damn it to hell!" Cougar burst out. He didn't want Swenson to complete his report. He knew what was coming next. Cal and Roz had ridden straight into catastrophe. And Cougar could guess who had become the defenseless hostages, abducted to keep the trailing posse at bay.

Cougar gouged his heels into his sturdy black mountain pony and took off like an exploding cannonball. His abrupt command sent the cats racing after him. John

Swenson was left to control his flighty mount when the pumas dashed past.

Flashbacks of the night Roz had been set upon by the scraggly ruffians leaped into Cougar's thoughts, putting a furious sneer on his lips. Cougar had sensed something strange about Vito Guerero's and Skeet Thomas's behavior, but he had been too distracted by the bewitching Yankee to heed his instincts. Unless Cougar missed his guess, and he doubted that he had, the Mexican and his tobacco-chewing companion had been monitoring the activities at the station, so as to estimate the strength of resistance against an attack.

Now Cougar knew why.

Another foul curse burst from Cougar's lips as he rode hell-for-leather toward the stage station. This was *his* fault. If he had stayed until after the gold shipment arrived, none of this might have happened. If he had been at the station, he could have picked off several of the thieves—starting with Jake Roche himself. Cougar wanted to see him tortured within an inch of his life— very slowly, very painfully, until he was screaming for mercy that wouldn't come.

Cougar wondered if that knife-happy Burney Adair was riding with Roche. Probably. Those two bloodthirsty Indian haters were as thick as glue. They had scalped Black Kettle after he and his wife had been shot down. Then they went about mutilating women, children, and old men.

Hatred twisted in Cougar's gut when the past collided with the present. He could hear the horrified screams of children calling to their butchered parents before the volley of bullets ended in bloody silence. Even the Indian agent who had been in the peaceful camp had been murdered to ensure his silence. Only Cougar and Gray Eagle had managed to bury themselves in the thick grass along the river and avoid detection when they returned from hunting to hear the whining bullets and haunting screams.

This time Cougar promised himself that Jake Roche and Burney Adair would meet their bad end, even if his own life was the price to be paid. And if either of those bastards laid a hand on Roz or Cal, they would become short-lived testimony to the worst kind of torture devised by white man or Indian!


Jake Roche flung up a gloved hand to halt the procession of riders and captives when darkness descended in the mountains. "We'll make camp here for the night," he declared. "Skeet, you ride back down the trail to see if we're being followed. Burney and Colby will stand first watch."

"And I get first turn with the woman," Vito insisted, leering at Roz.

"No one gets the woman tonight," Jake told him sharply.

"Why the hell not?" Vito grumbled in question.

"We're still too close to Howard Station to risk distractions. I intend to be prepared if that posse comes storming after us. Burney already assured me the riders were at the station when he doubled back to check on them. The posse sent one of their men south. They could be telegraphing messages along the route to give lawmen our general location."

When Vito cast Roz another hungry glance, she forced herself to ignore the disgusting promise in the Mexican's dark eyes. So help her God, she would become stone cold, just like Cougar, in the face of danger. He had the remarkable ability of switching off his emotions—to respond to nothing but instinct without allowing sentiment to cloud his thinking. He became as predatory as his cats and so would Roz. And until that moment when she was forced to subject herself to the lusts of these heartless cutthroats she would do all within her power to see Cal free of this nightmare.

"Give the boy a horse and let him go," Roz demanded, lifting a belligerent chin. "You need only one hostage."

Jake swung from the saddle and swaggered over to where Roz sat tied to the gray mare. When his hand curled around her thigh, Roz forced herself not to react, not to feel anything except controlled contempt.

"You're offering to whore for us to save this scrawny kid?" Jake smirked.

"Kindly mind your foul tongue," Roz admonished. "There is no reason to subject a child to your offensive language."

Jake reached up to untie Roz's hands from the pommel and then freed her feet. "Just where do you hail from, woman, to have acquired such a snippy accent?" he asked as he dragged her from the saddle.

"New York."

Jake chuckled as he passed a hand over her bosom. "New York? Then I don't suppose you've ever had a *real* man, have you, honey?"

"I've only met one in my life," Roz fired back at him. "You aren't him, Mr. Roche."

Gray eyes clashed with blazing blue, and Roz felt the sting in her cheek when he backhanded her for sassing him. Even when Jake roughly jerked her back onto her feet, her senses still reeling from the blow, she refused to be intimidated. Jake Roche may have been bad to the bone, but he was nowhere near as foreboding as Cougar in his black moods. If she could deal with a man like Cougar, then she could most assuredly handle this despicable bastard.

Jake cocked a dark brow and regarded the lovely blonde for a ponderous moment. He liked the woman's spunk, even if she did prey on his quick temper. Jake was going to enjoy taking his turn with this delicate but feisty female. He wondered how long it would be before he and his men broke that haughty spirit of hers.

"While you're cooking our meal, I'll consider your offer," Jake told her.

Roz tilted her chin a notch higher and stared down her nose at the five-foot-ten-inch desperado, who sported a wicked smile. His pale gray eyes indicated no potential for kindness or consideration. In short, he was as appealing to Roz as a rattlesnake.

Roz wormed from his imprisoning arms and made a spectacular production of fluffing the wrinkled sleeve of her dress. She drew herself up to dignified stature, determined never to cower to these ruffians. "I don't cook well, Mr. Roche."

"You will learn," Jake vowed as he wrapped his hand around her hip to give her a disrespectful pinch.

"Leave her alone!" Caleb wailed.

"Shut up, kid, or you'll find yourself beaten black and blue," Jake snarled.

"If you lay a hand on the boy I swear by all that's holy that—"

"All right," Jake scowled when Roz twisted away from his groping touch. "Take the kid with you to gather firewood and keep him quiet. If you do as you're told, I'll go easy on him. But if he starts bawling his head off like a damned baby again, I'll shut him up permanently."

With her hands bound in front of her, Roz strode off to gather wood while Hudson Caine monitored her activities with a loaded rifle. Roz told herself to look past her hatred, to think rationally. She was going to have to keep Cal alive by her wits. She had to be headstrong enough not to be coerced into submission unless submission worked to her advantage. She had to devise a way to outsmart her captors. Somehow, she had to provide Cal with an opportunity to escape. And she had better conjure up a workable plan pretty damned quick!

"Cougar! Thank God you're here!"

When Francene flung herself into his arms, Cougar asked himself when anyone had ever thanked God or anybody else that he had arrived. While Francene squeezed the stuffing out of him and unleashed the tears she had contained since her first good cry that afternoon, Cougar surveyed the demolished trading post. He hadn't given the posse outside the time of day before he strode inside to check on Francene and Gideon. The posse was left to control their alarmed horses while the cats stalked around, sniffing the unfamiliar visitors.

"The Roche gang took Caleb and Roz," Francene whimpered. "They'll scare poor Caleb to death, and what they have planned for Roz—"

"Where's Gideon?" Cougar broke in quickly. He had no desire to hear his own apprehension voiced. It had frustrated him to no end while he thundered back to the station.

Francene pushed away from the solid bare chest that was crisscrossed by two bandoleers and then wiped the streams of tears from her cheeks. "Gideon is confined to bed. I can't dig out the bullet in his leg." She nodded toward uplifted hands that shook uncontrollably.

"What about the stage guards' and passengers' wounds?" Cougar questioned.

"They were minor injuries that I could handle."

"Boil some water," Cougar requested. "The bullet has to come out of Gideon's leg before gangrene sets in."

When she turned away, Cougar zigzagged around the strewn supplies to enter the cabin attached to the back of the trading post. He found Gideon ensconced on the bed, scowling darkly.

"Those worthless sons-a-bitches," Gideon muttered. "They were going to take Francene. If I'd have lost her, my life wouldn't have been worth living."

Cougar sank down on the edge of the bed to unwrap the bandage Francene had applied. He was well aware that Gideon valued his wife, though Cougar couldn't fathom caring so deeply for a woman himself. But still, Gideon had always made it known by deeds and words that Francene owned his very soul. Cougar would well imagine Gideon's towering fury when those raiders tried to steal Francene away from him. Gideon was lucky to be alive if he had resisted.

"I know what I'm asking of you, Cougar." Gideon grimaced when Cougar touched the fiery red flesh around the wound. "And I wouldn't blame you for turning me down, but I don't think that posse has a prayer of tracking Roche's Raiders through the mountain passes. You know this country like the back of your own hand. You and your cats are more competent than those ten detectives put together. They'll be about as much help as the Denver volunteer fire department that managed to save a few foundations when the whole damned town burned down in sixty-three."

"How many men are riding with Roche?" Cougar questioned as he inspected the bullet wound on Gideon's thigh.

"Five. Vito Guerero and Skeet Thomas were with Roche. The bastards must have been informants and scouts. I thought there was something odd about their behavior. All they did while they were here was keep an eye on everything and everyone who moved. They were casing the station."

"I figured that out a little too late myself," Cougar grumbled.

"The stage supervisor said there was forty thousand dollars in gold and bank notes in the strongbox. The gang made off with all of it—ouch!" Gideon hissed. "Go easy on that leg. It's the best one I've got left."

"I don't remember your being too gentle when you were poking around to find the bullets imbedded in me a few years back," Cougar snorted.

"I was in a hurry," Gideon defended himself. "You were all but dead, as I recall. A few more hours and you would have had a headstone standing over you for eternity."

Cougar nodded, remembering how close he had come to dying and how fierce was his need to survive to have his revenge on the men who had bushwhacked him. He still wore the scars from Gideon's passable surgical skills, but the men who'd attacked Cougar had suffered more than scars. Cougar hadn't bothered to bury those desperadoes. He hadn't felt very merciful or generous at the time.

"The gang took all the supplies they could carry on the horses I bought from you." Gideon glanced up when Francene scurried into the room, carrying a pot of steaming water and her butcher knife.

Cougar intercepted the glance that passed between husband and wife. He couldn't imagine anyone caring for him the way this long-married couple cared for each other. Their feelings were almost tangible, filling the room with a warmth that Cougar wasn't sure he fully comprehended.

"Francene, you better wait outside," Cougar suggested.

"No," she refused. "I intend to be by Gideon's side, just as I always have been."

Cougar took the sterilized knife in hand to make the incision. "I hope you've got a strong stomach and a lot of whiskey left to numb Gideon's pain."

"Forget the whiskey." Gideon braced himself against the headboard. "Just dig out the bullet as quick as you can so you can be on your way. Cal and Roz need you and I'm slowing down progress."

Ignoring the beads of perspiration that gathered on Gideon's forehead, Cougar probed for the lodged bullet. Gideon's face turned as white as milk as pain seared through him.

"Damn, Cougar, you're worse at gentleness than I was!" Gideon gritted out through clenched teeth.

"That's a matter of opinion, friend. At the time, I swore dying would have been less painful than you and your knife."

"Ow . . . goddamnit!" Gideon roared when blistering pain shot down his leg and numbed his toes. "Hurry up, Cougar. This is beginning to make me sick."

"Don't watch," Cougar instructed. "Feeling is bad enough."

Francene eased in front of her husband like a human shield. Gideon's hands clamped on her forearms, anchoring himself against the agony that was a repetition of suffering his war wound. The room turned fuzzy gray and Francene's face swirled into a cloud of black.

When Gideon slumped lifelessly on the bed, Cougar shoved the knife all the way to the bone to reach the deeply imbedded bullet.

"Bring me the whiskey," Cougar ordered. "I want this wound packed with antiseptic before I stitch it up. If infection sets in, he'll lose his leg."

Francene darted off and then returned with the last bottle of liquor in the trading post. Cougar doused the open wound, grimacing at the smell of whiskey that reminded him of his bout with the bottle the previous night. He had drunk himself blind and unconscious in hopes of forgetting his fascination with that delicate blonde who now found herself on the pathway to hell . . .

Cougar discarded the thought immediately. He could not allow sentiment to clog his thought processes. As soon as he had patched Gideon up and had given Francene instructions for making a healing poultice—Indian-style—he needed to be on the trail. Every hour he delayed put Cal and Roz at greater risk. Roz was the one who would suffer the worst physical abuse while Cal endured mental torment, Cougar predicted. Neither of them knew what had become of the Howards or the other victims of the robbery. Cougar had to find a way to give Cal and Roz hope of survival until he could rescue them.

When the wound had been stitched and Gideon was resting as comfortably as possible, Cougar inhaled a fortifying breath. He needed to devise a plan to deal with the Roche gang. He couldn't let his hatred for Jake Roche make him impatient and careless.

*Stealth and cunning,* that was what the Cheyenne preached when they prepared their warriors for battle. Although Cougar relied upon his white heritage when it worked to his advantage, he was going to become all Indian now. He had to be attuned to his surroundings, living up to the name his clan had given him. He would *become* the cougar, and when he went in for the kill, Jake Roche was not going to walk away unscathed. The Cheyenne curse that had been placed on Custer and the Seventh Cavalry was not quite complete. Jake Roche and Burney Adair had escaped unscathed . . . until now . . .

# Nine

Cougar strode out of the trading post to find the posse lounging on the porch. General David Cook surged to his feet. His wire-rimmed glasses sparkled in the lantern light that slanted through the open door. His gray mustache all but concealed his upper lip as he set his mouth in a grim line and approached Cougar.

"John Swenson tells me he never got a straight answer from you. Are you going to help us track down Roche's Raiders or aren't you?"

Cougar did not reply. His expression was as immovable as stone.

"The reward for their capture has escalated weekly," Cook continued. "The supervisor of the stage line, who found himself dragged through the dirt this afternoon, assures me that his superintendent will match the reward that Wells Fargo has offered. Even if we split the reward eleven ways, you will be well compensated for your trouble."

Cougar stared at the stout, square-jawed commander of the Rocky Mountain Detective Agency. Cook was a reasonably competent man, but his tracking ability left a lot to be desired—in Cougar's opinion. Cook and his men did not possess the killer instinct needed to deal with extremely dangerous criminals. No way was Cougar going to attach himself to this group of men. His three cats were twice as deadly when given commands. When they pounced, animal savagery took control. That was what Cougar had learned to rely upon in perilous situations. These men were too human to cope with demons like Jake Roche and Burney Adair.

"I'll make you a deal, Cook. I'll track the renegades and you can have the credit and the reward."

Cook blinked in surprise. "You think you can bring all six men in by yourself?"

"Easier than ten riders who make more noise than a marching band," Cougar smirked disrespectfully.

Cook expelled an audible sigh as he stared at the cantankerous half-breed. Cougar was not an easy man to deal with. He was not an easy man—period. Cougar never cut anyone any slack and he had no tolerance or respect for white men.

David Cook tried to take all that into consideration, but he was tired, frustrated and a little irritable himself after three weeks of this futile manhunt. "Now look, Cougar. The lives of a boy and a young woman are at stake here—"

"Exactly." Cougar took an ominous step forward, looming over Cook like an unyielding ponderosa pine.

One sharp command from Cougar sent six hundred pounds of lean muscle, dagger-lined jaws, and sharp claws lunging onto the wooden railing. The three black mountain lions sent up unholy screams that had the detectives scattering like quail. If the sound effects weren't enough to prove his point, Cougar barked another indecipherable command and the cats leaped down to pen the men against the wall.

"Holy hell, General!" John Swenson croaked as he peered at the glistening golden eyes and sharp fangs that were bearing down on him. "One more command and we'll all be in bloody shreds. Make him call off his cats."

Cougar did nothing of the kind. The cats stood guard on their prey, poised to attack if the command came. "Well, *General,* whose army seems more effective to you? Or do you need further demonstration?"

Cook jerked his head back around to stare at Cougar, whose voice had taken on a hollow, echoing resonance. In the blink of an eye this brawny giant seemed as much the predator as his well-trained cats. Cook wondered what would become of him if he dared to lay a hand on Cougar, or even *look* as if he intended to make a physical strike. There was definitely something eerie about this half-breed. Cougar had lived with his cats so long that he'd practically become one of them.

"All right, call them off. You've proved your point."

A hushed command sent the black shadows leaping over the railing to crouch below the porch. Eleven men breathed noticeable sighs of relief.

"I intend to track the outlaws into the mountains after I've collected supplies and extra clothes for Cal and Roz," Cougar informed Cook. "You and your men can skirt the foothills to block their escape to the south."

"And I suppose you know exactly which route they'll take?" Cook scoffed.

Cougar nodded his raven head. "They'll go where I force them to go," he affirmed. "There are only a few known trails through the mountains, ones that can be blocked off with a stick of dynamite. I'll send the men your way on one condition."

"And what condition is that?" asked Cook.

"Roche and Adair are mine." Cougar's voice dropped to a deadly pitch. "No matter what else happens, no matter who else comes out alive, Roche and Adair receive the Cheyenne brand of justice."

"I intend to see these men stand trial," Cook objected. "I want them to become an example for every two-bit crook who decides to prey on the stage lines and mining camps."

Cougar shook his head. "No deal. I'll hold court as I see fit, just as I have always done. I live by the code of the men I stalk, same as before. If you want results then you'll have to let me do this my way."

Cook muttered under his breath. To his knowledge, this half-breed had only one way of doing things—his way. Cougar didn't know the meaning of the word *compromise*.

"All I want is Cal and Roz out of the mountains alive," Cougar said stonily. "I don't give a damn who I have to kill to get them out. If you're looking for examples to parade through Denver, go track someone else who can make you look good."

"I'm not after glory, damn it," Cook blustered.

"Glad to hear it, General," Cougar replied as he ambled off the porch. "Neither am I." He paused to survey the clump of men whose profiles were outlined by the dim shaft of light. "I can't honestly say how many outlaws I can hand over to you. My cats have to have fresh meat while tracking, you know. I'm not going to have a helluva lot of time to take them hunting, now am I?"

When Cougar sauntered off to collect supplies and spare clothes, John Swenson turned to Cook. "He's kidding . . . right?"

Cook stared after the sinewy half-breed who walked with the silence of a shadow. "I don't think so, John, not if all those tales I've heard are even half true. Cougar takes no prisoners. And to my knowledge, he's never brought a fugitive back alive . . ."

Cougar's hand froze above the frilly undergarments in the top dresser drawer when he spied the clean but torn chemise Roz had been wearing the night Vito and Skeet attacked her. Apparently she hadn't taken time to mend the garment. But then, judging by the stack of neatly arranged unmentionables that filled the drawer to overflowing, Roz didn't need to bother. That woman had a wardrobe befitting a queen.

Cougar haphazardly scooped up a handful of undergarments and crammed them into the feed sack that held Cal's modest garb. Then he rolled up three of the simplest dresses he could find and shoved them into the sack.

He hoped Roz and Cal lived to enjoy changing into the clean clothes he had packed for them . . .

Cougar's attention settled on the collection of sketches that Roz had placed in the bottom drawer of her dresser. Curiously, he picked up the stack, silently admiring her talent . . . until he came to the half-dozen drawings she had done of himself. Damn, she had certainly made him look fierce, he thought as he studied the sketches.

Did he actually look that cold and vicious to her? To the rest of the world? Well, he had good reason to wear such a harsh expression, Cougar silently defended himself. There was very little pleasure in his life. Danger had eaten away at him until emotion had become unnecessary baggage he couldn't afford to carry around. Haunting memories were more abundant than happy recollections. What the hell was he supposed to do? Wander around with an idiotic smile on his face, as if the world were coming up roses instead of a patch of cactus needles . . . ?

"Cougar?"

He pivoted to see Francene poised in the open doorway of Roz's quarters.

Francene unfastened the gold chain from around her neck and moved toward Cougar. Her hands shook involuntarily as she opened the engraved, heart-shaped locket attached to the chain, revealing the picture of her and Gideon. "Give this to Cal when you find him. Tell him we love him more than words can say." When Cougar frowned, Francene expelled her breath. "Oh, for heaven's sake, it isn't going to kill you to say those words, especially if I'm not asking *you* to say you love that child who believes you hung the moon."

Cougar jerked up his head to meet Francene's misty gaze.

"Didn't you know that Cal worships the ground you float over? You're all he talks about before you show up and long after you go away. You even overshadow his pride in his father and that takes some doing, because Gideon is almost as fearless as you are. He nearly got himself killed today. But of course, Cal wasn't here to see that. All Cal can see is you, the idol he wants to pattern himself after."

"You don't have to make a big fuss about it," Cougar grunted as he tucked the locket in his pocket. "I'll do everything within my power to bring the boy back."

"And Rozalie?" Francene prompted.

Cougar's gaze dropped as he tied a leather strap around the bulging sack of clothes. "She may not wish to come back alive," he said quietly. "I don't have to tell you what they're planning to do with her."

Francene blanched, nervously toying with the folds of her skirt. "Then it's going to be up to you to restore her feminine pride and her self-respect if the worst happens."

Cougar scoffed at that. "You know I'm not the sentimental sort. I don't have an overstocked supply of sympathy."

"Well, you had better acquire some," Francene demanded. "If the truth be known, Roz is as alone in this world as you are. Caleb told me what Roz said about her father and his lack of affection for her. Somebody has to care what happens to that poor girl while she's up in the mountains, surrounded by a pack of worthless thieves. You'll be the only one up there who *does* care."

"Who says I do?"

*"I* say you do," Francene snapped, annoyed with his callous attitude. "And don't try to convince yourself that you don't, damn it. Roz is the symbol of lovely innocence. Would you see that destroyed by men's abusive lust?"

Cougar expelled a rough sigh. "It almost was already," he confided. "Vito and Skeet tried to molest her the night they disappeared. I got to Roz in the nick of time. I wanted to slit the other half of Vito's throat and take off one of Skeet's legs, but the Yankee was foolish enough to order their release. Now she is paying for her generosity."

"Good Lord!" Francene groaned in dismay. "Why didn't someone tell me?"

"As you said," Cougar replied as he slung the sack over his broad shoulder and strode off, "The Yankee doesn't think anybody really cares, and it wasn't something she wanted to rehash."

"*Make* her care again, Cougar," Francene implored him, tears stinging her eyes. "If it hadn't been for Roz, I would have been the one carried away. And it's my fault Roz and Cal were away from the post. I might have been able to hide them if they had been here. But I asked Roz to take Cal with her while the stage supervisor made his inspection so he would give a good report to the new superintendent. What Roz is suffering at those scoundrels' hands could have been *my* plight!"

When Francene succumbed to another round of tears, Cougar quietly closed the door and let her vent her grief. Odd, as much as he admired and respected Francene, her sobs hadn't gone through him with the same devastating effect that Roz's had. The sound of Roz's tears had touched something deep inside him. Cougar wondered if Roz was in tears now, wondered how long the brigands would wait before they took their fiendish pleasure with her.

The thought caused Cougar to quicken his step. It

was imperative that he let the Roche gang know they were being followed by another, more deadly, posse of one. He wanted them glancing over their shoulders, speculating on his plan of attack, constantly trying to stay one step ahead of him.

Roche had served with the Army of the West for several years, Cougar reminded himself. That bastard followed customary procedure. Cougar expected Roche to keep at least one guard trailing behind to scout for trouble and one man riding ahead to survey the path they took through the mountains. And one by one Cougar would lessen the odds until he could retrieve Cal and Roz without further endangering their lives.

After the posse of detectives trotted south, Cougar swung into the saddle and prepared himself for a battle of wits and wills. The behavior he halfheartedly observed while he mingled with civilization fell away as he ascended into the mountains with one packhorse following behind him and three black cats at his side. Cougar conditioned himself to become the man he had been when he conducted his forays to apprehend fugitives. He had always taken the most difficult cases, using all the Roches and Adairs in this world as his scapegoats. Now Cougar was pursuing the true source of the hatred that had been poisoning him for eight years.

And there would be no mercy . . .

Roz glanced over her shoulder to see Hudson Caine standing as posted lookout while she and Cal gathered firewood. "Caleb, I need your help," she whispered as she knelt to collect kindling. "Do you know which of these plants are edible and which are poisonous?"

Cal scooped up kindling, discreetly pointing to the broad-leaf plants and herbs that grew in the underbrush. "Cougar says lambs quarter is edible, but that plant over there isn't." He gestured his tousled head toward the pale green foliage that clung to the rocks. "And Cougar says any cactus with milky liquid inside will make you sick."

Roz smiled to herself as she pulled several plants up by the roots and tucked them in her pocket.

Cal frowned at her. "That's not the good stuff."

"I know." She grinned impishly at him as she reached over to break off the prickly cactus beside the trail. "Our wicked friends are going to get a dose of the bad stuff."

When Cal realized her intentions, he smiled for the first time since their captivity. "We're going to make them sick, right?"

"Right," Roz quietly confirmed before she rose to gather more weeds and wood. "We're going to do everything within our power to slow these men down until help arrives. And every opportunity either of us have to get near the saddles and bridles will be the chance to work the straps and buckles loose."

Roz could see Cal regain a smattering of his youthful spirit now that he was given a mission to distract him from his perilous plight. She had to provide him with a reason to fight for survival so that he wouldn't wallow in misery.

When Cal ambled over to pluck the leaves off the fever plant, horehound and mountain tobacco, under the pretense of gathering kindling, Roz cast him a wry smile. He had obviously found more ingredients to spice up the stew she intended to prepare for supper.

"Hurry it up," Hudson demanded impatiently. "I'd like to have my meal before it's time to bed down for the night."

"As I told Mr. Roche, I am hardly an experienced cook," Roz said to the heavily-bearded guard. "You will have to be patient. Cal and I are going about this the best way we know how."

Hudson stepped aside to let Roz and Cal pass on the narrow path and then fell into step behind them. While Cal stacked wood for the fire, Roz fished into the sacks for the ingredients for her stew. Although her planned revenge might not provide her and Cal with the opportunity to escape, she sincerely hoped their captors spent a miserable night battling nausea. The worse they felt, the better Roz was going to like it.

"Gawd," Jake Roche muttered after he swallowed his mouthful of stew. "I've had skunk meat that tasted better than this!"

Roz tried to look properly offended. "I told you that I'm not adept at cooking, Mr. Roche. I'm sure I'll get better with practice." She took a bite of the stew she had prepared for Cal and herself. "It tastes perfectly fine to me."

Cal nodded in agreement and swallowed his grin, along with his spoonful of stew.

"Obviously you have yet to acquire a taste for Eastern

cuisine," Roz added, before munching on the stewed meat.

"If all citified food tastes like boiled cow dung, I'll never acquire a taste for it," Vito Guerero chimed in.

Roz shrugged and ate her meal, silently snickering at the awful faces the men made. They were chasing each bite of stew with a guzzle of whiskey. The combination, she predicted, would leave them all swearing their bellies would explode before the night was out.

"Shall I save a plate of stew for Skeet?" Roz questioned Jake. "He'll be hungry when he returns to camp."

"He won't be *that* hungry," Hudson Caine guaranteed before taking several gulps of liquor.

"Well, there is nothing in the supply sacks but hardtack," Roz pointed out. "Your man Skeet may not appreciate being overlooked after spending the past few hours watching our backs. It seems to me—"

"Will you clam up, woman," Burney Adair scowled. He jerked his dagger from its sheath and waved it in Roz's face. "I don't like chatterboxes. You'll serve your purpose well enough for me with your tongue cut out."

Roz surveyed the burly brute's puckered, scarred face. The man who rarely spoke had a sinister look about him and a fanatical fascination with knives. Roz couldn't help but wonder how many lives had fallen beneath that nasty-looking blade that Burney constantly sharpened.

In the distance a panther screamed its unnerving call and the group of men fell into silence. Only the crackle of the campfire penetrated the stillness of the night.

"Cougar . . . ?" Cal murmured, his wide eyes darting to Roz.

"This rough country is filled with them, kid," Colby Jordan snorted as he tossed his empty plate aside. "They make meals of scrawny, whey-faced little whelps like you—"

"Pay no attention to him, Cal," Roz cut in.

Colby sneered and cracked his whip against the hem of her skirt. Not to be outdone, she sneered back.

"And furthermore," Roz continued, undaunted, "Mr. Jordan obviously has poor taste, judging by the company he keeps. As for myself, I would prefer the companionship of mountain lions to this wayward flock."

Vito shifted uneasily on his pallet. "I heard that sound a few nights back. It still gives me the willies." He massaged the mending wound on his neck and glanced apprehensively around him. "Burney, are you sure that half-breed and his cats rode south?"

Burney nodded mutely, his attention focused on the knife he was forever sharpening on a lump of whetstone. "The bastard Injun is gone, so quit fretting, Vito."

Ah, if only it *was* one of Cougar's cats that had screamed down the night, Roz thought whimsically. She could rest easier knowing Cougar was tracking these cutthroats. It was obvious that Cal had taken heart when he heard that distinctive wild scream.

Roz wondered if she would sound exactly like the panther's terrifying cry when her time came. The dismal thought prompted Roz to glance around the circle of captors who were keeping her and Cal on rope leashes to prevent their escape. The next time she doctored these bandits' food with poisonous herbs, she would apply stronger doses. It might be her only consolation, because every hour that ticked past left her wondering if she would be able to descend from the mountains alive.

# *Ten*

Skeet Thomas snapped his repeating rifle against his shoulder when he heard the unearthly squall in the darkness. He had positioned himself on a rock ledge above the bend in the trail. If anyone had dared to follow the gang into the mountains, Skeet could pick them off before they knew what hit them.

A horse's whinny drifted in the night wind. Skeet spit an arc of tobacco and focused his full attention on the moonlit path. He squinted down the rifle sight, his finger poised lightly on the trigger, waiting to greet the unwelcomed intruder with a bullet between the eyes.

The clomp of hooves grew louder with each passing second. Skeet smiled wickedly as he waited for the kill. When a horse trotted around the jutting rocks, Skeet squeezed the trigger. The riderless horse reared in fright, but before the black gelding's front hooves hit the ground, Skeet felt a cold steel blade between his legs, prodding the most sensitive part of his anatomy. The barrel of a pistol rammed into his neck, making it impossible to move in any direction.

Skeet promptly swallowed his wad of tobacco.

"Drop the rifle," came a hushed voice from behind Skeet.

Skeet did as he was told.

"Now back up nice and easy. I'd sure as hell hate to see you stumble off this cliff and break your neck."

Skeet gulped down his catapulting heart as he inched away from the edge of the rock platform that overlooked the trail. He could feel the cold, dark presence behind him, but he wasn't sure if it was man or monster breathing down his neck. With each movement he made, Skeet had the uneasy feeling that his captor was as close as his own shadow.

Although nothing touched Skeet except the gun barrel and the sharp blade of a knife, he had the odd sensation that the creature behind him was crawling into his skin. Every step Skeet took was shadowed by a deadly calm, an eerie imagery of spirit that he was helpless to describe. And that voice! Skeet swore it came to him from a tunnel, a voice so quiet that it left him to wonder if he were hearing his own thoughts.

Cougar reached down to ease Skeet's dagger from his gunbelt and tucked it inside his bandoleer. After he had plucked up the long-barreled Smith and Wesson pistol that protruded from Skeet's boot, Cougar nudged his captive along the ridge.

"I don't want no trouble," Skeet babbled nervously. "I was just trying to defend myself."

"You're riding with the wrong kind of men if you aren't looking for trouble," Cougar replied in a voice as cold as the grave.

"Cougar . . ." Skeet gulped when he finally realized who had seized him. "I—"

Skeet's voice dried up when three fleeting shadows scrambled down from the rocks, prowling around him like demons that had come to collect a tormented soul. Skeet was afraid to turn around, for fear of staring death in the face.

"Where's the woman and the boy?" Cougar demanded

"I don't know what you're talking about—" Skeet sucked in his breath when Cougar hissed a command that sent the cats lunging toward Skeet's booted feet. His gaze landed on the glowing golden eyes and opened jaws that were poised inches from his flesh.

"I don't think the cats approve of your answer, Skeet. Would you like to try again?"

Skeet gulped hard. "The kid and woman are in camp."

"How far away?"

"A few miles."

"Be specific," Cougar growled in his ear.

"Five miles, maybe six," Skeet wheezed when the cats snarled up at him and the dagger between his legs pricked tender flesh. He breathed an audible sigh when Cougar stepped away from him.

Cougar moved nonchalantly toward Skeet's horse to collect the ammunition from the saddlebags. The ease with which Cougar strode off had Skeet swearing to himself and massaging the last wound he had suffered when he clashed with this ruthless half-breed. If Skeet dared to jump Cougar when he turned his back, Skeet could expect to be pounced on by the growling cats. It was as if Cougar were daring him to move, providing a reason to finish him off.

"What are you gonna do to me?" Skeet asked nervously.

"Me?" Cougar glanced over his shoulder. He smiled—if, by any stretch of the imagination, one could call that menacing baring of teeth a smile. "Why, I'm not going to do a thing . . ." He paused to flash Skeet another diabolical grin. ". . . Except feed my hungry cats."

Skeet's eyes widened in horror and he took an involuntary step backward. "You son of a bitch—!"

When Cougar barked a command, Skeet knew what was coming. With a wild curse he wheeled around to hobble down the trail on his gimpy leg. He heard the unholy screams behind him the instant before he felt those deadly jaws clamp down with bone-crushing force.

Cougar didn't so much as flinch when he heard Skeet's bloodcurdling wails. The man was paying his penance for what he had tried to do to Roz. When Skeet's curses transformed into agonized whimpers, Cougar issued a command to the cats and they immediately came to heel.

In stony silence, Cougar strode over to stare down at his fallen foe. Skeet's thin face was a mass of bloody scratches and his clothes had been partially ripped away, revealing the vicious bites he had sustained. His broken arm lay at an unnatural angle and his various wounds were bleeding profusely.

Slowly, Cougar turned away to retrieve the sack he had tied to his horse. When he had stuffed the contents into Skeet's saddlebags, he returned to the downed outlaw who was still whimpering in agony.

"I have a message for Roche. Tell him to let the boy and woman go," Cougar said, slowly and distinctly.

Skeet found himself jerked roughly to his feet and

propelled toward his horse. Every muscle in his gnawed body throbbed as he was slung over the saddle and tied in place. His vision blurred as he fought to remain conscious, but the feat proved impossible. Skeet slumped over his horse, hearing the thud of hooves pounding into a silence that was broken only by the unearthly scream of the cougar . . .

Cougar watched the horse disappear into the distance before he swung into the saddle. He had used similar scare tactics on gang members in the past. When renegades saw one of their own kind returned to them in bloody shreds, compliments of the cats, they became exceedingly nervous about their own fates. General Cook spoke of examples to discourage criminals, but this was the only kind of example murderers understood, because it drove home the vivid point that they could be next in line as a meal for man-eating cats.

Reaching into his saddlebag, Cougar fished out a stick of dynamite. Before the night was out, he intended to blast away the portion of the trail that led northwest to the ghost town that had been abandoned by discouraged miners. Roche's raiders would have to turn south toward the location where General Cook and his detectives blocked the route out of the mountains.

For a moment, Cougar allowed his thoughts to turn to the delicate blonde who had been on his mind far more than she should have. Cougar remembered Francene's plea to provide the comfort and sympathy Roz would need if she survived this ordeal. Cougar had been trained to kill, not regenerate broken spirits. He wondered how good he was going to be at it. Tenderness wasn't something he gave or received in this dark hell he called his life. How did a man teach himself to feel when all the kindness and goodness had been burned out of him, leaving only scarred memories?

Well, he had damned well better get to Roz and Caleb before both of them needed something from him that he wasn't sure he had in him to give. He would pursue Roche with a relentlessness that prevented the merciless butcher from taking his frustration out on his captives. Cougar vowed to make his presence known with every step Jake Roche took into the higher elevations of the mountains. Before long, Cougar's name would become the curse Roche wished would go away . . . and wouldn't until the Cheyenne prophesy had finally been fulfilled . . .

Jake Roche swore profanely when his stomach coiled in another knot. He had only slept a few hours before nausea awakened him. Obviously he wasn't the only one suffering the effects of Roz's cooking. The other men were doubled up on their pallets, groaning in unison.

Panting for breath, Jake crawled on hands and knees to fling himself over the nearest boulder. His stew tasted as foul coming up as it had going down. The sound of his men groaning and gagging caused another upheaval in his belly. He would have to acquire a lead-lined stomach if he was going to survive that incompetent female's cooking.

Roz lifted her head to glance at Cal whose teeth gleamed in the dwindling firelight.

"Next time I'll gather more Black Nightshade," Cal whispered conspiratorially. "Cougar says it's the worst."

"We're going to have to find another herb to kill the taste," Roz murmured. "We're also going to have to pretend to be ill or the men might become suspicious."

Cal nodded and sank back on his pallet, moaning as miserably as the men. Roz called upon her acting ability and pretended to lose her supper. The desperadoes were too sick to notice whether she had or hadn't.

The sound of pounding hooves overshadowed the bandits' groans. Roz glanced up to see the hunkered form of a man draped half on, half off his steed. She grimaced distastefully when the horse halted by the campfire. The faint light revealed the claw marks that shredded the skin on Skeet's face and shoulders. Roz couldn't help but wonder if the mountain lion they had heard screaming earlier had attacked and chewed Skeet within an inch of his life.

"What the hell happened to you?" Jake choked out, staggering to his feet.

Skeet Thomas uttered not a word. His head dangled limply against his horse's neck. Jake wobbled over to give Skeet a sound shaking.

Nothing. The renegade was all but dead.

"Burney, help me get Skeet out of the saddle," Jake ordered.

"I'm not sure I can stand up without throwing up," Burney mumbled.

Despite his nausea, Burney managed to drag his legs beneath him and weave unsteadily toward the lathered horse. With considerable effort, Jake and Burney untied Skeet from the saddle and lowered his mutilated body to the ground.

"*Dios mío,*" Vito breathed when he spied the claw

marks and penetrating bites. "It's Cougar! I was afraid that bastard wasn't gone for good. He's following us!"

"Calm down, Vito," Jake growled. "Skeet tangled with a panther, that's all."

"A half-human one," Vito clarified. "I tell you, that half-breed is on our trail. This is his handiwork. I'd have looked exactly like Skeet if the woman hadn't called Cougar and his cats off."

Jake scoffed at the wide-eyed Mexican. Before he could reply, an explosion shook the night and falling rock rumbled in the distance. The earth shook and a cloud of dust rose into the night sky. The scream of a mountain lion pierced the air.

"Cougar . . ." Skeet Thomas rasped as he opened his eyes to stare dazedly at the black sky. "He told me to tell you that you better let the kid and woman go."

Jake glanced down at the mauled man who had roused just long enough to relay the message.

"I told you," Vito muttered apprehensively. "Didn't I tell you? He's coming to get me!"

"Good, then *you* can stand the next watch," Burney snapped.

"I'm not going out there by myself," Vito refused. "First Skeet, and who knows who will be the next victim!"

"All right then, you take the watch at the edge of camp," Jake ordered as he wobbled back to his pallet to collapse. "As for the rest of you, I suggest you sleep with one eye open and a pistol in hand."

While the men drew their revolvers from their holsters and settled on their bedrolls, Roz peered over at Caleb. For the first time since their captivity a sense of

hope stirred inside her. Cougar was out there somewhere, prowling the darkness like an avenging angel.
He would find a way to rescue them.

But it was going to be up to Roz to provide a distraction. The thought prompted her to reach for the jagged tin can lid she had retrieved while her guard wasn't
looking. If she could saw the rope loose from her wrists
and free Cal, they might be able to manage an escape.
With any luck Cougar's gunfire could supply cover for
them. And if not . . .

Roz refused to consider the bleak alternative of being
shot in the back while she dashed toward safety. But at
least she could provide a shield for Cal. Cougar would
ensure the boy was returned to his family—if he still
had a family left.

Thank God Cal hadn't seen Francene sprawled atop
Gideon. The poor child would be beside himself, wondering if either of his parents were still alive.

At least there was someone in the world who cared
what became of Caleb Howard. Roz wondered what it
was like to be wanted and to be missed. As far as she
knew, no one would lament her passing. She was simply
an extra person in the world.


"Damn." Gideon grimaced when he tried to prop
himself up in bed. "What did Cougar do? Cauterize my
whole blessed leg?"

Francene smiled at the puckered expression on
Gideon's face. He had been in the foulest mood since
he had awakened. The laudanum Francene had forced
down his throat had kept him oblivious throughout the

night. She had checked on him hourly, applying poultices to the wound and wrapping the leg with fresh bandages. Thus far, infection had not set in, but Francene was keeping a close watch for the first sign of trouble.

"Actually," Francene said as she spooned chicken broth down her husband's throat, "Cougar did a fine job of stitching you up. Much better than I could have done when my hands refused to stop shaking."

Gideon gulped his soup and stirred restlessly. "I need to see to the chores. There is a stage due at noon."

"You aren't going anywhere. Cougar said to keep you in bed for at least three days."

"Cougar isn't my boss," Gideon said crankily. "I've been shot up before, after all."

"Yes, and you weren't allowed to heal properly," Francene reminded him. "This time you're going to take the necessary bed rest to heal and recuperate. The other men who feel up to it are seeing to the chores. General Cook promised to send a telegram to the main stage office in Denver. As efficient as the new superintendent is reported to be, I'm sure he will send an assistant to replace you until you have recovered."

"What? Some lazy freeloader who won't earn his keep?" Gideon snorted, disgruntled.

Francene crammed more soup in her husband's mouth. "Just relax, Gideon. This stage station isn't half as important to me as you are. All I care about is you and Caleb—"

Francene's cheerful facade wavered and she forced herself to inhale a fortifying breath.

"Cougar will bring them both back," Gideon assured

her. "If anyone can do it, he can. You know that, honey." He reached out to give her trembling hand a comforting squeeze. "There isn't another man like Cougar in the territory."

Francene blinked back the mist of tears and smiled as she bent to press a kiss to Gideon's lips. "Yes, there is, my love. There's you . . ."

Odd, wasn't it? Gideon mused as he held his wife close to his heart. Soft words from Francene very nearly succeeded in making him forget the pain in his leg. *This* was what he had defied death to save. This one very special woman gave his life purpose after serving in that hellish war that had torn the nation apart. And if only Cougar could bring Caleb back to them, all would be right with the world again.

Jake Roche clambered to his feet, greeting the sunlight with a scowl. He couldn't remember having hangovers that felt worse than the aftereffects of eating Roz's foul-tasting stew. His head was throbbing and his queasy stomach was sloshing like a barrel. Damn, that woman's attempts at cooking had nearly been the death of him. His only consolation was hearing her and the kid groaning while Jake tossed his supper in several courses.

When Jake had nudged his men awake, he strode over to gouge Roz in the ribs. "Get the fire started and fix us some coffee," he ordered grouchily. "And it better not taste like that sickening stew you served us for supper."

Roz levered up to see the leader of the gang snarling at her. "My coffee is better than my cooking."

"Good," Jake snorted. "And your cooking had damned well better improve by tonight—or else."

"When are you going to let the boy go?" Roz demanded as Jake hauled her roughly to her feet.

Jake yanked on the rope attached to Roz's wrists. "Just fix the coffee so we can be on the trail."

Roz gathered enough kindling to start the fire and brew coffee. What little herbs she had left from supper were discreetly dumped into the pot. She heard Skeet moaning in pain while the men rose to saddle the horses, but no one bothered to check on the injured outlaw. And to her amazement, Jake shoved Vito aside when he attempted to hoist Skeet onto his horse. Skeet was left lying on the ground like a misplaced doormat.

"Aren't you taking him with you?" Roz questioned after she had been placed on the gray mare and secured to the pommel.

Jake cast a cold glance at Skeet's barely recognizable face and then reined west. "Skeet is on his own. He's of no use to us now."

"Jake! Don't leave me here!" Skeet hissed as he tried to roll onto his side. "That bastard will kill me for sure."

"That's what you get for not taking care of Cougar when you had the chance," Burney snapped unsympathetically.

The procession rode off to the sound of Skeet's hoarse curses. To Roz's dismay, Caleb was placed on Skeet's horse rather than on hers. She had hoped to use the jagged tin-can lid to cut both her and Caleb's ropes. If Roz managed to free herself without being noticed, it would be difficult to rescue Caleb when she attempted escape.

Roz sat in the saddle, inconspicuously rubbing the jagged lid against the ropes that were coiled around her wrists. The men were too preoccupied trying to recover from their poisoned supper and doctored coffee to pay her much attention—thank goodness.

With any luck Roz could cut her way through the rope before the procession stopped for their noon meal. *How* she was going to make her escape and rescue Caleb while he was tied to his own horse was going to take some deliberation. She had to use the element of surprise since it would be the only advantage she had. Ah, if only she had acquired half of Cougar's skills, she mused as she frayed the rope. She and Caleb might have escaped during the night!

Cougar halted his steed beside the sprawled outlaw who had been left for dead. There was not an ounce of sympathy in Cougar as he stared down at the battered form of the man who lay in the middle of the path.

The instant Skeet spied the towering mass of cold vengeance towering over him, he tried to crawl away. But he had lost too much blood to muster the energy to do more than roll onto his knees and elbows.

"Left you for dead, did they?" Cougar asked in a voice devoid of emotion. "Kinda makes you wonder about the friends you have, doesn't it, Skeet?"

Skeet's only response was a weak curse to the world at large. Cougar grabbed Skeet by the nape of his shredded shirt and hoisted him onto weak legs.

"What are you going to do?" Skeet wheezed as Cougar hoisted him on the packhorse.

"Consider yourself fortunate, Skeet. I'm giving you the chance to repay your so-called friends."

With no more explanation than that vague remark, Cougar called to the cats and followed the old Indian trail that wound through the trees. The shortcut would allow Cougar to position himself in front of the gang, which would have to backtrack after they encountered the avalanche of rock that now covered their path ahead.

The previous night, Cougar had scrabbled over the rugged terrain to reach the fork in the road. The explosion he had set off had sent tons of rock cascading across the trail. Roche's raiders couldn't turn northwest unless they sprouted wings and flew over fallen boulders.

Cougar had bought himself some time while Jake was reversing direction. The bandits would have to remain on the move, and that was exactly how Cougar wanted them—moving.

One at a time, Cougar promised himself. He would reduce the odds until he could get Jake Roche exactly where he wanted that murdering son of a bitch. That satisfying thought prompted Cougar to quicken his pace through the clump of trees and up the steep embankment. If all went well, Cougar would have Roche and Adair penned down by dark. And when Cougar had rescued Roz and Caleb, he was going to launch those murdering bastards back into hell where they belonged.

# Eleven

"What the hell—" Jake Roche muttered vile obsceni-ties when he came upon a cascade of rock where the trail should have been.

"Cougar . . ." Vito grumbled, shifting uneasily on the saddle. "He must have set off the explosion we heard last night. That half-breed intends to box us in and pick us off."

"Will you shut up," Burney snarled, flashing his knife in Vito's face.

While the men were grumbling and changing direc-tion, Roz was sawing the rope with the can lid. Her wrists were nearly raw from her persistent attempts to free herself, and her arms ached from holding them steady to conceal her movements from the surrounding men.

When the procession turned south to follow the only route available to them, Roz found herself next to last in line. Jake Roche led the way and Colby Jordan brought up the rear. Caleb was directly in front of Roz, making it easier for her to saw on the rope without being detected.

After an hour of cutting the frayed strands and ig-noring her aching muscles, Roz managed to free her hands. She was careful, however, to keep the rope wrapped around her wrists. One quick jerk would allow her the freedom she needed to make her escape.

Roz had conjured up a plan. A dangerous one, to be sure, but feasible nonetheless. As soon as Jake called a halt to rest, Roz would hold her position until all the men dismounted and someone walked over to pull her and Caleb from their mounts. While the outlaws were on foot, Roz could spur her steed and grab the reins to Caleb's horse.

Hopefully the startled men would be too busy leaping out of the way to grab their pistols. Roz preferred not to catch a bullet in the back for her daring efforts. If things went according to plan, she could send Caleb clattering back in the direction they had come, using herself as a protective shield. Colby Jordan and his whip would be her main concern. He would be the only man close enough to lash out at her.

Roz inhaled a deep breath and assured herself that her plan would work. If Cougar was around somewhere, he might be able to open fire while Roz and Caleb galloped away. Damnation, Roz would give most anything to know if Cougar was up in the rocks, watching them. Her gaze lifted to the looming walls and scraggly trees on the outcropping of stone above her. If one of those black cats growled down at her, it would be the sweetest sound she could ever hope to hear . . .

A wild curse flew up from the front of the procession when they rounded the bend. A pistol shot shattered the silence. Horses collided on the narrow trail that encircled the mountain.

"Damn you, Jake!" came a hoarse screech, followed by another whining bullet.

Roz leaned sideways to see what was going on. Her eyes widened in disbelief when she spied Skeet Thomas propped against a boulder beside the road. His broken arm hung uselessly by his side, but his left hand was clamped around a .44 caliber Colt and he was firing at Jake and Burney with vindictive fury.

"This is what you get for leaving me behind!" Skeet snarled as he took aim at Jake's chest.

Skeet's left-handed shooting skills were sorely lacking and his sight was impaired by swollen claw marks, but he was determined to fill Jake Roche full of lead for abandoning him.

The pistol blast had Jake howling in pain and cursing a blue streak. Despite Skeet's inaccuracy, he did manage to inflict injury. Jake had taken a bullet in the shoulder before Burney Adair could get his wild-eyed horse under control and open fire on Skeet.

The echo of gunshots and curses raced around the canyon rim. Horses reared and sidestepped to prevent being shoved off the narrow path. While the outlaws were trying to bring their horses under control, Roz jerked her hands loose and nudged her steed toward Caleb.

"Damn it! She got loose!" Colby shouted, grabbing for his whip.

Chaos broke out when the crack of an unseen rifle exploded in the air. Horses and bodies circled and collided with each other in a frantic attempt to take cover. Gunfire ricocheted off rock, mingling with the unsettling screams the outlaws had come to associate with the legendary manhunter who had placed a death threat on their heads.

The desperadoes were trapped on the road, bounded on one side by perpendicular slabs of rock that gave way on the other to a wild tumble of boulders and trees that lined the plunging canyon below them. The cunning half-breed had them exactly where he wanted them and the smell of blood was in the air . . .

Cougar cursed mightily when Roz attempted to wedge her way between the men to grab Caleb's startled mount. Her blond head kept getting in Cougar's way each time he attempted to take Colby Jordan's measure on the rifle sight. If Cougar fired again he would risk hitting Roz or Caleb.

Hell, what a time for that Yankee to display such foolhardy daring! She was going to get herself shot and there wasn't a damned thing Cougar could do to stop it!

Another salty curse erupted from Cougar's curled lips as he bounded from boulder to boulder, hoping to gain a better vantage point to ambush the gang members without blasting Roz out of the saddle. Before he could locate a better position, Burney Adair barked the order for Colby to use his whip to drag Roz off her horse.

Cougar darted a quick glance toward Jake, who had slid from the saddle to use his horse as his protective shield. Cougar had noticed the bloodstains on the shoulder of Jake's chambray shirt, indicating he had been winged before Burney put Skeet out of his misery forever.

Although Cougar had taken the shortcut through the mountain meadow and had left Skeet in a perfect position to have his final revenge after being left for dead, Roz had bungled his attempt to pick off the outlaws. Cougar had half a mind to shoot Roz himself for foiling his well-laid plans . . .

Cougar's spiteful musings scattered when Roz's wild scream split the air. His heart stalled in his chest as he watched Colby plow his way between Caleb's and Roz's mounts. The two horses collided, penning Colby between them, making it impossible for him to lash at Roz with his whip. In desperation, Colby snaked out his free hand to grab Roz's hair, nearly ripping it out by the roots in an effort to unseat her.

A snarl exploded from Colby's lips when Roz's gray mare stepped on his foot. Colby popped his whip against the horse's rump, sending it dancing sideways, leaving Roz clinging to the saddle by sheer will alone.

Cougar forgot to breathe while he watched disaster unfold on the narrow ledge. He knew what was going to happen, even before the inevitable struck. Problem was, Cougar was helpless to prevent it.

Colby had forced Roz's gray mare sideways, but there was no place for the alarmed horse to set its feet. The mare stumbled on the loose rock beside the path and toppled off balance.

"Miss Gaylord!" Caleb wailed in horror as he strained against his confining ropes.

Roz's scream went through Cougar like a lightning bolt, knotting in the pit of his belly until it burned like fire. In frustration, he watched horse and rider teeter on the ledge that overlooked the chasm below. An unfamil-

iar sensation twisted inside Cougar's gut as Roz clawed
at the air in attempt to anchor herself to an outflung
tree limb . . . and failed . . .

The mare's shrill whinny echoed around the canyon
as it tumbled backward over the jutting rocks and disappeared from sight.

It was then that Cougar realized not every emotion
inside him had withered and died. Watching Roz plunge
over the cliff had paralyzed his thoughts and turned him
wrong side out. For those unending seconds he came
to grips with the horror Roz was experiencing and felt
the terror he heard in Caleb's voice while the boy
sobbed Roz's name until he was hoarse.

Jake scrabbled to his feet and trotted off with his
horse in tow. "Let's get the hell out of here!"

Cougar grimaced, listening to Caleb's horrified wail.
The procession of men disappeared from sight, seeking
the protection of trees and boulders as they made their
escape. For a moment, indecision warred inside Cougar.
He was anxious to track down Jake Roche and rescue
Caleb, but he couldn't pursue his prey without knowing
Roz's fate.

Never had such a perfect scheme gone bad so fast.
Cougar swore foully as he leaped over the pile of rocks
to reach the abandoned stretch of road. A quiet call sent
the cats bounding gracefully over the boulders to join
him. In bleak resignation, Cougar strode over to the spot
where Roz had plunged into the tangle of tree branches
and craggy rocks that overlooked the valley. From his
location, Cougar could see very little except dense foliage and more rock, none of which made for a soft
landing.

"Damn daring Yankee," Cougar muttered as he stamped eastward, searching for a place to descend the wild tumble of rocks.

Cougar shoved pine and cedar branches out of his way as he sidestepped over the boulders that formed an improvised ladder down the embankment. He already knew what he was going to find when he reached the site directly below the spot where Roz had fallen.

Gideon had asked Cougar to rescue Roz and Caleb, but it seemed as if the misplaced Yankee was going to be buried up here in this mountain landscape that she was so fond of painting.

Another curse tripped from Cougar's lips when he found the gray mare's mangled body sprawled over the ledge that rimmed the twisting ravine. The mare whinnied in pain and tried to gain its feet, but its front leg had been broken during the fall and chips of bone protruded from the seeping wound. Cougar drew his dagger from his belt and cut the mare's throat to end its agony as quickly as possible.

Rising, Cougar balanced on the thin ledge and stared down at the trees that blocked his view. There was no sign of Roz, no sound to alert him to her condition.

But then, Cougar reminded himself bleakly. *Death* had a unique sound all its own . . .

The crackle of twigs caught Cougar's attention and he pivoted to peer up at the canopy of cedars and pines that covered the embankment above him. There, clamped onto an overhanging branch, was a tangle of petticoats.

"Yank?"

The only response was a shuddering sigh, muffled sniff and the rattle of pine needles.

"Yank? Can you see me?"

"N—no . . ." Hiccup, sob.

Roz inhaled a shallow breath and tightened her grip on the spindly branch that stood between her and a quick drop into the jagged boulders below. Her hip had collided with stone and timber during her fall. Excruciating pain shot down her leg and throbbed in her knee. The fabric covering her elbows, as well as the left shoulder of her gown, had ripped away, and Roz suspected that bloody patches of her dress and skin were stuck to the slanting boulders she had cartwheeled over before she managed to latch onto the tree limb.

Roz was terrified. Her muscles were frozen in the kind of intense fear she never knew existed. The first half of her fall had been a horrifying whirl, followed by a series of flashbacks that were her life—a life that had not in any way prepared her for the challenge she now confronted. She was hanging on by her fingernails—all of which were broken—fearing the branch would snap at any minute, plunging her into oblivion.

Cougar craned his neck to study the cluster of petticoats and the dangling leg that were visible in the overhanging tree. If Roz managed to pull herself back onto the limb it might crack beneath her weight. If she didn't, she would lose her grasp and Cougar hated to venture a guess as to where she would end up . . . and in how many pieces.

Roz was so frightened—and with good reason—that her sobs were interrupted by hiccups. Cougar had witnessed her near-hysterics the night Skeet and Vito had attacked her. Now it was even worse because she didn't have solid ground beneath her, only a narrow ledge cluttered with a dead horse. Damn.

"Yank, you're going to have to jump," Cougar said as calmly as he knew how.

When Roz braved a glance over her shoulder, she couldn't see Cougar, only the teeth-like boulders that promised to chew her alive.

"I can't!" she cried.

"Yes, you can," Cougar told her. "I'll catch you."

He hoped.

Cougar had damned little leeway to work with on the ledge. If the projection of Roz's downward flight took her too far away from him, Cougar wasn't going to be able to maintain his footing. They would nose-dive into infinity together.

That was not a comforting thought. Cougar had made a pact with himself to live long enough to ensure Roche and Adair enjoyed their personal brands of torture.

There was a whimper from above and then Roz spoke with the sound of tears in her voice, "You might miss me."

Cougar gnashed his teeth and struggled to prevent frustrated impatience from seeping into his own voice. "I will not miss you. You'll be safely in my arms before you know it—"

"Or stone-cold dead," Roz mumbled and hiccuped. "I injured my hip and leg."

"I'll patch them up as soon as you come down from the tree."

Roz squirmed frantically when her arms threatened to give out. The prickly branch bit into her hands and only stark fear gave her the strength to hold on. She considered letting go, but paralyzing terror riveted her again. Her painful fall was still too fresh on her mind, and on her bruised and bleeding flesh.

"Yank, we don't have all day. Caleb is still in serious trouble and those outlaws are making tracks while we're standing here yammering."

"I realize that." Roz gulped hard and tried to imagine the horror Caleb was experiencing. Unfortunately, her battered body was selfishly considering *her* plight and her immediate death.

Cougar decided he had two options. He could navigate his way up the cliff and crawl out to where Roz clung to her flimsy branch. If he chose that alternative, he might shake Roz loose from her limb and there would be no one to catch her when she dropped. Furthermore, while he was making his way toward Roz, she might deplete the last of her energy and slip from her precarious perch. Unfortunately, the end result would be the same.

The only other possibility was for the cats to frighten Roz into letting go. Cougar glanced down at the animals that were making a meal of the dead mare. Cougar had no intention of informing Francene that her favorite mount had become a feast.

Cougar barked a sharp command to the cats. Although they were reluctant to leave their meal, they had been trained to obey every order Cougar gave them. When one contrary cat doubled back to the horse, Cougar's abrupt shout sent the cat slinking off.

The mountain lions sprang lithely onto the rugged boulders, snarling their displeasure at being interrupted during feeding. Cougar met three pair of green-gold eyes with his own menacing growl. Another brisk command sent the pumas bounding up ten feet of perpendicular wall toward the overhanging tree.

Roz's shriek assured Cougar that the cats had reached their destination. They were poised on the branches, screaming their heads off. Cougar set his feet and braced himself. There was little margin for error on this ledge that was rimmed by solid rock and a seventy-five-foot drop into oblivion. If Roz's momentum pulled Cougar off balance—

Cougar didn't finish the pessimistic thought; he concentrated on the bundle of petticoats above him.

When Cougar sent the cats a sharp, whistling call they snarled and swatted at Roz with their dagger-like claws. Roz's frantic scream blasted Cougar's eardrums. The cats tilted their broad heads upward and wailed like banshees. But still Roz didn't release the limb and drop into Cougar's waiting arms. He had no choice but to put the panthers on attack.

Upon command all three black cats lunged onto the branch Roz clung to. When the excessive weight of the cats caused the limb to snap, Roz's bloodcurdling screech transformed into a howl of terror.

Cougar watched Roz fall through the air and make desperate grabs at every protruding branch she flew past. For a harrowing moment Cougar wasn't sure he would be able to latch onto Roz without being launched over the cliff. When she whizzed by, headed for catastrophe, Cougar clamped one hand around her hip and the other around her waist.

Flinging himself backward, Cougar slammed into the rock wall, clutching Roz tightly to him. Her legs were anchored around his waist and her arms fastened around his head, unintentionally pressing his face into the tattered bodice of her gown. All Cougar could see and feel was her heaving bosom against his cheeks. He braced his legs and encircled Roz in his arms, waiting for her to realize she had not met her death.

It took a while.

According to Francene, this was when Cougar was supposed to manufacture sympathy and compassion. Yes, Cougar did feel sorry for this misplaced Yankee who'd had the wits scared out of her more times than she probably cared to count. Unfortunately, the sensations assaulting Cougar, while his face was mashed against Roz's soft breasts, and her lush body was wrapped around him like a glove, leaned more toward arousal.

Roz was still hiccuping like crazy when Cougar slowly eased her down his body to let her feet touch solid ground. That turned out to be a mistake. He could feel every curvaceous inch of her gliding against him. His senses, already on full alert, reacted as fiercely to her as they had to the shock of watching her plunge off the path, barely escaping death. That haunting incident drove home the point of how precious each moment of life was, how quickly it could be stripped away . . . and how glorious it felt to be holding Roz so closely that she was like a part of his own skin.

Roz's scraped arms fastened around Cougar's neck and she clung to him as fiercely as she had held onto the branch. And then all her bottled fears came gushing out like an erupting geyser. Cougar could not believe the woman had such an inexhaustible reservoir of water inside her. Roz was pouring tears all over his chest, and his meager attempt to soothe her was having no effect whatsoever. Her fingers dug into his shoulders like spikes, and he could feel her hiccups vibrating through him as if they were his own.

Cougar's traitorous male body reacted instantaneously to the generous curves and swells that were molded to him. He and Roz were plastered so tightly together that he could feel her heart hammering against his chest, feel the imprint of her barely concealed breasts, hear the raspy curl of breath gliding over his neck like a lover's caress. When Roz lifted her tear-stained face, Cougar's gaze dropped to her quivering lips. He was stung by the thought that he needed to kiss her as badly as she seemed to want to be kissed. What she needed, what they *both* needed, was to treat their minds and bodies to sensations that were far removed from fear, to forget her near-fatal fall.

Cougar yielded to temptation. He kissed Roz as if there were no tomorrow and she immediately responded, clinging to him, welcoming him like a long-lost lover. Their breath mingled as one, as their bodies clamped closely together.

Here, nestled in his encompassing arms, was the woman who prevented him from satisfying his needs with the doxy at Finnegan's Station. This blonde stirred him, activated emotion he would rather not feel. Her memory refused to let Cougar lose himself in another woman's arms when he had the chance.

How in the hell could a woman pose such an impossible distraction when he had trained himself to feel absolutely nothing?

Good question. Cougar wished he had a reasonable answer.

Cougar broke the stimulating kiss and came up for air, battling like the very devil to control his unruly male body and wayward thoughts.

"Are you about finished flooding the mountains?" Cougar rasped, his voice nowhere near as steady as he had hoped.

"Y—yes." Reluctantly, Roz eased away from the security and strength provided by the muscular wall of his chest. She inhaled a shuddering breath and made the mistake of glancing sideways to see the cats feeding on the mare. "Oh, God . . ." Roz promptly buried her head against Cougar's shoulder, sickened by what she saw.

Cougar scooped Roz up in his arms and inched away from the feeding panthers. To Cougar, the sight was natural and expected. This sophisticated Easterner found the situation to be vulgar and offensive. The incident emphasized the colossal cultural gap that separated them. Cougar lived in an austere world where survival was a vital part of life. Rozalie Gaylord was accustomed to civilized ways, not to the harsh reality of the wilderness.

"Ouch! Blast it, that hurts!" Roz hissed when Cougar set her on her feet to make the difficult climb up the embankment. "You'll have to rescue Caleb without me."

Cougar stared at her as if she were insane. "And what do you plan to do? Feed with the cats until I get back?"

Roz propped herself against the boulder and attempted to put weight on her left leg. She winced when pain speared from ankle to hip. "We have no choice. The longer we delay, the farther we fall behind. I'll stay here and . . ." Roz glanced back at what was left of the gray mare and gulped audibly. "I'll work on my journal. My sketch pad and painting supplies are attached to the saddle."

Cougar muttered something unrepeatable under his breath and reversed direction to fetch Roz's paraphernalia. "Come on, Yank. Let's find level ground so I can examine your leg."

When Cougar lifted Roz onto the slab of rock above him, her leg crumpled beneath her. "This is as far as I can go," she told him in panting breaths.

"Maybe under your own power."

When Cougar bounded up beside her like a graceful cat and swooped down to jackknife her body over his shoulder, Roz received an upside-down view of the yawning valley. She squeezed her eyes shut and hung onto Cougar while he carried her like a feed sack, weaving around rocks and latching onto protruding tree roots to make the climb to the road. When he finally reached level ground he eased Roz down into a patch of grass and grabbed the hem of her skirt. Her hand clamped over his, refusing to let him raise her gown. Roz wasn't sure she could allow him to touch her familiarly, not when his kiss on the ledge had sent her senses reeling to such a degree. She was entirely too receptive to this man.

Cougar expelled an impatient sigh. "This is no time for modesty. If you have wounds that need tending then I'll tend them."

"In New York, a physician never examines a female

patient without having another woman present," she said as an excuse to conceal her true concerns.

Cougar snorted, flinging his arm in an expansive gesture. "This isn't New York, Yank, and I'm no doctor."

Too bad he wasn't, Cougar thought. Maybe then he wouldn't find it so difficult to remain impersonal. This woman aroused him, that was a fact. It was *not* going to be any easier for him to look under her skirt than it was for her to let him.

Cougar well remembered the feel of her silky flesh, her natural responses, the passion he had sensed simmering inside her that night he had come dangerously close to stepping beyond the point of no return. Everything about this delicate beauty put his senses on vivid alert. He was as keenly aware of her as he was attuned to his surroundings in times of peril . . .

That thought shocked Cougar . . . and worried him to no end. His inability to control himself when he was with Roz was what had sent him trotting off to Finnegan's Station to ease his male needs. He had wanted Roz so badly that leaving was all that prevented him from satisfying his obsessive craving.

Cougar inhaled a determined breath and told himself to ignore his unappeased needs, to concentrate on locating Roz's injuries. "Turn over, Yank," he ordered abruptly.

Up went that skinned but defiant chin. "No."

Cougar muttered sourly and shoved Roz's upturned nose into the grass. In one swift motion he jerked up the back hem of her skirt and tugged on her shredded petticoats. Sure enough, the jolt of seeing the satiny curve of her hip and the creamy flesh on the back of her thighs sent a stab of awareness throbbing through him. His hand slid over her soft skin and he told himself that he was simply searching for knots and bruises.

There he went again, lying to himself—thanks to his corrupt white heritage. Cougar scowled and tried to keep his mind on the matter at hand, but it was the skin *beneath* his hand that was his undoing. He had wanted Roz too much too often during the past week. Then this entire ordeal had unearthed emotion Cougar thought he had buried so deep inside him that he had smothered all feeling. Obviously he thought wrong.

Cougar was tired of fighting for self-control where Roz was concerned. He wanted to expend this nervous energy in pleasurable release, but damn it, this was not the right time and place, and she was certainly not the right woman for him. How many more times was he going to have to tell himself that before his contrary male body began to believe it . . . ?

Cougar made the mistake of glancing down at her shapely backside, watching his fingertips glide over her hip. Where Rozalie Gaylord was concerned, he had exhausted all his willpower the night Skeet and Vito attacked her. He would have to stitch his eyelids shut not to cherish the alluring sight of her. He would have to chop his hands off at the wrist not to enjoy touching her.

Cougar sighed, very much afraid he had engaged in a battle he couldn't win . . .

# Twelve

"Well?" Roz prodded, her face turning every color in the rainbow. "How bad is it?"

Bad? There was nothing bad about the tantalizing view of satiny flesh, Cougar mused as his gaze roamed freely over Roz's well-shaped legs and curvy hips. His hand drifted up the back of her thigh, over the swell of her bottom, wondering when the pads of his fingertips had become so sensitive, wondering when he had felt anything as soft and lush as this.

"Cougar?" Roz prompted when he didn't reply.

Cougar inwardly groaned as he felt his pulse pounding in the lower regions of his anatomy—pounding out a forbidden message that was rapidly destroying rational thought. He wanted to strip Roz down to her lovely skin and touch her everywhere at once. And when he had discovered every inch of her, had memorized every texture and contour, he wanted to start all over again—for all the times he had deprived himself of what he wanted most.

Roz felt the seductive flight of his hand over her flesh and fought against the wild sensations his tender touch aroused. "Cougar . . . what are you doing?"

She rolled over to face him, and Cougar found himself staring down into wide sapphire eyes, feeling her flesh tremble beneath his hand. Another electrifying jolt sizzled through him.

His gaze met hers and Cougar felt himself succumbing to the needs he had too long denied. "What am I doing?" he repeated hoarsely. "I'm wanting you . . ."

Roz's eyes never wavered from the hungry expression that matched her own. "I'm wanting you, too, Cougar . . ."

Cougar felt himself magnetically drawn to those heart-shaped lips, felt his hand stroking her with a gentleness that only she could call from him. The feelings she engendered drew even more tenderness from him, left him yearning to please her as much as he sensed she could please him when he was surrounded by her soft, feminine flesh.

The thought left Cougar quivering with a vulnerability that he didn't like but couldn't help. He had nearly lost this dainty beauty. He would never have known the exquisite pleasure that her luscious body promised. He had nobly restrained his own needs and removed himself from her to prevent taking complete possession of her. He had been as noble as he could possibly be for entirely too long. Self-denial had taken its final toll.

And now, taking her, feeling her feminine body pressed intimately to his, was all that seemed necessary and right. The sensible side of his brain reminded him that Jake Roche was slipping away with Caleb in tow. The other half of his mind was focused on his overwhelming need for this enchanting nymph.

Roz was in no condition to travel just yet, and probably in no condition to accept in full his ravenous desire for her. But nothing seemed as important at this moment as feeding the fire that had been burning Cougar alive since he first laid eyes on this stunning female. Her supple body called out to the man in him, and the man in him could no longer refrain from answering the burgeoning needs that were as intense as his instinct of survival . . .

Before Cougar realized it, his mouth had slanted over hers, rediscovering the addictive taste of her dewy lips. His hand glided to and fro, skimming along her most sensitive flesh, drawing from her quiet gasps of pleasure. Cougar absorbed the scent of her, the delicious taste of her, the scintillating feel of her heated responses. He could hear her ragged breath matching his own, feel the warmth of need he summoned from her as quickly and easily as she aroused it within him.

When his delving fingertips discovered the warm rain of her desire, Cougar felt every muscle in his body clench. He had never been so hopelessly infatuated with a woman. He could not remember feeling such a fierce driving force spurring him, not even when he fought to survive the three bullet wounds that nearly cost him his life.

And yet, despite the primal need that thrummed through him, he was conscious of Roz's frailty. To have what he wanted more than he wanted breath itself he had to become the personification of tenderness. Hurting this delicate beauty, discomforting her, would deprive them both of ultimate pleasure. To take what he wanted, demanded that he give himself up to unhurried gentleness. Cougar knew he had to become the kind of man Roz needed and deserved. That was the sacrifice demanded in exchange for unrivaled pleasure.

To that dedicated end, Cougar transformed masculine force and superior strength into what he perceived gentleness to be—the whisper of the summer wind, the brush of a butterfly's wings and the taste of spring rain—all things delicate and soothing. Just as he had taught himself to become the ferocious predator in times of extreme danger, he had to teach himself to become winds, wings and rain. He offered this dainty woman what she could understand and respond to. He became the contrasting parallel of everything he was, for this space out of time.

Cougar's attempt at tenderness was rewarded tenfold. Roz responded to the feathery kisses that grazed the pulsating column of her throat. She arched upward to accept the gliding path of his tongue and lips. And when he eased her from the torn chemise to delicately feast on the velvet crowns of her breasts, Cougar could feel her body quivering beneath his lips, feel her breathless surrender become his own.

As hungry as Cougar was to devour her, to possess her, there was still a compelling need within him to shower Roz with effusive pleasure. Having her want him beyond reason had somehow become as essential as masculine possession. He reveled in the feel of her feminine body beneath his lips, against his skin, under his questing fingertips. He savored each sensation that sizzled through her when he gently suckled at her breasts. His fingertips glided lower, deeper, until he held her quivering in his hand.

Cougar doffed his bandoleers and breeches before

guiding her silky thighs farther apart to position himself between her legs. Despite his own raging needs, Cougar was aware that Roz had suffered injuries and that she was voyaging from maidenhood to womanhood. It was within his power to make this unprecedented journey a fantasy come true or nightmarish reality.

But Cougar had never dreamed the path to mutual fulfillment could be so arousing. He, too, was learning the difference between appeasing mere lust and exploring the mystical realm of lovemaking.

"Cougar?" Roz's voice wobbled in helpless response to his seductive caresses. "Please . . ."

He felt her shimmering around his fingertips, felt secret rain drenching him. Cougar told himself to be extremely gentle and patient as his body settled over hers. He stroked her as the hard length of his arousal replaced his probing fingertips. But as tender as he tried to be, he could feel her unclaimed body resisting him, hear her pained gasp shattering the breathless silence.

The haunted look in those luminous blue eyes cut into Cougar's chest like a knife. He felt utterly helpless to ease her pain . . . and utterly helpless to stop himself from taking her.

"This I promise," he whispered hoarsely, before he transformed her pained gasp into a kiss as he sheathed himself deeply inside her. "Though I cannot help but hurt you once, I never will again . . ."

He paused to give her time to adjust to the penetrating invasion of passion, to search for the pleasure that had been overshadowed by the initial pain of masculine possession.

"Yield to me," Cougar murmured as he slowly, carefully withdrew and then glided over her again. "Hold me in the most secret ways you have never held another man . . ."

Roz peered up into those flaming golden eyes that hypnotized and beguiled her. With each gentle motion, she felt her body accepting his possession, welcoming it. Roz gave herself up to Cougar, trusting him to be as tender as he had when he had first touched her. Her hands scaled the rock-hard wall of his chest, gripping his powerful shoulders. Her gaze locked with his. It was from this man, and this man alone, that Roz wanted to discover the mystery of passion, because there was no other man like Cougar.

There was no need for Roz to murmur words of acceptance. Cougar knew the instant she surrendered to him. He could feel her melting around him like a liquid flame. That silent, sensuous response was enough to drive Cougar mad with unbearable wanting. He held her in his arms, molding her into his muscular contours, teaching her to move with him until reality was a distant shore beyond a rolling sea of indefinable pleasure. Waves of passion crested and swirled as he drove into her, feeling sensation upon incredible sensation swamp and buffet him . . .

And then Cougar lost track of time, of rational thought. Inexpressible need pummeled him and he clutched Roz so tightly that he feared he would crush her with the intensity of his uncontrollable desire. Each hard, penetrating thrust cost him another measure of restraint, until there was nothing between him and mindless passion, nothing but a need so devastating that he became its willing prisoner.

Passion, such as he had never known, pulsated through him when Roz's feminine body contracted around him. She was taking him over the edge, plummeting him into a churning sea of indescribable sensations. Cougar forgot to breathe and suddenly couldn't think of one good reason why he needed to. His heart was hammering against his chest like a madman driving spikes. And as his male body clenched in wild, numbing release, Cougar felt himself drowning in such mind-boggling pleasure that he couldn't determine which way was up. He was lost in a dark sea, the captive of sensations he never even realized existed . . . until now . . .

Making love to Roz had cost Cougar everything he was, made him into something he had never been—a tender, caring lover who wanted more than the satisfaction of his own selfish needs. That was the price demanded of possessing the forbidden. Without asking, Roz had taken all he had to give, had changed him to meet her feminine needs.

Cougar, the legendary predator who called no man master, had become a purring pussycat who couldn't muster the energy or the will to move away from his greatest temptation. He had met defeat—tamed by the gliding stroke of Roz's hand down his back and hips, the soft whisper of her breath against his neck.

Cougar struggled to bring his heart rate back to normal, to breathe without gasping. He tried to tell his sluggish body to move before he inflicted even more pain on the fragile woman beneath him.

He tried and he failed.

"Dear God . . ." Roz murmured as she pressed a

fleeting kiss to his shoulder. "Nobody told me it would be like this."

Cougar gave an abrupt crack of laughter that echoed through their joined bodies. To tell the truth, he didn't know what the hell he was even laughing about. What could possibly be amusing about committing the unforgivable sin of stealing Roz's virginity beside a mountain trail while Jake Roche and his raiders were putting more distance between them?

Hell! Had he lost the good sense he had spent thirty years cultivating?

Cougar braced his forearms beneath him and eased away, noting the evidence of Roz's lost innocence clinging to him. Damn, how could something so wonderfully satisfying feel so ashamedly wrong in the space of a laugh?

Cougar wondered if he should give the command for his cats to feed on *him*. They certainly couldn't devour him more thoroughly than passion had devoured him. And now that the fog of maddening desire had lifted, what was he supposed to say to this deflowered sophisticate who was injured, bruised and undoubtedly aching in places she hadn't known could hurt?

Words sounded like flimsy excuses to explain what had transpired between them. Cougar felt incredibly awkward. Ordinarily, when he appeased his needs, he got up and walked away without looking back or reflecting on the woman he left behind. But there was no walking away from Rozalie Gaylord . . . or from the nagging voice of his newfound conscience.

When Cougar glanced back at Roz, he noted the embarrassed blush that stained her cheeks, the self-conscious way she gathered together the garments he had peeled away one at a time to feast on her scented flesh before he took ultimate possession.

This was not a situation that Cougar was accustomed to handling. There would be no exchange of coins, no impersonal farewells. Damn it all, he felt every bit as self-conscious as Roz did. One would think that this was Cougar's first time, considering the way he was squirming around, searching for distraction. But he could not deny that this was his first time with a woman's first time. He didn't know how to deal with the situation except to ignore it. Subtle finesse and diplomacy weren't even on the list of his saving graces. Hell, most folks swore he didn't even have saving graces.

Cougar's lack of response put another humiliated blush on Roz's cheeks. She didn't know what had come over her. One minute she was waiting for Cougar to make his diagnosis about her injured leg, and the next minute she was melting beneath his unbelievably tender caresses and begging for his kisses. And when she had willingly surrendered what no other man had taken from her, Cougar couldn't even bear to look at her! She had all but announced the moment they shared had bordered on phenomenal splendor and Cougar behaved as if he regretted every familiar touch, every intoxicating kiss, every—intimate—thing.

Roz squeezed back the mortified tears and fumbled to cover herself. "I'm sorry."

Cougar jerked up his head and frowned at her. "For what, Yank?"

"I didn't know what I was doing."

"The Great Spirit help us all if you ever figure out what you are doing," he grumbled as he fastened his buckskin breeches and reached for his hastily discarded bandoleers.

Roz glared at his muscular back. "And what is that supposed to mean?"

"Nothing," Cougar muttered sourly. "Just forget it."

"Fine. It's forgotten. Nothing happened." Roz surged to her feet in a fit of temper and humiliation. A yelp exploded from her lips when she put her weight on her leg. She crumpled to the ground, landing on the tender joint of a knee that felt as if it had been ripped from its socket.

Cougar expelled a rough sigh and strode over to inspect her leg the way he should have, before he forgot everything except appeasing a hunger that had been eating him alive for over a week.

*You think you've satisfied your obsessive craving once and for all?* his newfound conscience asked him. *Think again, Cougar.*

Cougar scowled at the inner voice that nagged him. Damnation, and here he thought hell had nothing new to teach him. As it turned out, Cougar was discovering all sorts of ways for guilty souls to be tortured.

A quick inspection, allowing only the briefest of touches, indicated Roz had bruised her hip and strained the tendons around her knee. Cougar didn't dare force Roz to straddle a saddle, not after their experience together.

Roz needed time to recuperate. That was obvious.

Cougar needed time to mentally kick himself for succumbing to unruly desire.

"I'll take you to the stream in higher elevations," Cougar insisted as he smoothed her gown back in place. "You can rest there while I track Roche."

Her lashes swept up to meet his grim expression. "You know Jake Roche?"

Cougar's face closed up. Haunting memories rose from their shallow graves. "I know him and Burney Adair all too well. Thus far, the Cheyenne curse has eluded them, but no longer."

Roz frowned, bemused by the icy tone of his voice. "What curse are you talking about, Cougar?"

Cougar stared back through the window of time, feeling burning hatred channel through him, reliving the anguish that had stripped away his very soul. "Roche and Adair rode with Custer when the cavalry charged into the peaceful Cheyenne camp on the Washita. The People had already survived the Sand Creek Massacre four years earlier. Although Black Kettle and White Antelope had gone to Denver to sign a peace treaty, Colonel Chivington attacked our village.

"Of the one-hundred-twenty-three victims of the Sand Creek Massacre, ninety-eight were women and children. White Antelope ran toward the invading troops with his hands raised, ordering Chivington to halt. He was shot down, and one of the soldiers cut off his privates to make a tobacco pouch."

Roz cringed at the horrible picture Cougar was painting.

"Black Kettle managed to escape the bloodthirsty invasion by moving upstream along the underbrush and reeds. His wife had been shot nine times that day, but she survived the butchery," Cougar continued in nothing more than an anguished whisper. "Sand Creek was nothing less than heartless murdering and mutilation by Federal troops against Indians who were led to believe they were under the protection of the Army after their peace talks. It was a cold-blooded slaughter that white society preferred to ignore."

"The Army did nothing about the atrocity?" Roz questioned, stunned.

"The Secretary of the Interior declared that the practice of extermination was a violation of humanity and a contradiction of Christian policy—or so he nobly said," Cougar added with a disgusted snort. "The hard fact was that supporting Indian-fighting regiments in the West was costing two million dollars a year in salary, weapons, ammunition, food and supplies. The government decided it was cheaper to keep Indians alive on reservations rather than kill them on the plains. Since the treasury had been drained by the Civil War, your Great White Chief decided to take the cheaper bargain."

"I'm sorry," Roz murmured as she peered up at Cougar's rigid stance, watching him stare into the distance, lost to the violence and atrocities that had been his life.

He spoke again as if he hadn't heard her. "Only one year after the peace conference at Medicine Lodge, Black Kettle and our clan had settled on the Washita River in the western regions of Indian Territory. This time it was Custer and the Seventh Cavalry who came charging in from four different directions. All of those who had survived Sand Creek sprang awake, praying that this wouldn't be a repetition of the slaughter in Colorado. But it was the same. Black Kettle died alongside his wife and his scalp was taken, along with many others."

"And you, Cougar? How did you survive the blood-letting?"

"Gray Eagle and I were just returning from hunting when we heard the shots, screams and shouts for mercy. What we saw was so terrible that words could not begin to describe it. Soldiers charged defenseless women and children, butchering them and leaving them in bloody heaps before hunting down other victims. Dead and wounded women and children were scattered along the river that ran with blood."

Cougar's gaze shifted to Roz who sat on the ground in front of him, her head downcast, her hands clenched in her lap. "Gray Eagle and I watched Roche and Adair commit crimes against the dead and injured, crimes whose vile description are not fit for your ears or your eyes, Yank.

"Those two bastards tore bodies to pieces, taking prizes with such disgusting pleasure that I have come to hate the memories, as well as the sight of those two men.

"What my cats did to Skeet Thomas cannot compare to what Roche and Adair did to defenseless Indian women and children. And all the while, Gray Eagle and I were forced to watch our clan being mutilated and murdered and chopped to bits. We couldn't even reach the survivors before they were herded off to the fort to be counted and numbered like sheep that escaped the slaughter."

Cougar inhaled a deep breath and cursed the visions that refused to die. "Oh yes, Yank, I know Roche and

Adair all too well. The Cheyenne curse that followed Custer and his cavalry to the Little Big Horn is the same one that follows Roche and Adair. Until those two butchers have been launched into hell, the victims of the massacre cannot rest in peace. Rescuing Caleb so I can take Cheyenne vengeance out on Roche and Adair is all that is going to satisfy me."

Roz did not doubt that for a minute, not if the frosty look in his eyes or the taut lines of his powerful body were any indication of his ultimate mission in life. Cougar had ghost spirits to appease. He saw himself as an extension of those helpless cries, the personification of the curse the Cheyenne had placed on men who had slaughtered them after they had given their vow of peace.

Roz said nothing as Cougar scooped her off the ground and placed her on his horse. After he had swung up behind her, he draped her across his lap so she wouldn't have to straddle the saddle. Roz squirmed uneasily, vividly aware of the sinewy arms encircling her, the hard, masculine thighs beneath her hips.

Too many emotions were riding high at the moment. Roz's near brush with death had left her savoring every minute, left her surrendering to Cougar's seductive touch for fear she might not live long enough to discover what passion and love were all about. Now she knew the incredible sensations that materialized out of nowhere. She knew the dark secrets of Cougar's past and she longed to comfort him, even as she knew that he wanted no more from her than he'd already taken.

Holding Roz close as he reined up the hill was arousing torment. Every time Cougar breathed he inhaled her scent and it reminded him of how close they had been just moments before.

Damn, Cougar really could kick himself to hell and back for taking advantage of Roz. He couldn't think of one appropriate comment to diffuse the awkward silence between them. Instead, in his effort to avoid the issue he had revealed the tragic tales of the Cheyenne, as he had to no other living soul.

At the moment, Cougar didn't know what he was feeling except guilt and frustration, but if Roz didn't stop squirming in his lap he was liable to do something he'd really regret.

"Hold still, Yank," Cougar finally muttered at Roz.

"I can't. It hurts."

"What hurts?"

Roz flashed him a glower that was colored with a crimson blush. "My leg. What did you think I meant?"

Cougar stared at the winding trail that zigzagged between the gigantic boulders. "I would expect you to be . . . um . . . uncomfortable after . . ." His voice dried up and he winced when Roz's blush turned a darker shade of red. He could almost feel the heat radiating from her lovely face.

"I'm fine, perfectly fine," she hurriedly assured him.

Cougar doubted that. Considering the difference in their size, he expected Roz was lying through her teeth.

"You'll have a chance to rest, bathe and change into the fresh clothes I brought for you."

"You were very considerate," Roz murmured, staring at the craggy mountain peaks above her. "Thank you for that."

Cougar said nothing. He didn't feel the least bit considerate. He felt like a rutting stag that couldn't control its male needs. The man of stone had definitely cracked.

Cougar dismounted beside a mountain stream that trickled from the wild tumble of rocks. As if he were handling fragile crystal, he lifted Roz from his horse and situated her on a pallet. For a moment, the tension between them eased. Roz's attention centered on the ribbonlike cascade of water that splashed over the rocks to form an inviting pool. Cougar could see her mentally sketching the landscape, admiring this peaceful retreat that few white men had discovered in this remote region of mountains.

This obscure valley had once been the site where the Cheyenne had often come to communicate with the spirits. Now this was the site of distant memories of a proud breed of people who had been hunted, herded and confined like livestock.

"This is beautiful," Roz whispered in awestruck fascination. "Would you fetch my sketch pad for me, Cougar?"

Cougar retrieved her supplies, watching her marveling gaze scan the rugged precipices and clumps of pines that reached up to bask in the afternoon sun. "Cheyenne Canyon is even more spectacular than this," he murmured as he studied her sketch.

"I cannot imagine that." Roz outlined the jagged peaks above her. "I wish Caleb could see . . ." Her voice trailed off and her hand stalled. "You better be on your way. Caleb needs to know that you're out here somewhere, watching over him."

And Cougar needed the time and space to clear his head, to regather the self-control that had deserted him two hours earlier. "I'll leave my rifle for protection. Do you know how to use it?"

"As well as Caleb does."

Cougar snorted at that. "The boy has much to learn."

"And I have a lot to forget," Roz mused aloud.

Pretending not to hear her, Cougar drew the rifle from its sling on the saddle and checked to ensure the cylinder was full of cartridges. "You'll also have the cats to watch over you while I'm gone. The rifle is only for show and for insurance."

Roz eyed the cats, remembering how they had hissed and pounced while she was dangling from the spindly limb by her fingertips. "I don't think your cats like me. They would have torn me to pieces earlier if I hadn't released the tree branch."

"Only because I ordered them to pounce."

Roz's tangled blond head came up and she stared incredulously at the brawny giant whose massive form eclipsed the sunlight. "You ordered them to attack me?" she bleated.

"You wouldn't let go. I had no choice," Cougar explained as he turned away.

Jaw gaping, Roz watched Cougar ride off. He had ordered his cats to attack her? Her wide-eyed gaze swung from the rider who disappeared around the jutting rocks to the pumas that had wandered to the pool to drink and sun themselves on the rocks. Sometimes the similarities between the cats and Cougar unnerved Roz. All four of them were true predators, reacting effectively but impassively to danger.

And yet, despite what Cougar was, he could become an incredibly tender lover. He had become like these panthers in repose for a short space of time, even if he transformed into a fierce and pernicious creature in the face of danger. Roz wondered if a man like Cougar could ever become human enough to feel the gentle stirring that had begun to fill her heart after he taught her the magic of passion and then fulfilled every pulsing need he had so skillfully aroused in her. Obviously this time Cougar had felt nothing but the appeasement of lust. When his male appetite had been satisfied, he recoiled beneath that hard shell that separated him from his fellow man.

While Cougar rode away without looking back, Roz was afraid she was falling in love with the legendary manhunter. It was a waste of perfectly good emotion, she knew. One-sided, dead-end fascination would only lead to heartache. Men like Cougar didn't fall in love and live happily ever after. Cougar was a loner, a man whose bitter past burned like an inextinguishible flame. And if Roz had a smidgen of sense, she would remind herself hourly that Cougar may have possessed her with his body, but his heart was not, and never would be, a part of the passion they had shared in a wild moment when circumstances and tangled emotion had gotten the best of both of them.

On that realistic but depressing thought, Roz settled back against the tree and committed the spectacular scenery to paper, telling herself she was every kind of fool for caring about a man who wouldn't know love if it walked up and bit him.

# Thirteen

After Burney Adair patched up Jake's shoulder wound, Jake tramped outside the cave, where they had holed up, to unsaddle all the horses. When Jake reached into the saddlebag that had once held Skeet's portion of gold, ammunition and personal supplies, he heard a hiss and rattle inside the leather pouch.

"Son of a bitch!" Jake Roche recoiled at lightning speed. He had come within a hairbreadth of being bitten by a rattlesnake.

There was no question that Cougar had planted that little surprise the night he had turned his man-eating mountain lions loose on Skeet Thomas. Jake was fortunate he had reacted quickly; otherwise, he would have suffered a nasty bite, adding complications to his existing wound.

That half-breed was proving to be a menace. Cougar had blocked off Jake's intended route through the mountains and he had caused Skeet Thomas to turn traitor. That kind of clever manipulation was dangerous. It caused dissension among the ranks of outlaws. The other men had seen Skeet firing at Jake who had been forced to return the gunfire in self-defense. Now that Jake and Burney had set the precedent, the other confederates knew they would be sacrificed if the situation demanded it. Cougar's wily technique had destroyed the unity of the bandits, leaving them casting speculative glances at each other, wondering if there was a loyal and trusted friend among them.

Cougar had also plugged Vito Guerero in the leg, as if the flighty Mexican wasn't already in bad shape. Now Jake and his raiders resembled a ragtag army of walking wounded. One man was dead, two were injured and one captive had plunged over the cliff. Hell and damnation—what had begun as a simple robbery at a remote stage station had evolved into a living nightmare.

Too bad the woman had fallen to her death, Jake thought as he carefully slid the infested saddlebag off the horse and carried it away on the barrel of his rifle. Jake had intended to take his pleasure with the uppity Easterner tonight. Now he was left to tend his throbbing arm and dispose of the snakes that had come dangerously close to making a meal of him.

At least he and his men would be safe for the evening, Jake consoled himself. The cavern they had located on a platform of rock would provide ample protection. There was only one entrance into the abandoned mine shaft that tunneled into the side of the mountain. If Cougar tried to attack he would find himself and his snarling cats filled with lead.

There was also enough room in the shaft to stable the horses so that blasted half-breed couldn't steal their mounts. With any luck Jake and his men could slip away before dawn, without being picked off like sitting ducks . . .

The unnerving sound of a screaming panther split the

afternoon air and prickled the skin on Jake's neck. He was really beginning to hate that sound. But as long as Jake had that bawling kid as hostage, he felt reasonably safe. And besides, he wasn't about to let himself be taken by a goddamn Injun! Somehow, he would set a trap to lure that half-breed in and dispose of him. As soon as the pain in his shoulder ebbed, Jake would give serious thought to dealing with Cougar.

On that determined note, Jake opened fire on the saddlebag that Cougar had sabotaged with live rattlesnakes. Jake pretended he was unloading his pistol on that pesky half-breed.

Soon, Jake promised himself fiercely, soon he would find a way to make Cougar exchange his life for that whimpering kid!

Cougar rose from a crouch and stood on the hillside, watching Jake Roche dispose of the rattlesnakes he'd planted in the saddlebags. If Cougar had had his rifle with him, he could have picked that bastard off. Unfortunately, Cougar had arrived too late and he had left the rifle with Roz as protection. Of course, Roche was no fool, Cougar reminded himself sourly. Roche was careful never to make himself an easy target by moving too far away from the horses.

When Jake led the last two horses into the cavern, Cougar let out a scream that rose to a high, howling pitch. He wanted Roche's raiders to know they were being watched and for Caleb to be aware that Cougar was lurking about like a cat that was rarely seen until a vicious attack was launched.

Leaving the haunting sound to echo around the stone walls like a curse, Cougar spun away. He had another route to barricade before he returned to camp. Roche's raiders would be squirming in their skin and leaping at shadows after Jake relayed the incident with the rattlesnakes. Mental warfare, Cougar had learned long ago, was as effective as physical attack. It left a man second-guessing his enemy until he lost sight of his intended objective. The Roche gang, like the dozens of men Cougar had tracked in the past, would find themselves with only one purpose—survival against a relentless predator.

However, Cougar vowed that even survival would be an impossibility for Jake Roche, Burney Adair and the rest.

Vito Guerero laid his head back against the rough stone wall of the cave and cringed at the unearthly scream that seemed to penetrate rock. The sound hung in the damp air like a tormenting curse. Vito took a gulp of whiskey and waited for Burney to apply his knife to the seeping wound on his thigh.

"I tell you, that devil cat is going to eat us all alive," Vito said between panting breaths.

"Shut up," Burney snapped as he laid his sharpened blade to Vito's flesh. "It's still five against one."

Vito yelped as he felt the point of the dagger touch his wound. Perspiration beaded Vito's brows and he hurriedly downed another drink. "I still don't like the odds," he hissed. "Cougar is dangerous now, but you haven't seen him when he changes forms."

"Changes forms?" Jake scoffed at the superstitious Mexican. "Men don't change forms."

Vito's pained gaze shifted to the lean, wiry leader of the gang and he clenched his teeth when Burney dug deeper. "Cougar is not a man—"

A thunderous noise swept through the mine shaft, drowning Vito's words. The walls vibrated and dust drifted from the supporting beams that braced the ceiling of the cavern.

"He's going to bury us alive!" Vito screeched. "He's—"

Burney used the butt of his knife and his fist to silence Vito. The Mexican's head slammed against the rock wall.

"I told you to shut up," Burney snarled. "If you don't, you won't have to worry about what that stinking Injun is going to do to if he gets his hands on you. There won't be enough of you left for him to bother with."

"The half-breed doesn't dare attack us as long as we have the kid," Jake reminded his men. "He's only trying to cause trouble for us, not bury us under a pile of rock."

Hudson Caine squirmed uneasily on his pallet as the explosive sounds rumbled down the walls of the canyon and clung to the air. "Maybe if we let the kid go, Cougar will back off and leave us alone."

Jake glanced at their pint-sized captive who had ceased his incessant sobbing the minute he heard the wild cry of the cougar. "That kid is our best defense," he insisted as he rummaged through the supply sacks for food.

"That kid is also our curse," Colby Jordan muttered as he toyed with his whip. "We're damned if we do and damned if we don't. And we all saw how Skeet turned traitor after Cougar sank his claws into him and poisoned his thinking. What if Cougar gets hold of another one of us? What if he—?"

"You're getting as soft as Vito," Jake growled at Colby. "You want to take your chances with that red-skinned bastard, do you? Go ahead. Walk out of this mine shaft and see if Cougar will give you a chance to defect before he slits your throat the way he tried to slit Vito's."

When Colby slammed his mouth shut and looked the other way, Jake breathed an inward sigh of relief. "We're all in this together. If we start doubting each other, we'll be playing right into that conniving bastard's hands. He's counting on us to turn on each other. While we're squabbling among ourselves, he'll pick us off."

"Turn on us like you turned on Skeet?" Hudson grunted sardonically.

Jake glowered at the grumbling confederate. "That was self-defense and you damned well know it. If Burney hadn't come to my aid, I would be lying dead and there would only be four of you left to outsmart that half-breed."

"But what guarantee do we have that you won't leave one of us behind again, just like you did Skeet when the cats chewed him to pieces?" Colby wanted to know.

Jake scowled and tossed hardtack to his men. He had already answered that question when he abandoned Skeet. Thanks to that cunning half-breed, there was no way for Jake to reassure the men who stared warily at him. Cougar had the desperadoes flicking glances at one another, wondering who would become the next doomed victim, knowing what little attention that victim would receive if he were seriously wounded.

"Cougar will come," Caleb murmured, staring past the small campfire that blazed at the mouth of the cavern. "No matter what else, Cougar will come."

The boy's unfaltering confidence had all five men shifting uneasily on their pallets. Every shadow that danced on the walls became the looming image of impending disaster.

Jake cursed the chills that ricocheted down his spine when another unsettling scream flooded through the cavern, causing the horses to snort and whinny. Flames leaped from the campfire and more shadows slid up the walls like dark demons rising from the pits of hell. Jake shook off his own nagging fears and vowed to make Cougar pay for the torment he was putting the Roche gang through.

"We'll ride out of here just before dawn," Jake declared to break the unnerving silence.

"Yeah," Hud Caine muttered, swiping a hand over the dusty beard that lined his jaws. "With any luck, this mine shaft won't become our grave . . ."


Mission accomplished, Cougar returned to the camp, just as the sun ducked behind the craggy peaks, casting purple shadows on the rock formations of the towering ridge. As much as Cougar wanted to launch a full-scale attack against Roche and his bandits, Roz's injuries had to be taken into consideration.

Leaving Roz behind was out of the question. Taking her with him would impede progress. The time Cougar allowed Roz to recover from near death would also provide the Roche gang with ample time to lick their wounds. Cougar hadn't planned on being so generous with Roche and Adair. Now he had no choice . . .

Cougar rode into the clearing where he had left Roz, and he halted his horse in its tracks. His pensive musings scattered like buckshot when he saw the tempting beauty gliding across the clear blue pool. Her unbound hair trailed down her back. Her bare arms glistened with diamond water droplets and instant arousal coursed through Cougar's veins. His all-consuming gaze swept over the enticing curve of Roz's back to the gentle swell of her hips. The pool was like a sheer wrapper that concealed just enough of Roz's curvaceous figure to torment and tantalize a man.

Although Cougar knew this stunning blonde was a weakness he could ill-afford, he felt a slow burn searing through him. Even the sharp reminder that it was his duty to take care of Roz, not take her for his pleasure, didn't cool the flames of his desire.

This woman was proving to be an impossible distraction. Young Caleb was in the hands of ruthless criminals and all Cougar could remember was the immeasurable satisfaction he had discovered when he had succumbed to his forbidden fantasy.

As of yet, Roz hadn't realized Cougar had returned. The panthers had left their perches on the rocks to greet him, but Roz was still frolicking in the pool as if she hadn't a care in the world.

Cougar's inability to control his desires irritated him beyond words. Roz's disregard of what transpired around her annoyed him to no end. The rifle Cougar could have

unloaded on Jake Roche was propped against a tree—
too far away to be of any use if danger arose.

Damn it, these mountains were jumping with wolves,
bears, snakes and who knew what else. Yet Roz was
oblivious to everything except her leisurely swim. Even
the distracted cats had been watching Roz swim and
splash around until miniature geysers erupted around
her like streams of liquid diamonds.

It had taken the cats a full minute to realize Cougar
had arrived. Some help those preoccupied panthers
were! Roz's antics had them bewitched.

Scowling, Cougar turned away from visual torment—
or at least he tried. When Roz noticed the cats had abandoned her, she swirled around in the water. With that
all Cougar's attempts to restrain himself vanished into
thin air. His gaze caught and held on the ivory column
of Roz's throat, the full swells of her breasts. The waist-
high water wrapped around her like a flowing caress
and Cougar felt as if he had taken a blow to the mid-
section when his eyes swept over every exposed inch
of her silky flesh.

"Cougar . . . I didn't know you were back."

Roz's attempt to modestly cover herself only made
matters worse. Cougar suffered another blow of instantaneous arousal when she wrapped her arms around her
chest and sank deeper into the pool. As if that could
conceal her from his hawkish gaze.

Even while Cougar was telling himself to keep his
distance, not to complicate matters even more than he
already had, he felt his betraying footsteps taking him
to the rocky ledge beside the pool. His gaze was transfixed on the tempting sight.

When Cougar unfastened the bandoleers that criss-crossed his broad chest, Roz assumed he intended to take a swim. Self-consciously, she turned her back and waded toward the reeds on the far side of the pool.

"The water is a mite cold, but invigorating," she informed him as she grabbed her clean chemise and wormed into it behind a dressing screen of underbrush.

"The colder the better," Cougar muttered as he kicked off his moccasins.

Roz strangled on her breath and tried to balance on her good leg when Cougar peeled off his breeches. She decided she was entirely too visual, especially when it came to this remarkable male specimen. Her artistic training had taught her to devour subjects that she sketched, to assess every intricate detail before committing shapes and dimensions to canvas. She should have looked the other way when Cougar stripped from his clothes. Should have, but didn't. He was utterly magnificent, a tribute to raw muscular power and sleek, bronzed flesh.

When she had surrendered to his astoundingly tender touch earlier in the day, she had been unaware of the full impact Cougar presented to the feminine eye. She had been adrift in a frothy sea of unexpected sensations. But now she was granted an unhindered view of a man whose body was a living work of art.

Cougar swore his knees had turned to jelly when he saw Roz peeping at him through the reeds that lined the east side of the pool. Her wide-eyed gaze swept down his chest to focus on the rigid length of him. No woman had ever peered at him like that. No woman had ever made him feel more of a man with an admiring glance.

Roz forced herself to turn away from the magnificent man who was poised on the stone ledge by the pool. She reminded herself that Cougar had no interest in her now that his needs had been appeased. On that dejected thought, she limped around the underbrush to stretch out on the pallet, purposely focusing her attention on the horse that had been left to graze. She didn't dare glance at Cougar, for fear she would succumb to the overwhelming urge to join him in the pool, to sketch every incredible inch of him—with her lips and fingertips.

Cougar breathed an enormous sigh of relief when the cold water began to work its desired effects on his overheated body. A bath was all he really needed, he assured himself sensibly. He had to keep his distance because that enchanting blue-eyed blonde was his Achilles heel. He had no defense when his male body overpowered his fumbling mind. Roz could make a liar of him in the blink of an eye, make him crave her without even trying.

A good while later, when Cougar had regained control of his needs, he heaved himself onto the rock ledge and strode over to where he had left the saddlebags. Once he had dressed in clean clothes, he set off to find fresh meat for their meal, granting himself time to deliver another round of lectures on the benefits of self-restraint. If he didn't watch himself, he was going to become a worse hypocrite than he already was. He had to remain focused on his ulterior purpose—rescuing Caleb and venting his fury on Roche and Adair.


"Gideon, I don't think you're ready to tackle your chores just yet," Francene advised as she watched her weak but determined husband lever himself up on the edge of the bed.

"Just fetch my canes, woman," Gideon demanded irritably. "If I stare at these four walls another damned day I'll go mad. And I will not have you tending tasks that are man's work."

"Man's work?" Francene sniffed as she handed Gideon two canes so he could prop himself upright. "This stage station belongs to both of us and I have no qualms about feeding the livestock or harnessing horses to the coaches."

"Well, I have qualms about it." Gideon braced himself on his bad leg to take the pressure off the worse one. A grimace bracketed his lips when he put weight on his most recently injured limb. His thigh hurt like hell and fire burned along the wound Cougar had stitched. "Damn, when did it turn cloudy outside?"

Francene glanced toward the window to see the sun beaming just as brightly as it had moments earlier. Her concerned gaze swung back to Gideon's peaked face. "The only clouds around here are the ones swimming in your eyes," she insisted, halting his progress before he could take another pained step. "Lie down, Gideon. You obviously haven't recovered your strength. All you're doing is making yourself dizzy. If you pass out, I'll be tempted to leave you sprawled on the floor."

Despite his determined spirit, his weak body failed him. Gideon felt the room tilt sideways and he sat down on the edge of the bed before he fell down. "Damn those raiders," he said weakly. "I hope Cougar stakes out every last one of them for the buzzards."

"I'm sure he has every intention of carrying out your

spiteful wishes," Francene answered. "And if you don't stay put until you have recovered, you won't be around to thank Cougar when he returns with Caleb and Roz."

Gideon floundered back on the bed. Once he had propped himself against the headboard and the room stopped swirling he expelled a weary sigh. "How is my replacement working out?"

Francene handed Gideon a slice of freshly baked pie. "Seth Radburn is proving to be very competent. He shooed me out of the barn this morning when I tried to help him with the chores. The young man is quite industrious, and exceptionally attractive."

Gideon's response was a mere grunt.

"Our female passengers certainly have given Seth all the attention a man could want," Francene commented as she sank down beside her husband.

"Just as long as it's only female travelers who are giving Seth Radburn the eye," Gideon grumbled before taking a bite of peach pie.

"For heaven's sake, Gideon. You know that I only have eyes for you."

"Maybe when I had at least one good leg beneath me," he muttered, staring at the far wall. "What use is a man to his woman when he isn't good on his feet or in bed?"

Francene gaped at Gideon. "Do you think that is all that matters to me?" she asked, highly affronted. "Well, if you do, you are wrong! You are my life and I intend to love you for better or worse. Without you I would have little reason to exist and you should know that, after all these years we have spent together. Do you think I'm so selfish and shallow that I would abandon you just because you were temporarily flagged by a bullet?"

Gideon handed his wife the empty saucer. When she set it aside, he pulled her into his arms and draped her across his lap. "I'd go crazy if I lost you. You know that, don't you?"

Francene peered up into those intense hazel eyes and looped her arms around his neck. "I know," she whispered as she drew his lips to hers. "And I don't want to lose you, either, Gideon. I just want things to be as they were before hell broke loose."

"They will," Gideon promised huskily. "Cougar will make everything right again. I know that as surely as I know I love you with every beat of my heart . . ."

When Gideon wrapped Francene in his arms and felt her lips melt against his, he forgot about the nagging pain in his leg and the handsome replacement who was making himself at home in the barn. For that moment Gideon held onto the most precious possession he had been granted in life.

He also sent up a silent prayer that his son would be returned to him, safe and sound. And never again, Gideon promised, was he going to consider himself too busy to answer Caleb's questions or neglect spending time with his son. Gideon was never going to take his wife or son for granted—ever. They were the most important part of his life and he hoped he never had to suffer a shot in the leg again to remind him of it.

# Fourteen

Roz munched on the tasty but unfamiliar meat Cougar had roasted over the campfire. For the most part, Cougar had been pensively quiet since his return, avoiding her as much as possible. But Roz was determined not to let him withdraw, not when she felt an extraordinary closeness to him. Surely he wouldn't be annoyed with her if she offered idle conversation.

Roz voiced the first thought that came to mind to break the silence. "I like the meat. Just what are we eating?"

Cougar glanced up from the tin plate in his lap. "Rattlesnake."

Roz sucked in her breath, causing a chunk of snake steak to lodge in her throat. Only after Cougar whacked her between the shoulder blades was she able to breathe again. She shuddered at the repulsive thought and wheezed, "Rattle—?"

"—Snake," Cougar finished for her, unable to stifle his amused grin. "I guess they don't serve snake in the restaurants of New York."

"Not if they can help it." Roz stared at her suddenly unappetizing meal.

Cougar's mouth quirked in a half smile. "I thought you were hungry, Yank."

"I was."

Cougar finished his meal and set his empty plate aside. "Look at it this way, the snake you eat is the one you know for certain won't take a bite out of you."

"If that is supposed to make me feel better it doesn't." Her appetite spoiled, she shoved her plate toward the cats that were lounging beside the pallet. While the cats feasted on her leftovers, Roz watched them.

"Where did you acquire your unusual pets?"

Cougar flicked Roz a curious glance, wondering at her need for irrelevant conversation. He was accustomed to silence, to the companionship of his own thoughts. Obviously Roz expected to chitchat over dinner. Cougar halfheartedly accommodated her.

"Panthers aren't unusual pets to the Cheyenne," he told her as he stretched out on his pallet. "According to the tradition of the People, in the days of long ago, we had no way of getting food other than obtaining it with our own hands. As the numbers of the tribe increased, acquiring food became even more difficult."

Roz sank down on her elbow, staring musingly at Cougar while he related what she suspected to be a fascinating Indian legend.

"Once, long ago, a Cheyenne woman lost the infant she was nursing to illness. Not long after the child was delivered to the Great Spirit on the Hanging Road into the Sky, the woman found a nest of young kitten panthers. While the mother panther was hunting food, the childless woman took one of the young kittens from its nest. The young panther gave a moan and whine that reminded her of the child she had lost. When the bereaved woman hugged the kitten to her breast the panther cub began to nurse."

Roz was thankful for the darkness that concealed the blush that worked its way up from her throat to her hairline. Although Cougar didn't seem the least bit uncomfortable discussing such matters, Roz felt self-conscious. But listening to Cougar's rich baritone voice was far better than the awkward silence between them. Roz swallowed her embarrassment and concentrated on his tale.

"Affection for this kitten panther sprang into the woman's heart and she raised it as if it were her own child. As the cub grew into a creature of strength and cunning, the panther killed deer and other large game, furnishing food for the Cheyenne," Cougar continued, relating the story as he had heard it told in his youth. "Other women in the tribe took kitten panthers and raised them as their own. With the help of the panthers, food was much easier to obtain and the tribe became stronger and healthier.

"Using flintstone that had been sharpened, the Cheyenne were able to clean the hides of the animals the panthers killed. The hides kept the People warm and made survival easier. Since the beginning, the People have come to respect the panther, to emulate its skills in hunting and battle."

Cougar smiled faintly at Roz, brushed his hand lightly over his body and then smoothed the ground beside him, just as Cheyenne protocol demanded. "This is the story of the Cheyenne's beginnings on Mother Earth. The tale is sacred and bears no falsehood, but those who are appointed to tell it must demand a vow from those who hear the Cheyenne's habits and customs. This history can be repeated, but the name of the one who told it to you can never be revealed. It is the way of the People."

Roz stared at the sprawled cats that could be perfectly harmless until they were given the command to attack. "And because the panther is part of your clan's tradition, you feel compelled to raise them as your own?"

Cougar chuckled at Roz's thoughtful expression. "Partly perhaps. Maybe it is my attempt to preserve the history of a tribe that has been forced to accept the ways of the whites while confined to reservations."

His smile faded as half-forgotten memories condensed in his mind. "As a young warrior in the village, the cougar was declared to be my totem, as well as my name. I was expected to train them and to react like the cunning cat that was my name. Four years ago, after I recovered from the ambush that left me with the scars, I found the orphan cats while tracking criminals near Cherry Creek. The cats have been with me ever since. But panthers are not the only animals revered by the Cheyenne. The tribe also claimed young wolves and wild dogs and domesticated them to protect the camps."

Roz reached out to stroke the nearest cat's head, only to have Cougar jerk her arm away. His stern glance indicated that he preferred that she left his cats alone, just as he insisted that she kept her distance from him. Roz decided Cougar would not be pleased to learn that she had petted his cats while he wasn't around to see her do it.

"I was never allowed to have a pet," Roz murmured. "My father wouldn't permit it because animals cost money instead of making it."

Cougar remembered what Francene had told him about the strained relationship between Roz and her money-hungry father. Although Cougar's fond memories had turned bitter, he couldn't help but wonder if Roz retained any happy recollections of her childhood, even if she were surrounded with every luxury that wealth could provide. He almost felt sorry for her. She had known little contentment, and Cougar wasn't making her period of mourning any easier for her.

But damn it, he had already made one colossal mistake with this woman. If he let his guard down for even a second, Cougar knew where they would end up—in a tangle on the bedroll. He was already walking a fine line, wanting Roz until he ached and refusing to let himself buckle to needs that should have been fully appeased but were still gnawing at him.

Cougar desperately needed a distraction. Staring too long and too closely at Roz, while moonlight danced in her unbound hair and cast shadows on her lush curves, was dragging his thoughts off in the wrong direction. Perhaps there *was* some useful purpose to conversation, Cougar decided, if he could keep his betraying thoughts from detouring down arousing avenues.

"Tell me about the men riding with Roche and Adair," Cougar requested. "It will make it easier for me to deal with them."

Roz absently massaged the knee Cougar had packed with a strange-smelling poultice and wrapped in padded bandages. "The only ones you don't already know are Hud Caine and Colby Jordan. They can be as ruthless and cruel as the other three. Colby is exceptionally fond of snapping his whip for intimidation."

Cougar remembered seeing the outlaw who lashed out at Roz with his whip. Too bad Cougar hadn't had the chance to shoot the renegade off his horse earlier in the day.

"And Hud Caine?" Cougar questioned curiously. "What is his specialty?"

Roz pondered the question for a moment. "I can't say that he possesses any extraordinary talents with pistols or knives. I think he must have been a gambler before he joined up with Roche. He spends most of his spare time shuffling cards rather than cleaning his weapons like the other men do."

Recalling her unpleasant ordeal with Roche's raiders made Roz oddly restless. With considerable effort, she climbed to her feet and ambled toward the pool that glowed like silver in the moonlight. There was a peacefulness about this secluded valley that Roz was happy to absorb.

Staring at Cougar left her remembering the shared intimacy that he preferred to ignore. She was fiercely attracted to Cougar, even though he made it clear that she had only been the place he had come for physical satisfaction. She was a shameless fool to want him the way she did. Putting space between them was the only way to ease these newly discovered longings that hounded her. Lord, she truly would have been better off if Cougar had left her behind while he rescued Caleb.

Sighing dispiritedly, Roz circled the inviting pool. Her footsteps halted when the angle of moonlight sprayed down on the miniature waterfall that cascaded over the outcropping of rocks. The mist that hung in the air was like a silver-studded cloud. Roz stretched her hand, watching the fine spray trickle over her fingertips. An indescribable sense of pleasure whispered through her as the mist rose like a floating spirit. Roz could understand why the Cheyenne considered this a place of visions. It was almost as if the waterfall was coming to life, speaking to her in bubbling whispers.

Cougar found himself entranced by the shapely silhouette poised beside the misty waterfall. Roz looked as if she were reaching out to him, and the whisper of the falls became the sultry sound of her voice, a voice that had become husky with passion when she called his name over and over again.

Despite the sermons Cougar had delivered to himself during the course of the day, he found his footsteps moving toward the enchanting vision beside the falls. Driving need pulsed through him, drowning every excuse as to why he should deny himself the pleasure he knew awaited him.

Roz flinched in surprise when she felt Cougar's lean fingers fold around her elbow, turning her to meet his somber stare. When she peered into those golden eyes, she knew he desired her again. It was evident in the angular features of his face, in the depths of those cat-like eyes.

And she wanted him. No other man had ever held such sensual power over her. But this man, this phenomenal creature stirred something so fierce and overpowering that rational thought abandoned Roz the instant he drew her to him.

No protest formed on her lips when Cougar's raven head dipped toward hers. When his hands glided over her hips, lifting her against his aroused contours, Roz felt familiar heat coursing through her body, answering the need she could feel throbbing through him.

When Cougar gently scooped her into his arms and pivoted toward the pallet beside the trees, Roz felt his warm breath whispering against the sensitive point beneath her ear. Inhibition deserted her as he eased her onto the pallet and joined her there. The look on his face was her undoing. The expression in those fascinating amber eyes sent need flooding through her body like a river overflowing its banks.

This dark, dangerous predator had a tender side that he reserved for her, whether he realized that yet or not. Beneath that ferocity which had become Cougar's way of life, he did possess gentle emotion. His feelings for her may have been only temporary, but they were real. They were simmering within him now and Roz responded, aching to draw even more tenderness from him, yearning to savor the pleasures he had exposed her to.

Cougar told himself he was making another disastrous mistake as his fingertips traced the slope of Roz's hip. He told himself that he should retreat before he drowned in the taste of her intoxicating kiss. But he couldn't so much as breathe without inhaling her alluring scent. He couldn't move without inching closer. The need she instilled in him was so tormentingly profound that dying would have been easier than backing away.

Ever so slowly, Cougar slipped the sleeve of her gown from her shoulder, drawing lazy circles on her smooth flesh. As he bent to take her lips beneath his, his hand glided to the stays of her gown. He treated every inch of exposed skin to feathery kisses and caresses, savoring her, wanting her.

"I've never seen anything so incredibly lovely, never touched anyone so soft and exquisite," Cougar heard himself say as his forefinger trailed over the rising swell of her breast.

To be considered as such by a man like Cougar was the greatest compliment Roz had ever been paid. When she smiled in response, Cougar actually smiled back. Soft laughter bubbled from her lips, even as her body reflexively arched toward his caressing hand.

"So you can do it after all," she whispered.

"Do what?" he rasped, entirely too distracted by the sensual responses he was drawing from her.

"Smile."

Cougar met her sparkling gaze and felt another grin purse his lips. This flirtatious game was new to Cougar, but he found himself enjoying it immensely. "There is a great deal about you that makes me feel like smiling. Such as touching you here and watching you respond."

Roz caught her breath when he gently stroked her nipple and then bent to take the taut bud into his mouth. "Don't do that, Cougar."

"Why not?" he questioned as his tongue flicked against the rigid peak.

"Because it makes me burn."

His hand drifted over her ribcage, peeling her gown away. His fingertips swirled over her belly, provocatively descending over the satiny flesh on her inner thigh.

"As much as this makes you burn?"

"Almost as much as that," Roz said in a strangled voice.

"And this?"

His fingertips traced her delicately, feeling the dewy

warmth of her reaction. When she shivered helplessly against his hand, Cougar smiled rakishly. "Burning again, Yank?"

"Mmm . . ." was all Roz could manage as his teasing fingertips penetrated and spread, holding her, stretching her until hot chills sizzled through the very core of her being.

When she closed her eyes for a moment, Cougar whispered her name, demanding that she meet his all-consuming gaze. "Look at me. I want to see what you're feeling," he commanded as he stroked her with the utmost care.

"Why?" Roz felt self-conscious about this newly discovered intimacy between them. This was far beyond the wild, explosive passion they had shared that afternoon.

His lips skimmed her mouth in the lightest breath of a kiss while his fingertips excited and explored. "Why? Because I have never been like this with a woman before," he told her honestly, marveling at the way she responded to each inventive caress.

"Never?" Roz whispered shakily.

"Not even once . . ." He bent to brush his mouth over her parted lips. "And just once, I want to know what loving might be like. I want to have all of you . . . in every touch, in each taste, in every sweet response."

"I don't think—" She paused when ripples of pleasure flowed through her as his fingertips probed and his thumb caressed.

"Don't think," Cougar commanded huskily. "I've worn myself out thinking for the better part of the day. All I want is to savor your sweet taste. I want you to teach me to feel again, by letting me feel what you experience when I touch you."

If any other man could have made such an intimate request, Roz would have rejected it. But what this man asked so sincerely was a plea to reclaim his own emotions, to escape the rigors of hell that had become his only reality. How could she deny him what lesser men had taken for granted? How could she deny herself the pleasure his touch aroused?

"Then love me, Cougar." She met those glistening golden eyes that burned over her like the radiant sun. "Love me until my only reality is you . . ."

Cougar wanted that more than he had wanted anything in his life. He recalled what Gideon had once said about touchstones. This fragile, misplaced beauty had become Cougar's touchstone. Through her, because of her, he was experiencing sensations too incredible to describe, enjoying the sweetest, purest ecstasy life had to offer. Each hot tremor that rippled through Roz scorched him. Each shared kiss was a new breath of life, an addicting taste of rapture. Roz had become the secret fire that inflamed him and he wanted to bathe all his senses in her until she became the only reality he understood.

This time, Cougar promised himself, he was going to cherish each caress and each shivering response. There would be no wild, heated rush to completion. Each touch would become a pleasure unto itself, like a sparkling kaleidoscope that changed from one enthralling image into another. And when Cougar learned every seductive technique to satisfy and arouse this innocent beauty, when she came unraveled in his hands and on his lips, then and only then would he unleash this ravenous hunger that would take him past the point of no return—again.

Cougar had seen the evidence of deep affection only once in his life. Gideon and Francene shared something Cougar had never experienced. If it really were possible for a man and woman to be half of each other's souls, then the Howards were that. Only now was Cougar beginning to suspect there might be some intangible bond like the one the Howards shared. He was feeling a heartwarming, unexplainable magic when he was in Roz's arms.

*Just once,* Cougar thought to himself, *let me know the elusive secret Gideon and Francene share. Let me understand what they feel.*

With dedicated care, Cougar taught himself to give pleasure after he had known only how to inflict pain and seek revenge. Roz's responses to his gentle touch astounded him, bringing a sense of power he had never experienced. The flight of his hands and lips were remarkable discoveries in sensuality that incited more breathless responses.

Cougar learned how, when and where Roz liked to be touched, when to retreat and when to advance. She was like a wellspring of endless reactions, a pool of shimmering heat that burned only for him. He, the deadly avenger who took life, was broadening the dimensions of life, learning to give tender pleasure. And in return, Cougar felt the pulsing desire he aroused in Roz and he wanted to shower her with every ecstasy imaginable . . .

Cougar heard Roz's shuddering gasp when his hand settled between her legs. He felt her body tremble as his palm splayed over her abdomen and he retraced his path with delicate care. He nearly moaned aloud when he felt the dewy heat of her response against his fingertips.

His tongue probed into her mouth at the same moment that his fingertip delved into the secret fire of desire he had called from her. He could feel her burning around his fingertip and it nearly drove him wild with need. He wanted to wrap himself in that dewy heat, to feel her sweet body contracting around him. He wanted to be as close as a man and woman could possibly get— heart to heart and flesh to flesh. He wanted to feel the sun warming his soul while Roz held him to her in the most intimate ways.

Roz strangled on a gasp when his seeking fingertips teased and tormented her almost beyond bearing. She found herself in the grips of sensations so wild and maddening that her body shuddered as if besieged by an earthquake.

"Cougar? What are you—? Dear God . . ."

He could feel her convulsing around his stroking fingertip, feel the wild crescendo of unexpected ecstasy engulfing her. He ached to join her in that far-flung universe where he had sent her, but he longed to pleasure her even more, if only once before they went their separate ways.

Cougar felt Roz tense apprehensively as he slid down her trembling body, relishing the soft contours of her flesh that were so unlike his own. But as his lips skimmed her abdomen, her hand descended, preventing him from proceeding any farther.

"I want all of you," he whispered. "I want to taste you . . ."

When her fingers lifted to comb through his hair, stroking him as she had tried to stroke the cats earlier, Cougar eased lower and lower still. His hand glided over her sensitive flesh and he heard her moan as his lips replaced his searching fingertips.

Her response was instantaneous. Need clawed at Cougar like sharp talons. Each flick of his tongue, each brush of his lips sent sensations spiraling through her and ribboning through him. Sweet intimacy blazed like wildfire. And yet, as eager as Cougar was to slide into that hot flame that burned for him, he wanted to arouse her again and again, for she had become his obsession . . .

"Cougar?"

Roz's wild cry sent shivers pulsing through him, matching the tremors that pulsated through her.

"No . . . please . . ."

Cougar felt her body trembling, and he knew her pleasure as his own again. Only then, only when her raging passion left her arching longingly toward him did he come to her, answering the need he had summoned from her.

Cougar promised to be the epitome of gentle possession . . . until Roz's hand enfolded him, urging him to her, holding him, caressing him with delicate care. He had permitted her liberties he had granted to no other woman. The cost was his self-control, every last ounce of it.

Her stroking fingertips would have brought him to his knees if he hadn't been there already. A killing blow couldn't have devastated him more than her gliding caresses. She had utterly defeated him with her own ardent need to have him buried so deep inside her that neither of them could tell where her passion ended and his ardent desire began . . .

Cougar lost the ability to form logical thought, to control the uncontrollable. He could only respond to instinct, only feel the sheathed warmth that was her, and now him. He drove into her, and she matched each possessive thrust. Each broken breath that caressed his shoulder became his name.

Dangers Cougar had faced countless times without paralyzing fear. But this! This helpless abandon transcended everything he could comprehend. Even the instinctive need for survival failed him. He could have died in Roz's silky arms with only one regret—that he couldn't die with her, a thousand times more. This amazing sense of inner peace and contentment defied explanation. Experiencing these phenomenal sensations was all that enabled him to understand and believe in what he never knew existed.

Even as pulsations of inexpressible passion racked him, Cougar swore he was still free falling through infinity. Indescribable warmth replaced the icy cavern of his heart and Cougar discovered the kind of satisfaction that life had never before offered him—blissful, uninterrupted peace . . .

Cougar fell asleep, knowing he had encountered the worst danger he could possibly confront. He had just discovered what he was better off not knowing: He had one very devastating weakness that went by the name of Rozalie Gaylord. When he had succumbed to need and the overwhelming desire to know what love might have been like, he was setting himself up for inevitable torment.

Learning to live again, to feel with every beat of his heart, to feel a stirring in his soul was an excruciating reminder of how much he had suffered in years past. To care was to become vulnerable. He could *not* allow himself to care so much that giving up this beguiling beauty would peel off another layer of his soul.

Cougar didn't have all that many layers left . . .

# Fifteen

Cougar awoke before dawn, counting the costs of what he had done the previous night. The price of enjoying heaven in Roz's arms was hell. He knew there was no future in this growing attachment to a woman who had no place in his world. When he stirred on the pallet, Roz's silky arm glided over his chest and she snuggled against him while he lay wedged between her and the cats that always slept on the left side of him. When he eased away, Roz's soft moan reminded him of the sweet sounds he had drawn from her in moments of unrivaled passion.

"What's wrong, Cougar?" Roz questioned when she felt the cool air replace the comforting warmth his body provided.

"I have to leave," he said tonelessly.

"Already? But you just got back." Or at least it seemed so to Roz. She had lost track of time when she cuddled cozily against Cougar.

"Coming back was another of my many mistakes," he muttered in self-contempt.

Roz levered up, favoring her tender leg that was worse for wear after a night's sleep on the hard ground. Silently, she feasted on the sight of his silhouette—all rippling muscle and lithe strides. The Greek gods, Roz decided, had nothing to compare with this sinewy specimen of living strength and catlike agility. He invited— and more than satisfied—feminine fantasies when he was in one of his gentler moods. Roz knew she would never be able to look at another man without making comparisons, without discovering that all other men fell short of Cougar's mark.

She loved him, even when she knew he could never return the depth of her affection. She wanted to be with him for as long as he would permit. This, Roz knew, was what had been missing from her life. Love. It was what her own father had never understood, that which she had craved as a child and never received. History was about to repeat itself. Edward Gaylord had never really loved her for what she was, but that had never stopped Roz from loving. And now, with Cougar, nothing could restrain the tender emotion after it had taken root and grew like a wild weed.

To all the world, Cougar may have been a deadly predator who terrified criminals. But Roz had discovered a very different man buried beneath fierce iron will and impressive survival skills. Life had forced Cougar to become hard and callous, but love could transform him. Even if Cougar would accept nothing else, Roz vowed that he would have her love, no strings attached. He needed to know he was appreciated and loved, that he was respected for something other than his unrivaled combat skills.

"I'm coming with you," Roz announced as she snatched up her clothes and hurriedly pulled them on.

*"No.* You won't like what you'll see, Yank," Cougar assured her as he strapped the bandoleers in place.

"Then I won't watch."

"I said no." Cougar's voice cracked like a whip.

Roz smoothed her gown into place, raised a determined chin and limped up in front of him. "Fine, leave me behind, but know that I intend to follow you. I want Caleb rescued every bit as much as you do."

Cougar snorted sourly. "Yesterday you were content to remain behind because you knew you would only slow me down."

"That was yesterday. This is now," she said as if that explained everything.

It made no sense to Cougar. But then, he had never claimed to understand the workings of the female mind, especially a white woman who had grown up in that faraway place called New York.

"And what, I'd like to know, has changed so drastically now?" Cougar demanded as he fastened his holsters in place.

Roz looked him squarely in the eye, even though he was glaring at her as if she were his worst enemy. She refused to be intimidated, because she knew he could be as gentle as he was fierce. He may have fooled the rest of the world, but he could no longer fool her. She knew him better than anyone.

"Well?" Cougar growled impatiently. "What has changed, Yank?"

"I love you and that makes the difference," she blurted out before she lost her nerve.

A breath of wind could have knocked Cougar flat. "You *what?*" he croaked, frog-eyed.

"You heard me. I love you."

He gaped at her as if she were insane. "Why?"

Roz frowned in frustration. "Do I have to have a reason?"

"I sure as hell think so," he muttered at her.

"That's because you're accustomed to dealing with hard truths," she said sensibly.

He scowled at her. "And what kind of truth is love? A woman's foolish fantasy?"

He was being exceptionally difficult. So what else was new? "Have you some reasonable objection to being loved?" she countered.

"I'm not comfortable with it," he grumbled. "And that wasn't what I wanted from you."

"Just exactly what did you want from me?"

Cougar swore under his breath, at a total loss as to how to handle this situation, having never before found himself in one like it. "I simply wanted what we had last night. Satisfaction. No complications, no obligations."

Roz almost felt for sorry for him, because he wasn't prepared to deal with her feelings for him. Difficulty he could understand. Fighting was what he did best, and Cougar was fighting now, she noted. Roz bit back a smile when Cougar awkwardly shifted his weight from one moccasined foot to the other.

"You'll get used to being loved eventually," she assured him.

He jerked up his head and his golden eyes glowed in the darkness. "You'll be gone eventually, Yank. That is reality."

"Not if you agree to let me stay here with you—"

"Which I won't," he said curtly. "You don't belong here and you damned well know it. What happened yesterday won't ever change that."

Cougar wheeled around and stamped toward his horse. He stopped short when he heard Roz tramping on twigs behind him. "I said . . . you aren't coming with me."

"And *I* said I was, even if I have to limp every step of the way."

Cougar bared his teeth and flashed Roz his most ferocious glare. "I could sic my cats on you, Yank."

"You could but you won't," she said with infuriating conviction.

Cougar expelled an audible sigh. Damned independent-minded woman. He knew she was trouble the moment he'd laid eyes on her and his prediction had come true. Now she had convinced herself that she was in love with him, just because he had taken possession of her body in moments of uncontrollable desire.

The next thing he knew she would try to convince him that he was more of a gentleman than he ever planned to be. Well, it wasn't going to happen because he had no desire to live up to her noble expectations. He was what he was and he had grown accustomed to what he was. Nothing was going to change him. This love business had to stop.

Scowling, Cougar lifted Roz onto his horse. He cursed under his breath when he noticed the self-satisfied smile twitching her lips. She wouldn't be smiling for long, he assured himself. Seeing him in action would cure this ridiculous fascination she had labeled as love.

Yes, Roz had made him feel emotion he swore was

dead and buried. But he and Roz were fated for different roles in life.

Setting his jaw in grim determination, Cougar urged his steed forward and called to his cats. He was going to break Rozalie Gaylord of any notion that they could share a future together, even if she did have the amazing knack of turning him wrong side out when they were in each other's arms. She wouldn't like what she was going to see, but Cougar would make her watch, if only to drive home the point that the stories circulating about him were fact, not fiction.

Roz wasn't being realistic right now, Cougar mused as he followed the Indian trail over the mountains, but she would be very soon . . .

While Cougar picked his way around the mountains, Roz slept trustingly in his arms. She had curled upon his lap like a kitten and nodded off a half mile earlier. Cougar muttered at himself when he realized he had nuzzled his chin against the tangle of silver-blond hair that spilled over his shoulder.

What the hell was wrong with him? He had an important task to perform. How could he mentally prepare himself to deal with Roche's raiders while he was lollygagging with this damnfool Yankee who had taken it into her head that she had fallen in love with him.

When Roz stirred and shifted on his lap, Cougar inwardly groaned at the tantalizing feel of her bottom. His spontaneous reaction had him scowling again. When Roz was underfoot—or in lap, as the case happened to be—he couldn't even trust his own body. Cougar had become too aware of her, had spent entirely too much time getting to know her, had become too attentive to her needs. If he didn't focus on his main objective he might miss the opportunity to lessen the odds and rescue Caleb from inevitable disaster.

"Wake up, Yank," Cougar murmured as he gently eased Roz away from his chest. "I've got things to do."

Roz purred drowsily and attempted to cuddle against his masculine warmth. Cougar grumbled at the tender emotion her gesture evoked. Curse it, he could not let this delicate female turn him into a tame pussycat. He wouldn't know what to do with himself.

"I mean it, Yank," Cougar growled in his most menacing voice. "Wake the hell up!"

When Roz didn't so much as flinch at his abusive tone, Cougar heaved an exasperated sigh and swung from the saddle. Off balance, Roz tumbled into his arms. Cougar quickly deposited her on the outcropping of rock that would provide her with a bird's eye view of the mine shaft where Roche's raiders had holed up for the night.

"What are you going to do?" Roz asked, her voice raspy from her nap.

Cougar steeled himself against that provocative tone. "I'm going to do what has to be done. Always that, Yank. Now, tell me which of the outlaws best compares to me in size and stature."

"No man compares to you, Cougar," she said without hesitation.

Cougar forced himself to ignore the compliment and the tingle of pleasure that accompanied it. "Which man?" he demanded to know.

Roz thought about it for a moment. "I suppose Hud Caine comes the closest to your height and build, but he has a beard and mustache."

Leaving Roz frowning at the reason for his inquiry, Cougar placed his rifle in her lap and spun away. With a quiet command to the cats, Cougar became one of the soundless shadows that loomed in the trees. He had to focus all mental and physical power on his purpose, to become a cunning predator, like his totem. He had to shed every ounce of wasted emotion and rely upon primal instinct. He could not allow Jake Roche to believe he would be safe anywhere in this range of mountains, not even in the mine shaft.

The only refuge Jake Roche would find from the Cheyenne prophesy was in the fiery pits of hell.

Cougar left the cats fifty yards from the entrance of the cavern and paused to smear coal on his face, arms and chest. He had already changed into dark breeches to transform himself into a living shadow that could pass undetected in the darkness. What he was about to do demanded unfaltering precision and the utmost silence.

From what Roz had told him, Caleb had been tied on a leash. Getting to the young boy who was certain to be surrounded by men would be impossible. But Cougar could get his hands on one of the outlaws and haul him away before the other men realized what had happened.

Inhaling a steadying breath, Cougar centered all thought, all action on single-minded purpose. He reached deep inside himself as the Cheyenne oracle had taught him to do, absorbing the power of the spirits that dwelt in these mountains since the beginning of existence. He called upon the great powers that ruled Mother Earth, immersed himself in the darkest depths that white men had not learned to draw upon.

Years of mastering self-control and dealing with perilous danger had prepared Cougar to attempt the impossible, to challenge overwhelming odds and succeed. When he transported himself to the innermost reaches of what he could become when necessity demanded, very few people recognized him because he no longer thought and reacted like a man. He became the cougar . . .

Hudson Caine rolled onto his back when an unexplainable sensation trickled down his spine. Caught between wakefulness and sleep, he stirred momentarily, relaxed and then roused to the odd chill that pebbled the side of his face, brushing against his beard. The campfire at the mouth of the cavern, near where he had bedded down for the night, had burned itself out, leaving a dampness in the dungeon where he slept. Only a thin shaft of moonlight hovered in the mine shaft. Hud was vaguely aware of the echo of horses' hooves thudding in the dust . . .

Another cold draft swept over Hud as a kerchief fluttered over the lower portion of his face. He sucked in his breath, inhaling an unidentifiable scent that quickly wrapped itself around his groggy senses. With each breath he took, the sensation of floating overwhelmed him. Hud had the eerie feeling that someone or something was climbing inside his skin with him. And yet, the overpowering scent that clogged his nostrils and throat prevented him from protesting whatever it was that was happening to him. The powdery taste in his mouth seemed to amplify the sound of his own breathing and bright colors condensed before his eyes. He felt as if he were falling into a strange trance, drifting beyond reality.

As if he had sprouted feathery wings, Hud felt himself coiling upward until his wobbly legs were beneath him. His head rolled against his shoulder. Sluggish instinct warned him to object when he was propelled toward the faint splinter of moonlight.

Venturing outside the cave invited danger, Hud remembered that much. But some indescribable force was urging him forward. For a half second, Hud balked, driven by the instinctive need to return to the darkness where the other men slept, but pain seared the nerve between his neck and shoulder like the abrupt prick of a knife. The sensation left him dizzy and disoriented. Hud felt himself half dragged, half carried from the safety of the cave . . .

Hud's breath lodged in his throat when the kerchief was drawn away and he saw golden eyes staring at him from the blackness of night. Hundreds of golden eyes . . . But that couldn't be, he thought dazedly. The night didn't have eyes . . . did it?

And then he heard the strangest, quietest voice calling to him, as if it were his own echoing thought.

"The ghost cats have come to collect another doomed soul . . ."

By the time the haunting words soaked into Hud's fuzzy brain, it was too late. He knew he was about to meet a most unpleasant fate . . .

* * *

Roz sat upon her stony perch, stung by an unnerving sensation that brought her fully awake. There was an odd stillness in the dark hour just before dawn, a silence she couldn't describe. It was as if there were some supernatural presence lurking in the shadows.

Flickers of gold blinked in the distance, as if the night had eyes. Roz shivered at the eerie wind that drifted over the mountains, and she tried to tell herself that her imagination was running rampant.

She hadn't seen Cougar enter the cave, but she spied Hud's sluggish form wobbling in the scant moonlight, accompanied by what looked to be no more than his own dark shadow. Roz clutched the rifle and held on tightly when another unexplainable sensation slithered down her spine. She knew, without knowing how she knew, that the floating shadow was Cougar.

How Cougar had crept into the mine shaft to locate the man she had described without disturbing the other raiders was beyond Roz's comprehension. But then, she recalled what Cougar had said about doing whatever had to be done.

To a man like Cougar there were no limits, no boundaries to contain him. What had to be done was his mission and he had the astounding knack of devising methods to succeed against difficult odds . . .

When Roz heard the unnerving screams of cats filling the darkness, she gulped audibly and clung to the rifle. The unholy sound seemed to echo around the canyons, as if hundreds of unseen creatures where chanting in chorus, refusing to let the haunting call die.

Roz felt as though she were sitting in the balcony of a theater, watching an unsettling scene unfold on a stage spotlighted by the first golden rays of dawn. Crouched shadows appeared from three different directions, condensing out of the night, gracefully leaping on the staggering man who flung up his arms in a futile attempt to protect himself.

Hud's terrorized screech sent icy tingles up and down Roz's spine, pricking every inch of her flesh. The vicious growls and snarls of attacking cats mingled with Hud's wails of pain. Roz watched Hud sink beneath the pouncing shadows, heard the strangled gurgle of his breath before his cries of horror drowned beneath muted growls.

Roz knew Hudson Caine had met his end before he had realized it himself. The desperado wasn't even allowed to breathe his last breath. It had been stolen from him by the cat that stood on his chest, its deadly jaws clamped around his throat.

Sickened, Roz turned away to inhale a shuddering breath. This, she decided, had been her punishment for daring to declare her love for a man who had very convincing ways of proving to her that he was not capable of giving or accepting affection, that he was only capable of vengeful retaliation.

But Roz knew better, despite what she had seen. She had experienced the tenderness of the man who lived inside that deadly shell. There could be more to Cougar than burning hatred and uncompromising revenge, if only he would permit himself to believe in the goodness inside him. And no matter how repulsed Roz was now, she reminded herself of the gentleness Cougar displayed when he touched her. All he needed was to give himself the chance to let love grow from the seed Roz had tried to plant. His killer instinct could be tamed if someone would only believe in him.

Roz believed in him.

She repeatedly reminded herself of that, while the menacing snarls faded into deafening silence . . .

# Sixteen

"What was that?" Vito Guerero jerked upright, staring in every direction at once. Another formidable scream pierced the night, on and on until Vito covered his ears and swore profusely.

"Get yourself under control," Burney snapped at the hysterical Mexican. When his terse demand went unheeded, Burney rolled to his knees to level a blow that sent Vito sprawling on his pallet. "If you don't shut your damned mouth, I'll feed you to Cougar myself!"

"You might as well," Vito muttered out the side of the mouth that wasn't swollen from the brutal blow. "That's what you and Jake are planning to do anyway, isn't it? You don't want to split the gold with us. That's why you sent Skeet back down the trail, letting Cougar have him for a midnight snack. You'll do that to every one of us before this is over."

"I said . . . shut up!" Burney snarled malevolently.

"I think we should let the kid go," Vito insisted. "It's our only chance of escaping alive."

"No," Jake denied. "The kid is our insurance. That half-breed can't get to us if we have a hostage."

"I want my cut of the gold and I want out," Vito demanded.

A steel blade flashed in the scant light. Vito swallowed his breath.

"You'll get your cut quicker than you think, amigo, if you don't curb your tongue," Burney promised in a deadly hiss.

Vito clamped his lips together and reached for the shirt he had left beside his pallet.

"We may as well mount up," Jake declared, rolling to his feet. "Hud, kick the stones away from the campfire so we can lead the horses through the shaft.

The command was met with silence.

"Hud!" Jake barked impatiently. "Get up and get moving!"

More silence.

Swearing foully, Jake stamped over to the dark niche beside the entrance to nudge his confederate awake. The toe of his boot connected with air. "Damn it to hell. Where did that fool go?"

Uneasiness descended over the cavern like a black cloud. Jake counted shadowed heads and came up one head short.

"Cougar got him," Vito whispered nervously.

Burney expelled a sardonic snort. "You think that bastard Injun floated in here and carried Hud off? Damn, Vito, your imagination is running away with you—"

The wild, eerie scream of a panther sliced across Burney's words.

"I wonder who's going to be his next victim?" Colby Jordan murmured to the darkness at large. "I'm beginning to think Vito's right. Those legends about the Cat

Man carry more truth than any of us would like to believe. I think we should—"

"You don't get paid to think," Jake scowled. "Just gather your gear and saddle your horse. We're getting the hell out of here before daylight. I don't intend to be picked off by a rifle. And the kid will be riding with me, in the middle of the pack."

"I'll take care of the kid," Vito eagerly volunteered.

"You can't even take care of yourself now that your imagination has gotten the best of you," Jake taunted.

"We should draw straws to see who's going to be the first one out of this hellhole," Colby insisted.

"We don't have straws," Burney snorted.

"You have sticks of beef jerky," Caleb piped up.

"Shut your mouth, kid," Jake snapped irritably.

Caleb stared toward the cave entrance, smiling to himself. "I told you Cougar would come . . . and keep on coming—"

A pained wail emerged from Caleb's lips when Jake backhanded him, sending him rolling to the end of his tether.

"You keep running off that mouth of yours and you'll be walking around with my dagger sticking out of your back," Burney threatened.

Caleb whimpered in pain and wiped away the trickle of blood from his lower lip. Before he could muffle another sniff, Jake jerked him to his feet and shuffled him toward the horses that had been hobbled in one of the side tunnels. Caleb was uplifted and then anchored in place before the raiders ventured outside.

"What the—?" Colby shrieked in surprise and shrank back when a dark hand shot out of nowhere to jerk the reins from his grasp. The horse trotted forward and Colby recoiled against the wall. Breathing heavily, he listened to pounding hooves fade into silence.

"The son of a bitch stole my horse!" Colby chirped after he regained his powers of speech. "I'm not going out there without a shield!"

"Go fetch Hud's horse," Jake commanded. "He certainly isn't around to use it."

"No, he's probably as deep in hell as a buzzard can fly in a week," Vito muttered. "And there's no telling who'll be joining him there next."

"Keep your pessimistic thoughts to yourself," Jake muttered at Vito. "We'll hightail it out of these mountains as quick as we can, and head for Mexico. Your kinfolk can put us up while we wait for things to cool down on this side of the border. The authorities can't get to us there."

"No," Vito agreed. "But Cougar can. He's a law unto himself and he won't stop hounding us until we give him the kid—if even then. I'd rather face those Rocky Mountain Detectives than Cougar. He's put a death wish on all our heads."

"Your first concern is going to be the death wish I put on your head if you don't stop spouting like Old Faithful," Burney snapped. "I'll save Cougar the trouble and keep your part of the gold for myself."

"That's just what I thought," Vito grumbled.

"Silence!" Jake demanded as he shoved Vito and his mount through the exit. "Together we have a chance against that half-breed bastard. Apart, he'll eat us alive. We're playing right into his hands by arguing among ourselves. I've dealt with enough Injuns to know their tactics.

That's what they all do best—sneak up when you're fool enough to turn on each other. Now get moving!"

With pistols drawn, the raiders skulked out of the mine, guarding each other's backs. They thundered down the trail as if the devil himself were nipping at their heels. Jake refused to slow the pace until he had put miles between himself and the living curse that followed them.

Jake swore profanely when he realized that another route had been blocked by falling debris, forcing him south toward the Garden of the Gods that was said to be one of the Indian's spiritual haunts. Jake wasn't about to set foot anywhere near the rising towers of rock, even if the area could provide protection against a hail of bullets. If there was the slightest bit of truth to the legends about that wily Cheyenne half-breed, Jake was taking no chances. And he wasn't slowing down until he reached the Mexican border.

"You did that on purpose, didn't you?" Roz accused when Cougar strode toward her.

"I did what on purpose?" he questioned, as he tucked the bag of secret charms in his pocket.

"Made me watch what you did to Hud. But it changes nothing. I want you to know that."

"It changes everything and you could see that if you hadn't taken the crazed notion that you have to love the man who deflowered you," he said brusquely.

Roz blinked and stared into Cougar's chiseled features, noting the harsh glitter in those amber eyes. "Is that what you think I think?"

"That's what I know."

"You are an authority on women, and on me in particular?"

"A greater authority than you are on men," Cougar muttered at her.

Roz studied Cougar's dispassionate expression for a pensive moment. "You did what you felt you had to do to discourage me, and I will do what I feel I must do," she said as she propped herself on the rifle like an improvised crutch.

Roz was developing entirely too much spirit. That wasn't good. Every ordeal she endured increased her self-confidence.

"Now is not the time for this conversation," Cougar said, ushering her down the hill toward the waiting horses. "We have plans to make."

"Maybe this isn't the time or place, but I am here to say that I know there's much more to you than meets the eye. You're not as unsociable and cantankerous as you would have the world believe. You can be very kind and gentle. Why can't you simply admit that?"

Cougar pulled up short and glared at the infuriating female who was trying to use the power of suggestion to transform him into something he was not. "Look, Yank, we had a roll together," he said bluntly. "I admit taking you wasn't the smartest thing I've ever done, but it happened. You could have been any woman and it would have made no difference to me."

Roz winced at the harsh declaration. Then she convinced herself that Cougar was only trying to discourage her by flinging insults. She was not going to knuckle under, no matter what he said. She simply knew him better than he wanted anyone to know him. He was battling her, just as he battled every obstacle he confronted. That was second nature to Cougar. But Roz was not backing down and she wasn't going to slink off in tears, either. Cougar was being deliberately cruel, and she was going to be deliberately strong-willed, so there!

When Cougar's harsh words didn't produce the results he expected, he flashed Roz a stony glare. "It wasn't love we made together, Yank. It was lust—pure and simple. If you'd been around, you would know that for yourself. Since you haven't been, you'll have to take my word for it. And when this is all over, I'm taking you and Cal back to Howard Station so you can go home where you should have stayed in the first place. The Colorado wilderness is no place for a wealthy debutante and I'm not the man you want me to be, not even during a quick tumble to ease my male needs." He stuck his growling face into her and added, "You got that, Yank? Physical satisfaction is all we shared and all we will ever share!"

Roz tilted her chin up a notch to meet his blistering glare. "You are not talking me out of what I feel, Cougar. I asked nothing of you in return. I gave you a gift—pure and simple. Just accept it."

"No."

"You're impossible!"

"That's what I've been trying to tell you," Cougar insisted as he scooped her up and tossed her, none too gently, on the horse he had confiscated from Colby Jordan.

Roz grimaced at the pain that shot down her leg, as she battled the sharp rejection Cougar had delivered and tried so hard make it stick.

"I have always been a woman who knows her own mind," she told him.

"I'm glad *you* do," he smirked sarcastically.

She ignored that. "I have been educated to the very limit of my intelligence, and I have spent the past few months learning to fend for myself—"

"—And doing a poor job of it."

She ignored that, too. "And I will have you know that I have been courted for my inheritance and ordered about by a domineering, uncaring father. But nothing has altered my basic nature."

"What a shame."

Roz glared at him. "I happen to know exactly what I feel. What we shared was warm and special and you are not going to convince me otherwise." She stared down at him in pure defiance. "I choose to give my heart to the one man who impresses me. That is my prerogative. You don't have to like being loved, but you are stuck with it!"

Cougar scowled at her. "Twice, you have seen what I can become when necessity demands. That is part of what I am, damn it! A rich aristocrat from New York doesn't belong with a half-breed who has blood on his hands and no soul to speak of."

Her chin went up again. "We're wasting daylight. Roche's raiders have a head start. Do you plan to chit-chat all morning or are we going to leave?" She glanced back at him momentarily before focusing her attention straight ahead. "You claim to be a man of action. Now, are you or aren't you?"

Cougar gnashed his teeth at Roz's stubborn defiance. "I am beginning to think I would have been better off if I had left you dangling over the canyon until your arms gave out. You're really starting to irritate me, Yank."

"You made the choice," Roz took great pleasure in reminding him. "Now you have to live with it."

Yes, he had made the choice, Cougar thought sourly. But by the time he finished proving to Roz Gaylord that all those unnerving legends about him were based on fact, she would be more than ready to shake the Colorado dust off her heels and head home. She hadn't seen the worst in him yet. Those who had, never lived to tell about it.

Roz would be the only one who would . . . for her own good . . .

Gideon Howard made it as far as the porch of the trading post before he was forced to sit down to catch his breath. His injured leg was killing him and his war wound didn't feel much better. The long days of lying in bed and existing only on chicken broth and an occasional slice of pie had sapped his strength.

"Damn it to hell," Gideon grumbled as he shifted his stiff legs and squirmed on the hard chair.

"I told you to stay in bed," Francene chided, staring into her husband's wan face. "The station is running smoothly, just as I said it was." She pointed toward the tall, dark-haired man who emerged from the barn with fresh horses. "Seth can hitch the team in nothing flat. The coaches are rolling out of here on schedule."

Gideon squinted into the sunlight to appraise his replacement. All right, so Seth Radburn was no slouch when it came to working quickly and efficiently. But Gideon still didn't appreciate lounging around when he was accustomed to keeping a brisk pace. He was going stir-crazy lying in bed with nothing to do and all day to do it.

When Seth noticed Gideon sitting on the stoop he gave a friendly wave and broke into a smile. Gideon sat there like a stump, feeling resentful and utterly useless.

Francene suppressed an amused smile when she glanced down to see Gideon's sour expression. "How long do you intend to sulk?"

Gideon watched Seth fasten the harnesses in place and guide the team into position to await the incoming coach. "I'm not sulking."

"It certainly looks that way to me," Francene observed.

Gideon heaved a frustrated sigh. "This inactivity is ruining my good disposition," he finally admitted. "And just who the hell is that man trying to impress anyway, scurrying around as if hitching teams was some kind of damned race?"

Francene lifted a curious brow. "You're complaining because Seth is highly efficient? I thought you would approve."

"Not if he's hoping to become my permanent replacement," Gideon scowled. "Let him get his own stage station. I've built this one into what it is."

"Oh, for heaven's sake, Gideon. Nobody is trying to put you out to pasture, just because you took a shot in the leg. Seth says the superintendent of the Colorado division is only trying to make things easier on us. Seth seems to be very well acquainted with the superintendent."

"Wonderful," Gideon scowled. "Seth Radburn is probably trying to score points with his friend the superintendent."

"Quit being so suspicious," Francene admonished. "I happen to like the man. He's quick with a helping hand and a smile. There is something oddly familiar about him, though I swear we have never met before. And when Roz returns," she added with determined optimism, "I think the two of them will hit it off grandly."

Gideon jerked up his head and frowned at his wife. "I thought you had visions of matching Roz up with Cougar."

"And you insisted that Cougar has lived alone so long that he will never be the marrying kind," Francene pointed out. "Roz is going to need someone to distract her after her ordeal. I have decided Seth has definite possibilities. For some unexplainable reason, when I see Seth, I automatically think of Roz."

Gideon rolled his eyes and sighed heavily. "Woman, you are beginning to change your mind faster than the weather. And if you don't keep your nose out of other people's affairs you're liable to ruin their lives."

"Is there anything wrong with seeing other couples as happy as I am with you?" Francene questioned, her green eyes shining down on him.

Gideon reached out to give her hand an affectionate squeeze and then glanced back at the lean, blue-eyed young man who was whistling as he worked. "I guess Seth is doing all right," he said, albeit begrudgingly.

"Of course he is," Francene agreed with an impish smile.

"He seems awfully confident for a lowly assistant," Gideon said. "Are you sure that's all he is? I have the feeling there is something he isn't telling us."

"Now you are imagining things, Gideon," Francene replied. "Seth came here, knowing he had a large set of boots to fill and he is only trying to live up to your expectations and gain your respect. I, of course, made mention of the fact that you had been praised as the best stage agent in the territory. But that was nothing new to Seth. He claims the new superintendent has nothing but compliments about the efficiency of our operation. Now, would you like a formal introduction before the noon stage arrives?"

Gideon nodded agreeably, wondering how Francene always managed to raise his spirits, even when he felt like hell warmed over. Of course, nothing would make Gideon feel better than to glance west and see Cougar riding down the trail with Caleb and Roz in tow. Maybe lounging around the trading post with two stiff legs while Seth Radburn put Gideon to shame wouldn't seem half bad.


Roz gasped in amazement when they descended from the timbered slopes to view two miles of huge sandstone formations. It looked as if God himself had hurled stone spears into the earth. The monolithic stones gleamed in the sunlight, set against a backdrop of whispy clouds and towering mountain ridges. The stunning contrast of red rock, thick underbrush and blue-green cedars created a spectacular landscape. Roz twisted on the steed that once belonged to Colby Jordan and retrieved her sketch pad, compelled to add this panoramic scene to her collection.

Cougar cast Roz a brief glance while she hurriedly sketched the impressive Garden of the Gods. "This is another of my clan's spiritual refuges," he informed her.

"I can certainly see why." Roz stared at the jutting stones that resembled cathedral spires reaching toward heaven. "This is absolutely magnificent."

"Kissing camels."

Roz frowned at him. "I beg your pardon?"

Cougar directed her attention toward the ridge of stone that was reminiscent of two camels sitting face to face on the peak of the cliff. Then he pointed toward the bald mountain that scraped the fleecy clouds. "That's Pike's Peak in the distance."

Roz smiled, enjoying the picturesque view.

"Balance Rock is over there."

She surveyed the huge mound of stone that was perched on a narrow base, rising up from a monstrous clump of rock. "Spectacular," she breathed in awe. "I've never seen anything like it."

"Compared to the majesty of Cheyenne Canyon, these are mere stepping stones that lead to the Earth Mother's unrivaled beauty," Cougar assured her, his voice taking on an odd resonance that drew Roz's curious stare.

"Will you show it to me?"

"I'm not sure that's a good idea."

"Why not? Is it too far out of the way?"

"Yes, too far removed from New York, that's for certain," he murmured enigmatically.

Roz was left to ponder Cougar's meaning while he led the way between the magnificent columns of stone and ascended into higher elevations, blazing his own trail to make up for lost time. When Cougar halted on a lofty ridge, he directed her attention toward the distant cliff dwellings etched on the platform of rock. Roz frantically sketched another piece of Mother Nature's fantastic handiwork before Cougar pulled her off her horse.

"I wasn't finished," she complained.

"You can sketch later. There is something here that you must see to believe."

Cougar told himself that he was only killing time until the Roche gang reached the section of the mountains where he would launch his attack. When he charged into the enemy's camp, the late afternoon sun would be at his back, playing deceiving tricks on the desperadoes. Cougar had no intention of allowing the outlaws to recognize him until it was too late to react . . .

"My God!" Roz choked out when Cougar paused at the entrance of a cavern. "What is this place?"

"The Temple of Silence." Cougar stepped inside the musty tunnel to retrieve a makeshift torch, consisting of rags, kerosene and tree branches.

Roz caught her breath when the torch blazed to life, revealing the mystical underground wonderland of stalagmites and stalactites. Crystal onyx, calcite and alabaster sparkled in the torchlight. She had never seen anything so fascinating. True, she had read the accounts of adventurers who had discovered caverns buried deep inside the earth, but words were inadequate to describe the fantastic formations of limestone or the distant murmur of water swirling through the darkness beyond her.

"The Secret Valley of Dreams," Cougar murmured as he held the torch high above his head.

The light speared into the dark recesses and Roz's eyes widened in sheer delight. "This wild, untamed country is an adventurer's paradise! So many remarkable sights to view, to sketch, to experience! How can I ever be satisfied within the confines of civilization after seeing this?" she mused aloud.

Her gaze drifted to the imposing giant beside her, who was also admiring the incredible scenery. And how, Roz asked herself, was any man ever going to satisfy her after she had become so intrigued with this phenomenal creature who didn't know the meaning of fear—or love?

Her life had become a challenging adventure that brought all her senses to life and taught her the importance of living one day at a time, reaping pleasure from every moment. She was no longer existing; she was thriving, learning to become self-reliant, testing the depths of her character, striving to reach her potential.

What a shame that Cougar wasn't willing to give her the chance to become the woman he needed, because she wanted to love him as no other woman had dared to do—not just with her body but with her heart and soul as well . . .

"Here, Yank, hold this," Cougar insisted, jostling Roz from her whimsical thoughts. "We may as well take our meal here before the action begins again."

When Cougar handed her the torch and ambled off, Roz smiled after him. "I love you."

Her soft voice echoed around the cavern, coming at Cougar from all directions at once. He halted abruptly and wheeled around to glower at the lovely but infuriating female who was determined to see something in him that wasn't actually there.

"Stop saying that. I don't want to hear it."

The gruff sound boomed around Roz like thunder, but she refused to be dissuaded. She had vowed to teach this mulish man what love was, even if it was the last thing she ever did.

Still grumbling over his inability to convince the woman that he wasn't the man for her or anybody else, Cougar stamped out to fetch pemmican from the supply sacks. He supposed he should be flattered that an alluring debutante like Roz Gaylord fancied herself in love with him. Instead, it made him uncomfortable. Cougar knew he was unworthy of a woman from her elevated status on the social totem pole. She was the crème de la crème of elegant society; he was rumored to be the devil's henchman. She was a romantic dreamer; he was a realist. She was the sunlight; he had become a creature of darkness.

They had nothing in common but an ill-fated passion that had burned out of control . . .

Cougar's leisurely gait became a dead run when he heard a shriek reverberating inside the cavern. The cats screamed in unison and romped at Cougar's heels as he plunged into the cave. Cougar stared into the darkness, trying to locate the torch he had handed to Roz a few minutes earlier. He could see the golden glow glistening on the shiny limestone wall that was blocked by a cone-shaped stalagmite.

Considering Roz's injured leg, there was no telling what kind of difficulty she had stumbled into. As much as Cougar hated to admit it, he was beginning to see the advantage of keeping that insanely curious imp on a short leash. If trouble didn't find her, she had the unsettling knack of tromping off to look for it. After all she had endured the past week, he would have thought she would have become extremely cautious.

That's what he got for thinking, Cougar decided as he felt his way around the slippery stalagmites to retrieve the flickering torch and the woman who had ventured off to explore rock formations on her weak leg.

# Seventeen

"Cougar?"

"I'm coming, Yank."

Cougar rounded the ten-foot-tall stalagmite, slick with mineral deposits, to see Roz wedged between two shiny boulders. The improvised torch lay on the uneven stone floor, illuminating the niche Roz occupied. Her foot had slid across the slippery deposits and dropped into a crevice between the stalagmites that were separated by a narrow water channel that trickled into the deeper recesses of the cavern.

"Is that your good leg or bad leg?" Cougar questioned as he studied her jackknifed form that was draped over the rocks.

Roz raised her head. "It *was* my good one," she amended, grimacing in pain.

Cougar grumbled under his breath. "You're going to be a lot of help with two lame legs." He cautiously stepped onto the slippery patch of deposits and anchored himself against the conical boulder. "Next time you tromp off to explore unfamiliar territory, remember that curiosity often carries costly consequences."

"I am not a child," Roz huffed, offended by his condescending tone.

"Then stop behaving like one." Cougar positioned himself on the slanted floor beside Roz's lodged leg. When Roz tried to worm her foot loose from the crevice, Cougar gave his dark head a shake. "Just hold still. If I can untie your shoe, you might be able to slip your foot free."

Contorting his body, while attempting to maintain his balance, Cougar groped into the inky crevice to locate the laces.

"I'm sorry about this," Roz apologized. "But I've never been in a cave before. It's fascinating."

Cougar's reply was a muffled snort that could have meant anything.

"I envy your adventurous life in these mountains," she said while he blindly wrestled with the lacings of her shoe. "I could get used to investigating such places as this."

"Not damned likely you'll have another chance. This is dangerous territory. If you venture deeper into the cavern, you'll find the skeletons of those who got themselves stuck and never made it out alive."

"Perhaps I could hire you as my guide," she ventured.

"I've got better things to do." Cougar tugged on the tongue of her wedged shoe. "Pull your foot out, Yank."

Roz braced her injured leg and tried to wriggle her foot from the shoe. It was no use. Her left leg was still too tender and swollen to bear all her weight.

When Cougar heard her quiet hiss of pain, he surged back to his feet, extending himself to grab Roz by the elbows. Before she could object, Cougar gave her a hard, quick jerk, dragging the upper portion of her body across the slick rock. Roz yelped, but she popped out of the crevice like a cork from a bottle. Cougar hoisted her off the floor and wrapped her legs around his hips to give her a piggyback ride to safer ground. When he leaned down to retrieve the torch, they both went sprawling on the mineral deposits that were as slick as glass.

Cougar's chin bounced along the rock floor, causing him to bite his tongue and curse vilely. When Roz tried to lever off him, favoring both injured legs, Cougar caught an elbow in the spine.

"Damn but you're clumsy," he scowled into the floor.

"You don't have to be insulting," Roz muttered at him. "I'm injured, you know."

"Self-inflicted injuries," Cougar reminded her as he came up on hands and knees. "Like I told you in the beginning, Yank, you're out of your element. You wouldn't last a month in this unforgiving wilderness all by yourself."

His comments cut to the quick, but Roz refused to take them to heart. She knew Cougar was doing his damnedest to discourage her from caring about him. But she was not giving up on this man. Somehow, she was going to convince him that having her love him wouldn't be a fate worse than death.

"Climb on, Yank, let's try it again," Cougar said, picking up the torch.

Roz draped her legs over the arms he curled into a makeshift sling and she clamped her hands on his broad shoulders. Surefooted though Cougar was, he had to perform a balancing act to trek over the slimy, sloping floor to reach the entrance of the cavern. Once he had set Roz on a pallet, he reversed direction to retrieve her shoe. She had wolfed down two pieces of pemmican by the time he got back.

Despite his attempt to act the cantankerous grouch who found fault with Roz at every turn, Cougar felt a betraying smile quirk his lips. Roz was ensconced in the corner of the cave on her pallet, looking quite content.

"When we free Caleb, I'm coming back here to paint these caverns," Roz declared between bites.

"No, you aren't," Cougar contradicted. "Very few white men know about this place and I plan to keep it that way."

"Then I'll leave a trail of crumbs like Hansel and Gretel—"

"Who?"

"Never mind."

It was obvious Cougar was unfamiliar with fairy-tales. Maybe that was why he was so cynical about dreams coming true and happy endings. He was a terrible cynic, but Roz forgave him for that. If she had endured all the torment he had encountered, she might have turned out to be as hard and skeptical as he was.

When a muffled howl whistled through the tunnels, Roz jerked upright, eyes rounded in alarm. "Dear God! Do you think someone might be stranded in the dark corridors beyond this cavern?"

Cougar chuckled at her wide-eyed expression. "Possibly, but I suspect it's only the rustling wind that is known to whisper through the cave. Indian legend has it that the spirits reside here. My people also came to this place to pray, fast and await visions."

Roz munched on her meal and listened to the wind echo through the darkness. It was eerie, yes, but utterly fascinating to have discovered such a remarkable place. She could think of nothing she would rather do than set up her easel and paint this colorful wonderland . . .

*Nothing, except earn Cougar's respect and win his love . . .*

The thought caused the contented smile to slide off her lips.

"What's the matter, Yank?"

"You see too much, Cougar," she murmured, smiling ruefully.

"That's what has kept me alive the past eight years—"

"And turned you into the world's sourest cynic?"

Cougar ignored the question and glanced toward the cave entrance to estimate the time of day by the location of the sun. "We better get moving."

Roz came gingerly to her feet, testing the ankle that had been scraped raw when Cougar jerked her loose.

"Are you all right?" Cougar questioned when she gritted her teeth and hobbled forward.

"Considering all the times calamity has struck, I'm in reasonably good condition. But, as you have taken excessive satisfaction in pointing out, I am not accustomed to dealing with these kinds of adventures. This, after all, is your stomping ground. If you were in New York, you probably wouldn't know what to do with yourself. It's all a matter of geography."

Cougar snorted at the unappealing thought. "I have no intention of winding up in New York—ever. I happen to know exactly where I belong, unlike some people I know."

Roz rounded on him, having reached the limit of her patience. "It isn't going to work, you know."

"What isn't going to work, Yank?"

"Your constant attempt to sabotage my thinking, belittling me every chance you get," Roz flashed. "Maybe I'm not as competent and self-reliant as you are—"

"Maybe?" Cougar scoffed. "There ain't no maybe about it, honey. You're as helpless as a newborn cub."

It was a credit to her self-control that she didn't whack him on the head. "Is that what you want?" she challenged him. "For me to become as dispassionate and self-contained as you are? Well, fine, Cougar. From now on, you'll look at me and see your own reflection."

"As I recall, you threatened to do that already," Cougar mockingly reminded her. "But, of course, whites were never worth a damn about keeping their word."

That was the last straw! "All right, Cougar, you have your wish. If you want cheerful and optimistic you'll have to provide it. I'm going to start looking for the worst, never the best!"

"I've been living without cheerful for years, thank you very much. Who needs illusions?" Cougar grunted as he stalked off.

Roz glared daggers at his back. "You will be dreadfully sorry that you drove me to this, Cougar. And one day, I'll hear you beg me to be myself again rather than the spitting image of you!"

"Doubt it, Yank. I always did prefer my own company."

When Roz had limped toward the tethered horses— with no help from Cougar—he was nowhere to be seen. The rustling in the underbrush prompted Roz to pivot around to identify the sound. In disbelief, Roz watched Cougar emerge from the bushes, dressed in the shredded, bloody clothes Hudson Caine had been wearing when he met his dismal fate.

"What in God's name are you planning to do?" she bleated.

Cougar ambled over to retrieve the chunk of coal from his saddlebag and smeared it on his jaw and upper lip, painting on a beard and mustache that resembled the one that had covered Hud's face—before the cats got hold of him.

"Hudson Caine is about to come back to life," Cougar informed her.

"Any particular reason? Or do you derive sadistic enjoyment from impersonating the dead?"

Cougar lifted Roz onto his black gelding. "Hud is going to return to Roche's raiders, the exact same way Skeet Thomas did."

Her blue eyes widened in concern. "You're going to ride into the midst of them? They'll kill you!"

"I don't think so."

"Well, you're the only one around here who doesn't," she sniffed.

"Roche and his men won't be surprised to see Hud's clawed body draped over the horse I stole from them this morning," Cougar said reasonably. "I purposely established the precedent with Skeet. The bandits will try to second-guess me, but they won't realize I'm impersonating Hud until it's too late. At best, I can retrieve Caleb. At worst, I can pick off one or two men before they get off a shot."

"Or get yourself killed," Roz felt compelled to warn him. "And if you do, what am I supposed to do? Paint Caleb and myself out of difficulty?"

"Take the opportunity to mourn my passing," Cougar smirked as he swung onto the mount he had swiped from Colby Jordan. "I'm sure it'll last—at most—through the afternoon."

Roz glanced sharply at him and frowned. "I do not find you the least bit amusing, Cougar."

"I never claimed to have a sparkling sense of humor," he replied before leading the way through the wild tumble of rock to cut the Roche gang off at the pass.

Although Cougar noticed Roz grimacing in discomfort as they scrabbled across rugged terrain and skidded down the trail at steep pitches, he said nothing. He had to stop taking Roz's needs and frailty into consideration, had to ignore this conscious awareness that had him glancing in her direction every other minute to determine how well she was holding up under rigorous conditions. Now was certainly not the time for dangerous distraction. He of all people knew the hazards of walking into perilous situations without being totally focused.

Cougar had less than an hour to forge his way down the stone embankments to reach Roche and his men. He was not riding into the jaws of hell with a confounded woman on his mind! There was only one reason why a man needed a woman on occasion, Cougar reminded himself fiercely. And there was no reason whatsoever why Cougar needed this misplaced debutante, except for the usual reasons.

Cougar headed down the mountain, refusing to risk distraction by monitoring Roz's progress. After all, she was riding his well-trained pony, and that particular horse knew its way around this rough wilderness as well as Cougar did.

* * *

Cougar swore he smelled Roche coming long before he set eyes on the wiry, murdering bastard. As predicted, Roche had strapped Caleb on the saddle in front of him like a protective shield. The other men were left to fend for themselves in case trouble broke out—which it was definitely about to. Rescuing Caleb would be difficult. Cougar was going to have to bide his time and be content with picking off as many men as time permitted before he thundered off again.

"The man who is bringing up the rear of the procession is Colby Jordan," Roz whispered when they halted on a platform of stone that overlooked the winding trail. "He's the one who enjoys intimidating people with his whip. Make sure you don't veer too close to him." She directed Cougar's attention to the lead rider. "Burney Adair threatened to cut out my tongue with his knife. But then, I suppose you are well aware of the man's sadistic penchant for daggers."

Cougar glanced sideways when he noted the lack of inflection in Roz's voice. She was emulating him better than anticipated. Odd, Cougar thought he would appreciate the transformation. He didn't. He hadn't realized how much he had come to enjoy Roz's unshakable optimism . . . until it vanished.

"Roche has no soul whatsoever," Roz went on in a neutral tone. "One look in his beady gray eyes told me that much. His only concern is for himself. Roche would turn on his own men in the blink of an eyelash if it would save his own skin."

Roz had summed up Roche's loathsome characteristics

perfectly. Cougar knew Roche to be a man without a conscience, without mercy. Jake Roche's time would come,
Cougar vowed. Perhaps not now, but soon.

"Vito is the most unstable man of the lot," Roz continued as the unsuspecting procession filed along the
path. "You already have your bluff in on the Mexican.
He's certain you intend to make him pay dearly for what
he tried to do to me."

"He will pay dearly for that," Cougar muttered in
promise.

Roz stared straight into those amber eyes that had begun to take on an icy glitter. "Did you mentally slit your
own throat because of what we did together, Cougar?"

Cougar made an awful face. Roz was too damned
perceptive. He was sorry as hell that he hadn't been
able to control his lusty urges where she was concerned.
He had tried to keep his distance from the beginning,
and he had failed miserably. Since then he had been
mentally punishing himself—and her—because he
found her so compellingly irresistible, even when he
knew damned good and well that they had no future
together.

"You're harboring regrets," Roz speculated in a bland
tone. "And because of it, you are taking your frustration
out on me. But you can stop punishing yourself, Cougar.
I do not hold you responsible for what happened. If I
hadn't wanted your touch, I could have stopped you."

Cougar emitted a snort that indicated he didn't agree.
And he didn't. Cougar hadn't even been able to stop
himself from taking Roz. How the hell did she think
*she* could have stopped him?

"Fine, have it your way. Now that I have adopted

your cynical philosophy, I won't invite your affection again." Roz propped herself against the nearby boulder and stared pensively at the men who plodded along the path below her. "After all, I no longer feel anything, need anything or anyone. I simply exist, just as you do."

Cougar muttered under his breath. He didn't need to deal with this right now.

What was he complaining about, Cougar asked himself. He had driven Roz away from him—physically and emotionally. Now she realized there was nothing about him to love. He had accomplished his purpose. That should have made him immensely happy. So how come he felt as if someone had just pulled his feet out from under him?

Cougar didn't have time to probe the depths of that disturbing question. He had things to do.

"Be careful, Cougar. Don't come back as bloody as the shirt you're wearing."

The request was spoken without emotion. Cougar cringed. Is that how he sounded? Like a talking rock? Damn, if Roz kept this up much longer she would have him hating himself!

Turning away, Cougar made the necessary mental preparations for his attack. He focused completely on the riders on the path below him. There was nothing Cougar wanted more than to destroy Jake Roche and Burney Adair, to fulfill the Cheyenne prophesy. He had lived for this opportunity for years on end.

When Roche and Adair were dead and gone, maybe then Cougar could put his nightmarish past behind him. Maybe then the mournful screams of innocent victims in the camp beside the Washita would fade into silence and the lost souls would finally find peace.

Clinging to that encouraging thought, Cougar left Roz and the pumas among the boulders and led his confiscated mount down the embankment. It was time to let Roche's raiders think Hudson Caine had been returned to them, just as Skeet had . . .

Jake called a halt to water the horses at the meandering creek. He had just issued the signal to mount up when he heard the clatter of hooves on the road.

*"Caramba!"* Vito howled when he saw the lifeless body doubled over the stolen horse. "That spawn of the devil siced his cats on Hud, too!"

"Colby, check to see if Hud is still alive," Jake ordered as he swung up behind Caleb to veer down the grassy slope.

Colby nudged his steed toward the path, grimacing at the shredded shirt and blood-stained breeches that indicated Hud's painful fate. To Colby's shock, the seemingly unconscious rider jerked upright in the saddle and swooped down on him. When icy golden eyes zeroed in on him, Colby automatically reached for his whip. Before Colby could grab his favorite weapon, it was snatched away.

In desperation Colby groped for his pistol, but the snapping whip curled around his neck. Colby reflexively grabbed hold of the whip that constricted his throat, gasping for air. The cry of alarm he had intended to voice never made it past his lips. Wild-eyed, he watched

Cougar rein his mount in a circular motion, keeping the whip so taut that Colby couldn't draw breath.

A quiet snarl that was reminiscent of a pouncing panther penetrated the silence. Colby felt a terrified shudder ricochet through him when he met the deadly scowl that looked as if it were etched in granite. There was no mercy in those chiseled features, in those glistening amber eyes, in the rigid clench of Cougar's jaw. It was just as Skeet and Vito had said: This creature was almost inhuman when he launched an attack.

Although Cougar possessed the keen wit of man, Colby swore this manhunter had the ferocious instincts of a four-legged predator. The look on Cougar's bronzed face decreed that death was the penalty demanded for the crimes Colby had committed. Colby also knew that he wasn't going to enjoy the luxury of breathing his last breath. It was being choked out of him . . .

With an abrupt jerk on the whip, Colby found himself dragged over the rump of his horse by his own weapon. When he tried to pull his tangled foot free from the stirrup, Cougar yanked him sideways.

With no more than a silent scream, Colby plunged off the side of his horse, face down. He tried to spit the dust and pebbles out of his mouth, but he didn't have any breath left. Colby inwardly cursed his fate. He knew he was going to be dragged down the road, just like the men who had been tied behind the stage. And worse, the vision that followed Colby to hell would be that of a dark, snarling face embedded with tawny eyes that promised no mercy . . . and granted none . . .

Cougar never changed expressions while he watched the startled steed bolt forward to gallop down the path, dragging its upended rider behind it. The Rocky Mountain Detectives would be waiting to make an example of what was left of Colby Jordan. It was the best Cougar could offer. He wasn't looking for examples; he was looking for results.

"Colby!" Jake shouted from the sheltering grove of trees. "Is Hud still alive or not? Did that half-breed send another message?"

Cougar offered a muffled response as he slid onto the side of his mount and headed for the clump of pines that skirted the creek. His astute gaze focused on the shadowy figure that lingered by the stream. Just as the panther set its sights on the weakest quarry in a herd of elk, Cougar veered toward Vito Guerero. The Mexican was nursing an injured leg, a stiff trigger finger, and he couldn't swallow without remembering the feel of Cougar's knife at his neck. Vito had gotten off easy . . . until now . . .

Jabbing his knee into the plodding steed, Cougar made a beeline toward the unsuspecting Mexican. When Vito recognized the expert horseman who slid back into the saddle, clutching a knife in his fist, he screamed at the top of his lungs—or tried to. The attack was so swift, the slash to the throat so accurate that the only screech Vito voiced was one of fatal silence . . .

When Vito pitched forward to the ground, sprawled face down in the grass, Cougar swung around to locate Roche and Adair. Since Colby and Vito had proved to be such easy prey, Cougar decided to press his advantage. Nothing would satisfy him more than to launch his full fury on Roche and Adair, here and now.

Revenge was pumping through Cougar like venom.

Killer instinct spurred him to strike hard and fast. He wanted blood—Roche's and Adair's.

Watching Vito cut down brought out a cowardly streak in Jake Roche. When those stone-cold eyes focused on Jake, he bailed off his horse in nothing flat. Surrendering his hostage was the sacrifice Jake had to make to save his own hide. Swearing foully, Jake slapped his horse on the rump and watched it thunder down the embankment with Caleb lashed to the saddle.

"Burney!" Jake frantically motioned for the last surviving confederate to retrieve him.

Burney trotted his horse forward, pausing only long enough for Jake to bound up behind him.

"Let's get the hell out of here!" Jake hissed as Cougar charged toward them.

Burney didn't have to be asked twice. He spurred the sidestepping steed and shot off like a speeding bullet, leaving Jake to hold on as best he could. The unsettling sight of Vito being all but beheaded in less time than it took to swallow was enough to drive him on to escape as far away as possible.

# Eighteen

Cougar cursed mightily when Jake and Burney galloped hell-for-leather across the meadow. He had no time to determine if the fleeing riders had veered north or south after they disappeared over the hill. Cougar only had time to chase down the runaway mount that carried Caleb. He regretted subjecting the young boy to such vicious brutality, but Cougar was accustomed to dealing in extremes. Straying from that policy always proved to be a costly mistake.

Like his namesake, Cougar had learned to go for the throat, to strike swift and fatal blows before his enemy had time to recover and retaliate. A man who had been trained to kill knew no other way to fight. That was what Cougar had tried to make Roz understand when she got off on that wild notion about falling in love with him.

Manhunters learned to kill or risk being killed. Cougar had come close to dying once and he had lain flat on his back for days on end, reminding himself that there was no margin for careless errors in this line of business. The ruthless murderers he encountered were the ones who wrote the code Cougar had been forced to live by.

Cougar imagined that he had successfully driven home that shocking point to Roz when she sat on the outcropping of rock, watching him deal severely with Colby and Vito. And still Roz had not seen him at his very worst. Cougar wondered how she would cope with . . .

"Cougar! HELP!" Caleb wailed in the distance.

Cougar leaned against his steed's neck, clenching his fist in the flying mane to maneuver the horse around the obstacle course of jutting boulders. This horse was nowhere near the animal Cougar's sturdy black gelding was. This mount lacked stamina, speed and agility. Cougar wished he could grow wings and fly down the side of the mountain to reach Caleb before catastrophe struck.

Caleb's wild yelp sent birds fluttering from the overhanging branches. Cougar cursed his mount's lumbering pace. There was no burst of speed when Cougar dug in his heels. He would have to remember not to take his black gelding for granted in the future. That mountain pony was one of a kind, and he wished he was riding it now!

A sense of urgency pulsated through Cougar as he slapped the mount on the rump, demanding more—as much as the horse could give. Caleb was still anchored to the pommel, but he had been knocked out of the saddle during his wild ride. The terrified boy was trying to slide his short legs onto the galloping horse, but to no avail. If Cougar didn't catch up with Caleb—and quickly—the boy would be scraped raw by the jutting rocks.

* * *

Roz cast one last glance in Jake's and Burney's direction before she limped toward the black gelding. Her greatest concern was for the helpless child who could not gain control of his runaway mount. Roz clamped herself around the gelding, despite the tenderness in her knee and ankle. When the steed trotted off, dodging obstacles in its path, the cats bounded from boulder to boulder to remain at Roz's side.

"Dear God!" Roz gasped when she saw Caleb's horse skirting the stone ledge that rimmed the canyon.

Caleb's horse panicked and scrabbled to regain its balance. Its wild scream riveted Roz to the saddle. The terrifying sensations Roz had experienced when her gray mare plummeted over the cliff returned to haunt her. She knew exactly what Caleb was feeling and what his fate would be if he was launched over the cliff, anchored to a falling horse. He would be crushed to death.

Roz heard the frightened horse whinny again and she prayed for all she was worth. Through the tangle of tree limbs she could see Cougar charging straight toward the scrambling horse. His arm shot out as he rode by, clamping onto the bridle. The forward momentum of Cougar's own mount provided the additional balance to prevent Caleb's steed from losing its footing—and not a second too soon.

Breathing an enormous sigh of relief, Roz trotted down the slope to see Cougar cutting Caleb free of the ropes. With a wild wail, Caleb flung himself into Cougar's arms and buried his head against his rescuer's shoulder.

The faintest hint of a smile traced Roz's lips and tears misted her eyes as she watched the frightened lad cling to Cougar like a barnacle to a ship. There was a moment of awkwardness while Cougar adjusted to having the boy hang onto him for dear life.

Tears trickled down Roz's cheeks when she saw Cougar relax enough to wrap his brawny arms around Caleb who was sobbing in great gulps to relieve the pent-up fear that had sustained him for almost a week.

From Roz's viewpoint, the scene was as touching as it was insightful. This hard-as-nails avenger of justice was learning to accept affection and provide compassion, whether he realized it or not. It was simply matter of changing the kind of company Cougar had been keeping for the past eight years. Once Cougar realized that the world wasn't populated exclusively with murderers, scoundrels and thieves he could adjust to the gentler, more civilized side of life.

Watching Cougar comfort Caleb gave Roz hope. Maybe she wasn't woman enough to earn Cougar's love, but maybe others could. Although Roz had vowed to treat Cougar the way he tried to treat her, she would be herself around everyone else. With any luck, that pigheaded man would wake up and realize that expressing emotion and sensitivity was not a symptom of vulnerability, only that he was receptive to giving and accepting love.

Roz reined the black gelding to a halt and gingerly eased down on her tender leg. She drew the sobbing lad from Cougar's arms and cradled him lovingly against her, stroking his tousled head and accepting the tears that dampened her shoulder.

"You're alive!" Caleb blubbered, clinging fiercely to Roz. "I thought—"

"I did go over the edge, but Cougar rescued me, just as he rescued you. We're both going to be just fine, Caleb. And did I mention how proud I am of the way you handled yourself in the face of trouble?"

"N—no," he murmured between shuddering breaths.

"Well, I most certainly am. And you have had a real adventure, haven't you?" She gave Caleb an affectionate squeeze and dropped a kiss to his clammy forehead. "I'm so glad to have you back, Caleb. Cougar tells me that your parents are anxiously awaiting your return."

Cougar had stepped aside to watch Roz work her magic on the terrified lad. He had felt a mite self-conscious about having the stuffing squeezed out of him by the bawling boy, but Roz had nuzzled against Caleb, stroking him, reassuring him. Caleb had instantly responded, and in a matter of minutes, Roz had dissolved his petrifying fear. The touch of her hand and the tenderness in her voice were soothing balms that healed Caleb's emotional wounds.

While Roz was murmuring quietly to Caleb, Cougar glanced in the direction Roche and Adair had taken. He felt compelled to give chase, but he knew he couldn't drag an injured woman and young boy—who'd just been scared witless—with him.

A month ago, Cougar wouldn't have considered a compromise while tracking murdering cutthroats. Roz had definitely influenced him, reluctant though he was to admit it. Of course, he could never change to such extent as to be labeled civilized, but his encounters with Roz had alerted him to the fact that he could still feel emotion, even though he was uncomfortable with the long-forgotten sensations.

Remembering the locket Francene had given to him, Cougar strode toward his black gelding. "Your mother asked me to give this to you when I found you."

Caleb raised his tear-stained face to see the gold chain dangling from Cougar's index finger. A smile curved Caleb's lips as he reached up to clasp the engraved locket, hugging it to his chest.

Cougar felt funny when Caleb opened the locket to stare at the miniature photographs. What the hell was wrong with him? Cougar asked himself. He was feeling all mushy inside. That hadn't happened before. This was no time to be turning soft, not when Roche and Adair had escaped him.

"Your mother said to tell you . . ." Cougar floundered on the words he had never spoken. "She said she . . ."

Roz glanced up, watching Cougar shift awkwardly and stumble over his own tongue. He was so uncomfortable with conveying messages of affection that he was squirming in his skin.

"Your mother said to tell you that she loved you and she can't wait to have you back. Neither can Gideon," Roz assured Caleb while Cougar struggled to formulate the unfamiliar words.

As Roz looked at Cougar, he saw her smile vanish and the sparkle evaporate from her eyes. All the affection and compassion she offered Caleb was purposely being withheld from Cougar, just as he had demanded. Cougar should have been immensely satisfied in knowing that his attempt to place barriers between himself and her had been successful.

*Should have been . . . but wasn't.*

*It was for the best. This was as it had to be,* Cougar reminded himself sensibly. As he had told Roz in the beginning: there was nowhere for them to go, except their separate ways.

After Roz had rejuvenated Caleb's flagging spirits, the boy stood up on his own two feet. Cougar watched Roz limp back apace, her smiling gaze fixed on the lad who had been forced to grow up faster than he rightfully should have, thanks to his unnerving ordeal. Cougar stood in the shadows, compelled to offer comfort and yet unsure how to go about it. The technique seemed to come so naturally to Roz. But then, Cougar reminded himself, Roz was all heart. He'd had his ripped out almost a decade ago.

What difference did it make if he had lost his heart and soul? Cougar asked himself sourly. All he had ever wanted was to seek revenge on Roche and Adair. He wasn't planning to make a place for himself in civilized society, so why was he fretting about his awkwardness? He had a mission to accomplish, one that required no charm or emotion. He would leave the tenderness and compassion to Roz. After all, she was a lot better at it than he would ever be.

"I didn't have the chance to doctor the outlaw's food the way you did," Caleb told Roz as he brushed his thumb over the locket.

Cougar's thick brows lifted curiously as his gaze bounced from Caleb to Roz.

"The men were setting too swift a pace when they discovered you were on their heels," Roz replied as she plucked up the pine needles that clung to Caleb's tattered shirt. "If not for Caleb, I wouldn't have known which herbs to sprinkle in the stew to make them nauseous." She chortled softly, her blue eyes twinkling with mischief. "But we did have our own brand of revenge on them, didn't we, Caleb?"

Caleb nodded his head and tucked the locket in his pocket. He mopped away his tears with his shirtsleeve and lifted his gaze to the looming giant who stood a noticeable distance away. "Can we go home now, Cougar?"

Cougar peered into those doe eyes that were clouded with a residue of tears, wishing he could grant Caleb his fondest wish, but knowing he couldn't. Not yet, not as long as Roche and Adair were running loose. Other lives could be at stake. Cougar had waited eight years to locate those murdering bastards. Caleb was going to have to wait a little longer to be reunited with his family.

"I'm sorry, Cal, but this isn't over yet. I made a promise to track down every last man. Would you have me go back on my word?"

Caleb inhaled an audible breath. "No, sir. Indians always keep their word."

"You have always wanted to see my ranch," Cougar tempted Caleb. "I could take you there while I hunt down Roche and Adair. Would you like that?"

Caleb perked up immediately. "Could we? Really?"

Cougar scooped the boy up and sat him on the gelding. "Consider it done, kid."

"And Miss Gaylord can come, too?" he asked hopefully.

Cougar glanced at the rumpled beauty whose expression altered the instant their eyes met. He could see the transformation taking place, and he felt the warmth drain out of him. He experienced an odd sense of loss when he stared into that bewitching face. Was that how she felt when she looked at him? Was she left yearning for what he refused to offer?

Cougar turned away from those thick-lashed eyes that had recently offered love and now offered only the reflection of his own rigid restraint. Damn it, that woman was making him crazy when she changed right before his very eyes. Now she had Cougar questioning what he wanted and expected from her.

Conflicting emotions—no, conflicting thoughts, Cougar hurriedly amended—were warring inside him. He wanted what he knew he couldn't have. It was completely out of the question to become enamored with Rozalie Gaylord, wealthy debutante from New York. And he had the inescapable feeling he was going to regret leaving Roz at his mountain cabin while he tracked down Roche and Adair. In the days to come, her memory would linger in his own home. Visions would come to haunt him, no doubt about that.

So what was new? Cougar asked himself dourly. He had been tormented for years and he had been cursed before, plenty of times. He just hadn't expected hell to devise new ways to torture him. But sure as the devil, he was going to be cursed for stealing the innocence from this blue-eyed nymph, a woman who deserved far better than the likes of him.

Jake watched Roz pick her way down the side of the mountain, accompanied by the three pumas. "I thought the woman was dead," Jake muttered to Burney. "I'd love to get my hands on her for insurance."

Burney said nothing. He kept visualizing the slash of Cougar's knife and the gurgling whisper that had become Vito Guerero's last breath.

Jake gestured toward the riderless steed that grazed in the distance. "Let's fetch Vito's horse. Vito sure as hell isn't going to need it or the gold in the saddlebags anymore."

Nudging his winded steed, Burney clung to the shadows of the trees to reach the meadow where the riderless mount had dropped its head to graze.

"I'm going to kill that bastard Injun if it's the last thing I do," Jake ground out as he swung onto the spare horse. "Cougar has most of the gold, but he also has the kid and woman to slow him down. I don't know about you, Burney, but I'd rather do the chasing than have that wild half-breed breathing down our necks. We'll never make it to the Mexican border."

Burney nodded grimly. "Tracking Cougar will be the last thing he expects from us. We'll give him a taste of his own medicine for a change. And the first chance I get, I'm picking off those damned cats. We'll see how daring that Injun is without reinforcements."

"We'll let Cougar think we headed down the mountain," Jake insisted. "This time we'll follow him and take him by surprise."

"That's one savage that I'm anxious to see walking barefoot through hell," Burney muttered before he trotted away.

While Roz and Caleb were taking their turns bathing in the stream and changing into fresh clothes, Cougar disposed of Vito's remains. When Cougar returned to the stream, Caleb was doing what he did best—posing questions. Roz smiled patiently while she sketched Caleb against the backdrop of the rippling stream that was flanked by cedars and pines.

"Make yourself scarce while I bathe," Cougar requested as he strode down the creek bank.

"How come?" Caleb questioned. "I've seen you bathe before."

"I prefer my privacy," Cougar insisted.

"I'll find something for us to eat," Roz volunteered.

When she limped away, Cougar peeled off the blood-stained shirt that was two sizes too small and tugged off his moccasins. He glanced up to see Caleb perched on a fallen log, despite the request to make himself scarce. Since Caleb had been forced into silence the past few days, Cougar figured the kid intended to make up for lost time.

"Cougar?"

"What, kid?"

"How come the sparkle goes out of Miss Gaylord's eyes when you come around?"

Cougar scowled at the overly observant boy and then he peeled off his breeches. "Maybe she just doesn't like me."

Caleb gave his head a contradicting shake. "No, she said you were the most remarkable man she ever met and that she owes you her life. I think you should marry her."

Cougar splashed into the stream and reminded himself to be patient with the boy. After all, Caleb had never been able to keep his thoughts to himself. It was his nature to yammer incessantly. "Let's talk about something else."

"Why?"

"Because I said so—" Cougar bit his tongue and tried to employ tact—for once. "Fact is, Yank and I are cut from different scraps of wood. She belongs with her kind in the East. Nothing is going to change that . . ."

His voice trailed off when he caught a glimpse of Roz's blond head shimmering in the sunlight that splattered through the surrounding trees. She was poised on a boulder, sketching him while he stood waist-deep in the creek. While Caleb rattled incessantly, Cougar's attention was transfixed on the dainty imp. Despite the cold water, Cougar felt hungry need simmering inside him. He could stand here until he turned blue, but he wasn't going to be able to curb the desire that forbidden memories incited every time he glanced in Roz's direction. He could almost taste those honeyed lips from here, feel her silky skin beneath his questing fingertips.

Cougar stifled a groan and turned his attention back to Caleb. The kid was safe. The way Roz made him burn was dangerous.

For the next several minutes, he listened to Caleb jabber. Cougar refused to let himself dwell on memories that should not have been. He could not lose sight of his purpose. As soon as Roz and Caleb were settled in his cabin he would track Roche and Adair. Satisfying his revenge after eight long years would be his compensation for turning his back on the one woman who could make him burn like a human torch.

Cougar told himself to be content with that.

* * *

General Cook restlessly paced the perimeters of the camp he and his men had established in the foothills. They had waited several days, hoping for some sign of Cougar or the men he tracked. Although Cook had given his word to block off the trail, he was ready to saddle up and charge into the hills. Any number of things could have happened. Not knowing what was going on was making him stir-crazy.

The clomp of hooves put the troop of detectives on their feet, staring anxiously toward the mound of rock that concealed them from passing travelers. Well-armed and waiting, the detectives watched the laboring steed trot into view, dragging its rider behind it.

"Holy hell!" John Swenson croaked, shoving his Colt into its holster. "Cougar did the same thing to this outlaw that the Roche gang did to the stage passengers. Do you suppose this is the only one left?"

General Cook strode over to halt the horse. He peered bleakly at the battered remains of Colby Jordan who had descended from the mountains with his own whip wrapped around his neck. Cook wondered if this particular criminal was the one who had gotten off lightly. Considering the legendary tales he had heard about Cougar, Cook wouldn't have been surprised.

"Do you think Cougar will be sending other members of the gang to us?" one of the detectives questioned soberly.

"I think," Cook said as he loosed Colby's booted foot from the stirrup, "that we're looking at the only example Cougar intends for us to have—his only concession." His gaze lifted to the craggy peaks. "We may as well gather our gear and head to Denver. I doubt there will be enough left of the other desperadoes to bother with."

John Swenson stared at Colby Jordan, a man who had left a trail of bloodshed in his destructive wake. Colby was about to make his final journey, jackknifed over the back of his horse, verifying Cougar's theory that there was only one way to prevent murderers and thieves from repeating offenses. John was beginning to agree with Cougar. This was a surefire deterrent to discourage outlaws. For certain, Colby Jordan and his biting whip were never going to cause anybody pain and suffering again . . .

# Nineteen

Cougar halted on the cliff overlooking seven spectacular waterfalls that cascaded over a natural ladder of stone, plunging fifteen hundred feet into a picturesque canyon.

Roz gasped in bewildered amazement. "What is this place? Paradise?"

Beyond the canyon lay a magnificent valley that boasted several miniature waterfalls and shady nooks. Of all the scenic sites Cougar had shown Roz during their trek through the wilderness, this V-shaped box canyon and the sprawling valley to the west were the most spectacular. Quartz, feldspar and black mica glistened in the looming walls like sparkling treasures.

"Wow!" Caleb hooted as he surveyed the incredible panorama that spilled before him. "This is where you live, Cougar? No wonder you only come down from the mountains a few times a year!"

"It's a wonder you come down at all," Roz murmured. "I'm not sure I ever would. This is almost heaven."

"This is Cheyenne Canyon," Cougar announced, tamping down the odd sense of pride Roz's words stirred in him. "Before the white men drove my people onto reservations, Cheyenne, Sioux and Shoshone tribes gathered here for the Indian Nation Olympics."

"Just like the Greeks did?" Caleb questioned interestedly.

Cougar nodded his raven head. "We also stampeded buffalo into the canyon when food was needed."

Roz sighed as she stared into the rock chasm that was filled with fir and pine trees. If not for Caleb, Roz doubted she would have been allowed to see this wondrous valley and awe-inspiring canyon. For some reason Cougar had not intended to let her venture here. She couldn't help but wonder why. Did he think she would steal something from his ranch by painting this beautiful scene?

Probably, Roz decided. She had heard that some Indian tribes were leery of having their photos taken. Cougar had certainly objected to being sketched. There was supposedly some superstition about photographs stealing souls from the subjects. Perhaps Cougar felt that same protective need to preserve this glorious canyon that had been the spiritual haunt of Indian tribes. But beauty such as this deserved to be recreated on canvas. To see it was to be compelled to paint it, to savor each fascinating rock formation, each sparkling droplet that cascaded into the misty pool below. What artist could resist such breathtaking landscape?

Before Cougar could lead the way down the trail, the ominous form of an Indian warrior emerged from the shadows cast by a thick grove of cedars. Roz halted her steed to appraise the brawny, dark-skinned man, dressed in fringed buckskin, who looked to be about the same age as Cougar.

Without casting a glance at Caleb or Roz, Gray Eagle spoke quickly to Cougar in the Cheyenne tongue. Cougar was aware that his blood brother was apprehensive about inviting anyone into his sanctuary in this canyon, but Cougar felt he could trust Roz and Caleb with the secret. Of course, Cougar might have to threaten to stitch Cal's mouth shut, but the boy wouldn't divulge the long-kept secret if Cougar ordered him not to. It was what Cougar would demand for saving Cal's life. That, the talkative lad should be able to understand.

"You bring white guests to our sanctuary?" Gray Eagle questioned.

"They will keep our secret," Cougar promised. "They will be safe here while I track down Jake Roche and Burney Adair."

Gray Eagle went as still as the stone walls of the canyon. "They are here?"

Cougar nodded grimly. "They kidnapped Caleb and Rozalie after stealing the gold shipment from the stage station. Both the boy and woman barely escaped death at their hands."

That was all it took to convince Gray Eagle that Cougar had made a wise decision in bringing the boy and woman to this haven in the wilderness. Cougar knew Gray Eagle yearned to fulfill the Cheyenne prophesy as much as he did. They had both witnessed that heart-wrenching massacre on the Washita. They had survived and escaped the confinement of reservations. But neither of them had forgotten their tragic loss.

"Caleb, Rozalie, this is Gray Eagle, my Cheyenne blood brother," Cougar introduced them. "This is his refuge, his home as well as mine. But if white authorities learn of his presence here, he will be taken to the reservations in Indian Territory, no longer free to live in the land that was once ours by right of birth and possession."

"A renegade?" Caleb paraphrased, staring at the lean, angular-faced Indian who stood only two inches shorter than Cougar.

"A misplaced warrior," Gray Eagle corrected in stilted English. "And you must be the boy Cougar has spoken of, the one with the runaway tongue."

Caleb slammed his mouth shut and raised his skinned chin. "I can keep your secret," he said with great conviction." I will keep your secret. I swear it as an Indian because Indians do not lie."

Gray Eagle's dark brow quirked upward as he glanced at Cougar.

"I've been working with the boy every chance I get," Cougar said to him in Cheyenne. "He is our link to future generations of whites."

Gray Eagle nodded agreeably before turning his obsidian eyes on the beautiful woman in pink. His appreciative gaze moved over Roz's curvaceous figure, lingering on the flesh exposed by her scoop-necked gown.

Cougar shifted in the saddle, stung by an unfamiliar sensation. He felt offended by Gray Eagle's gimlet-eyed perusal. On one hand, Cougar was relieved to know that his infuriating preoccupation with Roz was a natural male reaction. On the other hand, he was jealous of his blood brother's probing stare. That was absurd.

"It is my pleasure to meet you, Gray Eagle." Roz extended her hand in cordial greeting. "I cannot blame you for seeking refuge in such a place. It is the most extraordinary sight I have ever seen."

Cougar watched an odd reverence overcome Gray Eagle as he clasped the delicate hand extended in a gesture of friendship and acceptance. *Trouble in the making,* Cougar predicted. Gray Eagle had been practicing celibacy for several years because he had no choice. There were times when the two of them had ventured to Colorado Springs, and they both dressed as white men and employed darkness to conceal their identity. But Gray Eagle had not dared to ease his male needs with the harlots in the town's red light district. Cougar had the feeling Gray Eagle was beginning to suffer the side effects of restraint. It was also glaringly apparent that men from all walks of life were intrigued by this lovely female, whether she was out of her element in Colorado or not.

"You shine like the morning sun, *Vee-hay-Kah,*" Gray Eagle murmured.

*Definitely trouble,* Cougar thought, shifting in the saddle. No doubt about that. "Why don't you climb on behind Cal so we can take our guests to the cabin," Cougar ordered.

Gray Eagle noted the brisk tone and glanced up to appraise the twitching muscles on Cougar's jaw. "Is that a command or a request?" he asked in Cheyenne.

"Take it however you wish, but mount the horse," Cougar replied crisply.

The Cheyenne warrior swung up behind Cal and cast Cougar a speculative glance. "You are angry with me. Why?"

"Because your interest in her is very apparent," Cougar scowled at him.

"She is a beautiful woman and I am a man."

"She is a white woman," Cougar clarified.

"Is she spoken for?"

"No," Cougar grumbled.

"I have many fine horses to trade for her," Gray Eagle said as he took the reins from Cal and reversed direction.

"That isn't the way it's done in the civilized world."

"Well, it should be," Gray Eagle declared. "The way of the Cheyenne is the best way."

"Try telling that to the Great White Chief in Washington," Cougar snorted. "If he believed that to be so, the Cheyenne would not be confined to reservations."

Gray Eagle glanced speculatively at Cougar who took the lead, trotting into the valley where the stone and timber cottage was nestled in a clump of cedars. "You are warning me away from the woman. Why? Is she your woman?"

"No!" Cougar exploded in bad temper.

"How come you two don't speak English so we can understand you?" Caleb demanded to know.

Cougar expelled his breath and struggled to reclaim the reins to his temper. "We were having a man-to-man discussion."

"Oh," Cal said. "What about?"

"Many things," Gray Eagle replied, casting another discreet glance at Cougar. "One day, when you are a man, we will discuss such things with you."

Caleb lapsed into silence and Cougar was eternally grateful. He was not in the mood for twenty questions.

His thoughts were on the two butchering men who had eluded him and the difficulty he foresaw with Gray Eagle's fascination with Roz. He was going to have to be told that this sophisticated female was off limits to him, just as she was to Cougar. Unfortunately, Gray Eagle knew so little about white culture that he wouldn't understand why he couldn't trade a few good horses for the woman he desired, provided the object of his fascination found him worthy and appealing. To Gray Eagle, it was a simple matter of taking what he wanted after respectfully offering a comparable prize.

Cougar and Gray Eagle were going to have a nice long chat the first chance they got.

While Cougar was prowling with his cats and Roz was sketching the scenery, Gray Eagle prepared a pallet beside the hearth for young Caleb.

"Have you been hiding in the mountains all these years?" Caleb questioned.

The warrior nodded affirmatively. "While Cougar pursued his manhunts, I tended the livestock. It would have invited trouble for me to venture too deeply into your civilization. I have no wish to be sent to the reservation when none of my clan is left."

"Cougar says I should learn all the ways of the Indian, like he learned the ways of the whites."

Caleb surveyed the weapons and trinkets of beads, bone and conchos that hung above the mantle. The war club, battle hatchet and war bonnet momentarily captured his interest. Then his attention shifted to the buckskin case that contained a bow and arrow and a shield adorned with the colorful Thunderbird.

"If I would have been trained like a warrior, I could have escaped from those men . . ."

Caleb's voice trailed off and Gray Eagle was quick to note the mist of tears that clouded Cal's eyes. "The true test of a man, my young friend, is his ability to learn from his trials, to invent ways to escape. Cunning is the way of the Indian."

"Will you teach me the Indian ways?" Caleb requested, staring hopefully at the muscular warrior.

"Cougar and I will both teach you," Gray Eagle promised. "And you will teach me the ways of the white man. Do we have a bargain?"

Caleb nodded enthusiastically. "What would you like to know about the white man?"

Gray Eagle smiled wryly as he gathered more quilts for Cal's pallet. "How does a man go about courting a woman in your world?"

Caleb considered the question for a long moment, recalling how the men at the trading post bowed over Roz and scrambled to pull out chairs at the table for her. "The first thing a man must do is to be especially nice."

"Nice?" Gray Eagle frowned, bemused. "In what way?"

"By giving compliments," Caleb instructed, recalling the comments he had overheard at the stage station. " 'Your dress becomes you. Your eyes are like twinkling stars,' " he quoted. Then he thought of the affection Gideon and Francene displayed toward each other when they didn't think he was looking. "And then comes the hugs and kisses."

Gray Eagle blinked, surprised. "Those things are allowed in courtship?"

Caleb nodded confirmation.

"It is the Cheyenne custom for a man and woman not to touch or exchange too many words or glances. To do so indicates that you have not been taught the proper rituals. If a woman finds a man to be an acceptable suitor, she tells him that she would like to associate with him sometime in the future."

"What does that mean?" Caleb questioned.

"It means that she finds him pleasing."

"Why doesn't she just say so?"

"Because it is not proper," Gray Eagle patiently explained. "If a man comes to visit an Indian maiden at her family's lodge, she never allows him to stay overly long. Occasionally, a match is made by a woman's father after he visits the camps of other clans."

"You mean people get married without knowing each other?" Caleb asked. "Whites don't do things like that very often. I've heard of mail-order brides, but most folks do their courting in person."

"Then it is permissible to hug and kiss the woman you wish to court?" Gray Eagle persisted. "This is not taboo in your culture?"

"Naw, grown-ups hug and kiss all the time." Caleb tired of the topic. His gaze swung back to the weapons hanging over the mantle. "Will you teach me to use the bow and arrow? Cougar tried to teach me to handle a rifle, but he says it isn't my kind of weapon."

"If that is your wish." Gray Eagle lifted the bow from its hook and turned toward the door. "We must also find a name for you, young warrior."

Caleb beamed in delight as he trailed behind Gray Eagle, chattering nonstop. Gray Eagle pulled up short, causing Caleb to ram into him. "The way of the Indian is silence. We learn from the creatures that live in accord with nature. You must also listen if you are to understand the ways of the People." He smiled slyly. "I do not think you would like to be given the name of Thunder Mouth."

"I won't say another word," Caleb vowed determinedly.

Stifling an amused grin, Gray Eagle watched the boy clamp his lips together. "We will see if you are a man of your word."

"Of course I am—"

Gray Eagle arched a challenging brow.

"Sorry, I forgot already."

"Do not forget again, my young friend," Gray Eagle said as he strode out the door.

He recalled what Cougar had said about the talkative Caleb Howard. It was going to take considerable effort to break the boy of chattering, just to hear the sound of his own voice. But Cougar had also hit upon an important truth when he claimed this young lad was their link to future generations of whites. Caleb was also Gray Eagle's link to the curious customs of civilization, and more particularly to the courtship rituals that would gain him notice with the bewitching blonde known as Rozalie Gaylord.

# Twenty

Cougar propped himself against a tree and studied the shapely silhouette perched beside the miniature waterfall west of his cabin. Roz had made herself an improvised easel of string and branches to sketch the sprawling valley and the herd of cattle that drank from the stream. Although Cougar vowed to keep his distance, refusing to tempt himself again, he could not stop himself from observing Roz. He liked looking at her, envied her talent of creating rather than destroying.

While Gray Eagle was getting Caleb settled and Roz was sketching, Cougar had wandered off to collect more healing herbs to apply to Roz's injured leg. The cats had accompanied him, but sensing his restlessness, they wandered off to hunt, while Cougar found himself circling back to find Roz. He needed to drive home the point that they had made a careless mistake by becoming intimate.

While Cougar went in search of Roche and Adair, Gray Eagle could accompany Roz and Caleb back to civilization. That was best . . provided Gray Eagle didn't get some crazed notion about keeping Roz for himself.

Pushing away from the tree, Cougar silently made his

way toward the woman who was bent over her sketch in profound concentration. "Yank, I've decided—"

Roz was so preoccupied with her work that she nearly came out of her skin when the voice resounded from out of nowhere. Her knee bumped the easel, causing it to topple over. When Roz tried to grab the paper, her pen scraped horizontally across the sketch on its way to the ground.

"Blast it, Cougar. Will you please stop sneaking up like that!" she muttered, staring at her ruined drawing. "I have been trying to stay out of your way because I know that's what you want. And when I do avoid you, here you come to destroy what I painstakingly created."

"I'm sorry."

"I doubt you know the meaning of the word," Roz grumbled irritably.

"I brought a poultice to take the swelling out of your knee and ankle," he said in the way of compensation.

Roz didn't glance at him. Looking into his eyes made it even more difficult to pretend indifference, though God knew she had tried exceptionally hard to be as impassive and unfeeling as he was. "Thank you. I'll apply the salve after I complete my illustrations."

"Look at me, Yank," Cougar demanded when she continued to avoid his direct stare.

"I'd rather not."

"Why? Because you have come to realize that I am too destructive and vicious for your tastes?"

Roz jerked up her head to stare at the towering mass of sinewy masculinity. True, she did cringe each time she watched Cougar take on that dark, dangerous aura that accompanied him into battle. And it was also true she had been forced to accept the fact that he struck his enemy without mercy. But what tormented her most was her inability to convince him that love could replace the bitterness that haunted him. He stubbornly preferred to remain like the lone cedar she had been sketching against the backdrop of a rolling meadow and trickling stream. Perhaps that was why she was compelled to commit that solitary tree to paper, because it symbolized the man who refused to accept her love.

"If you came by to remind me that we have nothing in common, you have said it often enough already," Roz replied, forcing herself to speak without a trace of emotion. "The way you deal with adversaries has nothing to do with you and me."

"It speaks of what I am," Cougar told her somberly.

"Fine, you are a man of stone, a creature without a heart or soul. You have been trying to convince me of that since the day we met. Now that you have made your point, please go away. I would like to sketch this scene while there is still enough light."

Cougar watched Roz set her flimsy easel upright and he sighed heavily. "I'm only trying to do what is best. Can't you see that?"

"Don't bother doing me favors. I have no desire to be more beholden than I already am. I already owe you my life and I offered you my love—which you refuse to accept—"

"Damn it, Yank," Cougar muttered, grabbing her arm, forcing her to meet his level stare.

Roz steeled herself against the instantaneous effect of his touch, wishing for more of it and knowing Cougar preferred less of it. "Damn it, Cougar, if you don't want me, then simply go away. All you're doing right now is tormenting me when you know perfectly well how I feel about you."

Cougar felt his determination deteriorate when he stared into those expressive sapphire eyes. The unshed tears Roz fought so hard to conceal from him peeled away another layer of his resistance. This was neither the time nor the place to indulge the insatiable needs this beguiling woman aroused in him. But knowing that he was leaving at dawn to seek his revenge left Cougar with an unfamiliar sense of desperation.

No matter how hard he tried to deny it, he wanted one last memory to savor for months to come. He could already feel his betraying body reacting when his arms involuntarily contracted, molding Roz into his muscular contours.

At his touch all of Roz's self-restraint melted like thawing snow. In her heart she knew she wanted to fight for this one man's love, to prove to him that he could make a change for the better, that there was more to life than the hell he had known. She also knew without asking that he was going away, leaving her and Caleb behind while he exacted his long-awaited revenge against Roche and Adair.

This was Cougar's way of saying good-bye forever. She would never see him again . . .

That tormenting thought provoked Roz to lift her lips toward him, aching for the taste of his kiss, for the tenderness she knew was buried beneath that hard, defensive shell. She wanted to touch him, to please him, to leave her memory burning long after he sent her away.

"Just once . . . and for always," Roz whispered to him.

Against his will, Cougar was drawn into the spell of sparkling blue eyes and honeyed lips. Her soft words went through him like a white-hot shimmer of light. Just one last taste, he thought as his head dipped toward hers. Just one more touch and he would walk away without looking back. He would bury the blazing memories in stone, remembering a time when he had dared to be more human than his hellish life had allowed him to be. He would not take complete possession of Roz again, because making love to her demanded too much from him. But he would leave with the taste of her on his lips, her scent on his skin. Those were the only luxuries he could afford . . .

A husky groan tumbled from Cougar's lips when Roz's slender fingers ventured beneath the bandoleers. The leather straps fell away from his chest, leaving him vulnerable to her gentle touch. Cougar was helpless to resist her sweeping caresses that melted him from stone to liquid lava.

He had never realized there was such overpowering strength in a woman's tenderness. Roz had the ability to leave him aching for more of her whispered kisses, her bone-melting caresses. He should push her hands away and retreat into his own space. He should voice his last farewell and walk away from this forbidden illusion that would inevitably torment him until the day he died.

But he couldn't walk away, didn't want to walk away.

The compelling lure she held on him was like a delicate spiderweb entrapping a defenseless fly. Cougar's mind and body could not agree on what they wanted, not when indescribable sensations coiled, expanded and pulsated through every nerve and muscle.

And then, like an unearthed spring bubbling to surface, pleasure channeled through every fiber of his being, stripping away good intentions. Suddenly only one thought rang true, drumming with every accelerated beat of his heart. He wanted this woman more than he wanted breath, beyond all rhyme and reason. Just once more . . .

When Roz's bold caresses trailed down his belly to sketch the fabric that concealed the throbbing length of his desire, Cougar groaned in unholy torment. He remembered how she had stroked him before he had come to her in a blaze of mindless need, remembered the feel of her fingertips surrounding him, welcoming him until she was all he could think about, until she was all he could feel, all he could taste, all he wanted and needed to survive.

"I want to know you, all of you," Roz whispered as she urged him down onto the carpet of grass. Wanting him was more overpowering than pain, more precious than breath. Loving him in every inventive way imaginable was her greatest desire. "I want to know you in all the intimate ways you have known me, Cougar. Just once . . ."

Cougar went down in utter defeat, because remaining on his feet demanded more strength than he could muster. Her intimate kisses and caresses were drawing upon his strength, turning flesh to liquid and bone to mush. She was devastating him with one kiss and caress at a time.

His breath hissed from his lips when pleasure so intense that it felt like delicious torture encompassed him. Her hands moved nimbly over the lacings of his breeches, caressing him as she released the hard evidence of his need. The first gliding touch of her lips on his aroused flesh nearly drove him into oblivion. His hips instinctively moved toward her, and he squeezed his eyes shut against the wild heat that inflamed him.

When her flicking tongue teased him he heard himself whisper *no* and heard her murmur *yes*. His male body responded to her moist kisses with a dewy drop of need. Cougar forgot how to breathe when she bathed him with his own desire for her, measured him with her loving touch, aroused him until he was shaking with the need for her.

"Stop, Roz," Cougar begged hoarsely.

"Stop wanting you?" she whispered against the pulsating length of him. "Don't you realize that it's impossible, loving you the way I do? I will have this memory if I have nothing else. At least this, Cougar. At least this . . . because I love you with every beat of my heart . . ."

When Cougar tried to curl upward, her hand flattened on his laboring chest and then swirled over his male nipples. Cougar sank back into the grass, feeling utterly helpless. He had never known a woman's tender touch before, never wanted to be at anyone's mercy, but he could no more contain his mindless wanting than he could soar to the moon. Roz's loving touch had made him a willing pawn.

The feel of her soft lips and warm breath hovering over the velvet tip of his manhood left Cougar gasping, trying to drag air into lungs that felt as if they were clogged with sand. He wasn't going to survive this incredibly erotic assault, he was certain of that. Roz was costing him every ounce of energy, forcing him deeper into her sensual spell.

When her kisses trailed across his belly and chest to skim his lips, Cougar knew he had been conquered. He could taste his need on her tongue as she traced his mouth, just as her fingertip traced the moist tip of his desire for her. She had taken him so deep into the turbulent sea of passion that every sensation, every answering throb of his pulse was her whispered name.

"I need you," he groaned in mindless desperation.

When Cougar drew her up to meet him, she yielded without hesitation, meeting each urgent thrust of his body, clinging to him as if he were her only salvation. Ecstasy drenched her as they moved as one, spiraling above the towering mountains and tumbling over the seven magnificent falls that murmured in the distance. And when she felt his body pulsing in ungovernable release, she answered him in the most intimate of ways, holding him as they shuddered together and drifted into rapturous infinity.

In the aftermath of the kind of passion Cougar had never experienced, he opened his eyes to find himself staring at the crimson rays of dusk. He was fully naked and Roz was still dressed in the pink muslin gown he had brought from Howard Station.

Cougar inwardly groaned in frustration. She had made him so wild and hungry for her that he hadn't even taken the time to fully arouse her before he pulled her down on top of him to ease the ardent needs she had instilled. She had given him everything and . . . he had offered her nothing in return.

Cougar cursed himself up one side and down the other. What was it about this bewitching woman that demolished every shred of self-control? How could he keep breaking one promise after another until they were as close as two people could ever get without crawling inside each other's skin?

Roz had been through him until she had discovered every place he liked to be touched. She had unchained his greatest enemy—himself—and he had surrendered without so much as a skirmish before she took possession of his mind and body with a gentleness that mastered his imposing strength. She had cherished every inch of his body, savored him as if he were a priceless gift, and he had been able to do nothing but respond in wild abandon.

Each time they had made passionate love Cougar swore it had to be the last, because Roz kept walking away with yet another sliver of his shriveled soul. There would be absolutely nothing left of him when he sent her back where she belonged. He had been an empty shell before she came along and now she had drained what little life he had left in him. She had turned him inside out so many times that Cougar wasn't sure he recognized himself these days. She evoked feelings that defied explanation, left him contradicting himself until his promises were as unreliable as a white man's.

She called it love; he called it tormenting defeat.

"Roz, we have to talk," Cougar insisted in a half-strangled voice.

"You don't have to say anything," Roz whispered

against his muscular shoulder. "I asked for no promises. All I wanted was you. Just the memory, Cougar. Please don't take that away from me, too. You already have my heart and soul."

"Hell," Cougar muttered as she stirred provocatively above him. "Don't move, Yank. I'm having enough trouble getting myself under control as it is."

Roz grinned when she felt his immediate response. "I like you best when you are completely out of control," she confided.

"Why? Because you know you have mastered me?"

Roz raised her head and a waterfall of silver-blond hair tumbled over his shoulder like a sweeping caress. "No, because only then do you know how I feel each time you touch me."

Cougar marshalled his determination. "What we do to each other changes nothing, Yank. Nothing is ever going to change. I can't give you what a woman like you deserves. You've seen what I can become, and yet you haven't really seen what I am at all—"

Her index finger brushed his lips to shush him. "None of that matters, Cougar."

"It matters," he countered, nipping her fingertip to prove a subtle point. "What I have learned to become in order to survive is not a gift but a curse. When I reach deep down to summon the powers the Cheyenne oracle taught me to recognize and command, I sometimes wonder if I can return from those dark depths. Even now, I can sense danger lurking, just as my restless panthers do—"

The hiss of an arrow sliced across Cougar's words, putting him on swift and immediate alert. Before Roz knew what happened, Cougar set her away from him and snatched up his discarded breeches. His dagger leaped into his hand in the time it took for Roz to blink. An arrow shot straight into the sketch of the lone tree that sat upon Roz's easel and the unstable object pitched sideways into the grass.

"What in the hell—?" Cougar swiveled his head around to see a second arrow sailing toward them. With a muffled curse, he latched onto Roz and rolled sideways before the arrow could strike human flesh.

"Stay down," Cougar ordered as he sprang to his feet to jog toward the clump of trees.

# Twenty-one

Roz hurriedly rearranged her twisted clothes and then set her easel upright. Her sketch of the lone cedar beside the creek had suddenly become two dimensional.

When she heard Cougar's voice clamoring in the wind, she pivoted to see him stalking toward her, half carrying, half dragging Caleb. Behind them was Gray Eagle, toting a leather case of arrows and a bow.

"Do you see that?" Cougar growled at Caleb. His arm shot out to direct the peaked-faced lad's attention to the sketch. "You could have hit one of us just as easily, and damned near did! From now on, watch what the hell you're doing!"

Caleb's eyes clouded with wounded dignity after being taken to task in front of Roz and Gray Eagle. Caleb had not had a good day. But enduring captivity was nowhere near as demoralizing as having his idol dress him down in front of an audience.

"I was only trying to learn to use a bow," Caleb murmured as he stared at the damaged sketch from which his arrow protruded. "I just wanted to be able to do something well." He inhaled a shaky breath and peered up at Roz. "I'm sorry."

"You damned well should be," Cougar muttered.

Debra Falcon

"You're lucky you didn't hit me instead. I would have had your scalp."

The comment started Caleb's tears flowing.

Roz flung Cougar a disparaging glance, knowing that he was taking his frustration for her out on Caleb. Cougar resented succumbing to the needs she had evoked from him and now Caleb was receiving the brunt of Cougar's bad temper.

"It was only a preparatory sketch for an oil painting," Roz said as she limped over to wrap a consoling arm around Caleb's shaking shoulders. "Besides, the drawing was damaged before your arrow struck it."

"This is still a serious matter," Cougar contended. "The boy missed his target by a mile."

Roz arched a delicate brow and smiled wryly. "Did he? I thought you said Caleb was aiming at a tree."

"He was," Gray Eagle piped up.

"Well, he did hit a tree, didn't he?" she asked, indicating the arrow that struck the lone cedar in her sketch.

Gray Eagle apparently saw the humor; he smiled broadly. Cougar, however, didn't; he glowered.

"Fetch your arrows, Caleb," Cougar commanded. "And next time, make damned certain there is no one within shooting distance while you're practicing."

Crestfallen, Caleb trudged over to retrieve the two arrows that had gone astray. When Cougar pivoted around to rake Gray Eagle over the coals for turning an unskilled apprentice loose with a bow, his eyes widened in disbelief. Gray Eagle had launched himself at Roz. Without so much as a by your leave, the Cheyenne warrior wrapped Roz in his arms and hugged the stuffing out of her. And then to Cougar's astounded outrage,

Gray Eagle planted a kiss, right smack dab on Roz's gaping mouth.

"What in the hell do you think you're doing?" Cougar hooted.

Gray Eagle glanced over his shoulder, extremely pleased with himself. "I am courting—white man's fashion, of course. I am told this is proper procedure to make my intentions known."

"Who told you that?" Cougar demanded gruffly.

Gray Eagle didn't bother to reply. He gave Roz another endearing hug and kissed her again—-most zealously.

Cougar responded without thinking. His fist knotted in the sleeve of Gray Eagle's doehide shirt, swinging him around to receive a blow that snapped his head back and lifted him clean off his feet.

Gray Eagle hit the ground with a thud and a grunt. "Why did you do that?" he mumbled in bewilderment.

Cougar stared at his doubled fist in stunned amazement. In all the years he and Gray Eagle had been friends, he had never struck a blow. They hadn't even quarreled, not even once since they had staked their claim on this mountain valley that had once been a favorite camping ground for the Cheyenne.

Cautiously, Gray Eagle gathered his feet beneath him and stood up, feeling his split lip. His dark eyes fixed on Cougar, trying to comprehend what had caused his friend to launch such a painful attack.

Cougar cursed the three pairs of eyes that focused on him as if he were crazed. "I'm . . . sorry . . ."

"As you should be," Gray Eagle insisted. "Friendship

does not invite attack. We are of the same spirit, Cougar."

Cougar shifted awkwardly from one foot to the other, refusing to meet those three probing gazes. The odd restlessness he had felt earlier was gathering intensity, accompanied by newfound frustration. Cougar had experienced instinctive possessiveness when Gray Eagle pulled Roz into his arms and kissed the breath out of her. Roz carried Cougar's taste, his scent.

*She belonged to him.*

The thought struck like a hurled lance and Cougar immediately rejected it. Roz Gaylord did not belong to him. All they shared was forbidden passion. He was going to send her away as soon as he convinced Gray Eagle to become her escort . . .

*More trouble waiting to happen,* Cougar thought in exasperation. If he sent Roz off with Gray Eagle, there was no telling what this misinformed warrior would do in his attempt to court Roz.

Gray Eagle glanced from his scowling friend to the alluring blonde who had aroused his long-denied male needs. "I wish to claim this woman as my own, as it is done in her world."

"You don't just waltz up and hug a woman who appeals to you in white man's society," Cougar snapped more harshly than he intended.

Gray Eagle frowned, confused. "Little Bear says it is so."

"Who is Little Bear?"

Gray Eagle gestured toward Caleb. "It is the name I have given our young warrior. He is teaching me the ways of white culture while I instruct him in the ways of the Cheyenne, just as you suggested."

Cougar stared goggle-eyed at Gray Eagle. "You took the word of a child whose only experience in courtship is watching his parents display affection for each other?"

Gray Eagle stood there, stunned. Caleb sniffed miserably at another of his blunders and Roz burst out in laughter.

"This is not funny, Yank," Cougar muttered at her.

That was his opinion. Roz thought the entire incident was hilarious. And furthermore, her laughter relieved the bottled tension that had sustained her since the day she had been taken captive. The thought of Caleb instructing Gray Eagle on courtship rituals had Roz snickering again. Gray Eagle had been exceedingly proud of himself in thinking he had learned proper protocol, but his reward had been a bloody lip, compliments of his best friend's doubled fist.

"I didn't know Gray Eagle was asking about courting Miss Gaylord," Caleb hurriedly explained. "I thought—"

The crack of a rifle was followed by the scream of a panther. The sound rose to piercing intensity, ringing through the gathering night like a pealing bell. Roz's alarmed gaze swung to tawny eyes that burned with instant fury. The expression that claimed Cougar's bronzed features caused Roz to step back apace. It was almost as if Cougar had taken the shot himself, as if the wild scream that penetrated the twilight was his own wail of agony.

Four rapid-fire shots exploded and more terrifying screams swirled through the long shadows cast by the looming mountains. Before Roz could think of moving,

Cougar was shoving her toward the protection of the cabin, thrusting a pistol into her hand. His touch was like frozen stone and Roz shivered at the strange aura she felt gathering around him.

Roz had experienced those same unnerving sensations before, and she recalled what Cougar had been trying to explain to her before the stray arrow whizzed past them. The slightest threat triggered his killer instinct, sent him plunging into the cold depths where emotion did not exist. Even the sound of his voice, ordering her and Caleb to run for cover, had altered to an alarmingly hollow and unrecognizable pitch.

Roz wasn't certain what was happening, but she had the unshakable feeling that an attack had been launched on the cats. And those black cats were one with Cougar in times of danger. He was responding to the threat with the kind of murderous rage that spawned the legends circulating about him. The man she had come to know in tender moments had vanished before the agonizing screams of the panthers died into silence.

Driven by a sense of perilous urgency, Roz grabbed Caleb's hand and darted into the cabin, shutting and bolting the door and windows as Cougar had ordered her to do . . .

Cougar wheeled and crouched, feeling Gray Eagle's presence behind him. Danger lurked in the lengthening shadows that draped the mountains. The strained whistle calls of the cats put Cougar on full and vicious alert. He knew instinctively that Roche and Adair had grown tired of being hunted. They had come for revenge, striking first at the unsuspecting cats before turning their seething fury on Cougar.

The pained screams and calls that filtered through the air triggered haunting memories of dawn on the Washita River. Cougar could feel the same frustrated rage that had pulsed through him while he and Gray Eagle lay buried in the grass to avoid the murdering troops that searched for survivors of the massacre. Gray Eagle's quiet snarl suggested that he, too, was remembering that awful dawn when Cheyenne blood ran like a river.

Again Roche and Adair had invaded a peaceful domain, turning laughter to screams of death and destruction. But those murdering bastards were not going to enjoy the final victory, Cougar vowed fiercely. They would not take Roz and Caleb captive again. Cougar had barely been able to tolerate the thought of his best friend touching Roz. Having Roche and Adair abuse her was unthinkable.

Even if Cougar had to reach so deep inside himself that he could never navigate his way out of the stone-cold corridors where animal and killer instinct reigned supreme, he would execute the whispering curse of the Cheyenne who had fallen to these fiendish butchers.

There would be justice—Cheyenne justice—at any cost.

Cougar sent a hushed command to Gray Eagle. Like two shadows skipping through the trees, they crept off in opposite directions, remaining within the concealing underbrush to reach the rocky embankment, searching for the men who had fired the shots that downed the panthers . . .

# Twenty-two

Jake Roche smiled triumphantly when he saw the mountain lions tumble one by one. "That should limit that half-breed bastard's power." He shoved his rifle into its sling on the saddle and crouched behind a large boulder to ensure both pistols were loaded. Jake wished he and Burney had spotted the grazing black gelding and located the secluded cottage earlier in the afternoon. He would have liked nothing better than to ambush that son of a bitch who had picked off his gang members. Jake wasn't going to be satisfied until he had filled that Injun with lead and taken his lusty pleasure with that Eastern bit of fluff.

One step at a time, Jake told himself. Now that the cats were incapacitated, he and Burney could close in on the cabin and reclaim their hostages. Then Cougar would have no choice but to sacrifice his life in attempt to save the captives.

On that promising thought, Jake grabbed his horse's reins and moved toward the location where Burney had positioned himself for the ambush that had dropped all three cats.

* * *

"This is all my fault," Caleb whimpered as he huddled on the pallet beside the hearth. "I never say and do the right things." Tears pooled in Cal's eyes as he curled into a tight ball, clinging to the locket Francene had sent to him. "Everybody was arguing and Cougar was throwing fists. I didn't know Gray Eagle wanted to court you. And now Cougar has lost his cats because of me—"

Roz sank down to cradle the dispirited boy in her arms. "It wasn't your fault," she consoled him. "If it was anyone's fault it was mine. Cougar and I were having a debate while you were taking target practice. I was the one who distracted him and left him unprepared for approaching danger."

Caleb huddled against Roz, staring apprehensively at the closed window. "It don't—doesn't feel right. It's too quiet. What's happening out there, Miss Gaylord?"

Roz followed Cal's worried gaze. "I wish I knew, Caleb. I wish we both knew . . ."

Roz flinched when she heard an unidentified noise outside the door. She had closed and bolted the door and windows as Cougar had instructed her to do, making it impossible to determine what was going on. Her attention riveted on the door, wondering if Roche or Adair had sneaked to the cabin.

"Don't let them in," Caleb whimpered when scratching noises and quiet growls drifted toward him. "Someone might be trying to play a trick on us."

Those were Roz's exact thoughts. It sounded as if the cats had returned, but Roz wasn't even sure the poor creatures had survived the gunfire. The muffled sounds could have been an imitation. If she unlocked the door, she could find herself staring down the barrel of an enemy rifle. The possibility kept Roz frozen to her spot, clinging as tightly to Caleb as he clung to her.

Somewhere in the distance a horse whinnied and another shrill scream shattered the night. The scratching at the door became even more insistent. Roz inhaled a steadying breath and attempted to control the fear that had her pulse pounding like a tom-tom.

"Make them stop!" Caleb cried as he buried his head against Roz's shoulder. "Please make them stop!"

Roz's heart went out to the young lad who had endured one nightmarish ordeal after another. What Caleb needed was the comfort of his mother's and father's sheltering arms. Unfortunately, Roz was the only one around to provide compassion, even when she could have used some moral support herself. She began to realize how much she had come to depend on Cougar's protective presence, even when he kept a remote distance between them. He was the man she wanted on her side when trouble broke out—as it had now.

A soft whistle call jostled Roz from her thoughts. For an uneasy moment she stared at the door. Roz inhaled a deep breath and relied upon her instincts. She placed her faith in what she believed, rather than what she feared. Gently, she eased away from Caleb's clinging arms and pressed a kiss to his forehead.

"What are you going to do, Miss Gaylord?" Caleb whispered anxiously.

"I'm going to investigate," she said, placing the pistol Cougar had given her in Cal's shaky hand.

"You know I'm no good with pistols, rifles or bows. What if—?"

Roz grabbed the war club that hung above the mantle and pivoted to stare at Cal with the same grimly determined expression Cougar often displayed. "There are times when we must do what has to be done," she told him quietly. "If we have been deceived then we must both respond accordingly."

When Cal opened his mouth to voice a protest, Roz touched her forefinger to her lips to demand his silence. "Cougar has taught you to handle weapons. Now is the time to test your skills. Do what you must do to protect yourself."

Clutching the club in her fist, Roz tiptoed toward the door—one apprehensive step at a time. If Roche and Adair had deceived her, Roz was never going to forgive herself for unlocking the door. And if the wounded cats had returned, Roz preferred to have them inside instead of yowling outside, drowning out other sounds that indicated even greater danger.

When Roz slid the bolt off the door, the sounds outside evaporated. All she could hear was her own thundering pulse and the prayer she sent heavenward. The time of reckoning had come. She hoped she had made a wise decision rather than a fatal mistake . . .

The instant she twisted the knob the door banged open. Roz was pinned against the wall when three black shadows spilled into the room, caterwauling in pain. Breathing an enormous relief Roz shut the door and slid the bolt in place.

Caleb's thin shoulders slumped and the barrel of the

pistol thudded against the pallet. His audible sigh filled the room.

Roz appraised the wounded cats. One of them had caught a bullet in the left front paw, tearing away a claw. The cat curled up by the pallet to lick its wound. The second black panther was unable to put weight on its hind leg. The injured animal eased down beside the first cat to inspect its injuries. The third cat's condition appeared to be more serious. The shoulder wound left the cat's shiny coat glistening with blood.

Although Roz never boasted nursing skills, she was forced to follow her own advice and do what she deemed necessary. She wasn't sure how the severely injured cat would react to human ministrations. Although Cougar had always warned her away from his panthers, Roz had defied him by petting each and every one while they had remained with her at the mountain spring.

"Cal, bring me that bucket of water by the stove," Roz requested as she carefully sank down beside the whining cat. Her hand hovered above the panther's broad head, despite the reflexive show of teeth. With soothing words, Roz lowered her hand and stroked the injured puma. By the time Caleb returned with the water, the cat had laid its head on its oversized paws, docilely accepting Roz's light stroking touch.

"There is whiskey in the saddlebags that Cougar confiscated from the outlaws," she murmured. "Fetch it for me, will you?"

"Ma says proper ladies don't drink."

Roz smiled reassuringly. "I was planning to mix the whiskey with water to sedate the cats," she explained.

"We need to tend their wounds without having our fingers bit off."

"Cougar said never to touch his cats," Caleb reminded her.

"That was before they were injured," she clarified. "This cat is losing a lot of blood. I think Cougar would appreciate it if we cared for his cats rather than let them die, don't you?"

Caleb's narrow shoulders lifted and dropped. "I don't know, Miss Gaylord. I've already made too many mistakes today."

"Well, if Cougar considers this a mistake, I will take the blame. Just bring me the whiskey."

Caleb did as he was told.

When Roz set the bowl in front of the panting cat, it sniffed suspiciously and then lapped up the potion. Roz was reasonably certain the animal was in such a state of shock that it reacted only to its need to drink. And as Roz continued to stroke the cats head, it made an odd sound that reminded her of a purr.

Another wave of sympathy filtered through Roz. As ferocious as these catamounts could be in the heat of battle, they were also gentle in repose. They *did* enjoy affection and compassion.

And Cougar would too if he would only give himself half a chance.

"Can I pet them?" Caleb questioned as he eased down on his knees.

"Yes, but carefully," Roz instructed.

"No sudden moves, right?"

"Exactly." Roz tore off the hem of her gown and

dipped it into the bucket. "If the cat objects to my cleansing the wound, you skedaddle before you're bitten."

Caleb nodded and kept his gaze trained on the cat while Roz dabbed the wet cloth on the wound. When the panther continued to make a purring sound, Cal gently stroked its head and whispered soothingly, just as Roz had done.

To Roz's relief, the bullet had only grazed the cat's coat, tearing out a chunk of bone and muscle without damaging vital organs. Once she had cleaned the wound, she offered all three cats full bowls of sedative. When they had drunk their fill, she replenished the bowls and cleaned the other wounds. Before long, all three cats were quietly purring and licking their wounds.

The animals were lucky indeed, Roz mused as she stroked the nearest cat. If Roche and Adair had been better marksmen, the cats would never have made it to the safety of the cabin.

Cougar would have a fit when he saw his docile cats curled up like kittens. In her estimation, these cougars were nothing but overgrown pussycats that lapped up affection as quickly as they lapped up the whiskey-laced water. Maybe these graceful, muscular creatures had been trained to herd livestock like a trio of dogs and had been taught to attack at Cougar's command, but they were not vicious to the bone. They were actually quite lovable . . .

Roz glanced toward the door when she heard a wild, haunting scream in the night. She would have given most anything to know where Cougar and Gray Eagle were and what was going on outside. Not knowing was making her crazy!

* * *

"Burney?" Jake whispered to his confederate. When Burney didn't respond, Jake trekked along the embankment to reach the spot where he had left his companion a half hour earlier. He knelt down to grope for the rifle cartridge beside the boulder. Burney had fired one shot before he moved to another vantage point. Where the hell was he now?

Apprehension flooded through Jake's taut body when an unearthly scream shouted down the night. He glanced around as the sound evaporated, leaving only the distant call of an eagle and the faint warble of birds in the trees near the cottage.

"Damn it, Burney? Where are you?" Jake muttered to the darkness at large.

# Twenty-three

Burney Adair grimaced uncomfortably as he was dragged backward, locked in hard, unyielding arms. His attempt to struggle had earned him a brain-scrambling blow to the back of the head. When he roused, it was to find himself being toted away from the concealment of the boulders. He hadn't been able to shout in alarm or warn Jake of attack. All he had managed to do was to claw his way out of the fuzzy darkness that had enveloped him.

A quiet snarl caused every muscle in Burney's bulky body to flinch. If he hadn't known better, he would have sworn the cats had returned to haunt him. But that was impossible. He had seen the panthers roll and fall beneath the shots he and Jake had fired.

Cougar contained his murderous rage as he maneuvered his captive onto the ground. The instant Burney had wilted beneath the butt of Cougar's striking pistol, he heard Roche calling to his accomplice. And very soon these two bloodthirsty bastards would be reunited, Cougar vowed.

A soft call in Cheyenne brought Gray Eagle from the underbrush to tower over the downed captive. Burney muttered into the gag Cougar had crammed in his mouth. If he had known Cougar had company, he would have headed for Mexico and never looked back.

"You don't remember us, do you, Adair?" Cougar hissed against Burney's rigid neck. "We saw you butcher our clan before we escaped from the massacre on the Washita. Gray Eagle and I have waited a long time to settle that score with you and Roche. And it will be settled, just as Custer paid his penance at Little Big Horn."

Burney trembled uncontrollably as Cougar levered him into a sitting position. The knife-happy butcher was scared. Good, thought Cougar. The bastard had every right to be. Cougar had waited eight long years to meet Burney Adair face to face. An eternity of hatred boiled inside Cougar, and he knew Gray Eagle was harboring the same vengeful fury. In that, they were of one mind and one purpose. Gray Eagle had been forced into hiding because of the massacre and captivity of the Cheyenne tribe. Although Gray Eagle would never truly have his freedom, he could enjoy the sweet taste of revenge.

"Let me have this one," Gray Eagle snarled as he stared murderously at Burney Adair. "Let me give him what he offered my wife and our clan—tormented death."

Burney's eyes widened at the cold voice that settled over him like a blanket of snow. He mumbled a plea for mercy into his gag, a plea that fell on deaf ears and burned in golden eyes that bore into him like the blade of a knife.

"I have plans for Adair," Cougar said in a hollow voice.

"I want his scalp," Gray Eagle demanded.

Burney very nearly swallowed his tongue. His heart

stampeded around his chest, making it impossible to breathe. Suffocating, he decided, would be a blessing. These two vicious Injuns were fighting over a piece of his skin and he could do nothing to prevent them from taking it.

"Fetch the rope from Adair's saddle," Cougar commanded, staring unblinkingly at his terrified captive.

Reluctantly, Gray Eagle pivoted to do as ordered.

Cougar tied one end of the lariat around Burney's wrists and then looped a noose around his neck. When Burney tried to roll sideways to avoid being bound up, Cougar's moccasined foot rammed into his soft underbelly, forcing out his breath in a muffled grunt.

Burney went as still as a tombstone when he glanced up into those burning amber eyes and heard the guttural snarl. He was a dead man. He knew it. There was no emotion in those piercing eyes, no mercy, only fatal promise. Burney remembered what Skeet and Vito had said about feeling close enough to hell to smell smoke when Cougar breathed down their necks. Whatever Cougar and his companion had planned was not going to be pleasant. Burney had the horrifying feeling that he was going to pay retribution for every man, woman and child he had cut to ribbons on the Washita.

Cougar squatted down beside Burney, feeling the apprehension pulsating through him, savoring the torment this bastard so richly deserved. Ever so slowly, Cougar eased Burney to his feet, holding the dagger against his throat to discourage sudden movement.

"I don't suggest you do more than breathe, Adair."

Cougar whispered so quietly that Burney couldn't decide if he had actually heard the words. Burney had the frightening feeling he was enduring the same torment Skeet and Hud had suffered when they found themselves in this deadly predator's hands.

Burney tensed when he was lifted by a pair of arms and positioned on his horse. He glanced down to see his own dagger lashed to the pommel of the saddle, the meticulously sharpened point glistening in the moonlight like a deadly spike aimed at his belly.

Before Burney could hurl himself sideways off the horse, the noose that bit into his neck squeezed the air from his throat. He was shoved back onto the saddle, and the loose ends of the lariat were secured to the bridle. If Burney's mount dropped its head, the contraption of rope would pull him down on his own knife.

"You ruthless son of a bitch," Burney sneered into his gag.

While Burney cursed his captors to hell and back—twice—Cougar fastened leather straps around Burney's elbows and tied them to his boots which had been lashed to the stirrups.

A slow satisfied smile worked its way across Gray Eagle's lips as he surveyed the contraption of rope and leather straps that Cougar had ingeniously designed for Burney's personal brand of torture. This was ironic justice for a man who took fiendish delight in using his knife to carve his victims into bite-sized pieces. Step by step, Burney Adair would be reminded of each thrust of his own blade, each victim he had ripped to shreds. Cougar had arranged for this heartless scoundrel to endure the same brand of torture he was so fond of wielding.

"I need one last piece of rope," Cougar requested.

Gray Eagle dropped the twisted braid into Cougar's

hand. With eyes like chips of cold golden nuggets, Cougar turned back to lash the rope around the horse's flanks. The tight band prompted the steed to prance sideways and toss its head. Burney expelled another horrified curse when his steed dropped its head, scraping his belly against the point of his own dagger.

"Burney? Where the hell are you?" came a quiet voice from the darkness.

Icy claws of terror raked Burney's flesh when Cougar let out an unnerving scream that nearly punctured his eardrums. Burney's steed bolted forward, bucking in objection to the confining band that encircled its belly. The horse pranced and kicked its way around the obstacle course of rocks to rejoin the steed that whinnied in the distance.

Cougar heard Burney's pained howls drifting in the wind, but he felt no remorse for the man. Cougar felt nothing but the harsh satisfaction of long-awaited revenge. Burney Adair would understand how each of his victims felt when he had thrust at them in cold blood. Each slash Burney received was a grim reminder that he was dying a little at a time for every life he had taken that day on the Washita.

"Now there is only one," Cougar whispered as Burney's muffled wails faded into silence.

"And the personal punishment for Jake Roche?" Gray Eagle questioned. "Will it be ironic justice as well?"

Cougar nodded bleakly before turning away. "Jake Roche will remember the massacre in his own special way, because we are going to reenact it for him. But this time Roche will be on the opposite side of death, fighting a battle *he* cannot win."

Gray Eagle followed in Cougar's footsteps, committed to the same deadly purpose—annihilating the last of the men who tried to wipe the peaceful Cheyenne clan off the face of the earth forever.

Jake Roche ducked behind the concealing rocks when he heard the clatter of approaching hooves. With both pistols drawn, he waited to determine if he was encountering friend or foe. Even after Jake recognized Burney's horse, he didn't let his guard down. Jake and his men had learned the hard way that Cougar often relied on illusion. It could be Burney who was slumped over his saddle—and then again, maybe not. Jake prepared himself for anything . . .

But he was not prepared for this!

The horse pranced to a halt in front of Jake. Burney did no more than raise his chin from its resting place against his mount's neck. "Kill that son of a bitch for me," Burney rasped with his last breath.

Jake grimaced when Burney sagged against his horse, fastened in place by a contraption of rope and leather straps. When Jake untied the rope attached to the headstall of the bridle and cut the straps that anchored Burney's feet to the stirrups, Burney rolled off the horse and plummeted to the ground with a thud. Jake's eyes popped when he noticed the bloody dagger lashed to the pommel.

His stricken gaze dropped to the lifeless form at his feet. Moonlight glistened on the dark, wet stains that saturated Burney's shirt and the whites of his eyes that were fixed in a sightless stare. The unnerving sight of the torture Burney had endured at the point of his own dagger had Jake staggering backward, gasping for breath. Panic slithered down his spine. He was alone in unfamiliar territory, facing a vengeful devil who had proven that every fantastic legend about him was true. No matter what the odds, Cougar devised his own unique ways of dealing with his prey. That half-breed bastard had taken on six men and watched them fall—one by one.

Jake swallowed nervously as he glanced toward the cabin. If he could get hold of the kid and woman, he might have a chance of riding out of this valley alive . . .

Before Jake could bound onto the saddle, a hauntingly familiar scream penetrated the night. His heart catapulted to his throat when a shadow skipped among the pile of rocks below him. In fiendish haste Jake mounted his horse and reined east, abandoning his attempt to storm the cottage. He was stung by the inescapable feeling that Cougar would never let him reach the cabin alive.

The screech of an eagle came from behind Jake and he swiveled around to see another fleeting shadow approach. Jake remembered what Vito and Skeet had said about Cougar's phenomenal ability to change forms, but now it seemed this dark avenger could also split himself in half.

Jake gouged his heels into his horse and trotted off, picking his way around the boulders to reach flat ground. When he tried to veer north to retrace the path he and Burney had followed, he heard the unearthly screams coming from the direction he intended to go. Every time Jake tried to reroute his mount, he heard the cry of an eagle, the scream of a panther and saw ominous images emerge from the night.

Stark fear kept Jake moving along the path of least

resistance like a misguided current of electricity pulsing toward an unknown destination. All Jake knew was that he wanted to be wherever the cunning Cougar wasn't.

The roar of seven falls momentarily drowned out the eerie call of the eagle and the answering scream of the cougar. Jake spied the moonlight cascade that blocked his route and he veered around the rim of the plunging chasm. Each time he tried to thunder off on a course perpendicular to the crumbling canyon ledge, a shadow danced among the trees, barricading his escape. Jake was forced to follow the descending slopes, hounded by the eerie calls of the night.

Jake stared every which way at once, trying to decide where he was. Although Cougar had yet to close in on him, Jake felt trapped, driven. When he swerved sideways, he was herded by fleeting shadows that dictated his direction . . .

Jake's breath froze in his chest when an indefinable form dropped down from the tree in front of him. The crouched figure's guttural snarl caused Jake's winded mount to shift skittishly beneath him. The horse had sensed danger before Jake did. Eyes wide with alarm, nostrils flared, the steed involuntarily danced backward, avoiding the seething growl that rolled like thunder.

When Jake saw the crouched shadow bound forward, saw those golden eyes glint in the moonlight, his heart jumped to his throat. Panicking, he jerked his horse around and plunged through the trees, riding blindly away from the deadly creature that had materialized from the darkness.

Jake's breath sawed in and out as he dodged tree limbs that reached out like gnarled hands to snag him, threatening to snatch him off the saddle. The night had come alive to torment him. Shadows breathed and screamed. Rock formations took on supernatural qualities, standing like formidable sentinels against the starlit night. Jake was enduring all the torments of the damned. He was alone in a prison of imposing stone walls that rose a thousand feet on either side of him.

When he heard the roar of water ahead, he jerked on the reins, cursing the skipping cascade that formed another impassable barrier. Jake had unthinkingly ridden into the box canyon and now he was trapped.

Jake snatched up his pistols and turned his back to the falls, listening to the call of the eagle and screech of the panther. Frantic, Jake swung down from his laboring horse, using the animal for protection. The wound on his shoulder was beginning to throb with each accelerated beat of his pulse. Muscles twitched in response to each unfamiliar sound that was amplified by the surrounding walls of the chasm.

The hiss of an arrow caused Jake's mount to rear up and jerk loose from his grasp. Jake stumbled back when he saw the shaft of the arrow protruding from his saddle. When the horse bolted off in the direction it had come, Jake opened fire with both pistols. Twelve shots later he had nothing to show for his crazed efforts except smoking Colts and no ammunition. He swore foully when he realized the saddlebags that contained spare ammunition had left with his frightened horse. Now, all Jake had for protection was the dagger in his boot.

Jake shot off like a cannonball, running toward the falls, seeking cover among the trees and rocks, knowing that he, like each of his men, would eventually confront the legendary creature of doom.

"Damn you to hell, Cougar!" Jake bellowed.

The only response was a wild scream that came out of nowhere and resounded along the craggy peaks, circling, sinking and haunting Jake until his every breath was a vile epithet to Cougar's name.

And then came the eerie silence, broken only by the rush of water tumbling into the stream that flowed along the south wall of the chasm. Jake huddled against the rocks and waited . . . and waited some more. He didn't dare sleep, knowing Cougar would come for him. He had nothing to eat, only the nourishment of water from the creek. He had no hope, only the knowledge that any terms of surrender would be unacceptable.

Jake slumped against a boulder, squeezing back the image of Burney Adair's belly soaked with blood and an unblinking gaze fixed on the moon. Jake cringed, remembering the appalling sight of Skeet Thomas slashed to shreds by dagger-sharp claws and Vito Guerero's encircling necklace of crimson red. Jake didn't know what had become of Colby or Hud Caine, and he was glad he didn't. The other ghastly visions were more than enough to feed nightmares. Therefore, Jake refused to sleep, refused to let the unnerving memories take control of his mind. He was not going to allow Cougar to sneak up while he was unaware . . .

"Jake Roche!"

The rumbling voice prompted Jake to jerk upright, clutching his only remaining weapon in his fist. His wild-eyed gaze darted left, searching for the source of the sound.

"You have been hunted, herded and confined, just like the Cheyenne. This was their spiritual haunt before the Army descended on Sand Creek for the slaughter and rode on to the Washita to all but exterminate the Cheyenne."

Jake was instantly reminded of his tour of duty with General Armstrong Custer. Jake had relished watching those stinking savages crumple beneath his stabbing bayonet and the blast of his rifle. He had favored extermination of the heathens who had reclaimed the land Jake and his younger brother had taken as their own.

When James Roche had died with four arrows in his chest, Jake had vowed to punish every goddamn Injun on the continent. He had ridden with Custer and sought his personal revenge, swearing to destroy every living seed, until those red-skinned bastards were no more than a bad memory. But Custer pointed accusing fingers at Jake and Burney when superior military officers questioned the massacre on the Washita. Dishonorably discharged, Jake and Burney had been left to survive by their wits and their skills with weapons . . .

"Yours is Black Kettle's last revenge," came the booming voice. "The Cheyenne prophesy of living death is your destiny, Jake Roche."

Jake inhaled a shaky breath, realizing he wasn't simply suffering the backlash of kidnapping the boy and woman from Howard Station. Jake had the uneasy feeling that Cougar had been in the camp on the Washita River. Too bad he hadn't been killed with the rest of his clan . . .

Jake's heart nearly exploded in his chest when the underbrush rustled, not twenty feet away from where he sat. He glanced toward the sound and then reflexively swiveled around when he heard another voice calling his name. Jake let loose with a string of obscene curses when two ominous shadows materialized in front of him.

Cougar stared at the hunkered form of the man whose knife blade glistened in the moonlight. He could see the whites of Jake's wide eyes glowing with fear. As well they should, thought Cougar. Nothing could please him more than for Roche to remain in a constant state of terror, leaving his nerves frayed and his belly knotted with so much apprehension that his insides gnawed at him.

Cougar sensed the same fierce need for vindication pulsing through Gray Eagle. They both wanted revenge so badly they could taste it.

And they would savor each succulent drop while Jake Roche sweated blood . . .

"Enjoy your night in the valley where the Cheyenne spirits dwell," Gray Eagle hissed spitefully. "And remember how the Cheyenne were confined like cattle herds to be butchered. Their fate will become yours, Jake Roche. Knowing you have been humiliated, defeated and subdued will be your special brand of torture."

Jake's reply was a disrespectful curse that damned Cougar and Gray Eagle and all their kind to the fiery pits of hell.

"Come dawn," Cougar said in a hollow voice, "you will see that there are three trails leading out of Cheyenne Canyon. One path will lead you right to me. One will lead to Gray Eagle. The third will lead to freedom."

Jake felt a glimmer of hope replace the gloom of despair. "You will allow me to escape if I chose the right path?"

"If you make the correct choice, you will find your peace, Jake Roche," Cougar assured him.

To Jake's astounded disbelief, Cougar and Gray Eagle evaporated into the shadows, leaving him to mark time by the beat of his own heart. Hunger and apprehension gnawed at him, but Jake focused his attention on the towering stone walls, wondering where to find the trails that would allow him to escape the jaws of hell.

He knew one path led through the mouth of the box canyon, but would that be the trail to freedom? Jake had dealt with that cunning half-breed often enough to realize Cougar could leave a man second-guessing himself to death. Cougar was an expert at mental warfare and unnerving suspense. Just when Jake and his men thought they could accurately predict Cougar's tactics, the wily predator turned their predictions to his lethal advantage.

Jake knew without asking that an immediate escape attempt would prove disastrous. Cougar and his blood brother would be on him like starved wolves. If Jake dared to break the terms Cougar offered there would be no hope for freedom.

On that bone-chilling thought, Jake curled up like a snake beside the rocks, clutching his dagger in his fist, uncertain whether he could trust those savages, and yet, afraid not to. But no matter what, Jake refused to sleep. He had to remain alert, just in case those conniving

Injuns double-crossed him. For sure and certain, Jake wasn't going to depart from this world without trying to take at least one of those red-skinned bastards with him.

# Twenty-four

Cougar stood beside the tumbling falls, savoring long-awaited revenge. He derived supreme satisfaction from the irony of trapping Jake Roche in the very canyon that had once been a haven for the Cheyenne. Using nothing more than the intimidation of skipping shadows and haunting calls, Cougar and Gray Eagle had herded Roche exactly where they wanted him to go.

Now Roche knew what true captivity was like. Just as the Cheyenne had been starved into submission, Roche would experience ravenous hunger. Just as the Cheyenne, and all other Indian tribes, had been confined to hated reservations, Roche would understand what it was like to be surrounded and granted limited alternatives.

Despite how the falsified accounts read, there had been no battle at Sand Creek or on the Washita. There had been no attack against Chivington or Custer and his Seventh Cavalry. There were only mutilated bodies of defenseless women and children huddled together and then shoved into mass graves to conceal evidence.

The Army had used propaganda against the Indians since time immemorial. Newspaper reports failed to mention the atrocities against the Indians whose land had been invaded. The Indians had been lied to and cheated at every turn. The only accounts that white society read and heard were of Indian retaliation against injustice. All this to justify assaults against the Indians.

Cougar inhaled a cleansing breath and discarded his bitter thoughts. All that mattered now was that Jake Roche would spend a sleepless night, wondering if Cougar and Gray Eagle had deceived him, wondering if he could locate the other two trails that led up the canyon walls before starvation got the best of him . . .

Feeling a familiar presence, Cougar pivoted to see Gray Eagle moving silently toward him. A dark object dangled from the warriors fist. Cougar knew without asking where Gray Eagle had gone and what he carried in his hand. Gray Eagle had collected his bounty from Burney Adair—the man who had brutally stabbed and scalped Gray Eagle's young bride eight years earlier.

"I will stand watch over the canyon," Gray Eagle volunteered as he came to stand beside his blood brother.

"There is no need," Cougar insisted, staring at the seven falls that danced over its stone ladder. "Roche is being held captive by his own fear. He expects us to guard the only exit he knows. Darkness prevents him from exploring possible trails. He will wait until dawn to search for the other routes out of the canyon. Survival is all Roche understands now, and apprehension will prevent him from making what he considers to be a fatal mistake."

When Cougar pivoted toward the cabin, his thoughts immediately turned to Roz. Although Cougar was anxious to know the fate of his cats, he knew Roz and Caleb needed reassurance.

"About the *Vee-hay-Kah*," Gray Eagle murmured as

he matched Cougar's long, lithe strides. "I have decided to court her if she finds me acceptable."

Cougar scowled. "She is not yours for the asking. She belongs with her own kind in the East—not here, miles away from the luxuries of white civilization."

"She seems content to me," Gray Eagle pointed out. "Now that my wife's death has been avenged, I am free to take another bride. I find the white woman extremely pleasing. She will make a fine bride and I will provide for her."

"No!"

Gray Eagle stopped short at Cougar's one snarling word. "I do not think the decision rests with you, *Nisimaha*. The choice belongs to the woman, just as Cheyenne custom decrees. Is it proper to consult the *Veehay-Kah's* father?"

"She no longer has one," Cougar reported.

"Her brother then?"

"She doesn't have one of those, either."

"What family does she have?" Gray Eagle demanded impatiently.

"None. She is just like you and me—overgrown orphans."

Gray Eagle nodded solemnly. "Then the choice is hers alone."

"No, it is not!" Cougar blared. "I have become her protector and I say she will not stay here after we have concluded our dealings with Roche!"

"You are becoming angry again, Cougar," Gray Eagle observed, watching those slitted eyes flash like gold flames.

"I am not angry!"

"Then you are upset."

"I am not upset!" Cougar roared.

"The fuse on your temper grows short," Gray Eagle noted, an amused grin pursing his lips. "Only Jake Roche and talk of the white woman sparks your fury." His gaze narrowed perceptively. "Her memory affects you as strongly as your need to avenge the atrocities our clan suffered. Why is that?"

Grumbling irritably, Cougar wheeled toward the cottage. "Just forget those absurd notions you have about Rozalie Gaylord. You are going to escort her and Caleb to Colorado Springs so they can take a coach to Howard Station when this is over."

"You are not coming with us?"

"No, I'll tend the ranch and livestock."

Perplexed by Cougar's uncharacteristic behavior, Gray Eagle followed him to the cabin. There was something Cougar wasn't saying. Gray Eagle could detect that much from Cougar's sharp tone of voice. He wondered if Cougar felt their friendship was threatened by talk of taking a wife. True, other arrangements for a cabin would have to be made if Gray Eagle took Roz for his bride. He would not think of embarrassing the bewitching blonde by possessing her body while Cougar was within hearing and seeing distance.

"I will build my own lodge when I take a wife," Gray Eagle felt compelled to say. "But my friendship for you will remain strong and true. You know that I will always be your companion spirit, *Nisimaha*."

"There is not going to be a marriage!" Cougar all but shouted. "I absolutely forbid it! You will take Roz back to civilization and that is the end of it. If you bring up the subject again I will end it with the force of my fist!"

When Cougar stalked off, Gray Eagle stared after him. This encounter with Jake Roche and Burney Adair had certainly brought out the very worst in Cougar. He was snarling and growling like a wounded grizzly. Gray Eagle decided to bide his time before initiating another discussion about Rozalie Gaylord. Cougar would be in a more receptive frame of mind after Roche chose the path that led to his fate.


Cougar halted at the cabin door and expelled a frustrated breath. He should have been more explicit in his reasons for refuting Gray Eagle's interest in Roz. But confessing that *he* had possessed her body, and that she had taken possession of his in the most intimate ways, was not a topic Cougar could openly discuss. He had plenty of difficulty accepting it himself. The very thought of Gray Eagle lying with the woman Cougar had introduced to passion seemed like a sacrilege.

In the eyes of the Cheyenne, Roz already belonged to Cougar. Although his clan occasionally took more than one wife, a wife never claimed two husbands. A dying man could will his wife to a brother or friend, but two men did not share a woman. It was unnatural, unspeakable. To the Cheyenne, the unity of the family was honored and sacred. Only the death of one brother left a surviving brother with the responsibility of providing and satisfying the widow.

In this case, Cougar may have been all but dead inside, but the conscience—one he had recently discovered he still had—would not allow him to give his blessing to a match between Gray Eagle and Roz . . .

An idea hatched in Cougar's mind. He was coming at this problem from the wrong direction. What he should do was warn Roz away from Gray Eagle. The courting warrior would drop his suit if Roz rejected him. That would save Cougar from confessing to the intimate nature of his association with the woman Gray Eagle fancied.

On that encouraging thought, Cougar rapped on the locked door. "Open up, Yank."

Roz flinched and then instantly relaxed when she heard Cougar's voice. There was no way to imitate that brusque, clipped sound. And furthermore, no one but Cougar called her Yank.

Struggling to her feet, Roz unbolted the door. The instant she saw that Cougar was still in one piece, she flew into his arms—whether he wanted her there or not.

An odd sense of inner peace poured through Cougar while Roz clung to him, her cheek brushing affectionately against his chest. His arms reflexively contracted around Roz, holding her as tightly as she held onto him.

"Thank God," Roz murmured in relief. "Cal and I have been almost frantic, wondering what became of you. Is it finally over?"

"Not yet, Yank," Cougar whispered against the tangle of silver-blond hair. "But soon . . ."

His gaze darted toward the hearth to see his missing cats curled up like contented kittens. "What in the hell did you do to my cats!" Cougar growled in outrage.

Roz grinned at the rumbling vibrations in Cougar's broad chest. Stepping away, she peered into that bronzed face that was puckered with displeasure. Only then did she notice Gray Eagle standing in the doorway. The warrior was studying her intently, his obsidian eyes shifting to Cougar and then back to her again. Gray Eagle said nothing as he veered around Cougar and ambled soundlessly across the room, carrying—

"Good Lord!" Roz choked. "Is that what I think—?"

"Gray Eagle!" Cougar barked. "Put your trophy out of sight. Now!"

Gray Eagle frowned when the color drained from Roz's face. Without a word, he strode into his bedroom to stash the object that had caused Roz visible distress. His gaze darted to Caleb who also looked a mite squeamish. Gray Eagle decided whites were plagued with queasy stomachs. Their butchering soldiers had no qualms about scalping and mutilating Indians, but white women and children were appalled by prizes of battle.

There was much he had to learn about the contradictions of white society, Gray Eagle decided.

"Letting the cats in wasn't my idea," Caleb blurted out before he was accused of wrongdoing—again.

Golden eyes zeroed in on Roz. "Then it must have been yours, Yank. You aren't worth a damn at taking orders, are you?"

Roz tilted a rebellious chin. "No, and I don't ever plan to get good at it. And you are very welcome for my doctoring your injured pets."

Cougar stared at the docile pumas. Great! Just what he needed—domesticated pussycats. A fine lot of help they were going to be!

When Cougar called to the pumas, they did no more than raise their broad heads and expel wobbly purrs. Cougar frowned at their uncharacteristic behavior. Throughout their years of living and working so closely together, the cats rarely disobeyed his commands. Roz's influence was nothing short of treason! The last thing Cougar needed was a trio of house cats, lounging by the hearth, growing fat and lazy.

Cougar's second crisp command was met with feeble whistle calls and no physical response. He glared at his traitorous companions.

"They're drunk," Caleb explained.

"They're *what?*" Cougar hooted, owl-eyed.

"Drunk," Caleb repeated. "Miss Gaylord decided to calm down the cats before tending their wounds so we wouldn't get bitten."

There were times—like now, especially now—that Roz wished Caleb would keep his trap shut. When Cougar's glittering gaze pinned her to the wall, she squirmed uncomfortably.

"Well, what else was I do to?" she asked.

"You should have waited until I got back!"

"How was I to know when that would be? One of the cats was losing a lot of blood and I—"

"—Opened the door when you were expressly forbidden from doing so!" Cougar finished with a scowl. "You could have found yourself recaptured, raped and killed. Wasn't there room in your pea-sized brain to consider that possibility?"

Roz fully understood how Caleb had felt when Cougar had chewed him up one side and down the other for his inaccurate target practice. Cougar was making her feel all of two inches tall. Roz, however, had been building tremendous character and self-confidence throughout her ordeals. She refused to be intimidated, even by this brawny giant who was showing her his full set of teeth, leaving the glaring impression that he was going to bite her head off.

"Now see here, Cougar, I nursed and sedated your cats because I felt it was necessary. If you don't like it then that is just too bad! And furthermore, you are not my father, brother or husband and you have absolutely no control over me."

Cougar stared at Roz in astonishment; Gray Eagle's thick brows jackknifed and Caleb's eyes widened in shock. Cougar's authority was being openly defied.

Cougar grabbed Roz by the elbow and towed her out the door. When she yelped in pain, the inebriated cats caterwauled. Cougar slammed the door shut, picked Roz up in his arms and stamped off.

"Do not *ever* defy me in front of other men," he growled as he set her on her feet a good distance away from the cottage.

"And do not *ever* dress me down in front of witnesses, unless you wish to be defied," she countered in the same loud voice.

"I am sending you back where you belong as soon as I have finished with Jake Roche. Gray Eagle will accompany you and Caleb to Colorado Springs. Until then, I expect you to do as you are told, for your own safety, as well as Caleb's."

"I won't leave until I'm good and ready and you cannot make me. This happens to be a free country, Cougar."

"No, it isn't," he denied. "This is my country and you are intruding. You will be leaving, even if I have to bind you up and tie you to a horse. And on your way down the mountain, you can convince Gray Eagle that you cannot accept his courtship. He has decided he needs another wife."

Roz frowned curiously. "What happened to the first Mrs. Gray Eagle?"

Cougar did not mince words. "Burney Adair's scalp was compensation for what he took from Little Star at the Washita."

Roz swallowed visibly. "I'm dreadfully sorry to hear about Little Star. I will be sure to convey my sympathy to Gray Eagle."

"No, you will not mention her name," Cougar insisted. "The Cheyenne do not speak the names of the dead. It is taboo."

"You just did it," Roz didn't hesitate to point out.

"I'm only half Cheyenne and in this case, it is better to speak the loved one's name rather than have you commit an offensive blunder. It would be as inappropriate as the kiss Gray Eagle bestowed on you earlier tonight."

"I will keep my commiserations to myself, if you insist, but I am not leaving here. I happen to love you and you could learn to appreciate my affection if you weren't so infuriatingly stubborn. You need me, Cougar, and I believe you care in your own way. Why won't you admit it?"

Cougar steeled himself against the words that caused a tide of sensations inside him. "Hear me with both ears, Yank. *You don't belong here,*" he said gruffly. *"Not now. Not ever."*

His harsh rejection put a mist of tears in her eyes. Oh, what was the use? Roz asked herself. Cougar was exactly like her father—so set in his hard, unfeeling ways that he refused to change, refused to give her a chance to make a difference in his life. Roz longed to be loved for all the right reasons, to have the gift of her affection accepted and appreciated. But it never had been and it looked as though it never would be. It seemed that she had been doomed to love the wrong people.

Maybe Cougar was right, she thought, dejected. Maybe not caring was less painful than opening one's heart and having it crushed like a fragile blossom. Muffling a sniff, Roz stared into Cougar's shadowed face, wishing she didn't care so deeply for this hard, lonely man and knowing it was impossible to control what she felt for him—to the very bottom of her soul.

Roz pushed up on tiptoe to brush her lips over the firm set of his mouth, savoring the taste and scent of him. "Perhaps you can send me away, Cougar," she whispered. "But you can't make me stop loving you. Even you do not possess the power to perform that feat."

When Roz turned and limped away, Cougar expelled a rough sigh. Despite his sharp words of denial and rejection, he still wanted her. He would always want her, but Cougar could not permit himself to succumb to a foolish whim.

"I never meant to hurt you, Yank," he murmured.

Eyes glistening with unshed tears, Roz pivoted to face the looming shadow. "Then take my heart and soul and keep them here in this valley. That is all I will ask of you. But know this, Cougar, as long as I live I will never forget you. No matter where you go or what you do, you cannot escape a love freely given. My own father died, still refusing to accept my affection for him. But that didn't stop me from caring about him, from trying to convince him that there was no shame in feeling and demonstrating affection. But Edward Gaylord never cared for anyone but himself. That is the dispiriting truth that I have had to accept."

"Yank, that's not why—"

Roz cut in quickly, determined to say her piece, doubting she would have the privacy and opportunity to do so later. "And remember this, Cougar. Just as you swear you died with your clan at the Washita, so shall a vital part of me die here, for I would have preferred to stay in this valley with you. And damn all the obstacles you think stand between us!"

"Yank—"

Cougar's voice dried up when Roz burst into tears. He didn't dare go near her. He couldn't trust himself. He had to make a clean, decisive break, to convince Roz that there was no future for a wealthy debutante and a barely civilized manhunter who'd had so many layers stripped off his soul that he had nothing left to give anyone, especially not a warm, tender-hearted woman like Roz who deserved so much more.

Once Roz's starry-eyed fascination for him wore off, she would begin to resent him and long for the life she had known. Cougar preferred to live with her disappointment. He didn't think he could endure watching her become disillusioned. He knew she would leave him sooner or later. Sooner was better. In time, Cougar would forget his obsession, the forbidden fantasies. Letting go was best; holding onto the impossible was a fool's dream.

Cougar was many things, but he was not a fool . . .

# Twenty-five

When Roz awoke the following morning, Cougar was nowhere to be seen. After their confrontation the previous night, she suspected he was deliberately avoiding her. Roz decided to make it easy on him. She gathered her painting supplies, in hopes of making herself scarce before he returned. Before she walked out the door, Gray Eagle held up a hand to forestall her.

"Cougar said that you may sketch wherever and whatever you wish, as long as you do not go near the falls."

Roz frowned, disappointed, for that was to have been her destination. "And why did Cougar restrict me from Cheyenne Canyon? Because he knows that is exactly where I want to go?"

Gray Eagle shook his head, his expression grim. "No, *Vee-hay-Kah,* that is where Jake Roche is being held captive."

"Oh." Roz stared at the wall, feeling petty and foolish. "Then rest assured I will take great pains to avoid the area. I have no intention of encountering Roche again."

When she turned away, Gray Eagle's quiet voice halted her, "I did not intend to offend you last night. I only wished to make my interest known. But I have come to realize that it is Cougar you want."

Roz opened her mouth and then clamped her lips shut, deciding silence would be her contribution to the conversation. She was obviously transparent in her affection and Gray Eagle was too observant. There was no need to admit to something the perceptive warrior had figured out all by himself.

Gray Eagle glanced at the pallet where Caleb was sleeping, after a night of restless tossing and turning. The boy and the injured cats were peacefully sprawled by the hearth. Leaving the foursome to their sleep, Gray Eagle escorted Roz outside.

"My blood brother has suffered many trials in life," he felt compelled to explain. "All of our people have suffered greatly and it is not easy for any of us to forget. But it has been worse for Cougar. He embarked on his manhunts to provide the money to claim this land, according to the white man's rules and regulations."

"This really isn't necessary," Roz insisted.

"It is necessary when I can see that he is greatly troubled and that you have deep feelings for him. A man who has never learned to love does not know how to respond to affection. Cougar has become a ruthless fighter and that is all he understands. He has forgotten how to feel, how to care."

Roz smiled tremulously. "It seems you know him well."

He nodded. "I have seen him return from dangerous forays against vicious criminals too many times. The life he has led for eight years has taken a tremendous toll. He has come to expect the worst and he prepares himself for it—mentally and physically. He does not know how to look for the best."

Gray Eagle shifted from one moccasined foot to the other and stared into the distance. "There is something else you should know about Cougar that might help you understand why he is not like other men. It is because he is . . ." He floundered for an appropriate English translation. "Cougar is . . . different, charmed."

Roz's delicate brow lifted curiously. "Charmed?"

"For lack of a better word, yes. He was trained by the Cheyenne oracle whose powers were well known to our clan. The shaman was Cougar's maternal grandfather. The full impact of spiritual powers were passed on to him before the wise one ascended to the Hanging Road, after the massacre on the Washita."

"What powers?" Roz demanded.

"I cannot say, *Vee-hay-Kah*. It is not allowed. I am only permitted to tell you that these powers do exist and that they can be very demanding of the medium who controls and directs mysterious energies."

"And I suppose that if Cougar were to give himself to love, he would lose these secret powers?"

Gray Eagle smiled down at the enchanting face that peered up at him. "I am beginning to understand the wide gap that separates our world from yours."

"Not as wide as Cougar prefers to think," Roz contended. "I believe in what I cannot see and in what I feel. It is Cougar who contradicts himself."

"How so, *Vee-hay-Kah?*"

"He resents prejudices, but he blames everyone with white skin for the injustices he has suffered. And yet, you have assured me that he commands unusual powers."

"He does," Gray Eagle readily affirmed, though uncertain as to the point she was trying to make.

"If he does not believe in the power of love and he ignores the combined strength of two hearts beating as one, how then, can you consider him charmed? If you ask me, he is shamefully blind."

Gray Eagle chuckled. "I see your point."

"Well, you are the only one who does," Roz sniffed resentfully. "Your blood brother may be all-powerful, but in some things he can be exceptionally dense. But perhaps, it is my disappointment that clouds my thinking. Perhaps the truth is that Cougar sees nothing in me for him to care about."

"Then I would have to agree that Cougar is blind. You are a wise and willful woman. In fact," Gray Eagle said with a wry smile, "I do not recall seeing anyone stand up to Cougar the way you did last night. Very few dare to risk his wrath."

"And even fewer dare to win his love. I always seem to be the one who takes a fool's dare," Roz murmured before she limped off to paint the landscape she had sketched the previous night.

Gray Eagle stared pensively after Roz, admiring her beauty and impressive spirit. She would make a fine wife for the right man, he decided. Unfortunately, the right man had very strict rules about bridging cultural gaps and risking emotions he had buried. Gray Eagle had discovered the rewards of love in his youth. He knew the powers it held, the pleasures it provided. Cougar understood only anger, suffering and hurt. Now, he lived only to fulfill the prophesy that whispered to him.

Wheeling about, Gray Eagle strode back to the cabin

to rouse Caleb. When the exhausted lad had been fed and warned away from the canyon, Gray Eagle ambled off to locate Cougar. Gray Eagle was anxious to see if Roche had discovered the other two trails leading from Cheyenne Canyon. According to Cougar's calculations, Roche would spend the better part of the day searching for the routes that wound around the wild tumble of rocks to the narrow ledges on the granite walls of the canyon. By nightfall, Roche would choose his path and face the consequences.

By now, the man should be half crazed, half starved and totally frustrated. That was as it should be, Gray Eagle thought to himself. The Cheyenne knew those feelings well. And soon, the lost spirits of those who had not survived would return to watch Roche choose his destiny.


Cougar crouched in the dense underbrush that rimmed the south wall of Cheyenne Canyon. Since daybreak he had monitored Jake Roche's activities. With enormous satisfaction, Cougar watched Jake futilely explore the rock barriers that formed three sides of his prison. As predicted, Jake hadn't gone near the trees that lined the mouth of the box canyon. Jake had outsmarted himself. Cougar almost resented the fact that Jake hadn't attempted escape during the night. He would have enjoyed hunting down Roche again, for the sport of it—like a cat toying with a defenseless mouse.

Jake was becoming desperate, Cougar knew. The man was scrambling from one location to another, frantically searching for a trail along the canyon wall. Since Jake lacked an Indian's perception, he was having difficulty visualizing possibilities in the mounds of rock that encircled him . . .

The rustle of bushes signaled Gray Eagle's approach. Cougar glanced over his shoulder to see his blood brother pushing the underbrush apart to hunker down beside him.

"Has our captive discovered one of the trails yet?"

Cougar shook his raven head. "It will take him most of the morning," he predicted. "By the time Roche finds the second route along the cliffs he will have exhausted himself."

"Too bad about that." Gray Eagle smirked unsympathetically "He won't be able to put up as much of a fight as I had hoped."

"Like the Indian tribes that were confined and half starved by the Army, Roche will have to survive on desperation alone," Cougar muttered, remembering.

Gray Eagle was silent for a moment. "It is like watching ourselves become conquered by overwhelming numbers of whites, struggling for our freedom. I appreciate the irony you have created for Roche. By the time his ordeal is over, he will fully understand the plight of the Indian."

"Roche will have endured every torment the Cheyenne suffered," Cougar promised. "And he will learn the meaning of the freedom he has taken for granted."

Gray Eagle smiled dolefully. He understood the precious value of freedom, having lost it eight years earlier. Even the spiritual haunts of his people had become his prison. He was no longer free to roam the mountains without fear of captivity, not unless he decided to adapt the ways of the white man and alter his appearance. Even now, Gray Eagle was a fugitive, just like Jake Roche.

"Keep an eye on Roche," Cougar requested. "I'll relieve you from guard duty before noon."

Gray Eagle nodded agreeably, watching Cougar slink through the bushes. "Cougar?"

The quiet rustling stopped. "Yes?"

"About Rozalie Gaylord."

Cougar scowled. "I thought I made it clear that she is off limits."

"To me, yes," Gray Eagle agreed. "But you are the one she has chosen. I think—"

"—like an Indian," Cougar cut in. "And I keep telling you she is white."

"She is also a woman who knows her own heart and her own mind. You would be foolish not to accept the powers she offers."

"What powers?"

Gray Eagle smiled when tawny eyes peered at him through the underbrush. "Despite the secret powers you command, there is another source of strength at your disposal. It has a voice you refuse to hear. A warrior cannot be all-seeing and all-hearing if he is deaf to a driving force that waits to be tapped."

"You have spent too much time alone the past few years," Cougar snorted. "You've lost track of reality."

"I am not a soothsayer, *Nisimaha,* but even I can predict that your long-awaited revenge against Jake Roche will not fully satisfy you." Gray Eagle chuckled enigmatically. "In this, I have full knowledge that you have yet to acquire."

Cougar muttered at Gray Eagle's nonsensical riddles

and crept away. The Cheyenne warrior's isolation had definitely begun to affect his mental facilities. When Roche had chosen his destiny, Cougar would order Gray Eagle to fasten himself into the trappings of a white man and march down to one of the bordellos in Colorado Springs. Having a woman as breathtaking as Rozalie Gaylord underfoot had been too potent a reminder of what Gray Eagle had been doing without since he lost his lovely Cheyenne maid. Cougar promised himself, then and there, to get his deprived blood brother some much-needed relief.

# Twenty-six

Jake Roche slumped against a pile of rock and panted for breath. After several hours of scrabbling up perpendicular walls, finding footholds that led nowhere, he discovered the first trail along the outcropping of stones on the south wall. Though the path was precarious, Jake had dropped pieces of fabric from his shirt to guide him when he attempted escape in the veil of darkness.

Those bastard Injuns would expect him to wait until dawn, just as Custer's cavalry attacked at first light. But Jake intended to outsmart those stupid savages. They weren't going to play cruel tricks on him! By the time Gray Eagle and Cougar planted themselves at the end of each route, Jake would be long gone. Even if he didn't locate the other path that led out of the chasm, he could employ the ones he had discovered—if he didn't pass out from hunger first.

Muttering curses to his captors, Jake trudged to the stream to drink his fill. If he could locate the second path along the stone walls, he could choose the easiest route to travel in darkness. But there was no way in hell that he was going to exit the same way he came in. Cougar and Gray Eagle would be standing watch at the mouth of the canyon, just as they undoubtedly had the previous night.

When this living nightmare was over, Jake vowed to organize another outlaw gang and return to deliver his own death wish—one that would stick. It would be his revenge for the hell those savages were putting him through.


"It is time, Gray Eagle," Cougar's cold words dropped like stones in the silence of the cabin.

Roz glanced up to see Cougar poised in the doorway. He had avoided her all day, coming and going from the canyon, taking his turn at guard duty without sparing her a glance.

The glint in Cougar's amber eyes was enough to leave icicles on Roz's spine. She had seen Cougar in this cold, ruthless frame of mind often enough to know that he was mentally preparing himself for battle. Even Caleb was leery of speaking when he noticed the forbidding aura that hovered around his idol.

Without a word, Gray Eagle rose from the pallet to collect the Cheyenne war club, bow and arrows. The playful smile that had been directed toward Caleb vanished from the warrior's dark features the instant Cougar appeared. Roz didn't have the slightest idea what would become of Jake Roche, but if the expressions that settled in both men's faces were any indication, Jake Roche was about to encounter more trouble than he could handle—and then some.

Roz watched Cougar move silently toward the mantel to collect a leather poke. He reached inside it to retrieve an odd-looking necklace and long claws attached to leather bands. Roz gulped uneasily when Cougar slid the claw bands onto his fingers and flexed them like a cat.

Cougar's bandoleers fell to the floor with a thud before he pulled the stone and bead necklace over his head. Grabbing the spear that was decorated with conchos and feathers, Cougar pivoted toward Caleb and Roz who peered at him apprehensively.

"Under no circumstances are you to open the door," he commanded gravely. "No matter what you hear, or think you hear, no matter what you believe you see, do not venture outside. It will not be safe."

Roz wanted to ask why, but the stony expression on Cougar's face invited no questions. Her gaze momentarily shifted to Gray Eagle who had fastened a bone and feather breastplate over his bare chest and grabbed the Thunderbird shield. Roz remembered what Gray Eagle had said about Cougar commanding incomprehensible powers, but she had the unequivocal feeling that Gray Eagle could wield a few powers himself. According to Cougar, the Thunderbird—leader of the sky creatures—manifested tremendous power.

Cougar called to the cats and they obeyed his cold command without hesitation. The chilly draft that followed both men out into the night sent a skein of gooseflesh flying across Roz's skin. She recalled Gray Eagle's reference to Cougar's unspoken gift from the Cheyenne mystic. She also remembered the night that Cougar had somehow managed to creep into the dark mine shaft to abduct Hud Caine right out from under the noses of four desperadoes.

To this day Roz couldn't fathom how Cougar could have singled out Hud in the darkness without rousing the other bandits. But she did recollect the strange images she had seen floating around the canyon when Cougar sicced his cats on Hud. It seemed to her that hundreds of gleaming eyes had materialized from the darkness—watching, waiting for Hud's screams to be stolen from him, waiting until there was nothing left but ominous silence.

Roz shivered uncontrollably. She was ever so thankful not to be in Jake Roche's boots right now. She had the feeling Roche was about to pay his penance for the torment innocent victims had suffered at his hands. For each life he had heartlessly taken, Jake Roche was about to lose an inch of his worthless hide.

"Miss Gaylord?" Caleb gulped audibly, his wide eyes fixed on Roz. "What are Cougar and Gray Eagle going to do?"

Roz glanced at the young boy who looked to her for answers she didn't have. "I'm not sure, Cal. All I know is that Jake Roche is going to regret taking us captive and butchering Indians while he served in the Army."

Caleb's jaw gaped. "The whites murdered Indians after they signed peace treaties? Why?"

Roz sank down beside Caleb, looping her arms around his quaking shoulders. "There are too many Jake Roches in this world who prefer to exterminate people who claim the land and riches these other men desire. They do not wish to find workable solutions or stifle resistance. They seek to eliminate it with pistols, knives and rifles."

"But Cougar says Indians only take what they need

from the land and other living creatures," Caleb replied. "Cougar says the Indians only kill to protect and defend what is theirs and to supply food for their families. They live in harmony with nature, because it is a gift from the Great Spirit, the life source of all things. Why would whites kill the people who lived in this land long before settlers showed up?"

"Greed," Roz murmured. "In order to claim Colorado's wealth of gold and silver, the whites pushed the Indians off their land. And when the Indians retaliated against western expansion, they were massacred and driven to reservations."

"And Cougar says the whites will take all the Indian Territory one day, too," Caleb quoted.

Roz remembered hearing Cougar make the same prediction to her. He had no faith in white man's words of honor, no faith in promises that had been broken countless times. But Cougar was going to discover that when Roz Gaylord gave her word, she meant exactly what she said. She had confessed her love, even if that was the last thing Cougar wanted or expected. And even if he forced her to leave, there was nowhere he could go to avoid her vow of love. If that stubborn, cynical man learned to believe in nothing else the whites said, he was going to learn that Roz's promise was everlasting. He had her heart, even if he wasn't all that thrilled with her gift.

Jake Roche was feeling incredibly pleased with himself. By late afternoon, he had discovered the second winding trail that skirted the northern wall of the canyon. That was the path he had decided to take. Jake figured those savages had enjoyed watching him flounder around all day, meeting one dead end after another.

And there was no doubt in Jake's mind that he was being watched.

Since Jake had left a trail of torn patches from his shirt to mark the first route, he expected Cougar or Gray Eagle to block that path. Jake felt certain the obvious route through the mouth of the canyon would also be barricaded. Therefore, he would take the route those savages least expected him to use.

Before darkness descended, Jake had made himself a pallet of grass and brush, hoping to leave the impression that he was exhausted and intended to rest for the night. His captors wouldn't be able to spot him when he climbed through the trees to reach the slanting slabs of stone that led to higher elevations.

Jake would be gone before those stupid Injuns located him. And this time, Jake promised himself, he wasn't going to fall prey to Cougar's cunning. Jake was heading for Colorado Springs as fast as he could get there. Wearing a disguise, he could board a train that would take him miles from the Cat Man's haunts. Eventually, Jake would return to dispose of those savages who had put him through so much hell.

Jake crept over to the rippling pool to guzzle enough water to fill his growling belly. With his dagger clutched in his fist, he slipped into the thick underbrush beside the stream, circling toward the pine tree that would enable him to reach the overhanging shelf of rock above him. He pulled himself up onto the sloping boulders to find solid footing on the narrow stone path.

Twice, Jake came dangerously close to plummeting over the ledge, and twice he plastered himself against the face of the canyon to catch his breath. No matter how weak he was from hunger, he was going to escape this rock prison.

When Jake recovered from his near fall, he levered himself onto a higher stone ledge that took him up a sixty-degree incline to another uneven platform of granite. Tackling the steep grades over precarious outcroppings of rock depleted his energy. After two hours of rigorous climbing, Jake sank down to rest. If he could rejuvenate his strength he could reach the cliff in another three or four hours. Then he would be home free, slithering through the grass to avoid the prowling savages. He wished he could see the looks on those Injuns' faces when they realized they had been outfoxed.

Struggling for breath, Jake dragged himself over the abrasive boulders to reach the final stretch of trail that led to level ground. When he glanced up the pebbled path, a foul curse exploded from his lips. He had explored the whole damned canyon and schemed for nothing! Five formidable shadows condensed in the moonlight. Cougar and Gray Eagle, accompanied by the three panthers that Jake thought he had killed the previous night, blocked his escape route. Damn them one and all!

"You lied! You promised that you would separately stand guard over two of the trails and that one path would lead to freedom!"

Cougar stared down at the haggard white man who had scratched and clawed and dragged himself up fifteen hundred feet of rock. Jake had expended every ounce of his strength—and all for nothing. Cougar could see Roche's chest heaving from exhaustion, see the outrage in his gray eyes. It was fitting that Roche had struggled to resolve his problem and exhausted himself in a futile escape attempt. That was the well-deserved irony of Jake Roche's personal brand of torture.

Eyes, like chips of amber ice, burned into Jake's furious sneer. "I offered you a white man's promise," Cougar told him slowly and deliberately. "But just as there was no hope for the Cheyenne, there is no place on earth, no freedom for you, Jake Roche. No matter when or how you attempted to escape, Gray Eagle and I would have been waiting at the end of your difficult journey. You were cornered and starved and forced to live the Cheyenne's doomed plight. Your private curse was to have your role reversed. The Indian hunter has become the defenseless prey."

Cougar's face clouded with the inexpressible hatred that had boiled inside him for eight tortuous years. Jake Roche was a despicable excuse for a man and Cougar despised the very sight of him.

"The Cheyenne were given no way out, and you will not have your freedom." Cougar decreed, raising the ceremonial spear high above his head. He pointed the stone blade toward the starlit heavens. "The curse that followed Yellow Hair into the Battle of Little Big Horn now descends upon you, Jake Roche. Each life taken at your hands will seek vengeance upon you, each scream for mercy will come back to haunt you. This is your sentence of death—the same brutal torment you delivered to the Cheyenne on the Washita."

Jake tried to swallow but his throat felt as if it were clogged with dust. He was stung by unspeakable fear when Gray Eagle gave a haunting cry, lifted the Thunderbird shield and stepped back into the shadows. The prowling panthers came to Cougar, limping in endless circles at his feet, pausing only to snarl down at Jake when they approached the jutting ledge of rock.

Cougar's voice had taken on a much colder, more hollow sound with each word uttered. The icy decree hung in the air like winter frost. Jake braced himself against the rocks on the narrow trail, watching in fascination as Cougar, dressed in nothing but a loincloth and moccasins, twirled the uplifted spear in hands that resembled a cat's paws.

A ghastly scream surged from Cougar's chest, rippling across the V-shaped canyon, rising like an invisible curl of smoke toward the sky. The haunting sound went through Jake like a thousand pricking daggers and drummed in his ears until he swore he would go mad listening to that infuriating scream that had followed him every step of the way from Howard Station.

Jake shrank back when he saw the black pumas rear upon their hind legs, bracing their front paws against the brawny giant's shoulders. And suddenly, four unearthly squalls pierced the darkness like an unholy chant.

The terrifying sounds flooded in all directions. Like an echo, other voices erupted from nowhere, amplifying with such intensity that Jake covered his ears to block out the wild screams that pulsated in rhythm with his pounding heart. Frantic, he pivoted to inch back in the direction he had come.

Jake halted in his tracks when he encountered a phenomenal spectre that descended on Cheyenne Canyon like a black thundercloud.

Jake swore he could feel a cold draft penetrating his flesh and settling in his bones. He staggered back, blinking in disbelief when the walls of the canyon came alive with what appeared to be green-gold eyes. Everywhere he looked he could see eyes winking like fireflies— hundreds, thousands of them glaring condemnation at him.

He screeched vile curses, but the sound drowned beneath the howling chants of the Cat Man and his screaming panthers. Another swirl of shadows and whistling wind plunged into the canyon, rising up the walls toward Jake, surrounding him until all he could see were glowing eyes and all he could hear was the murmur of hollow voices.

Jake screamed in terror when the darkness became ghostly faces embedded with vengeful golden eyes. He heard his name being chanted in the echoes that reverberated around the canyon and he swore he would go mad before the deafening noises stopped, before the haunting eyes of ghost cats devoured him.

"It is the Cheyenne spirits themselves who will become your judge, jury and executioners, Jake Roche." Gray Eagle emerged from the shadows to loom on the stony precipice, his ceremonial shield held high. "You will be swallowed alive by the night of a thousand eyes . . ."

# Twenty-seven

"Dear God!" Roz choked out when she heard the darkness abounding with the sounds of the screaming panther and the cry of the eagle. Haunting noises rushed past the cabin like a billowing wind, gathering force and momentum with each passing second. Roz swore every mountain lion and fowl within a hundred miles had converged on the cabin. The wind swirled and tapped against the glass panes like drumming fingers marking time.

"What's going on?" Cal wailed, covering his head with a quilt.

"A gathering storm, Caleb," Roz murmured, her wary gaze fixed on the window.

"It sounds like a pack of cats," Caleb said from inside his cocoon of blankets.

Roz swallowed audibly and drew nearer the window. The sight she encountered very nearly buckled her knees. Incongruous shapes and images materialized from the howling wind. An incandescent glow formed pinpoints of light that illuminated the night. A frothy black cloud swallowed the moon and the unending screams filled the darkness like haunted souls crying from Beyond.

*Cougar* . . . Roz knew without explanation what was happening outside. She had witnessed a less intense but similar phenomenon once before. Gray Eagle had hinted at such an occurrence, but when Roz peered into the darkness that was amplified by strange sounds and unbelievable images, she was afraid to trust her eyes and ears. Cougar was wielding the omnipotent forces of the Cheyenne Spirit World, assembling the keen powers of the panthers that prowled the mountains—ghost cats that were heard but never seen until they pounced and devoured.

An uneasy tremor trickled down Roz's backbone. She clamped onto the windowsill for support, mesmerized by the countless pairs of eyes that winked in the darkness. The screams that filled the night left Caleb crying and begging for the sounds to cease. But Roz couldn't move away from the window to provide the comfort the boy desperately needed. She was frozen to the spot, staring at the glistening eyes that burned like twin flames in black ice.

The powers of the cougar and thunderbird had been summoned, converging into one unstoppable force. This, Roz was certain, was the consummation of the Cheyenne prophesy. This was the vendetta for those who had been slaughtered at Sand Creek and on the Washita.

"Miss Gaylord!" Caleb sobbed hysterically.

Roz turned away from the window, not in fear, but in bleak resignation. She knew Cougar had sacrificed himself to fulfill the curse that had begun with General Custer and which would end with Jake Roche. Cougar had reached into the darkest depths to appease the tortured Cheyenne souls.

This was what Cougar could never satisfactorily explain to Roz. She had never fully understood what he could become until she witnessed the staggering manifestations of unleashed power filling the night.

Cougar may have been born half white, but he commanded the unified soul of the Cheyenne who cried out for retribution. He had convinced himself that the consummate power he commanded—a force that changed him into a legendary creature—would alienate her, terrify her. But Cougar was wrong. He had only succeeded in assuring Roz that he cared deeply, passionately. This incident was living proof of his unlimited capacity.

Roz smiled ruefully as she scooped Caleb up from the quilts and cradled him protectively against her. She knew she was the farthest thing from Cougar's mind at the moment, but he would never be closer to her thoughts or dearer to her heart than he was now. No matter what he became to avenge his lost clan, he still owned her soul. Nothing, not even witnessing the eerie sights and haunting sounds of this night, would alter her feelings for him. If anything, Roz admired and respected him all the more, though she doubted Cougar would believe that.

"Miss Gaylord? Are they gonna get us, too?" Caleb whimpered.

"We're perfectly safe," she assured the frightened lad. "It is Jake Roche who has every reason to fear what the night has to offer. By morning, you will be on your way home to your family, Caleb. This ordeal is almost over."

"Do you really think so?" Caleb asked on a shuddering sob.

Roz hugged him close when the screams brought down the night. "I know so, Caleb. I know so . . ."

A tear pooled in the corner of her eye when Cougar's image formed above her. She could see the proud, chiseled face of the man who refused to see that her affection was unfaltering and enduring. Roz had done all she could do, in hopes that Cougar would eventually come to realize that she cared deeply for him and that he did harbor fond affection for her.

And she had failed to make him believe . . .

Roz cuddled Caleb close, wondering if Cougar would return at all, if there would be anything left of him after he gave himself up to the fulfillment of the Cheyenne prophesy . . .

Jake Roche wheeled around, panting to draw breath. The haunting eyes were behind him; the foreboding silhouette of Cougar was above him. The tormenting screams had finally driven Jake to demented fury. He knew he wasn't going to be allowed to leave this canyon alive, that he would suffer the fate of his men. There was nothing Jake wanted more than to take this vicious half-breed bastard with him.

With a snarl, he cocked his arm to hurl his dagger at the cursed savage who had wrought torment and destruction. "Damn you and all your kind . . . !"

"Cougar!" Gray Eagle bellowed in warning when he saw the knife blade glistening in moonlight.

A vicious sneer curled Cougar's lips as he coiled to launch his spear. The impact of the missile struck Jake with such tremendous force that he was carried off the ledge as if he were shot from a cannon.

Gray Eagle staggered forward, watching the swirling shadows converge on Jake as he plummeted into nothingness. The wild scream of the panther spiraled up from the canyon floor, rising and billowing until an icy wind floated across the ledge.

For a long, silent moment Gray Eagle stood on the towering cliff, watching the sights and sounds evaporate into deathly silence. In the distance, the warble of birds replaced the incessant screams that echoed through Cheyenne Canyon. For the first time in almost a decade, Gray Eagle felt a sense of peace. Those who suffered at Sand Creek and on the Washita had been fully appeased. At long last, the prophesy had been fulfilled.

Bitterness and resentment drained from Gray Eagle while he stared into the black canyon. What he had seen and heard bore testimony to his beliefs. The powers of the Cheyenne spiritual world were omnipotent. Gray Eagle had offered up his own powers, combining the Thunderbird's and panther's strengths. He knew that it was not he who had sounded the warning and it was not Cougar who had hurled the spear that launched Jake Roche off the cliff and into the darkest reaches of hell. It was the restless souls of the lost whose unified forces had cried out and then struck that final blow to satisfy the Cheyenne curse.

It was done. The revenent spirits vanished as they had come—in a cloud of darkness. The sentinels of the night, watching with a thousand golden eyes, had abandoned their earthly posts.

Wearily, Gray Eagle pivoted to see Cougar lying

prone on the rock ledge. The cats were lying by his left side, as was their custom, always leaving Cougar the freedom to fight with his dominant hand. Alarmed by Cougar's immobility, Gray Eagle knelt down, fearing Jake Roche's dagger had found its target.

*"Nisimaha?* Are you hurt?"

Cougar heard the familiar voice calling to him from across a foggy sea. He had no strength left to battle his way back from the fathomless recesses into which he had reached to satisfy the prophecy. Odd, he thought groggily. It was as if he were trapped in some gloomy dungeon that was his body, staring out through windows that were his eyes. Yet, he was unable to communicate with the man who peered at him with such grave concern. With Gray Eagle's combined power, Cougar had been driven too deep, had given all to appease the tormented Cheyenne souls.

"Cougar?" Gray Eagle reached out to give his blood brother a shake, but he jerked away from flesh so cold it burned to the touch.

Cougar felt nothing, saw only the hazy motion of Gray Eagle's retracted hand, noted the haunted expression on the warrior's face. Cougar tried to speak, but no words formed, no sound passed his lips. Cougar inhaled a shadow of a breath and heard it echo through his chest, as if it were an empty cavern. The energy required to breathe demanded more than Cougar could muster.

The only warmth he could feel was the steady pulse of the panthers that lay beside him. Cougar concentrated on absorbing the heat and strength they possessed, aching to speak and be heard from inside the dark reaches that imprisoned him.

"Leave me," Cougar shouted, but his voice was barely a whisper.

Gray Eagle strained to hear Cougar's words. He glanced at the lounging cats that stared into the night, silent and watchful. Hesitantly, Gray Eagle dragged his feet beneath him and stood up, exhausted from the demands made upon him.

Leaving Cougar sprawled lifelessly on the rocks went against his grain, but Gray Eagle did not argue with the hollow command. He knew Roz and Caleb were huddled in the cabin, tormented by the shrill, harrowing shrieks that had torn the darkness apart. It was up to Gray Eagle to provide reassurance.

What was he going to say when asked what had become of Cougar? How did one explain what one had to see and feel to believe? Could those who hailed from the white man's culture comprehend the powers of worlds that entwined and occasionally intersected?

With a heavy heart and weary soul, Gray Eagle cast one last glance at Cougar and walked off into the night.


The quiet rap at the door brought Roz to her feet. She had waited forever for the screams to fade into silence, for Cougar and Gray Eagle to return. When she unbolted the door, the grim-faced warrior paced inside to replace the war club, shield and bow on the mantel. The spear was mysteriously absent and so was the man who had carried it away.

"Where's Cougar?" Roz questioned anxiously. "Is he all right?"

Gray Eagle peeled off the feathered breastplate and laid it on the mantel, refusing to meet Roz's concerned stare. "Cougar is still on the canyon rim with the cats."

Caleb sat up on the pallet, his wide eyes fixed on the Cheyenne warrior. "He is coming back, isn't he?"

Gray Eagle smiled remorsefully.

"Gray Eagle?" Roz prompted when the warrior didn't respond immediately.

Another apprehensive moment elapsed. Roz could not endure the suspense; she sidestepped around the Indian warrior, headed for the door.

"No, *Vee-hay-Kah*." Gray Eagle snaked out a hand to pull her back to his side. "You must not go to him now."

"Why not?"

"I cannot explain."

"Where is he?"

"I cannot say for certain. He is somewhere beyond my own comprehension." When Roz tried to pose another question, Gray Eagle flung up a hand to forestall her. "You will occupy Cougar's room, as you did last night. At first light I will escort you and the boy to Colorado Springs. The stage will take you to Howard Station."

Before Roz could object—Gray Eagle shoved her into the bedroom and closed the door. He was in no mood for her protests. The events of the night weighed on his mind and soul, demanding that he rest and recuperate.

"Gray Eagle?"

"What is it Little Bear?"

"Miss Gaylord told me what Roche and the other soldiers did to the Cheyenne. I'm sorry . . ."

Gray Eagle crouched beside the doe-eyed lad and smiled fondly. "When you grow to be a man, perhaps you will understand what your own people cannot. There will be one kindred spirit to bridge the gap between your world and mine."

"And maybe when I become a man, I'll be better at explaining white customs to you."

Gray Eagle chuckled and ruffled Caleb's crop of brown hair. "The problem, Little Bear, is that you do not yet explain any better than I understand. In time, perhaps we will both become more familiar with each other's rituals."

Caleb yawned broadly and snuggled beneath the quilts. "You should have asked me about table manners instead of courtship. Ma saw to it that I'm good at those. Except for talking too much to stage passengers," he amended.

Grinning, Gray Eagle tucked Caleb in bed and trudged toward the room he and Cougar had shared in order to accommodate their guests. He wondered if Cougar would return to the pallet he had made for himself the previous night.

Gray Eagle sent a prayer heavenward, hoping Cougar would eventually return from whence he had gone. Wherever Cougar was now, it was a long way from the cabin sheltered by cedars and pines . . .

# Twenty-eight

Cougar fought his way up one grueling step at a time, desperately trying to reach places he remembered being before. He heard the quiet purring of the cats and eased toward them, savoring the warm flame that began to melt the ice around his soul—or rather what was left of it after so many forays in hell. But the cats could not provide all Cougar needed to feel again, to live rather than exist. There was only one place he could go to reclaim the shattered slivers of what he was.

Roz . . .

Cougar channeled all thought on the image of enchanting blue eyes and hair that shimmered like a silver-gold flame. Each time he had touched Roz he had come alive through her uninhibited responses. Each sensation of pleasure and satisfaction he had offered her had opened and unfurled inside him. If he could summon the energy to move, to reach the fire that breathed life back into what was left of his heart and soul, he could survive.

Cougar inhaled a determined breath and crawled onto hands and knees. He felt drained, more so than he had ever been. Knowing Jake Roche had paid full penance seemed hollow consolation. It was a knowledge Cougar accepted without the accompanying satisfaction. He would have to feel something—anything—before he could savor the fulfillment of the prophesy.

Roz . . .

If only he could hold her, feel her silky arms around him. Forbidden though she was to him, she was what he desperately needed right now. She was the beacon that lighted his way through darkness, his touchstone.

By sheer will alone, Cougar struggled to his feet. He felt as though he had lead weights strapped to his ankles, impeding his progress as he staggered along the canyon rim. It took an eternity to circle the falls and trudge into the valley. But with each step he felt a bit of strength returning, felt the flickering warmth he knew awaited him. Beyond the hill was his lifeline. If he could reach the cottage he could find himself again . . .


Roz flinched when icy fingers closed around her elbow. She had just drifted off to sleep after lying awake for hours on end, wondering what had become of Cougar. A gasp tumbled from her lips when she saw the shadow looming beside her—a shadow with eyes like the flickering golden flames she had seen burning in the night.

She remembered feeling Cougar's cold flesh once before, but never had it been as frigid as it was now. It was as if the chill of death had settled into him. The thought terrified her. She longed to hold him in her arms until she could feel his pulse beating against her chest, feel the warmth of his breath caressing her skin.

She would give all she had if she could bring him the inner peace she sensed eluded him.

"Roz, I . . . need . . . you . . ."

Cougar's voice rattled as he eased down beside her in bed. With each ragged breath he inhaled the sweet scent of her. He felt her lips graze his, felt her nestle familiarly against him as she drew the quilt over them. The three words of love that he had constantly rejected came to him in a soft, feminine whisper, and Cougar reveled in the contentment that rippled through him when she spoke the adoring phrase over and over again.

His hands moved on their own accord, rediscovering the lush curves and swells with a tenderness that only this one woman demanded from him without even asking. He felt her shiver beneath his sweeping caresses and he wondered if the touch of his hand brought a chill rather than pleasure. But when he withdrew his hand, Roz arched toward him, silently requesting more, not less of his touch.

With each gliding caress Cougar could feel strength regenerating, immeasurable pleasure infusing the empty vacuum that encompassed him. Each pulsebeat became a steady throb of burning need that assured him that he lived and breathed. Cougar felt every nerve and muscle contract and then relax as Roz returned each kiss and caress with a gentleness he could never emulate. The spell she cast was like a warm spring bubbling inside him, burgeoning until he knew beyond all doubt that he had escaped the dangerous recesses that had entrapped him. Desire hammered through him and Cougar welcomed it, reveled in the white-hot sensations that burned like fire.

His breath tore out of his chest when her hand closed delicately around the throbbing length of him, exciting him, arousing him almost beyond bearing. Cougar wanted to return the pleasure tenfold, for he had begun to live for the sound of her sighs, the feel of her satiny flesh beneath his roaming hands.

Roz's tender touch and eager response brought Cougar indescribable satisfaction. She was indeed the touchstone by which he measured the very heartbeat of his own existence. If not for Roz, Cougar knew he would never have been able to make the return trip from the icy depths of mind and body control. Through her eyes, her touch, Cougar could discover the effusive splendor of paradise.

Cougar concentrated all thought, all energy on pleasuring Roz as completely as she had always pleasured him. His sensitive fingertips swirled around the dusky peaks of her breasts, arousing ineffable needs that ricocheted through her and whispered into him. When he drew the taut bead of her breast into his mouth and gently suckled, he heard her breath catch. She arched up in silent request for more loving touches, yielding to him in complete abandon.

And suddenly, those frantic moments of uncertainty he experienced, while he lay on the edge of the cliff, vanished from his body and his mind. He couldn't get enough of the taste and feel of Roz's sweet, responsive body. He cherished each wondrous sensation that making love to Roz awarded him. He offered tenderness without impatience. He was ravenously hungry for her and yet oddly satisfied with savoring each profound sensation that rippled through her and shimmered through him.

How in the world was Cougar going to forget this incredible moment when he couldn't permit himself to remember what they had shared without driving himself insane? Touching her, holding her was bittersweet splendor. He, who well knew the torments of the damned, would be cursed with one more tortuous memory that would linger forever in his mind.

He didn't want Roz to go away, but he couldn't allow her to stay—for her own good. She was destined for better things in better places than this rough and tumble wilderness. She was meant for a man who could provide all the luxuries she deserved, a man who could love her with more than just the shell of his heart and what was left of his soul.

Yet, Cougar vowed as his lips drifted over the small indentation of her waist, no one was ever going to love Roz as reverently and completely as he would tonight. For all the times he had intentionally and unintentionally hurt her, he was going to offer all that he was to pleasure her. It was his gift to her—giving all of himself to her, for her, just as she gave so freely to rescue him from those indefinable depths.

Ever so gently, his hand glided between her thighs to caress the molten core of femininity that burned only for him. He stroked her, teased her until he felt the coil of liquid heat shimmering around him. Cougar relished the glowing flame that burst to life inside him, bringing him all the way back from where he had been—and far beyond.

An inexplicable tremor went through him as his lips

moved across her softest flesh. The gliding penetration of his tongue evoked her shuddering sigh and trembling response. Where there had been icy darkness hours earlier, now there was intense heat that burned him. Cougar knew without question that he could never possess another woman the way he possessed Roz. What they shared was too profound, too private, too remarkably satisfying.

The scent and taste of her saturated every cold crevice until he became a living fire. The feel of her pliant flesh beneath his hands and lips was survival itself. Her hot quivering responses were his very existence. Cougar had been the hollow darkness and Roz transformed him into the sun—the living, pulsing radiance of hunger that fed on her wild responses.

When he felt her body contracting around his fingertips, Cougar knew what it was like to be consumed by fire, to be so lost in pleasure that dying seemed a small sacrifice for giving of himself and receiving far more in return. He and Roz were tripping along the brink of wild, mindless abandon. He could hear her whispering his name like a quiet chant, calling to him to appease the ardent need he had summoned from her.

Cougar levered himself above her and peered down into that exquisite face that was alive with the need he had awakened. Until the day he died he would never forget the loving expression mirrored in those glistening blue eyes. And as hard as he tried, he would never forget those three words she murmured as he settled himself in the cradle of her thighs, feeling her burning around him, possessing him as surely as he possessed her.

The darkest hour before dawn came crashing down

on Cougar like a meteor shower, consuming all within its path. Ecstasy so intense, so riveting, streamed out in all directions. Cougar drove against her and felt her match him touch for most intimate touch, breath for shuddering breath. They moved in perfect rhythm, as if they had been designed for each other, as if they were of one body and spirit gliding on pinioned wings through paradise.

Rapture surged, swelled and crested until Cougar clutched Roz to him in frantic desperation. His powerful body shuddered above her, over and over again, until pulsations of pleasure encompassed him. This splendorous warmth and completeness was the only reality he needed. Here, within the circle of Roz's silky arms, was inexpressible satisfaction.

"I will always love you, Cougar. Know that, believe that. Remember . . ."

Cougar closed his eyes and held Roz close when his renewed strength abandoned him. But this time he didn't sink into cold oblivion; he lay quietly, enjoying the kind of inner peace he had never known. This stunning nymph, who hailed from a world far away from what he understood, had given him back his heartbeat and smoothed the wrinkles from his weathered soul. He could never repay Roz for what she had done for him on a night when a thousand vengeful eyes had come to seek long-awaited justice, executed through the powers he had been taught to command. Without Roz's loving, generous touch he would have been lost forever. Cougar had saved her life and now she had repaid the debt by rescuing him.

Cougar sighed tiredly, wondering if this delicate

beauty knew of the power she wielded. Just as she possessed the artistic talent to create, she had the phenomenal ability to heal the most tortured of souls.

On that thought, Cougar's hand glided over Roz's hip, molding her to him and he fell into exhausted sleep. This was the last time he would know incomparable contentment. Only the forbidden had been enough to satisfy him, revive him.

And the price Cougar was forced to pay was letting Roz go in just a few short hours—at that moment when darkness surrendered to the majestic golden rays of dawn . . .

Gray Eagle heard the quiet creak of the other bedroom door, saw the first glorious rays of dawn spill over the mountain and into his room. He glanced over at Cougar's unused pallet. Rolling quickly to his feet, Gray Eagle eased open the door to watch Cougar steal silently away from the room where Roz slept.

A sense of relief rippled through Gray Eagle when he saw his blood brother looking his old self again. After witnessing Cougar's condition the previous night, Gray Eagle had retired to bed with grave concern. He considered it highly significant that Cougar had gone straight to Roz to revive his strength and spirit. The deed spoke clearly to Gray Eagle, but he doubted his stubborn friend had accepted the truth of his feelings, because Cougar was convinced he no longer knew how to feel, how to care.

An amused smile pursed Gray Eagle's lips as he watched Cougar crouch beside the sleeping boy who lay before the hearth. Cougar reached out to trail his forefinger across Caleb's cheek. The boy stirred without waking and Cougar smiled fondly at him. That simple gesture convinced Gray Eagle that Cougar was undergoing change, whether he realized it or not.

Dressed only in a loincloth, Cougar rose from his crouch and made his way outside. Gray Eagle followed at a distance, curious about his blood brother's destination. When he heard the splash, Gray Eagle knew where he would find Cougar.

"So you have returned, *Nisimaha*. That is good. Last night I began to wonder if you would."

Standing waist deep in the stream, Cougar whirled around to see Gray Eagle peeling off his clothes. The warrior walked into the water, gritting his teeth at the cool temperature.

"You will take Caleb and Roz to Colorado Springs after they awake," Cougar commanded. "The Howards have waited long enough to know their son's fate."

"And what will you be doing while I'm gone?"

"Rounding up mustangs to break and train."

"And you believe this will satisfy you?" Gray Eagle queried.

"Hasn't it always?"

Gray Eagle grinned wryly as Cougar sidestroked across the channel. "Perhaps it has before. Now I'm not so certain. Things have changed."

Cougar stared at some distant point on the horizon. "I don't know what you're talking about."

Laughter erupted from the warrior's lips. "Yes, I believe you do, though you are not prepared to accept it yet."

"No more riddles," Cougar muttered at his smiling friend. "Say what you mean."

Gray Eagle ignored the crisp command. He completely submerged himself in the creek and then waded ashore. "In this instance, I think it is best to let *you* discover what I believe you already know, but hesitate to admit. You are a proud warrior who does not appreciate being told what to think. I only hope you come to your senses before it's too late."

After Gray Eagle dressed, he turned back to see Cougar standing in the creek, arms crossed over his massive chest, frowning pensively. "I will return to the cabin tomorrow, to see how long you last, *Nisimaha.*"

On the wings of that baffling remark Gray Eagle strode off. Cougar scowled. Gray Eagle kept smiling as if he harbored some amusing secret that he refused to share. And what, Cougar wondered, did he know that he had yet to discover for himself?

All Cougar knew for certain was that the previous night was brimming with memories. He had passed the milestone where his haunting past ended and his future began. He could make a clean break now that the Cheyenne prophesy had been fulfilled. He needed to give this ranch first priority, needed to begin again, needed to find long-awaited contentment.

The same held true for that misplaced Easterner, Cougar mused as he came ashore. Her long-suffering ordeal with Roche's raiders was no more than a bad memory. And when Roz recalled how Cougar had come to her in the darkest hour of the night—like a cold shadow in need of revitalization, she would realize he was not the kind of man who was worthy to be a part of her future.

Rozalie Gaylord deserved far more. That was the one truth Cougar could never forget. He had to set her free. In years to come, Roz would silently thank him for sending her back to civilization. It was the only sensible answer to a question that never should have been asked, to a forbidden memory that never should have been made . . .

# Twenty-nine

"We are ready to leave, *Vee-hay-Kah.*"

Roz heard Gray Eagle's quiet voice behind her, but she continued to stare across the peaceful valley, hoping for one last glimpse of Cougar and his magnificent black cats. All she had was the memory of his devastating lovemaking before he slipped from her arms while she slept. He wasn't coming back to say good-bye. Where his passion had ended the previous night, there also had Cougar bid her a silent farewell.

It was over.

Her words of love had not been enough to hold Cougar, to convince him that the only place she wanted to be was with him. She was not woman enough to sustain his interest after his desires had been appeased. He was sending her away . . . and he didn't care that he had broken her heart in a thousand pieces.

Turning her back on her shattered dreams, Roz mounted her horse. Absently, she listened to Caleb chatter nonstop while they trekked down the mountain path toward Colorado Springs. Gray Eagle ventured no further than the foothills overlooking the railroad settlement before he halted. There, he waited in the shadows of the trees until Roz and Caleb reached their destination.

With saddlebags heaping with the recovered gold from the robbery at Howard Station, Roz headed for the marshal's office. After she had purchased the stage tickets, she bought their lunch with the money she had left.

Roz barely remembered the trip to Howard Station. Her thoughts were elsewhere. The loneliness that accompanied her over the washboarded route was colored with images and memories that brought her close to tears. But Roz battled for composure, disciplined herself to conceal her emotions, just as Cougar was in the habit of doing.

It may have been over, but it was not forgotten . . . Loving Cougar would never be forgotten. Roz had come to care so deeply for him that he consumed her every thought . . .

"Caleb! Thank God!"

Francene's excited voice penetrated Roz's pensive trance. She glanced through the coach window to see Francene dashing off the trading post porch. Relief and love beamed in Francene's face. In all her twenty-one years, Roz had never received such a joyous homecoming, not even during her yearlong absences at boarding school. Her father had been too preoccupied and impassionate to demonstrate what little regard he had for her. As for Cougar . . .

Roz smothered the depressing thought. Thanks to Cougar she was alive and she was back where she started more than two weeks earlier. She had resigned herself to her losses and accepted defeat. It was time to return to New York. This stage station, nestled beside the picturesque valley and towering mountain peaks, triggered too many bittersweet memories. Roz would wallow in self-pity and misery if she stayed here, hoping, waiting . . . in vain.

*It was time to go home, to begin again . . .*

Roz frowned. For a moment she wasn't sure if that whispered resolution was the product of her own thoughts or a quiet voice that had been planted in her mind. It was an odd sensation, to say the very least.

"Caleb!" Francene flung open the door the instant the coach rolled to a stop. Before Caleb could say one word, Francene pulled him off the seat and into her arms, hugging him until his face turned crimson.

"Gee whiz, Ma, I'm a man now," Caleb protested self-consciously.

Francene glanced past her son to see Roz emerge from the coach. When their eyes met, Roz nodded reassuringly. Caleb had endured the kind of ordeals that made men out of boys. Those with less strength of character would have crumbled. Caleb, however, had simply developed more character along the way.

"Your son is a very courageous young man," Roz told Francene.

"Cal!" Gideon's booming voice echoed out of the barn. He surged outside, dashing toward his son, despite his mending wound.

When Gideon hoisted Caleb up to smother him in a bear hug, Francene tapped her husband on the shoulder. "According to your son, men do not go around hugging, especially each other."

"They don't?" Gideon set Cal to his feet and straightened the shirt that had been twisted around the boy's neck. "Oh, the hell they don't!" He snatched Caleb off the ground and clung to him for a long moment that put tears in Francene's eyes.

"There aren't words to express how glad we are to have you back, Cal," Gideon insisted. "Ask me anything, any time you please. From now on, I'll always make time for your questions, I promise, son."

When Caleb was returned to his feet, he peered up at his father with a newfound confidence. "I don't have as many questions these days," he proudly announced. "I have answers."

Gideon arched a graying brow, amusement dancing in his hazel eyes. "Do you indeed?"

"Me and . . . Miss Gaylord and I learned to depend on ourselves," Cal insisted. "We even saw Cougar—"

Roz discreetly jabbed Caleb in the ribs to silence him. The mere mention of Cougar's name was enough to destroy what little composure Roz had collected. All she wanted was a bath, a meal and the luxury of a bed—time to be alone with her thoughts and pretend she hadn't had her heart torn out by the taproot.

While Francene and Gideon bundled Cal off to hear what Roz was certain would be a lengthy, detailed account of their captivity and release, she strode off to her room.

"So you are Rozalie Gaylord, of the New York Gaylords," came an unfamiliar voice from behind her.

Roz half turned to see a swarthy, dark-haired man who looked to be twenty-seven—or thereabout—looking at her intently. The stranger was garbed in chambray and denim and he was leaning negligently against the corral. In curious fascination, Roz watched the man push away from the fence and saunter toward her.

"Well, well," he chuckled as he looked Roz up and down—again. "As I live and breathe, the bastard left his mark on you, too, didn't he?"

Roz frowned at the rude stranger, wondering where this peculiar conversation was leading. Who the blazes was the cocky rascal? There was something oddly familiar about him, but Roz couldn't remember ever meeting him.

It was the blue eyes, Roz decided. There was something intriguing about those eyes and the way the man's full lips curved up on the left side of his mouth. She knew this man. From where? When?

"I'm glad to know you returned from your traumatic ordeal in one piece, Rozalie. At first, I wasn't sure I cared one way or another. But, after replacing Gideon while he recuperated, and hearing Francene's praise of your stunning beauty and artistic talent, I'm wondering why I've harbored so much resentment. After all, you had to live with the bastard. I didn't."

Roz blinked, bewildered by the comments. "At the risk of sounding dense, just who the devil are you?"

Seth bowed elegantly before her and grinned as he rose to full stature. "I'm your half brother. Seth Radburn is the name."

Roz staggered as if she had taken a blow to the jaw: "You're my—?"

"—Half-brother," he confirmed, reaching out to steady her. "It's the eyes, I think. His eyes. I always resented that, too, until I got a look at you. Quite becoming in that bewitching face of yours, I might add."

Nonplussed, Roz stared at the man who claimed to be her half-brother. No one had told her Edward Gaylord had been married before. Was this wily adventurer trying to weasel his way into her inheritance? Probably. At least it was a novel approach. Roz gave him credit for his creativity. Most men offered marriage, not brotherhood.

Seth nodded knowingly when he noted the suspicion that clouded Roz's expressive eyes. "You're thinking I'm after the money since my mother wrote to inform me of Edward's death. I can't say I spent much time grieving for a father who didn't want me or my mother. We were much too plain and simple for the life Edward Gaylord aspired to when he left Philadelphia to settle in New York. I was only the mistake he skipped town to avoid."

Roz frowned warily. How did this man know her father hailed from Philadelphia? He must have done a great deal of research in order to convincingly portray her long-lost brother.

"All I acquired from my dear father was his blue eyes and the label of bastard," Seth added coldly.

Roz still wasn't convinced. "If you lived in Philadelphia, what are you doing way out here?"

"A reasonable question," Seth acknowledged, glancing toward the coach. "Unfortunately, I don't have time to answer it. I'm still employed here, much to Gideon's dismay. He thinks I'm trying to worm my way into a permanent position here. I didn't bother telling Gideon that I insisted on undertaking these duties the minute I learned of the holdup because I heard that you were one of the hostages abducted by Roche's raiders. Expe-

riences like you suffered give the company a bad name."
He smiled mysteriously. "The superintendent doesn't
like that. It's bad for business."

Roz was still standing there with her jaw gaping when
Seth strode off to hitch the fresh team of horses to the
whiffletree. Inhaling a steadying breath, she aimed herself toward her room and once there flopped down on
the bed. Her mind was still reeling when Seth tapped
on the partially open door and invited himself inside.

"What do you want from me?" Roz questioned as
Seth parked himself in the chair and propped a sinewy
arm on the edge of her dresser.

Seth shrugged nonchalantly. "At first, I guess I wanted
to rail at you for enjoying all the luxuries I did without,
to curse you and the woman who took my mother's place,
leaving her alone and pregnant and demoralized by a man
who had no concern for anyone but himself."

Seth knew Edward Gaylord exceptionally well, Roz
decided. He had summed up her father's selfish outlook
on life in a nutshell.

"Did your mother love you?" she asked out of the
blue.

Seth was taken aback by the question. "Of course,
she loved me. Still does, at least her letters say so. Why
do you ask?"

"If you grew up in a loving atmosphere, then you
received the better bargain. I should resent you."

Seth leaned back in his chair, crossing his booted feet
at the ankles. He studied Roz for a long moment. "He
treated you the same way he treated my mother, didn't
he? Like an object he ignored unless you could serve
some useful purpose?"

Roz nodded bleakly, remembering the frustrating years of trying to please and impress her father . . . and always failing . . .

Just as she had failed to make a difference in Cougar's life.

"I went to New York to see Edward ten years ago," Seth admitted. "I wanted to introduce myself to the man who turned his back and left the mother of his child destitute and humiliated while he languished in luxury. Edward presumed I came to blackmail him. He dropped a pouch of money in my hands to get rid of me. For my mother's sake, I took what he offered. I also accepted the job he promised me, even though I knew he was sending me West, hoping I wouldn't come back. With Edward's connections and investments in the Overland Express Company, he made arrangements for me to work at the headquarters in Leavenworth, Kansas."

"So you accepted what little he was willing to give and you stayed away? You deserved more than that after the shameless way you were treated."

"I didn't care for the man at all and I had no intention of trying to get close to him, not that Edward wanted any such thing," Seth said with a snort. "Besides, my mother had married a man who truly cared about her, and I had acquired a taste for adventure. I found the offer to my liking. I was promoted to the Colorado division last year. I'm sure Edward had something to do with that. The farther west I moved, the better he liked it."

Seth smiled and shrugged. "Now Denver feels like home. I inspect way stations and travel the routes that require maintenance. It provides an interesting life. I usually leave the management to company men who prefer to remain behind a desk."

"And just how far have you come up the ladder in the stage company?" Roz questioned interestedly.

Seth flashed her a mischievous smile. "Trying to get your hands on my money, little sister?"

Roz rather enjoyed that title; she also enjoyed Seth's playful banter. He was the distraction she desperately needed after Cougar walked away without looking back.

"Certainly not," she said with feigned indignation. "We Gaylords are stinking rich, you know, and spoiled rotten. In fact, there are those around here who refuse to associate with wealthy Easterners because we are pitifully out of place."

"The man called Cougar," Seth guessed. "Gideon mentioned that that half-breed gunslinger might be interested in you."

Roz hurriedly changed the subject, drawing Seth's speculative frown. Her association with Cougar was too painful to discuss. Gideon and Francene had probably told Seth more than Roz preferred he knew about Cougar, since they were so fond of him.

"I asked you about your position with the stage line. You didn't answer me," she reminded him.

Seth grinned wryly. "I do well enough."

"Be more specific," she demanded in a tone that would have done Cougar proud. He had taught her the benefits of never asking when one could demand.

"I'm superintendent of the division that covers the eastern half of the territory," Seth replied.

"Superintendent?" Roz was impressed.

"Headquartered in Denver. I probably should thank

Edward for ensuring I moved up the ladder to a position of authority so I would stay miles away from New York."

Roz frowned pensively, remembering her father's adamant request that no one other than a Gaylord would be allowed to inherit his money. Now Roz understood what it was that Edward refused to admit, up to and including the day he died.

"Maybe I should thank Edward," Seth added belatedly, "but I prefer to believe my hard work paid off. I certainly got little else in this world because of my father . . ."

His voice trailed off when he noticed the stack of drawings and canvas paintings on the opposite end of the dresser. Curious, Seth leaned over to scoop them up. His blue eyes widened as he appraised each picturesque landscape and detailed sketch.

"These are yours?" he asked.

Roz found herself extraordinarily pleased by Seth's appreciation of her sketches. "I came West to do a journal and illustrations for *Harper's Weekly* and *Scribner's Monthly.*"

Seth glanced up, impressed. "You are incredibly good at this, Rozalie."

"Thank you. My father considered it a waste of time."

"He would," Seth muttered as he studied the paintings. "You would have to paint hundred-dollar banknotes to impress Edward Gaylord. He valued nothing else."

Sad but true, Roz mused as she appraised her fascinating brother. Twelve hours ago, Roz was feeling lost and alone in the world. Now she had a family of sorts, one her father had purposely kept from her. Seth was here when Roz had needed someone. It made her wonder if there truly was something to fate and destiny. Life's difficulties had an uncanny way of untangling themselves. Cougar had become the answer to the Cheyenne prophesy and . . .

Roz thrust the betraying thought aside, refusing to let forbidden memories dampen her spirits. It would do no good to pine away for a man who refused to believe in love.

"It is a small world, isn't it, Seth?" she blurted out.

He paused from admiring her art work, looked at her and smiled. "Yes, I'd say that usually proves to be the case. You would be surprised how many Pennsylvanians turned argonauts I've met the past few years. With the progress of steel rails and stagecoach connections, people have become very mobile. The bridge between the East and West is narrowing by the year."

*But Cougar would never cross the bridge he had burned behind him,* Roz thought, despairingly. That was one twain that would never meet. All she had been to that mulish man was the place he came for physical satisfaction—and even then, with great reluctance.

Except for their last night together, Roz reminded herself. In that instance Cougar had come to her in hopes of finding his way back from where he had been after giving everything he had to fulfill the prophesy. But Roz would never be a priority in Cougar's life, because he refused to let himself care, refused to believe that he could revive his soul after so many excruciating trips to hell and back. He believed in the manifestation of Cheyenne spirits and even greater powers, but he refused to believe in the healing power of love. Some mystical oracle he was, Roz thought sourly . . .

"Rozalie, are you all right?" Seth questioned when the faraway look in her eyes turned to tears. "I know I shouldn't have sprung my identity on you so abruptly, but I've waited two weeks to see you." He smiled apologetically. "And I'm sorry for sounding so snide and cynical. I've carried around a lot of hurt feelings since I was a child, growing up with a father who preferred his personal success to raising his own son. I was prepared to dislike you because I saw you as part of him. But I was impressed by the things the Howards told me about you. When you stepped off the stage, you caught me off balance. Now, I rather like having a sister."

Roz eased off the bed, giving way to the impulsive urge to hug Seth and thank her lucky stars that she wasn't as alone in the world as she thought she was.

It was at that precise moment when Francene craned her neck around the corner to see Roz nestled in Seth's encircling arms. Francene had an idea these two individuals might hit it off. She just hadn't expected the fascination to take hold so quickly.

Part of her was disappointed Cougar and Roz hadn't been able to come to terms, for Cougar badly needed a sparkle in his life. But Roz also needed someone who truly cared about her. Francene had given Seth her stamp of approval after watching him work so industriously. She liked the man immensely, even if Gideon had groused and muttered about the possibility of losing the station to Seth who was young and assertive.

"Dinner is on the table," Francene announced, prompting Seth and Roz to self-consciously step back apace.

"Caleb is reciting every last episode of his adventure to the stage passengers. There will be nothing left for you to tell, Roz, if you don't show up—and quickly."

Roz followed Francene out the door, knowing there was nothing for her to say that Caleb couldn't relate just as well. Caleb would get exceptionally good mileage out of his exciting tale. As for Roz, she simply wanted to close the door on the past and find new direction, new purpose.

Although she was never going to recover from loving that golden-eyed giant who prowled the ravines and mountains, she had discovered that she had a second home in Denver. When she longed for the breathtaking scenery she loved to paint, she could board the train and come West again. It would temporarily relieve the restlessness Roz doubted she would be unable to outrun.

# *Thirty*

Cougar crouched beside the wild-eyed mustang that lay on its side, bound and secured with rope. The frustrated animal snorted its displeasure as Cougar reached out to stroke its quivering neck. Murmuring softly, Cougar brushed his hand over the pure white mare that had been forced to submit to him.

This was the horse that would replace Francene's gray mare. The instant Cougar had seen this powerfully built steed among the herd, he knew he wanted it as a prize, along with the strawberry roan stud colt that lay a few steps away, whinnying in outrage.

For two days Cougar had tracked the herd, steering the horses toward the mouth of Cheyenne Canyon. The wild race across plateau and side hills had kept him focused on his ultimate purpose—forgetting that Rozalie Gaylord had become an integral part of his life. Cougar approached that crusade with the same relentless determination that sustained him when he tracked fugitives like Jake Roche. Forgetting the forbidden was all that would salvage Cougar's sanity.

He funneled all his time and energy into capturing and training the mustangs that were penned in the canyon. The hours of concentration required to gentle the flighty herd was Cougar's therapy—although he was sorry to say that it wasn't one hundred percent effective.

The cats had not been much help during the breakneck chase. Their injuries had slowed them down and Cougar had been forced to put his black gelding through rigorous paces to turn the herd and keep it traveling in the direction he wanted it to go.

Now the pumas were sprawled in the sunshine, licking their mending wounds. They weren't obeying as quickly as they once had. Cougar blamed their contrariness on Roz. She had stroked, coddled and spoiled them. Next thing Cougar knew, those regal pussycats would expect him to fetch their meals for them . . .

When the cats pricked their ears and bounded to their feet, Cougar swiveled around, his pistol near at hand, his body on full alert. Warily, Cougar watched a tall, lean figure emerge from the shadows of the cedars. The man was garbed in denim, polished boots, a wide brown sombrero, shirt and leather vest. Holsters that sported pearl-handled revolvers hung low on his hips.

The face concealed beneath the broad brim of the hat had Cougar frowning in curious speculation. Only when white teeth flashed in a crooked smile did Cougar recognize the intruder.

"Gray Eagle, why in the hell are you dressed like that?" Cougar demanded.

"I'm turning white." Gray Eagle announced as he swept off the oversized hat and gestured to the thatch of coal-black hair.

Cougar nearly fell. The long raven strands that were usually adorned with a braid and feathers had been sheared off. Gray Eagle's ears were showing! Cougar was convinced that sexual deprivation, stimulated by having Roz underfoot, had sent Gray Eagle over the edge.

"One of the Hurdy Gurdy girls at Seaton's Palace purchased these clothes for me and clipped my hair. Do I not look like a white man to you, *Nisimaha?*"

"Why the hell would you want to?" Cougar snorted derisively.

Gray Eagle strode forward, mimicking the swaggers of the men he had observed on the darkened streets of Colorado Springs. "Why? Because it is time for me to adapt to what I cannot change. My only freedom will come in pretending to be part white—like you."

If Gray Eagle's nonchalant air and lazy smile were any indication, he had received more from the woman than a haircut and new set of clothes.

Cougar frowned. Gray Eagle had taken a great risk in venturing into town alone. Any number of incidents could have occurred. White men could have instigated a fight that landed the misplaced warrior in jail. From there, Gray Eagle could have been shipped to Indian Territory and restricted to the reservation. What had he done!

"Take those fancy duds off and help me with these horses," Cougar ordered brusquely.

"No."

Cougar spun around when the single word reminded him of Roz's refusal to obey him.

Gray Eagle grinned triumphantly. "I learned that from the *Vee-hay-Kah*. It is very effective."

"It is also extremely annoying," Cougar grunted.

The smile vanished from Gray Eagle's lips. "I am going away, *Nisimaha.*"

Cougar's hand stalled in midair, hovering a few inches above the wild-eyed mare. "There is nowhere for you to go without risk."

"But life is full of risks, is it not? Were you not at risk each time you hunted down fugitives for bounty? Did you not risk your life to see the prophesy fulfilled? Those who do not accept change do not grow; they merely exist. That is what I have done for eight years. Now that I can no longer fight the white man, I must become him, at least outwardly. There are many crude and lawless mining towns that will pay bounty for criminals. In that, my skills are comparable to yours."

Cougar stood there, trying to digest what his blood brother was saying. "Why would you want to leave when we have built this ranch together on our people's sacred ground, holding and defending it until the rivers no longer flow?"

Gray Eagle smiled cryptically. "There is another who belongs here now, *Nisimaha.* Soon, I believe, you will see that for yourself. And just as the chick comes of age to soar as the eagle was born to do, so must I find a place for myself."

When the Cheyenne warrior spun away, Cougar felt a knot of desperation twist inside him. Cougar was accustomed to having his blood brother around. He and Gray Eagle had been friends forever. His blood brother was the one man Cougar never doubted. They understood each other.

"When are you coming back, Gray Eagle?"

He half turned, striking a gunslinger's nonchalant

pose, his hand resting on the butts of the pearl-handled Colts. "The name is Grayson Engals. It is a fine name for a white man, don't you think?"

"I think you've lost your mind," Cougar scowled in frustration.

Gray Eagle raised his hand in Cheyenne custom. "Know that you will always be my friend, Cougar. And when you have made your own peace with yourself, I will return. Perhaps I, too, will find the one who cares as deeply for me as the *Vee-hay-Kah* cares for you. Then I can return to our sacred haunt and live in peace."

Cougar watched Gray Eagle walk away, mimicking the white man's cocky swagger.

The call of the Cougar filled the canyon, echoing around the granite walls until it faded into silence. The screech of the Eagle responded in a lone cry that drifted away in the wind.

"Crazed fool," Cougar muttered as he sank down beside the white mare. "Trying to become a white man, of all things! What self-respecting Indian would want to do something as absurd as that!"


Roz grabbed her bonnet, holding it in place, when Gideon clutched her tightly to him to bid her farewell. It was obvious the station agent had regained his strength after being wounded during the raid. Roz swore Gideon was going to crack her ribs before he finally released her.

At least Gideon and Francene were sincere when they declared they were going to miss her, Roz thought. In all her years, her father had never shown her this much affection. It was nice to know someone cared.

"You know you will always be welcome here, Roz," Gideon assured her. "And now that you've found this brother of yours, you have more than enough reason to return to Colorado."

Gideon turned to confront the young man who had turned out to be Overland Express's ambitious and very competent superintendent, as well as Roz's brother. "And as for you, *sir* . . ."

Seth chuckled when Gideon's hazel eyes narrowed on him. "I believe I sufficiently apologized for the deception. And I certainly worked hard enough around here to compensate for refusing to be completely honest in my motives. Station agents have a habit of putting on the dog when I announce my arrival. This way, I can determine the effectiveness of everyday operations."

"I could have slept a helluva lot better if I'd known you weren't trying to replace me permanently!"

Seth extended his hand to Gideon and grinned. "You can rest easy knowing the superintendent of Overland Express has nothing but respect for the way you and Francene run this station. I know exactly how hard you work, having assumed all the responsibility myself. In fact, I've decided to send you an assistant."

"I don't need help," Gideon snorted, offended.

"No, but you would make an excellent management instructor for prospective agents," Seth said diplomatically. "Of course, there will be an increase in your salary for training an apprentice. If every roadhouse was as efficient as Howard Station, and served such fine cuisine, we would probably drive the railroad out of business."

"Gideon accepts your offer," Francene said on her husband's behalf. "He has promised to devote more time to Caleb. An agent-in-training is an excellent idea."

"Then it's settled," Seth confirmed, winking conspiratorially at Francene. "Your apprentice will be reporting for duty within the week."

Before Seth could assist Roz into the waiting coach, Caleb charged out of the trading post with his shirttail flapping. "Miss Gaylord! I have something for you!"

Roz pivoted to see Cal waving a paper over his head. When he skidded to a halt, he presented her with the sketch he had made as a parting gift. Roz felt her heart twist inside when she stared at the drawing of a man poised on a platform of rock, surrounded by three lounging cats.

"It's Cougar," Cal said, as if she couldn't tell.

"A grand likeness it is," Roz managed to say without her voice cracking.

Seth studied Roz shrewdly, watching the sparkle dwindle in her eyes. His curious gaze drifted to Francene, who nodded in answer to the silent question. Seth said nothing. He didn't have to; Roz's crestfallen expression told all. She had fallen in love with her rescuer. The man was obviously a fool if he rejected the affection of a woman like Rozalie Gaylord. Seth was going to have a few choice words to say to the legendary Cougar if they ever happened to meet.

"My artistic talent is improving, don't you think, Miss Gaylord?"

"Absolutely, Caleb."

"Thank you for the easel, paints and sketch pad," Caleb added. "But are you sure you won't be needing them?"

"I'll buy replacements in New York." Roz smiled and reached out to brush his tousled hair back in place. "And I will always remember our adventure."

Caleb met Roz's surreptitious glance. They had made a pact not to divulge certain adventures to anyone. Roz had suggested they keep one incident in particular a secret. The night of a thousand eyes was a tale better left to Cheyenne legend. The sounds and sights they witnessed were too incredible to relate to those who hadn't witnessed them firsthand.

When Roz had settled herself in the coach beside Seth, the stage lurched forward, along with Roz's heart. She peered at the craggy peaks, knowing Cougar was out there somewhere, prowling the panoramic valleys that were only hers in sketches and bittersweet memories. She hoped Cougar found his peace, hoped he was happy after years of hounded torment.

She hoped at least one of them could be content . . .

# Thirty-one

Cougar was miserable. He had practically exhausted himself, spending every spare minute training the white mare. The serenity of his cabin was driving him mad. After full days of working with the mustangs, Cougar trudged back to the cottage and dropped into a chair. Tormenting visions assailed him. Everywhere he looked, blue eyes were peering at him and a hauntingly soft voice whispered to him.

It was over! How many times was he going to have to tell himself that before he started believing it?

It didn't feel over . . .

Cougar scowled and grabbed one of the whiskey bottles he had confiscated from the bandits. He lifted the liquor to his lips, hesitated and then set the bottle on the table. The last time he had pickled his brain in an effort to forget a forbidden fantasy, disaster had struck.

Restlessly, Cougar prowled the confines of his cabin. He should have been blithely content. He had everything he had ever wanted—the deed to Cheyenne Canyon, a prosperous ranch, the resolution of a prophesy . . . and deadly boredom.

These days, Cougar didn't appreciate his own company as much as he once had. And furthermore, the cats had become a nuisance. They kept rubbing up against his legs like kittens lapping up affection. Pussycats, one and all, Cougar thought sourly. If those pumas hadn't turned so cursed lazy they might have mustered the energy to be ashamed of themselves. As it was, they practically beat down the door every night to bed down on the pallet that still lay by the hearth.

And Gray Eagle, Cougar thought with a disgusted snort. There was no telling where that fool was now, or what kind of trouble he'd gotten himself into. That idiotic Indian was going to peel off the layers of his soul, the same way Cougar had. Then Gray Eagle would come dragging back, shot all to hell, and Cougar would have to cheer him up.

Cougar didn't know why he was in such a foul mood. He just felt uncomfortable, as if his own skin didn't fit anymore. And what was that nagging sensation in the pit of his belly that nourishment couldn't appease?

Heaving an exasperated sigh, Cougar surged out of his chair and stalked outside. Before he could close the door, the cats nearly bowled him over to park themselves on their newly established thrones by the hearth, just as Roz had allowed them to do . . .

The knot in his belly coiled like a clock spring. Cougar cursed. Even after all the consoling platitudes he had delivered he couldn't stop wanting that woman, couldn't get her off his mind or out of his system. She was like a mosquito bite that constantly needed scratching.

Damned infuriating female, all the time whispering that she loved him when he didn't want to hear words he didn't deserve, couldn't return . . .

*Couldn't or was afraid to?* came an annoying little voice.

"Who the hell woke you up?" Cougar muttered at his conscience.

Afraid? Cougar? That was ridiculous. He had taken on the devil's henchman so many times during the past eight years that fear was like a word in a foreign language. Except when Roz's life was in danger, Cougar begrudgingly amended. In those instances, Cougar had practically come apart at the seams. The only time he was able to feel anything was when he experienced life through Roz . . .

There it was then, Cougar realized dismally. That was the truth he had valiantly tried to ignore. Rozalie Gaylord, heiress to a fortune, a much sought-after Eastern debutante was the inspirational force that revitalized his life and put him back in touch with his emotions. She lifted him to higher plateaus, far above the cold, dangerous reaches of the hell he had endured. Right or wrong, Cougar was empty without Roz's bright smile and ringing laughter.

Maybe she did belong in some elegant mansion in the East. And maybe she did claim title to a fortune he could never match. But she loved him, damn it; and he . . . needed her. Nothing felt right since Roz went away.

And what if she were carrying his child? Cougar scowled, thinking how he had resented the fact that his father had come and gone from the Cheyenne camp, seeking only his own pleasure without accepting the responsibility of the child he left behind. Well, no child of Cougar's was going to be abandoned and unclaimed.

He certainly knew what that felt like. And he sure as hell knew how it felt to yearn for the woman who constantly came uninvited into his thoughts. Her memory was eating him alive.

*Soon, I believe, you will accept what you already know to be true. There is someone who belongs here . . .*

Gray Eagle's words resounded through Cougar's mind like a gong. A vision, poignant and clear, rose in the darkness. Before Cougar knew what he was doing, he had turned around in his tracks and marched back to the cabin to gather his gear.

Although the white mare was not trained well enough for Francene to handle, the animal would be manageable after a gruelling trip to Howard Station, Cougar assured himself. He would accept nothing less than well-mannered obedience from the mount he gave to Francene.

Cougar scooped up his supplies and called to the cats. He would probably have to spend a week gathering the cattle and horses that wandered away while he was gone. Without Gray Eagle to ride herd, the livestock would set their own boundaries. But Cougar didn't care. He was driven by the kind of desperation that no amount of rationalization could pacify.

Presenting the mare to Francene was the perfect excuse to see Roz before she left Colorado. This would provide Cougar with the opportunity to tell Roz how he felt. And he did feel again—because of her, through her. She was the essential link that had been missing from his life.

Leading the black gelding behind him, Cougar thundered off, forcing the half-broken mare to behave or risk having its neck twisted out of joint for refusing to go where Cougar commanded. Eventually, the mare learned to switch directions when Cougar applied light pressure with his knees and the reins.

In high spirits, Cougar aimed himself toward Howard Station. Very soon, he told himself, all would be right with the world for the first time since he could remember.

Cougar brought the winded mare to a halt on the rise of ground overlooking Howard Station. The morning stage had just rolled away, leaving a cloud of dust behind it. Cougar expected to see Roz poised beside her easel, but she was nowhere in sight. Caleb and Gideon were pitching hay to the horses and Francene strode off to freshen up the rooms for new arrivals.

"Cougar!" Caleb's excited shout wafted in the wind.

Cougar trotted down the hill, watching Caleb bound toward him like a jackrabbit.

"You're back already? Is it going to snow in July?"

"I don't think so," Cougar replied, his gaze scanning the area for a glimpse of Roz. "I came back early to bring your mother a replacement for the horse she lost."

When Gideon limped out of the corral, Cougar pivoted, staring past the agent, hoping Roz would emerge from the barn. Again, he was disappointed.

"I was hoping I'd get the chance to thank you." Gideon said to Cougar. He wrapped his arm around his son, giving him a quick hug. "Knowing that you were tracking those bandits was all that kept Francene and me from worrying ourselves sick."

When Francene heard the commotion outside, she rushed from the inn to fling her arms around Cougar's neck. Cougar had suffered through all the social amenities he could stand. Uneasiness was hounding him to no end. As much as he enjoyed seeing the Howards, he wanted to see Roz more.

"Where's Yank? I'd like to speak with her."

"She isn't here," Cal informed him. "She left yesterday with Seth."

Cougar frowned warily. "Who the blazes is Seth?"

"He's the one who filled in for Papa until he got back on his feet. And Miss Gaylord was sure glad to meet him, I can tell you that," Caleb jabbered. "Seth Radburn is—"

"Where did she go?" Cougar cut in impatiently. He was not in the mood to listen to Cal's long-winded yammering.

"She went to Denver," Francene supplied. "If you wanted to tell Roz good-bye, I'm afraid you're too late. She's catching a train for New York tonight."

Tonight! Cougar was going to have to make tracks to reach Denver before the eastbound train left town.

Enjoying the rare display of emotion, Francene watched Cougar scowl and mutter under his breath. "And I'll tell you something else, Cougar," she said in a lecturing tone. "If you don't reach the depot in time, it's your own fault for letting Roz go in the first place. I've thought all along that the two of you—"

Cougar didn't give Francene time to finish her motherly sermon. In frantic haste, he bounded onto his black gelding and called to the cats. He rode off in a thunder of hoof-beats, leaving the Howards to stare after him.

Caleb crammed his hands in his pockets and grumbled, disappointed. "I didn't even get to tell Cougar that Roz found out she had a brother."

An amused smile pursed Francene's lips as she watched Cougar disappear over the hill. She had not missed the shocked expression that claimed his rugged features and flared in his amber eyes when he learned Roz was on her way back East. Francene's prayer that Cougar would one day find a woman to breathe life back into him had been answered.

When Caleb wandered back to the corral to pitch hay to the horses, Francene looped her arms around Gideon's neck. "Cougar is in love," she announced with utmost satisfaction.

Gideon blinked. "And how, may I ask, did you arrive at that conclusion?"

"The look on Cougar's face, when hounded by the possibility of losing Roz, was the replica of your desperation the day Roche's raiders swarmed the station and attempted to take me hostage," Francene informed him.

Gideon gathered his wife close and dropped an affectionate kiss on her smiling lips. "And Roz? Do you think she feels the same way about Cougar?"

Francene peered up at Gideon with adoring green eyes and a loving smile. "Roz has always looked at Cougar the same way I still look at you . . ."

While Gideon and Francene were expressing their affection for each other, Caleb leaned against the fence, watching the hugging and kissing that was going on. Even if he had led Gray Eagle astray about the white man's courtship rituals, Caleb knew exactly how married couples responded to each other when they didn't think anyone was looking.

Too bad Gray Eagle hadn't asked Caleb about that. He could have given several firsthand descriptions after watching his parents in action.

# Thirty-two

Cougar made use of every shortcut across mesas, gulches, ravines and mountains to reach Denver before nightfall. He didn't even stop to eat, only to rest and water his horse. The rigorous pace he set made it difficult for the mending cats to keep up with him. They would disappear for an hour at a time to rest before using their own shortcuts to catch up.

There were times when Cougar was forced to climb down from the laboring gelding, leading it over rugged terrain, giving it time to catch its second wind. But as always, Cougar was relentless. His future happiness was at stake and he was fighting the clock to reach the railroad depot on time.

The sun was making its final descent when Cougar topped the hill overlooking the mile-high city that bustled with activity. Cougar stared at the steel rails that bisected what had once been a valley where buffalo peacefully grazed and the Cheyenne made camp.

"And they call this progress," Cougar muttered sourly. Would that he could live long enough to see the white men give this land back to the Indian!

The population of Denver had increased weekly, acquiring far too many citizens for Cougar's tastes. For a moment he hesitated, wondering if Roz would prefer the hubbub of the city with its opera houses, theaters and elegant shops. Well, he supposed he could make the concession of journeying into town when Roz yearned to mingle with society.

Nudging his weary steed down the hill, Cougar focused his attention on the curl of smoke that indicated the arrival of the northbound train. He had no time to circle Denver before the train reached the depot to board eastbound passengers. He was going to have to ride right through town.

No doubt, he and his cats would cause a disturbance, but that was just too damned bad. The fastest route that would get Cougar where he wanted to go was a direct line. Denverites could move out of his way or risk being run down on the street. Cougar was in a rush.

Sure enough, dogs yelped and took after the panthers, sending them bounding down the boardwalks. Passersby screeched in alarm and tried to dodge the cats. As usual, the panthers sent up their customary screams causing horses to balk and rear, and break away from hitching posts to scatter in all directions. Curses filled the street as man battled to control beast.

Cougar rode through the mayhem, ignoring the stunned glances and whispers that identified him to newcomers. His gaze was fixed on the train depot and the glorious blond head he had instantly singled out of the crowd.

Cougar knew how hot the flame inside him could burn—would always burn—the moment he spotted Roz. There were some battles a man couldn't win. His affection for that misplaced Yank was one of them . . .

A scowl curled Cougar's lips when he noticed Roz's handsome companion lifting her down from the carriage that was piled high with luggage. Cougar cursed mightily when Roz flung her arms around the attractive gentleman who was garbed in an expensive three-piece suit.

The curse got even worse when Seth Radburn—the bastard!—bent down to kiss Roz, right squarely on the mouth. For a half second Cougar considered reversing direction and riding hell-for-leather out of town. The man whom Roz was presently squeezing in two and kissing in front of anyone who cared to watch was definitely more her style than him.

Cougar grumbled, tormented by the unexpected scene. And Roz had admitted that she loved Cougar? Well, she had a strange way of showing it! She had certainly gotten over him soon enough!

A burning knot of jealousy and possession coiled in Cougar's gut as he watched Roz wave farewell to her latest beau and step onto the train platform. He really should turn around and ride home. But home had become an empty ache that was eating Cougar alive. If he wanted Roz with him from now until forever, he might very well have to fight for her. Considering the sour mood he was in, it wouldn't take much to provoke him into tearing apart that citified dandy limb by limb. That scoundrel was after more than Roz's money, Cougar predicted.

Cougar felt his heart drop to his knees when Roz turned away, answering the conductor's summons for all passengers to take their seats. Steam rolled from the engine like a fire-breathing dragon, and wheels creaked on steel rails. Everything in Cougar objected to seeing that beguiling female ride away. Damn it, he was going to lose her forever if he didn't do something—and fast!

A wild, piercing scream, accompanied by three haunting cries, brought all conversation and activity at the depot to a standstill. The sound went through every nerve and muscle in Roz's body. She halted abruptly and surged toward the platform that connected the railroad cars. Alarmed yelps and shouts flew up around Roz as she emerged from the passenger car. Goggle-eyed, she stared at the familiar profile, set against the backdrop of a blazing sunset. The dark shadows that swirled around the horse's hooves commenced screaming and the crowd parted to let the entourage of wild creatures pass.

To Roz's astonishment, Cougar very nearly ran Seth down as he charged toward the train. Seth dived toward the carriage, grabbing the reins before the horse bolted away from the growling cats.

Staring stupidly, unable to believe what she was seeing, Roz watched Cougar plow his way through the congregation of new arrivals who hovered around the steps.

Cougar brought the gelding to a skidding halt, sending passengers scrambling out of his way. He didn't have the time or inclination to apologize for scaring the white folks half to death. He was desperately impatient. The most precious part of his life was about to take the eastbound train.

"You can't leave, Yank," Cougar insisted.

Roz feasted on the unexpected sight of him, savoring every minute detail. "Why not?"

"Just . . . because," Cougar grumbled. "I . . ." The words he wanted and needed to say, words he had never uttered to another living soul, were stuck to the roof of his mouth.

"Just because?" Roz felt the makings of a smile tug at her lips. "That is hardly a reason."

"Just because is reason enough," Cougar said awkwardly. He felt as conspicuous as an actor on stage, surrounded by an eager audience that was hanging on his every word. Cougar shifted uncomfortably on his horse and stared at Roz. "I want you to stay, Yank."

"Why should I stay?" Roz asked him.

The fact that Cougar had raced after her, rejecting all his arguments as to why they couldn't enjoy a future together, caused Roz's heart to swell with so much happiness she swore it would burst. Cougar was here; that had to mean he cared. After all, Cougar was a man whose actions spoke louder than words.

Roz supposed she should have been satisfied with that, but she wanted more. If Cougar had come this far and had caused a commotion in the streets of Denver, then he could damn well admit to his reasons. And furthermore, this man who never cut anybody any slack was not going to get any slack from her. If he didn't say the words she longed to hear then she would reach down his throat and yank them out of him!

"Why, Cougar?" she asked with the relentless persistence she had learned from him.

"Because I—" Cougar swore under his breath when the unfamiliar words tangled with his tongue.

The whistle tooted impatiently and the conductor grasped Roz's arm, directing her to her seat. The train rolled forward and Cougar's heart nearly beat him to death.

"Because I love you, Yank!" Cougar bellowed to be heard over the piercing train whistle.

Cougar decided that embarrassing himself in front of a rapt audience was worth the radiant smile that blossomed on Roz's face. When she wormed loose from the conductor's grasp and attempted to leap off the train, Cougar reined his mount up beside her, scooping her onto his lap.

The world around him faded into oblivion when Roz peered up at him with sparkling blue eyes and an impish grin. Emotion flooded through Cougar, filling the once empty caverns that had been his heart and soul. The warmth that channeled through every part of his being put a broad smile on his face. He threw back his head and laughed with the sheer pleasure of being alive, of loving and being loved.

Roz's laughing voice harmonized with his as she looped her arms around his neck. "So you cannot only smile, but laugh as well," she said, absolutely delighted.

"Only for you, Yank, only for you," Cougar murmured, lost to the love shining in her luminous eyes. "Because I love you . . ."

The words that had been so difficult to utter came rolling off Cougar's tongue with surprising ease. And each time thereafter, it grew ever easier to say.

Cougar found that he actually enjoyed saying the words. It was as if a heavy burden had been lifted from his soul, a shadowy burden that—once lifted—allowed glorious light to replace the inky darkness.

The gelding sidestepped uneasily as the train pulled

away, bringing Cougar back in touch with his surroundings. He glanced down to see Seth Radburn propped leisurely against the carriage that was still heaped with Roz's luggage.

"When I saw him ride up," Seth said to Roz, "I didn't think there was any use of unloading your luggage. Although I assume this is the man called Cougar, I would appreciate a formal introduction."

Cougar glared at the self-confident man. "Do not ever let me see you kiss my future wife like that again," Cougar growled menacingly. To reinforce the unspoken threat of what would become of Seth Radburn if he didn't heed Cougar's advice, a command in Cheyenne sent the cats pouncing at Seth's feet.

"Call them off," Seth demanded, bounding into the carriage before his feet were chewed off at the ankles. "You obviously got the wrong impression."

"Perhaps I should introduce you," Roz agreed as she nestled against Cougar's bare chest. "Cougar, this is my brother, Seth Radburn."

Cougar's astounded gaze leaped from one pair of dazzling blue eyes to the other. There was definitely a resemblance, now that it had been called to his attention. "Brother? I didn't know you had one, Yank."

"Neither did I, until five days ago."

"Half brother, actually," Seth amended, staring warily at the cats that stood guard on him. When Cougar finally called off his pumas, Seth inhaled a relieved breath. "I have a cottage west of Cherry Creek. Perhaps you would like to join me there."

Cougar had other ideas about how he intended to

spend the evening. None of them included chitchatting with his soon-to-be brother-in-law.

"I can arrange to have a clergyman present," Seth said, sending Cougar a meaningful glance. "As Roz's brother, I am obligated to ensure that she receives all the courtesy and respect she deserves."

"In the eyes of the Cheyenne she is already my wife," Cougar assured Seth.

Seth picked up the reins and flung Cougar a parting glance. "Good for the Cheyenne. Now make it right in my eyes and I will give my consent. It's my place or no dice, Cougar. Which is it going to be?"

Cougar glowered at the rascal who was trying to make a simple matter unnecessarily difficult. "You are not making it easy for me to like you, white man."

"I'm not too crazy about you stealing away the sister I am just getting to know, either," Seth countered with an ornery grin. "It's my house and marriage—or nothing."

Cougar peered down into the enchanting face that formed the boundaries of all his future hopes and dreams. "Nothing is what I would have had without her."

When Seth smiled in agreement and headed toward his cottage, Cougar gathered Roz tightly in his arms, feeling a fragile blossom unfurl until no part of him remained untouched by the pleasure and affection promised in Roz's eyes. For all the forays into hell that peeled the layers off his soul and shriveled his heart, new life burgeoned inside him. *This,* Cougar decided, was the special power Gray Eagle insisted had eluded him. *This,* Cougar also realized, was the greatest source of strength any man could command—Indian or white.

Now Cougar understood the secret Francene and

Gideon Howard had shared through twenty-five years of marriage. When two hearts beat as one, there were no obstacles that could not be overcome. No one could outrun the all-encompassing arms of love. Cougar could see his bright future in those beguiling blue eyes that sparkled only for him.

"I love you, Cougar," Roz murmured, pressing a light kiss to his bronzed cheek.

"I know, Yank. That's why I'm here," He grinned playfully at her. "You're the only one who ever did."

"No," she whispered in genuine sincerity. "I'm the one who always will, because you are all I will ever want and need . . ."

Cougar rode through the streets of Denver, following Seth's carriage, causing another commotion. He was oblivious to the rumors and whispered conversations that were flying to the left and right of him. All he heard was the scream of the cats that had managed to clear the streets to let him pass.

Cougar glanced absently at the pumas before refocusing on Roz's adoring smile. He decided, there and then, that becoming a purring pussycat wasn't going to be all that bad, not when Cougar laid claim to the cat's meow . . .

This breathtakingly lovely Yankee was Cougar's woman—now and forevermore . . .

Dear Readers,

I hope you enjoyed Cougar's story. In November you will meet another dark and dangerous hero who goes by the name of Sin. When he arrives in Natchez, Mississippi rumors immediately start flying. Some folks say the ebony-eyed, midnight-haired newcomer to baronial society was once a privateer whose exploits have brought him untold wealth. Others whisper that Sin is freely spending the blood money he stole as a highwayman along Natchez Trace. There is also speculation that Sin might have been one of Jean Lafitte's pirates who came out of the swamps to settle on higher ground.

The truth is that Sin has come to Natchez with one purpose in mind—revenge. He intends to repay the three men who took everything he valued in life and set him adrift at sea eighteen years earlier. Just as Sin has methodically charted his course to exotic ports around the world and navigated the Seven Seas, he plots to ruin his enemies' reputations among the gentry. It is his intent to reclaim his lost inheritance and strip away the treasures each of the three men hold dear.

There is just one miscalculated hitch in Sin's plans—Angelene Sheridan, the daughter of one of his sworn enemies. Her appearance leaves Sin at a difficult crossroad where satisfying a long-held vendetta complicates his growing attachment for Angel. And it is then that Sin learns yet another hard truth in life: He cannot have his full measure of revenge without destroying his chance at love.

*Angel's Sin* is a story of choices, of consequences and one man's struggle to decide if fulfilling his promise for revenge is worth the sacrifice of his own heart.

Until November,

Debra Falcon